Hugo

Painter Place Saga 2

Pamela Poole

Inspiring Southern Ambiance
Published by Southern Sky Publishing

Cover Painting and Interior Illustrations by Pamela Poole

Southern Sky Publishing
southernskypublishing.com

Scripture references are from the Holman Christian Standard and NIV Bibles unless otherwise noted.

Print: ISBN 978-1-9956089-04-2
Print: ISBN 978-1-956089-11-0
Print: ISBN 978-1-956089-20-2
eBook: ISBN 978-1-956089-03-5

For my husband, with whom I endured the wrath of Hugo as we sat huddled in our living room with two small children. The Lord has seen us through many storms, and He works good out of them all.

Author's Note

The decade of the 1980's in America was "the best of times, and the worst of times." Americans were decadent and materialistic, spending money as if the world might end—for they thought it might. Designer labels were worshiped, fashion was scanty, colors were bold, hairstyles and makeup were brash and outrageous, and the realm of gadgets exploded. Nike brand encouraged everyone to "Just Do It," and they did! They danced, sang, and entertained themselves as if the world might end—for they wondered if it might.

Russia had us in the crosshairs of their nuclear weapons, Mt. St. Helens erupted, and John Lennon was murdered. Americans were enchanted as they saw Princess Diana's fairytale wedding on television. Music video channels were edgy, and Americans relished shows like *Miami Vice* and *Dallas*.

As the decade ended, the Berlin Wall came tumbling down, like the Communist governments around Eastern Europe where thousands sang "Just As I Am" at Billy Graham Crusades. A British scientist brought the world closer by creating the World Wide Web.

The Eighties also produced some of the most classic movies and music of any decade ever, and as those actors and musicians pass from this life, no one with their unique talents has come onto the scene to replace them. In my debut novel in the saga, *Painter Place*, and in the second novel in the saga, *Hugo*, this is the world my characters live in.

The young characters of *Painter Place* and *Hugo* ride the roller coaster that was the 1980's, forced to make decisions that test the relevance of their faith and influence. Turn the page for a trip into a turbulent era and hang on for the ride to survive the monster in the dark that ended the decade, Hurricane Hugo.

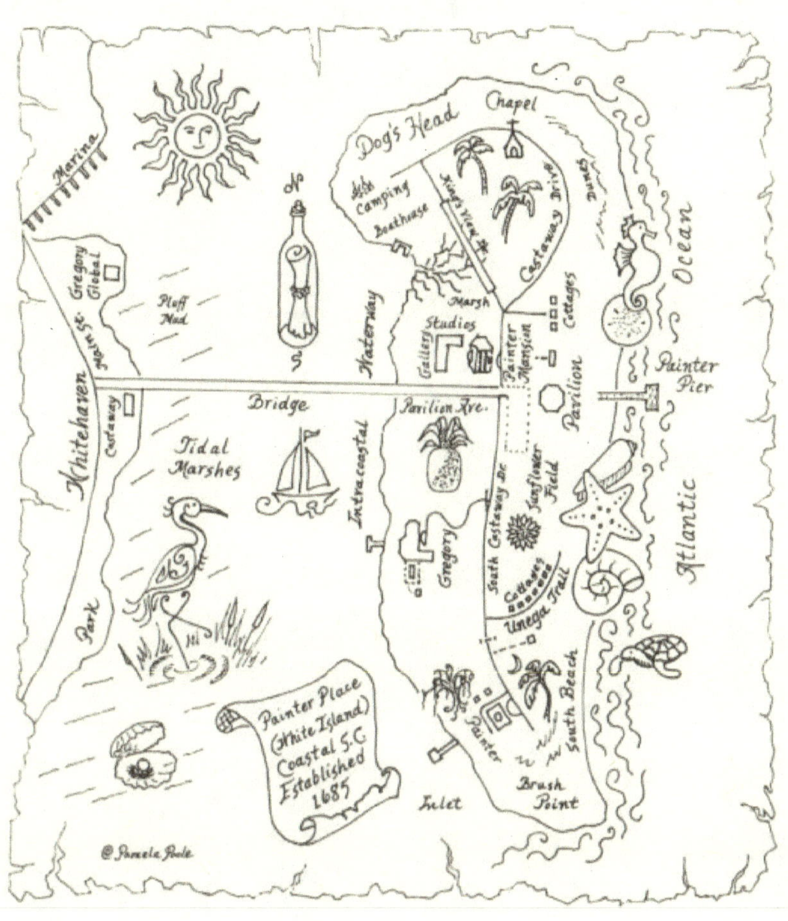

Map of Painter Place before Hurricane Hugo, 1989

Hugo

Prologue

Tuesday, September 19, 1989

Three disheveled men pulled someone from the rubble where a wall had just collapsed on a dozen American aid workers. Hurricane Hugo had decimated the island of Montserrat, and the Americans arrived that very morning to search for survivors. The three men guessed the rescuers had something worth taking on their bodies.

Gunshots at their feet sprayed sand, stinging their faces. They yelped and dropped the arms of the American, jerking around to see two dark-haired men in expensive suits and aviator sunglasses aiming at them. The three locals ran to find shelter in the ruins of what remained of the town.

The shooters kept their guns level in front of themselves, jogging toward the body. One got on a radio he carried while the other checked over the victim. It was weak, but he had a pulse and a nasty head injury. He was tall, lean, and strong, with calloused hands that had never worn a wedding band.

Feeling around in the young man's pockets, he found only scant identification and a humble stainless-steel cross. He scanned the name and details on the card and turned the smooth cross over in his palm. It was unremarkable except as a testimony to years of handling.

Finally, a man worth saving. He thought he saw a ghost earlier when he and his partner had done surveillance on the plane that landed with the aid organization. They tailed the young man ever since, satisfying their previous mission and discovering a new one. This man's demeanor and character was better than the man they would force him to replace. *Few men get to vet their future employer,* he mused.

The young man moaned.

"What's your name?" asked the dark-haired man. He stashed the ID card and metal cross into his own pocket and scowled in concern as he lightly touched the head wound, pushing aside sun-streaked, light brown hair that was a couple inches long on top. It was darker where it had been cut to taper short along the sides. It was perfect, and he anticipated the man opening his eyes. He hoped they were green.

The injured man tried to make his mouth form words. "Name?" he managed to repeat. He squeezed his eyes in concentration. "Not... sure..."

"Do you know where you are?"

The injured man barely shook his head before gasping in pain. He lost consciousness again, and his rescuer pulled the polo shirt with the aid organization logo up over his head to wrap around the bleeding wound. He swept away evidence of the man's blood in the sand.

Helicopter blades sliced the sky overhead. "God has let you live today," he said conversationally to the unconscious young man. "Congratulations on your new identity as the Jaguar, the beloved son and heir of a powerful man. It's not heaven, but his enemies will send you there soon enough. I pray that's where his real son went when they killed him two days ago. Thanks to you, the legend of the Jaguar that can never be killed will topple strongholds without effort, and those enemies will assume they've lost this battle in the long war."

Men with a stretcher spilled onto the sandy beach from the helicopter. The last ones in wiped away their trail and in no time at all, they made the cleanest get-away they ever pulled off.

PART ONE

Storm Warning

Chapter One

Wednesday, September 20, 1989

Chad Gregory stood in front of a wall of glass seven stories high. It would withstand winds of 250 miles per hour in a hurricane, and it made up one whole side of his office. His brooding stare was aimed at the island across the Intracoastal Waterway and the Atlantic beyond it. His home.

He started at the brisk knock on the doorframe of his open door, jarred from his ever-increasing unease, but remained standing with one arm across the chest of his cobalt blue polo shirt and the other propped with his fist under his chin. "Come on in, Dad."

His expansive, comfortable office was the twin to his father's, side by side on the top floor of Gregory Global. Phillip Gregory came in and stood beside him, unconsciously assuming the same expression as his son.

"It's hard to take a storm threat seriously on a beautiful day like this." Chad kept his eyes on Painter Place as he spoke. "The Big House—it's on a ten-foot gradual elevation on the island. The foundation puts the building up another twelve. Maybe we won't get the full force of a tidal surge because of the barrier island just south."

"It's up to hurricane codes, and the foundation pilings are on bedrock. But if that stained-glass dome roof in the rotunda shatters, the whole house will be open to torrents of rain. The mansion will have to be gutted, and the stained glass—well, that's priceless. The Painters shipped it out of England in the late 1600s from their original 1300s estate. We'll never be able to replace it with anything but a modern reproduction, like Andy did for his house. And if this hurricane hits this island as a Category 3 at high tide, the storm surge will take the gallery and studios. Forget the pier and the pavilion. Just pray they aren't slung like missiles into the mansion."

"Insurance. I assume you're planning for the worst that could happen?"

Phillip paused, biting his lower lip for a moment. "The insurance was all we could get on the property, but it won't replace the old cottages. Some things can't be covered. I handle the insurance file, since there are some policies that don't pertain to the structures. The time will come when I'll go over all that with you."

Chad frowned.

"It'll take months to recover if a big hurricane hits here," his dad continued. "Years, for some of the losses. Wyeth's frantic—his sixth sense is going berserk. He's spending big money to send every original painting and family antique on the island to the vaults inland, and he paid dearly to have the *Artistic License* hauled across the state to a dry dock to keep it out of the marina. He made the excuse that it needed professional cleaning that Andy doesn't have time to do. I trust his instincts, and I told him to do the same with our collection. We can't sit around and wait to see if the storm turns. This takes planning and time."

He and his dad continued to scowl out the window for a few moments before Chad spoke again. "Will Andy lose the marina?"

"Yep. And since he's next door, his boats will end up in this building." His dad blew out a breath and shifted his weight to put his hands on his hips. "I remember making it through Gracie and Hazel. Painter Place has surely been protected by divine intervention for over three hundred years. We've never lost the mansion. You've seen the photos of what was left when we made it through Hazel as a 3 when it hit farther north in '54, taking out every pier from Myrtle Beach to Wilmington. Your mom was hit worse that we were by Gracie in Charleston back in '59. It slammed into Beaufort as a 4, but it hit at low tide, so the surge was less than twelve feet. The tide makes a huge difference."

Chad unconsciously copied his dad's stance. "Of all the times for something like this to threaten me, this is the worst. The twins are due any day, so I can't put Caroline on a plane to London or Hawaii while I deal with the aftermath."

Phillip slapped his son's back lightly and attempted a smile. "That's in God's hands now. I'm sendin' everyone home and diverting business calls to Justin in London. I need to go convince your grandparents to leave Charleston."

Patrick Painter tucked his head in the door. "Hey, guys. Chad, lunch is at the Sand Dollar, since I just closed the Castaway. Everyone's hoardin' 'n' boardin.'"

Chad turned his face to his shoulder to acknowledge his brother-in-law, who was walking over to look out at Painter Place with them. They silently contemplated how different the view would be after a hurricane.

"Go on to lunch and head over to the island," Phillip said, his tone lighter than the mood in his eyes. "I've got a feelin' there's a long afternoon ahead of us."

Patrick pulled his marine blue Corvette into a space at the Sand Dollar Drive-In, shading the open T-top under the long aqua awning. Chad slid his aging silver Porsche 944 into the next space, then pulled off his Wayfarer sunglasses and took his keys from the ignition. He climbed into the passenger seat of the Corvette.

There were only three other cars parked in what was usually a busy venue at lunch time. Patrick pushed the button on the speaker to order, and the owner's voice crackled out, joking about Patrick not keeping his fancy restaurant open today and settling for a redneck meal.

"Yeah, well, if the big boss is takin' the speaker orders and harassing patrons, I predict you'll be closin' up after lunch," Patrick said into the slotted metal box. "I'll just add an extra ten minutes to my workout to get rid of the redneck meal and keep my Hollywood physique."

Rusty laughter blared from the other side. "You caught me! I've got one waitress left today, and she's only been here a couple of weeks. Trust me, she'll check out your physique. How about some of my famous chopped beef barbecue, on the house? I can't stand to see the fresh batch wasted when I close and board up."

Patrick looked at Chad, who nodded. "Sure, thanks. Add an order of fries and remember my extra pickle and Chad's extra coleslaw. Throw in a hamburger done Joey's way. He's meetin' us."

The speaker blurted a mocking protest. "I'm gonna have to raise my prices to cover yer extras. I ain't Maggie Jane, ya know. She spoiled you two rotten."

Joey's Harley-Davidson roared into the space beside them. He slung a leg over and set down his custom painted helmet, shaking out a sun-streaked chestnut shag haircut that hung in layers below his ears and on his neck. He wore frayed jeans and a *Point of Know Return* tee shirt, on which a ship sailed endlessly over the edge of the world.

"Hope you guys have an entertainment plan if we get trapped here, like Key Largo," Joey drawled. "Maybe some unexpected well-armed guests will show up."

Patrick pushed his Ray Ban aviators onto the top of his blonde hair. "The entertainment would be gettin' you into a Bogey and Bacall situation, so weapons might be necessary."

Joey's brows shot up and he shook his head. "No worries, boys. I'm enjoyin' all your misadventures over there on Ozzie and Harriet Island. I can't wait to see Chad joggin' behind a double stroller. Romeo's kept Caroline all to himself every minute for four years, makin' up for college and gettin' revenge on parents who beg for grandchildren. All that romance is about to come to a screechin'—and I mean that literally—halt."

Chad's broad grin flashed white against his tan, and his hair lifted gently in the gusting coastal breeze. "Just makin' up for lost time and lovin' life as the center of her attention. When kids come along, I'll have to share her."

A young, dark-haired waitress confidently carried a tray of food to the Corvette. Patrick remembered her boss' warning that the waitress would check out his physique. He made a point of flashing his gold wedding band when he handed her the bills folded between his first two fingers. She blinked dark brown eyes with heavy eyeliner and hesitated before taking the money and turning her interest to Chad.

Her gaze roamed appreciatively down from his face and over his chest to his thigh, where his left hand rested on his tailored khakis. The smile faded as she noticed the platinum wedding band on his ring finger. She ran her eyes up the muscles of his tanned left arm before meeting the frosty look he had waiting for her. Startled by the blunt rejection in his expression, she shrugged, tucking the money into an apron pocket.

"You look a lot like Sonny Crockett," she offered as an excuse.

"We like to say Crockett looks a lot like Chad," Joey answered evenly for his friend. He leaned back on Patrick's car behind the driver's seat with his arms folded. "He's also married to the artist at Painter Place and about to be the father of twins."

"You're kiddin' me! You're married to Caroline Painter?"

The young waitress shook her head as her expression transformed, shifting a spike of bangs in her pixie haircut. "Caroline's like—like Miss America, or that Uptown Girl, with a smile like Elle McPherson—like she's gettin' ready to make somethin' fun happen! She came to my tech school class to talk about art. I thought she was married to that gorgeous hunky guy she was with when I was leaving Millie's on Main a few weeks ago. He came in and swept her into his arms and asked how all his babies were, and they looked so—good together."

Chad rubbed his right hand over his face. Patrick grimaced and turned to him. "Derrick."

"Mr. Painter, please don't tell Caroline I was—you know," the waitress stammered. "I moved here in August to go to tech school, and I didn't know who you were."

Chad irritably ran his hand through his hair. "You still don't know who I am. I'm not Mr. Painter—that's her maiden name. I'm Mr. Gregory."

She flushed. "Are you related to the Gregory Global family?"

Chad nodded slowly and met her pleading eyes as she gushed. "Look, I made a mistake, jumpin' to a wrong conclusion about that guy. It was nothing but my imagination. Don't be mad at Caroline about it. Classy ladies like her don't—you know. I'm sure the twins are yours."

Joey burst into a lusty laugh, doubling over against the Corvette, and Patrick's shoulders shook as he pressed his lips together.

Chad's green eyes narrowed. "That guy's a family friend who was visiting. Caroline's twins are mine. I'm not mad at her and won't say anything about your—interest."

The waitress mumbled a relieved thanks and turned to Joey, who had regained control of himself. She tore off a page from her order book, quickly wrote down her phone number, and tucked it into the helmet on his motorcycle.

"Love hearing you on the radio, Joey. This is just in case the one I put in your pocket last week got lost in the washing machine." She curled her bright magenta nails around the tray and walked back inside.

Patrick snorted as Joey leaned over his shoulder to grab the burger. "It's been a while since the buddy system had to kick in. You're still quick on your feet, Joey. So, you and the waitress have history? I'm not askin' how, or where, she touched you long enough to put her number in your pocket. What was it like to have her eyes makin' out with Chad when you were last week's flavor?"

Now it was Joey who snorted, peeling back the wrapper on his sandwich. "That's how it's always been with you two. The flashy blondes get the attention, and it's been impossible to get noticed around Chad since Miami Vice. But in the end, it's the quiet ones like me you have to look out for."

He reached into Patrick's fries. "A better question is, how long will it take Chad to erase that mental image of Derrick that flashed through his mind? Guess that's part of the package when you marry someone who looks like a model and has a smile that makes people think somethin' fun's about to happen. Caroline keeps him stirred up all the time. There's a lot of wisdom in keepin' your stress down in life by marryin' an ordinary woman."

Chad pursed his lips. "Joey, had any check-ups lately? Or have you been too busy with the laundry?"

Patrick hooted before taking a bite of his barbecue. Lunch was turning out to be quite entertaining.

Joey grinned. "You know I'm not that kinda guy. Casey's thoroughly checkin' me *out*, though. I tossed the waitress' number in the trash before I washed my windbreaker. It was on my Harley when she tucked it into the pocket." He bit into his burger again and leaned back on the Corvette to chew leisurely.

Patrick swallowed his barbecue. "Glad you made such a good impression on the nurse that night at Chad's, at the women's Bible Study."

Joey took a sip from the straw sticking out of the lid covering his drink cup. "No thanks to you two clowns! I thought for sure they'd hear us after you both fell on the ground laughin' under the window, holding your mouths shut. When are we crashin' them again? I wanna know when Caroline leads it. Who else could begin a lesson on how Noah named his son 'Hot'? She was definitely makin' somethin' fun happen that night."

"No more teachin' for her until the kids are born and we settle into something that resembles a routine. And obviously 'hot' was on her mind because she was thinkin' of her husband." Chad smugly bit into his chopped barbecue.

Joey sputtered and Patrick swallowed so he could chime in. "Only, being thought of as 'hot' in this case was a bad thing, guys. It prompted a curse and things kept going downhill from there."

"Sure, but Caroline's comparison of what hot meant back then to a guy being hot now was based on a standard," Chad protested. "Casey understood the girl code—that Caroline thought I was the good kind of 'hot.' That's why she said it was amazing that *all* the Gregory and Painter men were hot, even the Big Three, they just weren't as hot as Joey Grayson. There's no accountin' for taste."

Patrick shrugged. "And it's a small town. Joey doesn't have any real competition now, since summer is over and the white collars went back to their real jobs." He looked back at Joey. "Is that why you're bein' so cool and stringin' her along?"

Joey took a deep breath, his expression suddenly serious as he gazed into the distance and chewed the last bite of his burger. "No, that's not why. Casey's got some maturing to do as a Christian. Caroline needs to keep teaching. It was brilliant of her to use that passage in Genesis to teach the Bible's view against nudity, applyin' it to art and photography, and against drinking alcohol, even in private when you assume it doesn't hurt anyone. In the Bible, the negative consequences of that on Noah's family impacted the whole world. Casey had never heard that kind of stuff before."

Chad and Patrick looked at one another with raised eyebrows. Chad turned and said, "Joey, seriously, are you romantically interested in her?"

Joey shrugged and looked at the toe of his boot as he kicked at the pavement. "Maybe. Just need to be careful. I don't know yet where she's been and who with."

Chad was startled by the déjà vu. "Hey, man, Caroline said that exact same thing about me when I'd only been back from college a few days. She assumed I was like her grandfather, runnin' around with women and endin' up in the society pages of the newspapers. But I wasn't. Other than the fact that she has a deep Texas drawl, we don't know much about Casey Austin yet. But at least the first thing she did was visit our church when she moved here for the nursing job."

Then he slapped his hand on the console. "I have a way you can get to know her better. Caroline's due any time, and there's a strong chance now we'll be affected by this storm. I'd like to have a nurse around if the worst happens. Could you see if Casey wants a job on the side, while the doctor's office is closed for the storm? You'll be with us too, while your family's gone."

Joey shrugged again, but his eyes kindled with interest. "Yeah, I'll be around. I had to use a few personal days at the radio station before the quarter was up, so I'm off until Saturday. I'll call her."

Chad looked toward the direction of his home. "Caroline hasn't gained enough weight, so the twins will be small. I haven't been too concerned until now. I can't believe she's due with a hurricane threat over our heads."

Patrick scowled. "What's goin' to be left if Hugo comes through? If the Castaway's damaged, there goes my job." He swiped his hand over his face. "And if our homes are torn apart, I've got a pregnant wife and a two-year-old to find shelter for."

"We built the Castaway to hurricane codes, it's insured, and your salary is guaranteed. If a big one comes in strong, the Castaway won't escape, and it won't make money for a while. That's part of the risk we took by building it on the water, remember? Its appeal is also its weakness."

Patrick's mobile phone rang. He picked it up while Chad and Joey put their wrappers in a bag to throw away. "Are you serious? Hold on." He looked at Chad, and alarm filled the blue eyes that were so much like his sister's.

"Hugo's in the Gulf Stream and it's exploding from a CAT 2 into a monster, heading straight to the Carolinas. It's expected to hit tomorrow. We've got to go make a bunker at the Big House."

Chad had heard Andy Painter's voice and raised his to be heard through the phone. "We need to find someone to board up the Castaway or do it ourselves."

Patrick told his dad they were on their way. He quickly hung up while Joey strode to the other side of his Harley and reached for his helmet. When the order slip with the waitress's number fell out, he scooped it up and turned to the trash bin.

"Hey Joey, give me that," said Chad, holding out his hand and opening Patrick's glove compartment with the other.

Joey hesitated before he walked back. He and Patrick raised quizzical eyebrows at one another while Chad searched for a pen. He took the paper from Joey and wrote something on it.

Chad looked up, saw their expressions, and rolled his eyes. "This girl's new in town and looks up to Caroline. Maybe she can invite her to church. The girl might be loose, but she knows Caroline isn't. That's a start."

"Seriously?" Patrick sputtered. "Chad, that's—awkward—and you're playin' with fire. Are you really goin' to send my sister down this trail and not tell her this girl was tryin' to—"

"It's just a hunch," Chad interrupted. "I haven't thought it all through yet. This storm's gettin' me rattled."

Patrick huffed and looked the other way, drumming his fingers lightly on the car door in agitation. He decided to turn back and reinforce his point. "If eyes were hands, Chad, that girl was all over you. Like Gloria used to do when she lived here."

The muscles in Chad's neck and jaw clenched with a memory he despised. Joey studied him before he blew out his breath and turned. "I believe in hunches, Chad. But I hope Casey won't get the wrong idea if this little chick comes in and nestles up beside me on a Sunday mornin' in worship service."

He briskly went to his bike and talked over his shoulder. "I'll call Casey, then board up the storm shutters at home and pack a bag. My neighbor will help me, then I'll meet you at the Castaway. If I can round up any more help, I'll send them over. Chad, I'm stayin' at your place tonight."

"Mama, can you ride around the island with me a little while? I want to take photos with Chad's camera."

Caroline held the phone receiver to her ear and shifted her position on the oversized buff leather sofa. But it was impossible to get comfortable with the twins staking their claim on so much of her body.

"Sure, honey. I'm like a cat on a hot tin roof anyway."

"You always say worry is a sin, so cut it out."

Her mother's laughter spilled into the phone, soothing the ragged edges around Caroline's peace of mind. "Just wait 'til you have kids and remind them to do as you say, not as you do. See you in a few minutes."

Valerie Painter drove Caroline's 1965 Mustang around the island. Her dad had restored it, mostly with his own hands, and had it re-painted in the original factory "twilight blue" because he said it was the color of her eyes. He and her mother gave her the car for her 16th birthday, and as she rode in the passenger seat now with the white convertible top down, she snapped photos of views around her beloved island.

Palm branches waved congenially at them and silvery Spanish moss swayed as it dripped from live oaks, like a Southern belle imagining distant music at a ball.

Caroline's mother studied her sad, wistful demeanor. "Honey, you're lookin' at everything as if it's for the last time."

"Mama, how can I stand it if everything is lost?" Tears stung Caroline's eyes and she blinked fiercely while she let the Nikon rest from its strap against her tie-dyed maternity tank top. "It would be like losing Poppy Noble. At least while Painter Place remains as it was then, I can see him everywhere."

Valerie groaned sympathetically in her throat and put her arm around Caroline's shoulders. Both stood a willowy five feet nine inches tall, and she touched her dark bob of hair to her daughter's blonde bangs.

"Nothing stays the same in life," she said soothingly. "And somehow, that's a really good thing. Remember, the end of anything is the beginning of something new."

She pulled back to see her daughter's face. "You keep so much inside yourself, Caroline. You used to be like Patrick, a happy-go-lucky open book. You've opened up a lot since marrying Chad, but sometimes I catch you with an expression that's haunted and mysterious, like some heroine in an old movie."

Caroline's mouth quirked with a smile at her mother's melodramatic analogy. "My perspective changed when Poppy was ripped out of my life. I began to dread losing Gran Vanna and Grandma Audrey when I should've been enjoying time with them. Then when Chad left four years later, I realized all over again that nothing is certain, and I had no choice but to carry on, no matter how I felt about it. When he came back and I found out why he'd left and stayed gone for four more years, I discovered that even my family isn't what I thought."

She knew this was a painful topic for her mother, so she hurried on. "I don't dwell on it. But I've never figured out how to handle the loneliness of knowing that in an instant, God can take away the blessings He's given me. No matter how much I love Him and understand that He knows best, that makes me uneasy."

Valerie linked her arm through Caroline's and walked her through the sand and shells that crunched under their tennis shoes. "I'm glad you finally let me in on this. Have you told Chad?"

"No, I'm embarrassed. Mama, is this going to get worse when the twins are born? Will I be fearful of God letting somethin' bad happen to them?"

They reached the spidery arms of an old oak they had entrusted for shade over the Mustang. Valerie turned to look straight into her daughter's eyes. "Honestly, this is where I become a bad example again. I know the right thing to say to you, but I can't live it out. Something happened when Patrick was a baby, and I began to fear that God would allow something bad. Your dad was worse than me, almost paranoid. But our fear drew us closer. We started to pray more together about our children."

She shrugged as if shaking off a memory. "Every time has its share of trouble, Caroline. Back then, Poppy Noble was alive. But there was still a lot of uncertainty. Your dad had to produce the heir to carry on here, since Wyeth's illness left him unable to have children and Juliette didn't plan to stay at Painter Place. We were more at peace as you three grew older. Then little Noble and TJ were born, the twins are due, and Patrick has another baby on the way. I'm back to those twinges of fear. Let's pray for one another to trust Jesus and have peace about whatever He allows into our lives. It's better to experience a blessing for a brief time than never to have known that joy."

They turned to see Chad's car pull off the road and into the shade behind the Mustang. Caroline inhaled deeply as she watched him get out and grin at her. She loved to see him coming to her as if she were the only important thing in his world at that moment and knew the expression in his eyes behind the Wayfarers.

Chad strode over to Caroline and her mother and kissed her forehead. "I was worried when I saw your mom's car at the house and yours gone. Everything okay?"

His perceptive gaze caught the look passing between them. He pushed his sunglasses up to the top of his head, waiting.

Caroline shrugged nonchalantly and smiled. "I'm feeling a little nostalgic, so I asked Mama to drive me around the island to take photos. You told me not to drive or go anywhere alone, and I always do whatever you say."

Chad guffawed. He hesitated, looking from one to the other. An air of confidentiality wafted thickly around them like a lingering scent.

"Storm jitters?" he offered, fishing.

Valerie glanced down at her watch. "Oh! Look at the time! Andy will be waiting. I'd better get back to the house to help with storm preparations." She turned to get in the driver's seat of the Mustang. "I'll drop off Caroline's car and she can come back with you when you're ready."

They waved and watched her drive away. Then Chad said, "Somethin's up. Time for show and tell."

He pulled Caroline to him, which was a challenge with the twins between them. The Atlantic breeze wrapped its tendrils around all four of them. His family.

"Will you take me to the pier and stand with me in the pavilion?" Caroline whispered.

This was no answer to his question, but he caught a glimpse of something that made him uneasy. She had the intuition that always marked the artists in the generations at Painter Place. It made her unpredictable. She was the most interesting person he had ever known.

Chad looked over her head as she rested it on his shoulder. As he ran his fingers through her hair, he murmured, "I'm glad you asked. I was comin' home to take you there and told Patrick I needed an hour before I join in the mad rush to board up the Castaway."

Ten minutes later, they stood at the end of the ocean pier, on the spot where they said their wedding vows. He brought her here on their fourth anniversary two weeks ago and told her he loved her even more than he had on their wedding day.

Now, he stood facing her again and holding her hands. "Tell me who I am."

This was a trap, she knew. But she decided to cooperate—creatively.

"You're Phillip Chadwick Gregory III. You grew up here, left for college, and returned after four years to crash the Island Summer Dance and my world again, promising you'd always look after my home for me." She looked down at the signet ring on his right hand and ran her finger over it. "You gave me this ring at the dance because you knew I'd need visible proof that you could be trusted. It has your motto engraved on it from Psalm 1:3, about a man who seeks God."

She paused, watching his scowl melt away. "You're the guy who met the heroic conditions set up by our parents for you to court me and be vetted as the next Gregory to oversee Painter Place. I assumed you left me and this life behind. Then you earned my trust again when my sister Marina sent you on a quest to prove you're not a frog, but a prince, and you had to do it all without a kiss."

She glanced down at their clasped hands, where the sunshine became caught in her diamond. "To prove you were my prince, you proposed to me with my dream engagement ring, a smaller version of the one Grace Kelly's prince gave her. You put it on my finger in our secret childhood place on the veranda of the Big House, where you'd dreamed for years that I'd say 'yes.' All of this happened in the summer of 1985—the summer when a magical spell fell over the island, resulting in seven other weddings, five of them before the year was over."

Caroline paused again, smiling up at him. Memories now danced in his eyes.

"We made history as the first Painter and Gregory to marry since settling Painter Place over 300 years ago. We had our first kiss here in this spot on our wedding day. My first kiss had always been yours, and your first kiss had always been mine. We've had four of the best years of my life together and it still takes my breath to know that you're all mine and always will be. I married my impossibly handsome prince, and he still only has eyes for me."

She moved his hands in hers to her stomach. "And finally, God used you in the first mix of the Painter and Gregory genes. I don't know what He's goin' to create with that concoction, but if it's anything like what He did with you, it has to be incredible."

Caroline watched him hold a smile in check before he said, "You're really good at this. I didn't see all that comin', but you proved my point. I'll still be all those things without the pier, the pavilion, or our cottage, right?"

She blinked as the trap snapped shut. Then she nodded slowly.

"Do you understand what I'm sayin'?"

She nodded again, not taking her eyes from his. "But we have a legacy to continue here. It's who we are!"

"And God willin', we'll do it with whatever He gives us to work with. Right now, though, if the Painters and Gregorys crash and burn in a hurricane, this is still Dad and Wyeth's time to salvage what's left."

The anxious feeling tightened her chest again. "I want things to stay the same," she blurted. "I want to walk with our kids around the island and tell them things that happened before, with you and me, and Poppy. I don't want them to be born on the day I lose everything except you and my family!" Her voice choked and she brushed away an errant tear.

"Caroline, remember who I am. Do you trust me? Tell me what else is goin' on."

She used the back of her hand to catch another tear and looked out toward the ocean. It took restraint not to comfort her, but Chad was not about to relent. It had taken years to get to this moment. They often read one another's heart and mind with an exchanged look. She only turned away from him like this when she didn't want him to see that far.

He waited while her flirty blonde bangs blew back from her brow. Her straight nose was poised like a ballerina over the soft indentation of her upper lip, where he loved to press his fingertip. Now it teased his eyes into following down to her slightly parted lips, to a mouth he once told her would bring tears of joy to a sculptor. Her pearly pink lip gloss reminded him of the delicate interior of a seashell. Her jaw line always reminded him of confidence, and he often found it irresistible to trace the back of his fingers along it.

Like now. He reached up under her ear, where an amethyst teardrop set in silver was swinging in a soft breeze. Then he traced her jaw before cupping her chin to turn her face slowly back to him.

She followed his touch, meeting him with eyes he always said were like the Atlantic on a clear day. His expression melted her resolve and she confided in him. He squeezed her hand. "I wondered when you'd ever work this out for yourself or find a way to tell me. Let's talk about it more tonight when we're alone. We can relax and focus."

He glanced around at the noisy activity at the Big House, then at his watch. "Let's go to the pavilion."

They strolled side by side on the path to the sprawling covered gazebo structure. Caroline brushed her hand lovingly over the weathered wood railing before following him to stand in the middle on boards well-worn from years of sandy feet.

Tears stood in her eyes, and he had to swallow hard before he could speak. "Dance with me," he said huskily, pulling her into his arms.

Caroline sniffed and raised her arms gracefully onto his shoulders. She gulped and whispered, "I pick you." Then, she closed her eyes and melted into his steps, just as she had done for as long as she could remember. "I'm imagining the Japanese lanterns, moonlit sky, and our solo spotlight dance to celebrate the night we got engaged."

"You read my mind again." The melody of the song they had danced to on that incredible evening became a soft rumble in his throat as he hummed. Years of unforgettable moments swirled and danced around them while they swayed together.

They prayed out loud together as they swayed, thanking the Lord for countless priceless memories and asking for protection over their twins and Painter Place.

As they walked hand in hand to the car, Caroline's heart was lighter from sharing her secret burden with Chad. But she was haunted by the feeling she said a bittersweet goodbye to things that were part of all she had ever known.

Chapter Two

It was one of those hot, silent nights, when people sit at windows, listening for the thunder which they know will shortly break; when they recall dismal tales of hurricanes and earthquakes; and of lonely travelers on open plains, and lonely ships at sea, struck by lightning.
-Charles Dickens, Martin Chuzzlewit, Chapter XLII

The phone lines buzzed without mercy at the Big House. Savanna Painter, the matriarch of the family, called her son Wyeth from a writing conference in Atlanta, where she was a featured speaker and would remain safely with friends.

Wyeth's long-time gallery manager, Shelly, and her husband, his studio manager, called from a show they were setting up in New York. Wyeth told them to stay out of danger and use the time to make connections and work on representing the Painter Gallery. They arranged for friends to look after their house and would keep in touch when phones were up again.

Phillip Gregory called his family in Charleston. His daughter Sandy assured him that his son-in-law, Joey's brother Ben Grayson, had a military shelter arranged for her and little Joshua. But Phillip's parents and in-laws were planning to hunker down together in a local shelter. It frustrated him to hang up without convincing them to evacuate.

Their live-in housekeeper traveled inland to stay with relatives until the storm was over. She put dinner on the table for Camellia and Phillip, tearfully hugging them goodbye and making them promise to keep her updated. Camellia pushed her meatloaf around on her plate, upset over the reports of the storm hitting Charleston and the governor urging coastal residents to evacuate.

"Your mom said your dad didn't tell you he doesn't have his strength back after that virus he's been so sick with, and Mama told me Daddy didn't tell us he'd banged up his leg working in the yard and isn't getting around well. How will they get to a shelter in traffic tomorrow? What if the shelters are full?"

Phillip squeezed his eyes shut. Of course, his dad would never mention being sick, knowing Phillip was working to protect Global and Painter Place from the storm. He understood the pressure. It was once his job, handed down from generation to generation.

Opening his eyes again, he ate what remained of his roasted red potatoes and green beans just to get something nutritious down to sustain him tonight. His thoughts tripped headlong over themselves into a chaotic tumble. Then, he glanced at Camellia and did a double take.

Her cool green eyes anxiously searched his before settling into a look that conveyed total confidence in him. He felt so inadequate to deal with this storm, but he could never disappoint her. Ever.

From the moment he met her eyes at a concert on the Battery over thirty years ago, that same look had made him feel like he could do anything. And he had, after measuring himself by how she saw him.

He pushed away from the table and stood by her chair to take her hand. She rose, wearing the smile reserved for him, and he pulled her close, swaying with her to the rhythmic island music on the stereo. He relaxed under her touch as her hands slid over his polo shirt, melting the tension in his shoulder blades.

"Cami, how can you be so exciting and so calming at the same time?" He nuzzled his face into her blonde hair, close to the diamond in her earlobe, and murmured, "I'm in over my head this time. I'm desperately goin' to need you to make it through the storm."

Before leaving for the emergency meeting at the Big House, Phillip called his dad and his father-in-law again to convince them to evacuate Charleston. This time, his dad confessed that he was too sick to drive in crawling traffic.

Then his father-in-law said traffic to get out on I-26 was like a parking lot. He planned to stay and protect his house on the Battery against looters.

Phillip envisioned the nightmare of flooding, flying debris and power outages his father-in-law would endure even if the storm did not destroy his house. He grimaced as his imagination concocted a mental image of Montgomery sitting with his gun aimed at the door.

He barked into the phone. "Cami and I are leavin' in an hour to be in Charleston tonight. We'll be at your place as soon as I can get Mom and Dad. We're not goin' unland on I-26, we're drivin' back to Painter Place so I can handle trouble here. Chad's not ready for this and Caroline needs him if she goes into labor. Cami will drive your car and follow me, so fill up the tank if there's a station open that still has gas. Be ready to ride most of the night. You know I'm not kiddin' when I say this, Montgomery—don't make me force you into your car in front of your wife and daughter."

Caroline held a cassette tape in her hands. Her bold painting of the cliffs in Mevagissey was featured on the cover of *Braking*, and she turned it over to return a smile at the face of the British band's front man before slipping the tape by Public Parking into the stereo. Baker Holmes' voice filled the cottage as he belted out an upbeat message that smoothed the crinkles of apprehension in her nerves. Her friend Baker was expecting his first baby, and Caroline prayed again for his wife Beth to have a safe delivery.

She loved this cottage on the Gregory estate, her first home with Chad. A hired crew arrived before lunch to carry away the most valuable and sentimental art and collections to be taken to a vault inland, and the empty spaces made her feel anxious. Brushing aside tears, she packed a box with non-perishable food and water bottles from the pantry.

Sliding the box beside another one full of supplies for a possible stay in the Big House, she absently sang along with Baker. The music floated upstairs as she climbed them to pack for an evacuation. There was a bag for nursery essentials in case the twins arrived before she could get home after the storm, and as she looked around the sweet room she and Chad created for the twins, a sense of loss swept over her. If the hurricane took this cottage, where would she raise her children?

In the master bedroom, she found Chad's khakis and polo tossed across a chair. He never left things lying around, and she smiled, remembering his hurry after spending too much time with her dancing in the pavilion. There was a jingle of coins when she picked them up. Still singing with the stereo, she felt around to see which pocket he missed emptying.

He had his wallet and keys, but left his business card holder, some change, and a slip of paper with her name on it. It was common for him to jot down things during the day on random bits of paper and tell her about them when he emptied his pockets—snippets to remind her of something, or a date he wanted to plan or put on her calendar. When they were brainstorming baby names, he was especially creative with the sources of paper for his ideas in his pockets, jotting down a serious name on one side and a silly name on the reverse.

This one was from the Sand Dollar, a long-time favorite local drive-in burger spot in Whitehaven. "Caroline" was written at the top in Chad's bold handwriting. Underneath her name, the receipt was a little confusing. In a different ink, curvy handwriting spelled "Call," and Caroline unfolded the paper to find a phone number.

Chad's handwriting picked up again underneath with the note, "waitress—new student at Tech—invite to church."

With a tilt of her head, she studied the note again. Apparently, Chad talked to a waitress at the Sand Dollar who had moved here for school and was looking for a church in the area. He knew it was more appropriate that Caroline be the one to invite her.

If this storm was the problem people were predicting, the young waitress might want to connect with their church for help. She picked up the extension phone by the bed and punched in the number on the paper. On the second ring, a female voice said hello.

"Hi, my name is Caroline. My husband had a note for me on a receipt from the Sand Dollar with this phone number, saying you were new in town and might be interested in an invitation to visit our church."

Raucous laughter blared out of the phone receiver. Caroline winced and held it out from her ear.

"I've heard some creative excuses in my day, but this is sheer genius!" A fresh wave of laughter followed, and Caroline braced herself.

"He must've met Krystal. She gives her number to guys she wants to go out with. I'm her roommate, and she's not home yet. Let me guess—he didn't give you this note. You *found* it. If your man had Krystal's number in his pocket, trust me, sugar, goin' to church was the last thing on their minds. You must be one of those wholesome Pollyanna types who believes everything he says. Poor thing—it's time to wise up."

Caroline slowly hung up the phone.

Chapter Three

Never be afraid to trust an unknown future to a known God.
-Corrie ten Boom

The air in the Painter mansion was electric with apprehension. The normally beautiful, gracious interior of the mansion had always looked like it was straight out of a magazine. Now, the walls, tables, and shelves were bare where art originals and valuable antiques were missing. The open, airy views were gone, gloomy now with draperies closed against boarded windows.

Phillip and Camellia stood near the door, packed to leave for Charleston to evacuate their parents and dreading being at the mercy of traffic and the weather to get them to safety. Phillip had no idea how long it might take and was on edge at leaving Chad in charge. His son lacked the experience it would take to handle a disaster on the island, and a mistake could mean loss of life.

Caroline reclined with her feet up on a loveseat. Her eyes were moody and troubled as she silently watched all the preparations and instructions.

Chad was exhausted as he sat on the floor in front of her, trying not to lean against the upholstery in his dirty work clothes. His hair had a dent all around from wearing the grimy Braves baseball cap on the floor beside him. Joey lounged wearily next to him.

Casey Austin had ridden over from Whitehaven with Joey. She settled into a dining chair pulled next to Caroline and her eyes were alert as she watched the activity. She tossed her head to swing the longest side of her trendy asymmetrical haircut away from her face.

Patrick's wife Natalie sat in a large wing chair holding their two-year-old son, Noble. He slept fitfully, his blonde hair flattened against his mother's shoulder, while race cars endlessly chased one another all over his onesie. He straddled the lump of Natalie's stomach, where his unborn sibling was also resting with their mother. Patrick sat on the floor a few feet in front of them, too tired to talk, absently toying with the adjustable strap on a sweaty racing cap that should have been in the trash can.

Caroline and Patrick's little sister, Marina, also sat on the floor with her husband, Danny Mitchell. Their daughter, Taylor Juliette, or TJ, as they called her, giggled as she trekked tirelessly between them with her newfound walking skills.

Wyeth held a checklist in front of him. "Well, it looks like we've done all we can on short notice," he observed. "If you didn't get dinner, Maggie Jane left some vegetable soup on the stove and some fresh bread on the cutting board. We'll finish last minute things in the morning and see what the weather report is, but it looks like we'll have to head to the shelter by the afternoon. Patrick, is the Castaway boarded?"

"Yeah, Joey and some friends from church drove by and stopped to help."

Chad gathered the energy to speak. "Casey Austin is part of our group now. She's stayin' to help Caroline."

"Glad to have you, Casey," Wyeth said with a nod to her. "We all feel better that you're here."

Danny announced that he and Marina had their cottage boarded and would go to Whitehaven after the meeting to help his parents. "We'll stay with them tonight," he said in his lazy drawl as TJ toppled onto him. "We'll meet you at the shelter."

"Okay, then. Let's have a prayer. I'll say somethin' first and then start. Anyone who wants to pray can jump in when someone else is finished. Andy will close."

He cleared his throat. "They say a storm like Hugo happens about once every 200 years. The foundation of this house is set in bedrock, which is part of the reason it's standin' after 300 years of storms. Painter Place was built by someone who had an eternal foundation on the ultimate Rock, and he dedicated this house, the island, and his life to that Rock. He trusted that whatever survived and thrived here in the years to come was all part of bein' in God's hand, the answers to his prayers for future generations. In Matthew 7, Jesus teaches us to build our lives on Him—a spiritual foundation. Verses 24 and 25 tell us that everyone who believes Jesus' words and lives by them may be compared to a wise man who built his house on rock. When the rain fell, and the floods came, and fierce winds slammed against that house, it did not fall. I praise God daily that everyone here has that foundation. Ultimately, we'll get through this storm, and whatever else God allows to happen to us."

Chad said goodbye to his parents, getting last minute instructions from his dad, a kiss from his mom, and an anxious hug from both. He turned to join Patrick and Joey in the kitchen for some of Maggie Jane's soup and homemade bread, then he picked up an apple from a bowl of fruit on the kitchen island. They carried laden trays back into the living room to sit on the floor. Chad made a tray for Caroline, cutting a part of his apple for her and encouraging her to eat.

The guys chewed in rare silence, and Caroline waited until they finished before she casually dropped her bomb.

"Who was the waitress interested in today at the Sand Dollar?"

Natalie sat up taller, alert, and wide-eyed. Casey scooted to the edge of her chair.

Chad froze in mid-bite of his last slice of the apple, hesitating before he chewed it slowly. Joey swallowed his last bite of bread and picked up his glass of tea to wash it down.

The three friends wordlessly exchanged looks. Chatter came from the kitchen, where Wyeth Painter, his wife Chrissy, and younger brother Andy gathered to answer phone calls and talk about how their dad once handled preparations. Valerie held her sleeping grandson Noble in her lap in another chair across the room, close enough to hear both groups.

The silence among the young men stretched awkwardly. Patrick read the warning in his mother's eyes. He looked back at Chad and blurted, "It wasn't a good idea."

"What wasn't a good idea?" There was an edge in Natalie's voice.

"Don't assume anything," Patrick replied over his shoulder to his wife, holding his left hand up in the air and wiggling his finger to emphasize the wedding band. "I made sure she saw my ring and she stopped there."

"Then who *did* she pursue, and what did you do about it?" Natalie looked past the back of his blue Castaway sponsored ball jersey at Chad and Joey. Chad closed his eyes under her scrutiny and took a long draught of water. The only sound was the ice in his glass chinking on the side. Joey suddenly found the swish logo on his dirty Nikes fascinating, running his finger along it over and over.

Patrick looked at his friends and said, "Look, we're busted, and I didn't promise not to tell, like Chad. So, let's air this out. I'm not fightin' with my wife or my sister tonight."

Chad and Joey exchanged a meaningful look, then Chad looked back down, tracing a pattern on his napkin with the Fleur-de-Lis on the end of his soup spoon. Patrick related what happened at lunch that day, beginning with the warning that tipped him off about showing the waitress his wedding band.

Then he looked at his sister. "I didn't think it was a good idea to have you call this girl without tellin' you what she was doin'. I watched enough cartoons to know Wyle E. Coyote dynamite when I see it."

Casey sat back in her chair and crossed her arms. She studied Joey's downturned face and then looked at Caroline. "How'd you find out?"

"Emptying Chad's pockets to put his khakis in the laundry. I found the number the waitress gave Joey. But it had my name on it and a note to invite her to church. I thought the phones would be down after the storm and this girl might need a church for help, so I called." She told them about her brief conversation with Krystal's roommate.

Patrick spontaneously laughed out loud at the comment about Chad and the waitress not having church on their mind, but quickly clamped his hand over his mouth. Joey fought a grin and turned his contorted expression away until he had control. Natalie gasped, eyes popping. Casey was indignant, huffing and squirming in her chair with the urge to set the record straight with Krystal's rude friend.

Chad raked his fingers through his hair in agitation. "I'm sorry about how this whole thing went south. When the waitress asked me not to tell you what she did, it was because she respected you and even defended you, assuming I'd be mad about Derrick. I agreed because she hadn't known who I was when she—" his voice trailed off. "You and I don't come home and tell one another every time someone—checks us out."

He tossed a tight smile her way as bait to get one back. "Not that I don't wanna know, I'm just afraid to ask."

Her expression did not change, so his smile vanished, and he sighed. "Look, I was repelled by the way she gave Joey her number. But when he was throwin' it away, it flashed into my mind it might be an open door. After all, he was given that number twice."

Cross-legged on the floor beside his tray, Chad's demeanor was apologetic and resolved to facing any consequences. In the dining room, Wyeth picked up the phone as it rang again.

Caroline shifted on the loveseat as the twins began a game of kickball inside her. "You were with your accountability team," she said. "That should be enough to help dismiss the rumors unless people lump all three of you in it. But when we get home, expect a private discussion about promising another woman to hide something from me. I'm your wife, Chad. She, her roommate, and whoever else they tell might wonder what other secrets you keep from me."

Chad gnawed his lip but did not break away from the look in her eyes. Behind him, Wyeth waved to get Caroline's attention with one hand over the mouthpiece of the phone. "There's a call for you. Do you want it over there?"

Caroline nodded. Casey handed her the phone from the end table. "Hi, this is Caroline." Instantly, she sat up. "Hello, Krystal. What a—surprise."

She rose clumsily from the loveseat. Chad almost rose to help her, but she shook her head. He settled in his place on the floor with his legs under him, watching.

"I see," she said into the phone, walking away. "Well, this is a good place to reach me or leave a message. My home phone is a private number." She reached the huge carved double front doors, keeping her back to the room as she talked.

Despite her previous rebuff, Chad got up to go stand contritely behind her. He hesitantly put his hands on her waist and leaned his head down near the phone at her ear, listening to Krystal's version of what happened.

"I appreciate the apology, and that you've told your roommate what really happened," Caroline replied into the receiver. "Warn her this Pollyanna has a way of dealing with rumors about her husband that isn't remotely like the 'glad game.' Are we clear on that?"

Chad instantly backed away to stifle his laughter, facing the wall and pretending to pound silently on it. Patrick fell over where he sat on the floor, covering his face with the dirty ball cap to muffle his laughter. Joey's shoulders shook as he buried his face in his folded arms across his knees.

"All right, then. I don't expect to hear any more about this." Caroline said in a tone that brooked no nonsense and reminded everyone of her grandmother Savanna. She shifted from one shapely leg to another as the twins seemed to gallop inside her. Her attitude softened.

"I know it took courage to call me." Caroline filed the edge off her voice, and then listened for a few moments. "That's sweet. I appreciate the kind words about my presentation. I hope you'll come to the gallery and remember that the invitation to visit our church is still open. Maybe you could bring your roommate."

Caroline glanced back at Joey, meeting his apologetic brown eyes before she turned again to the doors. "Listen, Krystal, can we talk a minute, girl to girl? Givin' your phone number out to guys you meet—how's this approach to findin' Mr. Right workin' for you?"

Chad quickly resumed his stance at Caroline's back so he could hear. "I—I'm not sure what you mean," Krystal said. "How will I find him, if I'm not out hunting?"

Caroline sighed. "The thing is most guys like to be the hunters. A relationship has less value to them if they didn't work for it. Something else you should know about Joey is that he's an authentic Christian. You could think of him as—a preacher."

Chad's body shook with suppressed laughter against her back and Patrick stifled laughter. She ignored them.

"What that means is, unless you can see yourself as a church leader's wife, he's not your type. If you knew him better, you might not have given him your number."

Krystal gasped in surprise at the other end of the line before Caroline continued. "I don't know if you're a Christian and believe in a divine plan, but you believe in something like fate, right?"

"Sure," stammered Krystal.

"So, if you believe fate will ultimately bring you and Mr. Right together, do you really think you could miss him, even if you tried?"

When Krystal mulled this over, Caroline went for the soft underbelly of her misguided approach to finding lasting love. "So, how many guys will it take before Mr. Right shows up? How many women do you want Mr. Right to—uh, spend time with—before it's *your* time? Don't you hope he's not runnin' around wild, but waitin' on you? And Krystal, if finding one another is inevitable, aren't you cheatin' on him? You've drawn the line at married men like my brother and my husband, but when you pursued Joey without knowing if you were suited for one another, you were tempting him to cheat on his future mate while you cheat on yours. I think Mr. Right would rather that you waited for him to find you, don't you?"

Behind Caroline, it was Casey's turn to gasp. Her eyes darted from Chad and Caroline over to Joey. Meeting a loaded look in his eyes, she blushed and looked away to Natalie. She whispered, "That's—brilliant! Where does she come up with this stuff?"

Chad's heart soared as he put his arms around Caroline from behind her and felt his rowdy twins kicking. They were strong. She was amazing. This was his family.

His smile of contentment faded when he remembered that he was in trouble once he left here. Like Wile E. Coyote, his plan had blown him up. He heard Krystal stammering around on the other side of the line.

"I know, it's an unexpected perspective on things." Caroline's tone sounded like she was talking to a special friend, not witnessing to a lost soul. "You won't hear logic like that in a song or on television, where most of us get our worldview. We let clueless people lead us into their own chaos because they dress it up to look so romantic and independent. But you know what I found out? What they're celebrating is brokenness and bondage, not freedom. The people we blindly follow on the road to regret aren't the ones who pay our consequences. But you can bet they will pay their own."

Caroline listened a moment while Chad seemed to lean on her in his exhaustion. She braced herself to prop him up, setting her free hand on his arm around her. She said into the phone, "Listen, if you'd like to think about this and talk more, let's plan to have lunch together at the Castaway after this hurricane is over. Right now, my husband's ready to fall off his feet from all the storm preparations. I need to get him home."

After Caroline said goodbye, Chad rallied energy to take the receiver from her to put it in the cradle on the table. He looked smugly over at Patrick.

"Okay, man, I get it," conceded Patrick, raising his hands in surrender. "Your hunch *might* be right, and this *might* work out in a quirky way. You win Round One with me. But soon you'll be in Round Two with my sister about promising another woman you'd hide something from her. Caroline's the one who saved the day for you and for Preacher Joey, who can now eat at the Sand Dollar in peace again."

Joey rewarded Caroline with a grateful look before bopping Patrick in the chest with his tossed ball cap. Valerie gestured to Caroline to come over to her and her sleeping grandson while the others continued their banter. She had tears in her eyes as she pulled her daughter's arm down to whisper to her. "I love you. No one else could have done what you just did."

Caroline pulled a light throw over herself on a blue sofa in the sitting area of the master suite, near the glass doors that opened to the waterway. Natalie had crocheted the cotton throw for her as a gift, and the colors were supposed to represent Monet's *Waterlilies* painting, which was the theme for the décor of the suite. Natalie tried to get Caroline to work on crochet projects with her while they all watched television or movies together, but usually Chad wanted her hand or arm. He never seemed to have caught up on the four years they were forced apart.

Now, as she settled into the sofa, hoping to get some sleep through the early morning antics of the twins, she peered through the darkness at the bed. Chad slept so soundly he had not moved since lying down. His handsome profile was outlined by the glowing face of the alarm clock, and she felt that squeeze of her heart and a rush of love that sometimes overwhelmed her. He was too good to be real. And he chose her. Of all the women he could have, he wanted her.

Earlier, while she made Joey and Casey comfortable around the cottage, Chad had showered and fallen asleep waiting for her to come back up. It seemed selfish to wake him, so she swallowed back all the things she wanted to say. He had planned to talk with her about what she told him on the pier, and she wanted to clear the air about what happened with Krystal.

It was the first time they had gone to bed with an unresolved issue between them since their marriage. In the morning, they needed to hit the ground running to safeguard Painter Place. Her thoughts and feelings must wait.

Chapter Four

Patrick saw the explosion as he drove down Pavilion Avenue, just before he reached the bridge from the island to Whitehaven. Instinctively, he slammed on the brakes and felt the tires leave the road as he hydroplaned sideways. But the Tahoe did not hit the bridge until Chad slid into him in the Jeep Cherokee, instantly followed by another jarring impact and sickening crunch of metal when Joey rammed Chad's jeep with his Nissan 300ZX.

Joey checked on Casey and helped get her seatbelt loose, then he was first out of any of the three vehicles. He ran to Caroline's door to see if she was hurt. She and Maggie Jane claimed to be fine, and Chad jumped out to run to Patrick's door. Joey checked on Natalie.

Chad scowled and groaned when he saw blood on Patrick's forehead near his eyebrow. He glanced across the front seat at Joey and Natalie. "I saw Patrick bang his head on the window when I slid into the side of him. I should've given him more space in this weather."

Patrick waved Chad off and Joey reminded him he had done the same, crashing into the Jeep and putting Caroline and the twins at risk. He told Chad they were both like a surfboard on water and could not stop. Then he gestured back to Casey to check on Patrick.

Natalie assured them that she and the baby she carried were fine, and little Noble was safe in his car seat, looking out his window at the flames and smoke on the bridge with a bewildered expression.

"I'm all right. Just a little dazed. I had my seat belt on," Patrick said, dismissing their concerns. Chad backed out into the rain to make room for Casey, who took Patrick's head to examine his wound. He protested and winced when she made him put pressure on a tissue she dabbed at his forehead.

Black mountains of smoke rolled over the bridge, but it was impossible to see what happened because the crest blocked their view. Chad tried not to slip on wet grass as he ran down to the beach beside the bridge to find the cause of the explosion. Joey followed him, and Patrick soon joined them. A large boat was burning, trapped under the bridge, caught on the pilings in high tide and rough water between the crest and Whitehaven. The bridge itself moaned as if it was human.

They watched in horror as a man in a life jacket jumped from the back of the boat into the churning water and never came up. Chad looked desperately at Joey as if he could invent a way for them to rescue the man, but Joey shook his head sadly. Patrick turned away and stepped over to an ancient oak tree, retching.

"He could have come up on the other side of the boat and tried to make the shore at the Castaway," Chad said hopefully. "He'd be close."

Joey nodded, but he looked doubtful.

"Andy made it across before the explosion," Chad said. "He may not know if Patrick was caught in it."

Seeing Patrick was sick, Casey watched her footing as she hurried down to check on him. She handed him a bottle of water and a small towel before running up to grab Chad's arm. "We have a problem. Caroline stood up and her water broke. She'll be in labor soon."

Joey groaned loudly, bringing both hands up to his forehead and raking back the wet hair from his face. "I hope I didn't do that when I hit the jeep."

Chad stood with rain dripping off the ends of his hair and chin, staring at Casey, uncomprehending. She shook his arm, and her hand slid on his wet skin. Her expression was urgent. "Chad, listen to me! If we can't cross the bridge, we need to get your wife back to the house."

At the same instant, she and Joey saw someone staggering toward them from the direction of the Gregory pier. Shocked and wide-eyed, she let her hand slip from Chad's arm. He turned to see what they were looking at, and all three stood transfixed. Curious at their reactions, Patrick wiped his face with the towel and came over. His jaw dropped in disbelief before he clenched his fist.

A tall, gray-haired man limped and held his ribs with his hand. He was dripping from more than the rain—he had come out of the water. A backpack was slung on the opposite shoulder from his injured side.

They stood speechless for the time it took him to reach them. "Hello, Chad," the man drawled. His gray eyes looked down to Patrick's balled fist before roaming up with a cordial nod. "Patrick."

"Dad told you years ago not to show up on this island again!" Patrick growled through clenched teeth.

"Not exactly. He told me never to come across that bridge again. I didn't use the bridge."

The man tilted his head out to the fiery boat. "The captain was an alcoholic who needed my money, or he'd never have taken the job of gettin' me here before the storm. He missed your pier, but he helped me jump out with a life jacket near the Gregory's. Hope he made it to the shore."

"Who are you?" blurted Casey, baffled at this bizarre interaction.

Chad cleared his throat and found his voice. "Casey, this is Dr. Anthony Rush. He's Patrick's grandfather."

Andy Painter saw a large boat struggling in the waterway as he crested the bridge, distantly following his brother Wyeth in a caravan heading off the island to stay at a local shelter. A surge of adrenaline shot his heart into his throat. Experience told him the vessel would never clear the bridge in such high and turbulent water. Before he could shout a warning to Valerie, he felt his F150 jump as if there had been an earthquake underneath it. The explosion boomed in his ears, and he floored the accelerator to put more distance between his truck and the flames that licked the bridge in his rear-view mirror.

The long bridge groaned and shuddered in protest. Valerie screamed Patrick's name while Andy slammed on the brakes at the end of the bridge, slinging the truck around on the flooded pavement so it faced back to the island. He grabbed Valerie's arm to keep her from getting out and commanded her to wait. He tried to dial Patrick's mobile phone with shaking hands. It took more than once to get it right. He held it with his left hand and grabbed his frantic wife's arm again to keep her in the truck.

Natalie answered. He could breathe again. Glancing at Valerie and nodding his head, he learned Patrick delayed getting on the bridge when he turned to check on Noble. He saw the explosion, reacted by hitting the brakes too hard, and hydroplaned, which set off a chain reaction for the others to slide into him.

"Patrick is a little banged up and shaken," Natalie reported. "He hit his head on his window when Chad knocked the Tahoe into the bridge, and he's got a cut over his eye that's bleeding. He bumped his shoulder when Joey hit Chad into us again. When he saw a man jump off the boat, he got sick, but Casey's not sure if it's from seeing the man drown or if it's a concussion. Everyone else seems to be okay, except that Caroline's water broke. And some man is here off the boat. He limped up from the Gregorys' place. They're here now at the car."

Andy's voice was incredulous. "Natalie, are you tellin' me a man made it off the moving boat—"

"Dad! This is Patrick. When can we get across the bridge?"

"Hold on. I'm goin' to see if there's any lane left."

Andy and Valerie both jumped down from the truck, heedless of the stinging rain and wind gusts. They took a few steps into rivers of water over the pavement before the concussion of a smaller explosion rocked them, sending Valerie colliding into her husband. She screamed and sobbed hysterically. "Get my children off that island!"

He hugged her tightly against his drenched shirt. "Okay, okay, baby. Calm down. I need to think."

She shook violently as she clung to him, and he smoothed a hand over her dripping dark hair. He kept the other arm wrapped strongly around her to soothe her, hoping she would not resist being led back to the truck. He opened her door and put her in before he settled into the driver's side and picked up the phone. Their clothes soaked the interior. "Patrick, listen to me carefully."

"Dad! Dad, are you okay?"

"Yeah, but that bridge is goin' to burn a while. Metal is melting. Can you smell it? Maybe this deluge will put it out. I'm taking your mom to the shelter to get her out of this weather, and I'll round up some help and come back in a few minutes. For now, get everyone in the Big House and set up as if you're goin' to ride out the storm. Is Chad close by?"

"Yeah, he's with Caroline. Casey says she's going into labor soon. We need to get her outta here, Dad. We need to leave. I don't want Natalie and Noble on this island tonight!"

Andy felt a stab in his gut. He had never heard desperation and fear in his son's voice before. "I don't want you there either, Patrick. I love you, all of you. Can you put Chad on?"

"I love you too, Dad. Tell Mom the same. She must be pretty scared."

Andy Painter heard a muffled sound before Chad answered.

"Chad, listen to me carefully. I don't know how hard a hit Patrick took, but he's not himself. He sounds rattled and panicked, and I've never seen him act like that—never would've expected it with you and Joey around. Have Casey keep an eye on him for concussion. I need you to be in charge until he settles down, do you understand? Are you steady?"

"Yeah, I'm—I'm steady. I'm just tryin' to adjust to a new scenario here. It seems to change by the minute."

"I understand, and I'm goin' to go get some help. Do not—I repeat, Chad, *do not* come onto that bridge to check the damage or try to cross it. If it can be done, I'm the one who's goin' to try it. Is anything drivable after the accident?"

"My Cherokee is—probably the Tahoe, we just can't open the passenger door on the driver's side."

"Chad, I'm goin' to be straight up with you. I've got nothing left in the marina that will survive comin' over to get you by water. But if that bridge isn't safe, you're a lot better off on the island in the Big House than in a vehicle falling into the waterway. Do you understand me?"

He heard Chad inhale sharply. Andy could tell his blunt word picture had the intended effect, so he continued. "For now, take everyone to the Big House, like when we ride storms out. Remember the plan? If I can't get to you and can't reach you again on the phone, don't stay on the first floor too late. High tide is just after two in the morning, and the surge could come up the foundation. Keep checking the radio and portable TV for alerts and bring the phones in from the cars. Bring in *everything* from the cars—they won't survive the surge. Get Caroline into Gran Vanna's suite when she needs it. Don't let anyone stand under the stained-glass dome in the rotunda. Has Casey ever helped deliver a baby?"

"She's assisted when she was training. Maggie Jane's helped her cousin, who's a midwife, but Andy, we have a doctor here now."

"*What*?"

The wind blew into the phone to make a pounding sound as he waited. Chad's breathing sounded like he was moving away from the others. "Patrick's pretty messed up about it. Get this! Of all people, Tony Rush swam up from the boat that crashed. He claims twins are a risky delivery and he didn't want Caroline to end up in a shelter without a doctor. I know he's a heart surgeon, but he's on standby when a patient delivers a baby, and he brushed up on any complications with twins. Only, he may need a doctor himself. He's limping and holding his ribs. His shirt is snagged like he was thrown against our pier by the current before he could climb up. Check the shoreline around the Castaway for the captain. We saw him jump out of the burning boat and we're prayin' he made it."

Andy opened his mouth, but his mind went blank at the audacity of his father-in-law's appearance in this crisis and the probability of anyone getting to shore in the wild water. His blue eyes darted to Valerie's anxious expression. She sniffed and dabbed her nose with a tissue. He decided not to break this news about her estranged father to her yet.

The wind made a pounding sound into the receiver. "Andy, I've walked away from the others. I don't—I don't know how this is all going to work out, but I do know it doesn't look good for us to get off this island, or for anything on this island to—to survive this storm. Will you tell my dad somethin' for me?"

Andy heard Chad's voice shake as he tried several times to speak. Tears sprang from Andy's eyes, and he turned away from Valerie to look out into the storm.

Chad's voice was a croak once he found it. "Cell tower reception might be down before I can call him. I need to get everyone back to the mansion. Caroline and I thought it would be more fun for everyone if we kept the twins' names and gender a secret until they're born, but now I want you to have people prayin' for them by their names tonight. Do you have somethin' to write with?"

Andy was choking with emotion as he asked Valerie to give him a pen and notepad from the glove compartment. "Hold on."

"Have my dad call Cole and Sandy. Tell Valerie to call Audrey and get Chrissy to call Gran Vanna and Juliette. Get us on every prayer chain you can network to. And Andy—your daughter and son—"

Chad's voice broke again before he continued in a strangled tone. "They're two of the best things that ever happened to me. I'll die protecting them."

Wyeth jerked open the door of his brother's truck, alternately looking from the fire and smoke on the bridge to his brother, who was crying and dialing his mobile phone with shaking hands. Valerie was inconsolable, clutching a piece of paper.

"What happened?" Wyeth shouted over the wind.

Andy looked at the phone as if it were misbehaving when no one answered. He let it fall into his lap and he wiped his eyes. "Help me get Valerie into your SUV. Chrissy needs to take her to the shelter to rally help and make phone calls. A boat hit the bridge, the kids are stranded, and they've been in a chain reaction accident that banged Patrick up and sent Caroline into labor. We need to rescue them, and maybe a survivor from the boat. I can't reach Phillip."

Wyeth ran to Chrissy, who got out of the Explorer with the hood of her purple raincoat pulled over her head against the pelting rainfall. They hurried to Valerie's side of Andy's truck, and Wyeth opened her door. Gently but firmly, he pulled her arm to help her get down.

She resisted, insisting she would not leave until they told her how they were getting her children and grandchildren off the island. But Chrissy convinced her she could help her children best if she rushed to the shelter to see if anyone might know what to do.

With that plan, Valerie let Wyeth put her in the passenger side of his Explorer, sobbing desperately as she looked out at Andy through the window. Chrissy's face was stricken and pale when she met

Wyeth's eyes through the window and started the engine. The keys jingled in her trembling hand.

Buffeted by wind gusts and driving rain, the Painter brothers turned away and jogged toward the flames and smoke on the bridge.

Camellia Gregory settled down onto a dark green sleeping bag her youngest son Cole used before he left for London. He stashed it away without washing it, and traces of his musky scent mixed with a hint of a smoky campfire as she unrolled the padded fabric. She smiled at the reminder of her youngest son. He was happy in London, but she wished he could come home.

Leaning back wearily against a wall of wooden gymnasium bleachers, she checked on her parents and her in-laws again as they slept in cots close by. "Did you let Andy know where we are?" she asked Phillip, who sat down beside her with tousled hair and a day's worth of beard stubble framing his face.

"Right after we stopped. They hadn't left yet."

"Were they calling again once they got settled?"

"Yeah. We should've heard somethin' by now. Where's the phone?"

Camellia rummaged under bags, searching to find the phone. She pushed Chad's number to check on him. Just when she thought there would be no answer, gusty wind blew into the receiver with her son's voice.

"Hi, honey. Why are you out in the weather?"

"Mom! Did Andy call you?" She heard him turn his face from the phone to answer Joey about taking something into the house.

"No, we couldn't hear the phone and just found it. Granddad's sick and we heard the highway was blocked. We had to settle into a shelter not far from home—near Georgetown."

"I need to talk to Dad. And Mom—I love you. God gave me the only mom in the world that was right for me."

Camellia's heart flipped over in fear, and she paled as she sat up straight. "I love you, too, honey, endlessly." Then she blurted, "And I'm so proud of you. I'm in awe of what God's done in your life. You're goin' to be a great dad."

Phillip watched Camellia's reaction with a scowl as he took the phone. "Chad, what's goin' on?" Static began to interfere with the connection.

"Dad, call Andy for the details. We're stranded at the Big House and Caroline's in labor. If no one rescues us, the twins will be born here in the storm. I want to give you their names. Call Cole and Sandy and get us all on every prayer chain you can."

Phillip felt his heart drop with nowhere to hit bottom, a freefall that left him breathless. He put out a hand to steady himself, but the sensation went on and on. He heard Chad answer a question from Patrick about whether they were leaving the wrecked vehicles in the parking lot.

His mind raced. Chad was in charge—something was wrong with Patrick. They were supposed to be a team in an emergency. There were wrecked vehicles.

More static grated. Phillip asked Camellia to find something to write on. She scrambled in her purse and handed him a pen and her pocket calendar.

"Dad?"

"I'm here. Is Patrick hurt?"

"Yes. Andy will explain. Let Sandy and Ben know Joey's stranded with us. We need prayers to get through tonight. Write this down."

Phillip trotted over to a spot by the door of the shelter to make calls. He was unsuccessful in reaching Andy Painter, so he called Wyeth's phone and talked to Chrissy. She explained the accidents and the explosion that damaged the bridge.

He looked back across the room at Camellia, who raised a tissue to her face as she cried quietly. Thankfully, their parents were sleeping. He dialed his daughter Sandy on her mobile phone, reaching her in a shelter. He told her what he knew about the situation and the names of the twins. Her husband Ben snatched the phone and barked into it with alarm.

"Phillip, tell me I heard wrong—Joey is *not* stranded on White Island tonight in this storm! I can't get anyone there in this mess." Then, Ben shouted in frustration and fear. "That island will be the Atlantic Ocean at high tide tonight!"

Static was the next blast in Phillip's ear. He lost the connection, but his son-in-law's reaction roughed up his own anxiety. He called his brother Justin in London.

"I may be disconnected any moment, so just listen," he said in a rush, breaking with emotion when he heard his brother's voice.

His son Cole picked up another line, and his words tumbled out breathlessly. "Dad! Dad, I'm gettin' the first flight out. I'll see how close I can land, then I'll rent a car or hire a helicopter or whatever to try to get in tomorrow. Tell me where you are."

"I'll come with Cole," said Justin. "We'll get the prayer chains linking. Hang tight, Phillip. Stop blaming yourself. You got Mom and Dad out of Charleston, and Cami's parents—you can't do everything for everyone! You and I, we've weathered hurricanes at the Big House together. The boys can, too. Let's pray right now together before I lose your connection."

Chapter Five

We must accept life for what it actually is - a challenge to our quality without which we should never know of what stuff we are made or grow to our full stature.
-Robert Louis Stevenson

Within the shelter of the garage under the mansion's raised foundation, Chad gathered Patrick and Joey. They were as soaked as if they came out of the ocean for an afternoon of surfing.

"We need to be realistic," Chad said, looking at them in turn and raising his voice over crashing sheets of rain. His nerves made his teeth chatter. "I'm scared, but I'm not showin' it to anyone inside. Let's keep things upbeat. Joey, will you handle the radio and that little emergency television for updates? Patrick, manage the mobile phones in case your dad calls. We're watchin' you for signs of a concussion, so take it easy and don't be a tough guy. And please—now's not the time to make things any worse with your granddad. We'll handle him later."

Patrick crossed his arms over his chest petulantly. "Yeah, well, God certainly has a sense of humor, letting Don Juan drop in on what will likely be the worst day of my life."

"It could be the *last* day of your life," Joey quipped, slapping his friend's wet sleeve companionably and splattering them all with water droplets.

"You're my brothers." Chad hooked each arm around their necks, pulling their heads to touch his. "I got through my toughest time because you stuck with me to see it through. If it all ends here, I'm glad I faced it with you."

Choking up and emotional, Joey and Patrick hooked their arms in a huddle. They spurted out their own sentiments before launching into praying together.

Setting their faces to look as normal as they could, they went inside to dry their hair and change clothes. Joey and Casey finished first and headed down to the ballroom, followed by Maggie Jane and Patrick. Casey ordered Patrick to a seat where she could watch him, then covered the cut on his forehead with a dry bandage. Maggie Jane handed him hot ginger tea from the kitchen to settle his stomach.

"Okay, gang," Joey piped up over the storm, looking through a cabinet with the music collection. "We're goin' to ride a monster. You know what that means."

"Hurricane Party!" Casey sang out, waving her hands in the air. "This is how we do things in Texas, too!"

"We'll mix our Southern party with your Texan party and see what happens without adults around," Joey winked.

"I beg your pardon, Joseph Daniel Grayson," said Maggie Jane sternly. "I'm here, and you're twenty-six, so it's high time you acted like an adult ya'self. No shenanigans."

"Awww, Maggie Jane, you're not like the others!" Joey's chocolate eyes sparkled as he stood up. "Come on, be my first dance tonight. Let's shake up our shenanigans! Then you can pull out that gourmet picnic you made to cheer us up at the shelter. I smelled those fried apple pies. Do we get extras since Andy and Wyeth aren't here? It might be my last meal."

She exaggerated a snort. "Ya better have more faith 'bout makin' it through this ole storm if ya wanna dance with me!"

"Hey, Dr. Rush is another adult who's hangin' around here somewhere," said Casey, turning from the music selections to Joey.

"He's not an adult—just an adulterer," retorted Patrick from his seat by a table as the guardian of the mute mobile phones.

Startled, Casey spun around, and her doe eyes were compassionate as she met his. "Oh, Patrick. How awful! I'm so sorry, I didn't know."

Joey spoke to his friend across the expanse of the ballroom with a warning in his eyes. "Come on, buddy, let's make the best of this."

Caroline's hair was dry and silky again, and she hung her wet clothes across the shower door with Chad's. She was ready to leave her grandmother's bedroom to join everyone else as he pulled a tee shirt over his head and caught her arm.

"I'm sorry we didn't clear things up last night, Care. I never wanted the sun to go down with anything between us. Let's make things right before our babies are born." *And in case we don't live through this storm,* he thought.

Her change of expression made him drop his hold on her arm. Debris slammed into the house near the shuttered windows for an ominous timing. She took his arm and pushed so his back was against the wall, positioning herself to stand closely at his side to face him. He drew a quick breath. He loved it when she demanded his attention this way. It was a good sign, despite the stormy look on her face. When the business side of this was settled, it would end well, and making up was his favorite part.

"You know I trust you, Chad. But you have a responsibility to represent us to the world as a solid Christian marriage with no secrets. You once taught your brother that hiding things can be the same as lying. Your hasty promise to Krystal would've upset your peace of mind. It would've changed things in your relationships, not only with me, but with Patrick and Joey. You involved them, and they were forced to choose loyalties against me, to keep from betraying you. That's why Patrick couldn't live with it."

His jaw muscle clenched at the truth in what Caroline was saying, and he braced himself. She was not finished.

"There are things you must be confidential about, because of your position at Global. I accept and respect that, Chad. But never favor another woman over me by promising to conceal her advances, implying that you hide things from me. Clear enough?"

Caroline's eyes were like steel in the dim light now, and for a fleeting moment, he was startled at the resemblance to her grandfather downstairs. Thunder cracked outside like the order to fire gunshots on a battlefield. Chad nodded and gulped at the stab of her point. He put the interests of a woman he never had never met ahead of the best interests of his own wife and friends. *Stupid,* he chided himself. A man in his position could not afford to make this kind of mistake.

He cleared his throat. "You're right. On the spot, I didn't think of it that way. I didn't realize the position it put you in or consider that it could go public. I was wrong, and I'm sorry. I'll apologize to Patrick and Joey."

Caroline's firm grip on his bicep relaxed, but her expression remained solemn. "Apology appreciated and accepted."

"Thank you. Now listen to me."

It only took one move to pivot, and her back was the one against the wall. He braced his weight on both hands spread flat on the wallpaper beside her shoulders, boxing her in to face him without leaning against the twins. Her brows were now the ones raised in surprise, and his eyes were the ones with the steel.

"I'm havin' a talk with Derrick when he calls me soon about some business with the Young Guns. He needs to watch how he touches you in public from now on."

His inhaled breath coincided with a clap of thunder. "It cut deep when Krystal raved about him and thought you were married, then stammered around to assure me the twins were mine. An image was planted vividly in my mind, and I'll have a hard time shakin' it off. I've never conquered jealousy where he's concerned, and it's time I admitted it. Now you know. Consider my feelings from now on."

Caroline slowly reached up and cupped her hand on his face. "There's no need to cause friction between you two. I handled it on the spot. I whispered to him to remember who we are in front of people. He wasn't making an advance, Chad. He's outgoing. He hugged ten other friends around us in Millie's."

The ice in his eyes was melting at her touch. He fought to make a last stand. "Don't pretend he's not different with you, Care."

Caroline stroked his clenching jaw muscles with the back of her fingertips. "That's a relational connection we have. He didn't disrespect you."

He saw her point and was ready for the making up part of this little session, anyway. "Just—save your heart for me. Are we good?"

"Not until we seal the deal, with a dangerous kiss."

Chad smiled faintly. This was his favorite part.

He wished no one was waiting for them and he had nothing to do but be alone with her. He anticipated the next minute and the intensity of her whispers about how the waitress had good reason for wanting him, but she would make sure he was so happy another woman would never distract him. In a second minute, he would fervently promise he was already that happy, and there was no one in the whole world for him but her. He admitted his jealousy, so he would promise she would never regret choosing him over a better-looking pro basketball player with an amazing personality.

Thunder shook the mansion and a blast of wind sent sheets of rain crashing into the boarded window. Chad hoped this was not the last time he would hear Caroline's declarations of how much he meant to her.

Noble's face lit up when he saw his father. He half skipped, half ran to him, then climbed into his lap and reached up to touch a fingertip to the bandage over his eye. Noble imitated an expression of extreme sympathy and patted his dad's head, his big blue eyes a study in concern. "Awight?"

Patrick grinned. "Yes, I'm all right," he said, kissing Noble on the blond hair so like his own. "Thank you for checkin' on me."

"I pwayed." Noble said. He pointed at the phones. "My Pawpa talked?"

Patrick grew solemn and stroked his toddler's hair. "No, buddy, not yet. Keep prayin'."

Casey jumped up with an album in her hand. "Let's play a song Maggie Jane likes, since she's Joey's first dance! We can take turns choosing songs."

Maggie Jane approached the open cabinet. "I'll show you what I want," she said. She pulled out an album and handed it to Joey.

"Whew!" he exclaimed with a laugh, looking over the worn cover. "Maggie Jane's ready to rock! This should drown out the thunder. Which song first?"

Maggie Jane heard Chad walk into the room with his arm around Caroline. She smiled and said, "'Roll Over, Beethoven' should get those twins loosened up, right Caroline?"

"That's the idea!" Caroline answered brightly.

Patrick smirked at Chad's demeanor. His brother-in-law had gotten last night's lecture. But when all was said and done, somehow, Chad won something he wanted. He always did.

Casey put the needle down in a smooth ring on a black vinyl record. Chad and Caroline joined Joey and Maggie Jane on the ballroom floor, while Patrick sat snuggling with Noble in his lap.

Then, Tony Rush strolled in after bandaging his leg. Patrick rolled his eyes, chafing at his grandfather's presence. But he grudgingly admitted to himself that he hoped to look half that good in a pair of jeans and a tee shirt when he was an old man.

Natalie came in next, and she went to stand beside Patrick and Noble. She clapped her hands to the rocking beat and sang along. Tony Rush acted every bit a Southern gentleman when he politely asked Casey if she'd honor him with a dance.

When Joey swung Maggie Jane in a turn, it startled him to see Casey with Patrick's suave grandfather. Dr. Rush favored his leg slightly, but he knew his way around a dance floor. Unlike most older men, he did not cover his gray hair. Now that it was dry, it was hard to imagine another color looking as good on him.

Joey's eyes scanned Dr. Rush. Maybe being a heart surgeon was encouragement to work out. This man kept beautiful women of all ages at his side, and his charming smile was focused on Casey.

"I'll get Dr. Rush, you get your girl," Maggie Jane murmured as the song ended and another began.

When it was time for someone else to choose a song, Chad called from across the room, "Hey, Joey, I have one. I know it's in the cabinet. Hang on."

Without the music, it sounded like someone turned the volume up on the wild storm. The lights flickered. Windows made popping noises, reminding the group of the popping in their ears.

Chad found the album and jogged back to the middle of the ballroom. He took Caroline's hand, but he addressed everyone there. "If we were in Charleston, I'd be renting a carriage to take my bride to South Adgers Wharf and Chalmers Street for the traditional bumpy ride over English ballast cobblestones. I'm told it helps Southern belles in her delicate condition. But we're not in Charleston. We can't even walk on the beach to shake things up like my mom did, and it inspired her to name my big sister 'Sandy.' But we have a ballroom and a stereo. So, we'll dance."

He turned to Caroline, brushing a strand of her blonde hair back. "Caroline Amanda Painter Gregory, I told you before we came downstairs about how happy I am with you. You've made me happy my whole life, ever since I was Noble's age, and you were born. I have the proof in an old photograph. Your Poppy let me see the new baby, and it was love at first sight. You didn't have much hair then, but you curled your tiny fingers around one of mine, staking your claim on my heart."

He paused to enjoy her smile, then gathered his thoughts. "You took happiness to a whole new level when you married me, and I couldn't imagine anything better. But I know you'll level me up again soon. When we tell the twins this story about the night they were born in a hurricane, I want them to know this was my song to you, from my heart to yours. I'll love you endlessly, Caroline, and I always have."

"'So let it be written, so let it be done!" thundered Joey, raising his fist for a Pharaoh-like pose to quote the movie *The Ten Commandments.* The others whistled and cheered.

Chad made their sign, the gesture of pointing from his heart to hers. She made the sign back to him, remembering the first time he did it at an Island Summer Dance four years ago. On the stereo, a band started singing an oldie about how happy love had made them.

Patrick got up and swayed, holding Noble facing out to Natalie. She held one of the toddler's hands as if they danced together, and to his delight, she sang to him. He tried to look up over his shoulder at Patrick.

"Daddy! You sing 'bout happy, too."

Tony Rush danced with Maggie Jane, but he watched his grandson and granddaughter as they interacted with their spouses. Maggie Jane smiled knowingly and said, "This is a blessed family, Dr. Rush. God does miracles with commitment."

Patrick danced his family over to the turntable and picked up an album as the song ended. He pointed to a selection so Joey would see it.

The old house shuddered against buffeting winds and rumbling thunder, and Noble turned his head for a view through a window. He found only closed draperies. Wide-eyed, he extended his arms as Joey reached for him so Patrick could take Natalie's hand.

Patrick escorted his wife to the middle of the room and stood face to face while he ran his hand up and down her arm, composing his feelings into words. "Natalie, I think of you a million times a day. Bits of songs everywhere remind me of how crazy I am about you, and what a miracle it is that you love me back. But this song is you all the way through. It's my dad's song to my mom—"

His voice cracked, and he swallowed before he could continue. "They taught me what real love is. It's not tripping and falling, it's something you evaluate and commit to, for your whole life. By the time I was a teenager, I thought it was over the top the way my dad stopped whatever he was doin' when this song came on and my mom was nearby. But secretly, I wanted to see him love her that way. He was provin' himself to her, assuring her she was his only love, and it made me feel secure, too. That's the love I want to show you, to show our kids, and our grandkids, and anybody in the world who's watching."

Patrick pulled Natalie into his arms. She closed her eyes and smiled against the shoulder of his tee shirt, wrapping her arms tightly around him.

Everyone started shag dancing with their partners to the beat of the song. Joey held Noble in a makeshift dance with Casey. The toddler put a hand to Joey's chin. "Joey! You sing, 'bout my girl, and bees, and birds."

Joey threw his head back and laughed. Casey glanced away, laughing and blushing. Joey watched her face and leaned near the little boy's ear. "Don't rush me, Noble."

The band claimed they didn't need money, fortune, or fame, because they had all the riches one man could claim. Patrick sang the words to Natalie, and as the song ended, Natalie leaned back in his arms for a fluid, graceful dip, her long dark hair spilling like liquid silk. He pulled her up to meet his kiss.

It was a magical, emotional moment for Patrick. He was apprehensive about what was ahead of them when the hurricane hit, and like Chad, he wanted to be sure that if he didn't survive, he wanted Natalie to know the depth of his love for her.

But when he opened his eyes, his grandfather had moved nearby. He watched them with a faint smile. Patrick quickly looked away.

Maggie Jane took Tony Rush's arm and announced that the "adults" were leaving to set out the picnic dinner. Joey asked Casey to choose the next song and dance with him before the flickering power went out. Soon the stereo speakers pounded with a song about riding a highway to the danger zone, and Joey cranked up the volume to compete with the roar outdoors.

"Andy, pick up the phone!" Phillip growled through clenched teeth and slapped his hand against the wall in a back hallway of the school shelter. Camellia leaned against the same wall while he paced to the open double doors to check on their sleeping parents.

He punched in the number again, and Andy Painter answered. Phillip heard Wyeth's voice shouting over the weather in the background, telling someone he was driving Andy back in the truck. He heard their pastor among other voices, and the sound lit a spark of hope in his heart.

"Andy, this is Phillip! Tell me you've rescued the kids." *Please, God,* he prayed.

The truck doors slammed, muffling the sound of the storm. "We can't cross the bridge. I don't know what to say."

Andy's voice broke into a sob and his brother Wyeth took the phone. "Phillip, there's nothin' anyone can do. If Patrick had followed right behind his dad, he and Chad's cars would've exploded, and maybe Joey's if he'd hydroplaned into them. It's a miracle they're stranded with a chance in the Big House instead of bein' killed on that bridge."

Phillip made a choking sound as he struggled to breathe. He touched his forehead to the cool concrete block wall and allowed pent-up tears to break free. The image of Chad's Cherokee exploding overpowered him.

But what fate was his son saved to? Drowning? Being crushed under debris from the house he had practically grown up in?

At his defeated look, Camellia guessed the news and wailed before she burst out crying. She staggered against the block wall and slid down to the floor with her face in her hands.

"Phillip, listen! Don't despair," Wyeth urged. "The boys know the drill, and they're resourceful."

But Phillip joined Camellia on the floor in the hall as they cried. He fiercely brushed away tears and prayed, *God, please don't take my son. Please! Take me instead.*

Andy grabbed the phone back from his brother. His voice was hoarse. "Phillip, my father-in-law is with them. It's his fault the boat was in the waterway to start with. He's been watchin' Caroline's due date and thought she'd get stranded without a doctor. Remember, I once told him never to cross that bridge again? It's just like him to blow it up! If this storm doesn't kill him, I might. We rescued the boat captain, and he's goin' to make it. He washed up in a life jacket under the deck at the Castaway. Mouth-to-mouth to revive a drunk isn't something I ever want to do again, but it proved if he survived, miracles happen. The kids—"

Static raked across the phone line like fingernails on a chalkboard, and Phillip squeezed his eyes shut in a grimace. When it cleared, Pastor Payne had taken the phone. He encouraged Phillip and Camellia not to despair and prayed with them before handing the phone back to Wyeth. Phillip could hear spotty sentences that sounded like Wyeth, saying he and Andy were going into the shelter.

The line went dead. Phillip let his arm go limp with the mobile phone in his hand, plopping into his lap.

Loud thuds and pops like gunshots told the little group of nine souls at Painter Place that trees and other objects were broken and hurled against the old mansion. The group huddled around the remains of their picnic, wary within their shelter as it creaked, cracked, sighed, trembled, and groaned with the brutal force of the blows. For the benefit of the ladies, Chad, Patrick, and Joey tried to appear calm in the increasing clamor on the island.

Patrick rubbed his forehead and left shoulder. Maggie Jane went to a cabinet in the kitchen for a small bottle of pain reliever and put two tablets in his hand. She gave the bottle to Natalie while he swallowed the tablets with some water and stared at his mobile phone, willing it to ring.

After glowing compliments about Maggie Jane's cooking, Tony Rush was quiet. His gray eyes watched Patrick, Caroline, and little Noble like a man soaking up water before a trip to the desert.

Caroline largely ignored her grandfather. She ate lightly and sipped an herbal tea Maggie Jane made for her. When she could hide her discomfort no longer, she told them she was going up to her Gran Vanna's room.

Chad alertly studied her face, then checked the Submariner on his wrist. There had been no phone calls or a rescue. They were on their own.

His spirit sank before he braced himself to be in charge. The group was in danger and his wife was in labor with his twins. "It's a good time for us all to move upstairs."

Tony Rush hesitated at the first step, staring up at the stained-glass dome depicting the six days of Creation from the book of Genesis. Casey came to stand beside him. Her dark hair fell back from her pretty, upturned features as she looked overhead, where lightning made the scenes visible.

"It's utterly magnificent when the sun shines through it and it glows. Isn't it amazing to think about? Christ created everything from nothing in six days, then He rested on the seventh. It's our model for work and rest, since He obviously didn't need it. He can look after us in this storm."

"Christ wasn't born yet. He couldn't have created the world."

"I used to think God did the creating and Christ was born later, too. But I hadn't read the first chapter of the book of John, and I didn't understand who Christ really is. Caroline showed me. John calls Christ 'the Word,' as in the Christmas verse about when the Word became flesh and dwelt with us. John says Christ was with God in the beginning, created everything, and He's the light of every man born into the world. Those who recognize and receive Him get to become children of God. I once thought everyone was a child of God, but when I studied scripture, I found out the Bible never says that. It says some people are children of the devil, so they obviously can't be God's."

She flashed him a warm smile and put her hand on the railing. "With your injured leg and all, would you like some help goin' up?"

He looked at her in surprise. "Thank you for the offer, but it's just a bruise and a scrape from bumping into the pier."

Casey chatted while he followed her slowly up the curving staircase to the second floor, where he found Maggie Jane beckoning his granddaughter to a rocking chair. "Here, honey, rock a little while. The motion will help."

Caroline's mouth was set in a line as she meekly obeyed. Chad tried not to pace the blue-green Persian rug in Gran Vanna's room that depicted the Tree of Life.

Tony Rush winced and grasped his leg as he got on one knee beside Caroline. He peered intently into her face and addressed her for the first time since arriving. "I think the twins are comin' hard and fast tonight. Old wives' tales about bad weather are connected to barometric pressure. All of us are feelin' it—ears poppin', headaches, and more."

He turned to get an acknowledgement from the others. Maggie Jane, Casey and Chad nodded, so he looked back at his granddaughter.

"Try to relax and take deep breaths, no matter what's goin' on around you. Let the tough guys worry about the storm. I brought somethin' safe for pain. It won't get rid of it, but it will take the edge off and help you relax. The only thing is, if you try to hold on and wait too long, it won't help."

Caroline only gulped and nodded. Chad mumbled, "Thanks, Dr. Rush."

The doctor rose stiffly. "I'm newly retired, so just call me Tony. I don't have any hang-ups about people younger than me owin' me respect. Titles put distance between people. I've had enough of distance."

Joey unrolled his shabby sleeping bag on the marble tile floor. The landing was designed to feel elegant, open, and spacious, with a railing overlooking the ballroom below. From where he was, they could see if seawater from the storm surge flooded the first floor of the Big House.

He checked a small emergency television, but there was no reception, so he clicked it back off to save the batteries. Nearby, Patrick sat quietly in a chair with his eyes closed as the pain reliever eased his headache. Joey peered into his face uneasily. His friend wasn't acting like himself at all.

"Feel like a game of cards?" Joey ventured.

Before Patrick could answer, Casey and Maggie Jane came out to the hall, followed by Tony. "Time to let Caroline have some space," Casey announced. "Noble wants her to draw with him before bedtime. He's jittery about his dad's bandage, this bizarre sleepover, and things hittin' the house."

"I was just askin' Patrick if he's up to a game of cards. He doesn't look so good," Joey observed as he pulled a deck of cards from his backpack.

"It might be from the extremes in the weather, but some of it's from the blow against the window this afternoon," commented Tony Rush as he walked to one of the open bedroom doors and listened when a thud hit the boarded window. "Does your neck hurt, Patrick?"

Patrick opened his eyes and nodded stiffly. "It's feelin' better now, though."

"That's just the pain killer. The problem will still be there when it wears off," his grandfather said. "May I?"

Patrick reluctantly nodded again. His grandfather studied the small cut over his brow by lifting the edge of the bandage and shining a flashlight on it. Then he deftly ran strong hands over Patrick's head, neck, and shoulders, prodding where Patrick's spine met his skull. He ran his hands down over the neck and pressed, as if setting something in place. Patrick winced. His grandfather made a grunt as if he discovered something, then he pulled lightly to stretch Patrick's neck and shoulder.

"I'm goin' to release some of this tension—you're havin' muscle spasms. I don't suspect a concussion, though you have symptoms. Those may be stress. Casey, will you make a flexible ice pack for Patrick from what we've got left in the cooler? Small bits, in a plastic bag, wrapped in a hand towel and closed with safety pins. You or Natalie give him a pain reliever every four hours so he can focus on—our situation. He can increase the dose if he needs to."

He worked with Patrick's neck and shoulder more as Casey followed his instructions. "Don't worry about a sliver of a scar over your eye," he drawled to his grandson. "It shouldn't be noticeable, but if it is, remember people love a guy who looks like he has stories to tell. It'll enhance that hint of a swagger you got from me. You're too handsome for your own good, anyway. A guy who can land a woman like Natalie needs to be brought down a peg or two now and then."

Patrick struggled against a smile that twitched the corners of his mouth. Soon, he sat with an ice pack on his neck and shoulders, his head back on the chair and his eyes closed, while Joey and Casey played cards around a small table nearby.

Chapter Six

Caroline got as comfortable as she could in her grandmother's wide bed, leaning on pillows against the headboard with her nephew on one side and Chad on the other. Noble reached inside his toy bag for a tablet of drawing paper, a pencil, and a box of crayons, then considered them carefully.

"I know," he said matter-of-factly. "I share with Unka Chad and Aunt Care."

Little hands carefully tore away two sheets of drawing paper from the pad, and he gave one each to his aunt and uncle. Looking Chad in the eye, he said solemnly, "You draw Lambo."

He turned his blue eyes up to Caroline. "You draw—"

Noble searched the room for inspiration. Caroline asked, "Can I draw Lady? She's with Aunt Marina tonight."

Noble beamed. He loved his aunt's collie. "Yes! You draw Lady. I can have it?"

"Yes. What are you going to draw?" Caroline kissed the top of his head, winced, and clenched her teeth at a contraction.

Noble searched the room and tilted his head. His eyes wandered to his mother, who was in the rocking chair, crocheting a fuzzy blue baby blanket. "I draw Mama." He handed Chad a pencil, Caroline a brown crayon, and he kept a blue crayon for himself.

Chad rose and stepped over to Gran Vanna's bookshelf, where he pulled off two volumes he and Caroline could use as a portable desk. Noble watched him curiously. When he saw they did not open the books, he looked down at his paper to draw. He said matter-of-factly, "No drawing in books. You have a story?"

Chad raked his teeth over his lip to keep from laughing as he drew on his paper with the book underneath. "That's right, Noble, no drawing in books. A smart man named Walt Disney once said that there is more treasure in books than in all the pirates' loot on

Treasure Island. He was talking about this book, *Treasure Island*, one of my favorite stories of all. It's about ships and pirates and a good boy. Ask your daddy to read it to you someday."

"Okay. My Daddy reads to me. You have a story, Aunt Care?" Noble drew a shape that was remarkably like his mother.

Noble's contour drawings always amazed Caroline. Watching him, she answered, "Oh. Yes, the book in my lap is a sad story called *The Old Curiosity Shop*. It's about a sweet girl who lived with her grandfather in an interesting shop with unusual antiques in it. Antiques are old things people keep. But he had a bad habit that wrecked their lives and they had to leave their home. She became so sick looking after him that she went to heaven. The grandfather wouldn't stop his bad habit, even though it was destroying their lives and even though he said he loved her..."

Caroline's voice trailed off as she realized what she was saying. She swallowed and looked at Chad, who put his hand over hers. His eyes were loaded with a startled apology for having selected that classic book from the shelf.

Natalie stopped crocheting and looked at her sister-in-law sadly. Noble noticed his mother's expression and followed her eyes. He noticed Chad's hand on Caroline's, and he gazed at his aunt thoughtfully for a few moments. "Your tummy hurts?"

Caroline nodded. "Yes, it hurts, but I'm all right."

Satisfied, Noble craned his neck to see his uncle's elaborate drawing of his Lamborghini Countach. Next, he checked on Caroline's drawing, and he reached up to pat her head. "Very good," he said in a lilting tone, the way a teacher would encourage a student. He went back to his drawing of his mother.

With a sudden gasp, Caroline hugged her stomach. Natalie laid down her crochet with an alert look at her sister-in-law. Noble saw his mom's expression. "Care awright," he assured her, and patted his aunt's arm. "The bad storm scares her babies."

Caroline breathlessly said, "Noble, let's sing while we draw. We'll sing to the babies in my tummy and your mom's tummy, so they won't be afraid. They can hear us."

The toddler's face lit up with delight. "How 'bout the world and the babies? You sing, Mama."

Natalie cautiously picked up her crochet project. She tried to smile at her son when she said, "Do you remember whose hands the world and the babies are in?"

Without looking up from his drawing, Noble nodded. "'Course! God's hands. Large and in charge."

Caroline giggled and Natalie started them off, singing as they drew and crocheted while the storm raged outside. They sang about God having the whole world in His hands, including the little bitty babies.

When they finished, Noble wanted his mother to have a turn choosing a song. "I've got the joy, joy, joy, joy down in my heart," she sang. When she got to the question, "Where?" Noble sang out the answer, pointing at his heart with the blue crayon.

Chad passed his drawing over to Noble when the song ended. Noble had many drawings of Chad's Lamborghini, but this one made him giggle. "Unka Chad, what's this story?"

Natalie got up from her chair to see. In this one, he and Caroline stood in front of a profile of his car, each with a baby in their arms. Chad pointed at the babies. "Having babies is a special occasion, so we drove the Lamborghini."

Noble grinned. His mother laughed and sat back down in the rocking chair with her yarn. He put Chad's drawing on the bed and went back to his own drawing. "Very good, Unka Chad. Now you have a song."

Chad started singing, and they quickly joined him. Noble's eyes lit up. He made gestures to the song with Chad.

"The wise man built his house upon the rock

And the rain came tumbling down.
Oh, the rain came down, and the floods came up...
And the wise man's house stood firm."

Noble yawned and glanced at the wall as a powerful thud came from outside. Wind screeched around the corner.

Caroline handed her nephew the drawing of Lady after signing it with "C. A. Painter." He sleepily smiled at her signature, ready to play their game. He put his hands over his eyes and then quickly dropped them to point at her, saying, "I see a painter! Very good, Care. Now you sing."

Wrapping her arm around him, Caroline sang. Noble sang a few words with her, rubbing his eyes and struggling to stay awake. He made a candle with his finger. "This little light of mine, I'm gonna let it shine."

The song was short, and when they ended, Natalie told Noble they were going to lie down in the next room. His eyes lit up when she reminded him of his new sleeping bag that looked like he was driving a race car when he was in it. Noble kissed his aunt on the cheek and giggled when Chad extended his hand to shake with Noble across her stomach.

Natalie took Noble's hand to leave Gran Vanna's room, then pulled up short when she encountered Caroline's grandfather just outside the doorway. Tony Rush leaned against the wall in the shadows and nodded cordially before he wished them a good night.

While Noble blew him a matter-of-fact goodnight kiss, Natalie's eyes searched Tony's face. He smiled sadly and let her read his expression. He had heard Caroline describe *The Old Curiosity Shop* to Noble.

After Natalie left to put his great-grandson to sleep, he wiped his hand over his face and sighed before stepping into the room to check on his granddaughter. Caroline was gripping Chad's hand, and she immediately asked him for the pain medicine he brought for her. At the doorway, he turned back when a moan escaped through her clenched teeth. He hoped she asked for help in time.

Patrick came to check on his sister after he tucked his son into the new sleeping bag. Caroline gestured to him to sit down, patting the bed where Noble had been. In two long strides, he smoothly settled in beside her and kissed her forehead before he teased. "You always create a sensation, don't you? Where are we goin' to survive when your next baby is born, a third world country during an earthquake? Or some cabin in the path of an erupting volcano?"

She grimaced and clenched Chad's hand until a contraction was over. "It's good to see your sense of humor is back. I need my brother again."

"I need you back, too, baby sister, when we see what daybreak reveals of what Hugo left us. It'll be a whole new take on the old saying 'morning has broken.'"

As if on cue, the mansion shuddered in a fresh torrential onslaught. The wind screamed.

"Patrick, your little Noble—he's the one."

Her brother tousled her hair and smiled knowingly. "You're assuming there will be something left for him after this storm. Yes, we'll keep a Painter as the artist in the Big House, with the same artist signature as Poppy's. You've got a big responsibility ahead to train him."

Beside her, Chad met Patrick's eyes over her head. "He's only the first one. We could have a Gregory in the house and studios, too."

"I'm sure of it. You'd never let me win without a fight."

Caroline gasped in pain and groaned again, a sound so unlike her it unsettled both men. They glanced at one another before Chad tugged her arm. "Come on, you need to walk or rock some more. You want me, or your brother?"

"You. Patrick is injured and medicated."

"Hey, wait a minute!" Patrick protested. "I might be a lot more fun on medication."

Their grandfather came in to give Caroline something for pain and approved of Chad's idea of getting Caroline moving. He left to find Maggie Jane.

Chad put his arms around Caroline and swayed as if they were slow dancing. "Gettin' back to what Patrick said, he's on to something. How can we plan for the next baby?"

"You two have a lot of nerve!" Caroline exclaimed through clenched teeth as she endured another contraction. When it passed, she gasped, "The last thing I want right now is to think about another baby. Two are enough!"

She stood straighter to look at Chad. "I'd rather think about how to make you pay for doing this to me," she blurted. "I promise it will be just as dramatic, slow and painful."

Patrick hooted from where he lounged on Gran Vanna's bed, slapping his hand on the headboard. "I love it when she sasses you!"

Chad laughed in delight, and his drive to win surged. "But I want a little Savanna Caroline," he pleaded. "My 'Carolina Painter' can give me a South Carolina artist who signs her paintings with 'S.C. Gregory.'"

Caroline moaned again and squeezed her eyes shut. Sweat beaded on her forehead as she clenched her teeth. Then she blurted, "You give *me* a little S.C. artist! I'm sure you handle pain better than I do, Golden Boy."

"Woah! She used the 'g' word," exclaimed Patrick. "You're in for it now."

Chad's white grin flashed at his brother-in-law and he swayed to an imaginary beat to keep his wife moving. "But I'm not equipped for that kind of miracle, Care, and you're the perfect little princess who likes to keep me happy. Just name your price, and it's yours—I'll lasso the moon like George Bailey."

"I'll take the moon, and a 1990 Ferrari Testarossa, like the one I saw in Dad's latest car magazine," Caroline retorted before drawing a quick breath and gripping his shoulder.

Chad halted, his eyes wide and jaw hanging. Patrick recovered first and threw back his head to howl in laughter, thumping the bed with his hand. Chad forgot to rock Caroline to ease the contractions.

She dabbed beading sweat from her forehead again and managed a smirk. "Don't make promises to distract me when I'm in labor with your children. I'm in the mood to ask for a whole lot of things right now."

"Caroline—baby—you've never asked for anything, ever! I couldn't have seen that comin'! I've waited four years for you to ask me for somethin', and it had to be a brand-new Ferrari? Come on!" Chad implored.

Maggie Jane cackled at Chad's dilemma as she came in and piled supplies on the dresser. Perplexed, he rocked Caroline again to an imaginary beat, and now she was not the only one with sweat on her brow.

Patrick sat up on the edge of the bed. "Maggie Jane, I'm feelin' much better now. My sister just made my day—maybe my whole year! Am I supposed to be boilin' water for her, or something useful like that?"

"No, you're supposed to rest under doctor's orders, and it's time for that ice pack again," Maggie Jane clucked at him. "Joey's boilin' water. Casey beat him in cards, and he's her slave for fifteen minutes."

Patrick snorted. "Good thing we're here watching 'em, then. I don't trust her with him, do you?"

"Don't trust who?" asked Casey, marching into the room with her arms full of linens. Joey followed behind her with boiled water in two large, insulated containers.

"You, that's who, with my buddy, Joey. Hey Joey, what were you thinkin', man?"

"When I let her win, I hoped she'd come up with somethin' remotely sexy or intellectual, like making me compose a sonnet about love bein' like a hurricane, or quote lines about overcoming the worst odds from The Lord of the Rings," Joey complained. "All she wants from me is work."

Casey rolled her eyes. "*Let* me win? What a sore loser!"

Patrick looked at Chad with exasperation and gestured to Joey. "He learned nothin' from us. Casey's checkin' out his brawn, not his brains. Brains come later if the package looks good and conducts itself well in public."

"He's not ready to be out on his own," Chad agreed.

Caroline gasped and moaned again, louder this time, gripping his arm so tightly he winced at her strength. But he paled when he saw a look in her eyes that reminded him of a cornered animal.

Tony walked in and caught Chad's startled glance at him over her head. Sounding matter-of-fact, he said, "Joey, Caroline needs something to help her relax. Got any music with you that doesn't do more damage to the inside of the house than it's already gettin' on the outside?"

"Baker," Caroline blurted.

Joey nodded and turned to leave. "I brought some of Baker Holmes' music."

"What I meant was, somethin' might be happenin' with Baker," she gasped again. "I can't get him out of my mind. His baby's due, too."

Chad searched her face. "I told Dad to tell Cole to get us on prayer chains. I'm sure he called Baker." He looked around at everyone else. "But they could be in trouble, too, and we need to be prayin' for them."

A sound like a mighty train sent them instantly to the floor. Chad and Maggie Jane shielded Caroline, Joey threw himself over Casey, and Tony landed across Patrick's back just before a deafening crash came from the front of the house. Wood splintered and glass shattered.

When they were sure nothing in the room had collapsed, Patrick scrambled up from under his grandfather and offered a hand to help him up. Then he bolted out the door to the next room to check on Natalie and Noble.

Joey ran out behind him to see if he needed help. The others sat up cautiously, and Caroline writhed in a contraction.

Chad kissed her forehead quickly as he rose. "You can do this, Baby!" He helped her up and put her into Maggie Jane's arms before he ran from the room, shouting at Tony. "I'll be right back. Stay with her."

Damp air forced its way through the mansion. "It was downstairs!" exclaimed Patrick over the screaming wind outside.

Storm Surge
by Pamela Poole

Chapter Seven

Joey, Chad, and Patrick stood indecisively at the top of the staircase, looking down into the darkness below. Drafts of air rose to stir their hair. Patrick and Joey looked at Chad like soldiers to their commander, ready to jump into action.

"That dome overhead is dangerous," Chad began, unconvinced that they should risk descent into the dark well.

"But we need to see what's goin' on," Patrick urged. "We might prevent more damage."

Joey reached for his flashlight. "I'll go. You both have kids. I'll stay against the railing."

Chad rubbed both hands over his face as if an answer would appear like a genie out of the top of his head.

"Listen!" Joey put his hand up. Other than the soft croon of Maggie Jane's voice singing an uplifting old spiritual to a gasping Caroline, the only sound was soft rain.

"Okay, quick! Scout around with the flashlight. Don't do anything—just report what you see," Chad ordered.

Chad and Patrick scarcely dared to breathe as Joey nimbly descended the stairs, slinking along the railing. His flashlight flitted like a lightning bug on a summer evening.

An incoherent cry of suffering from Caroline made Chad clench the balcony railing. It took all his resolve to stay rooted where he stood. Maggie Jane's voice calmly sang, soothing his jagged nerves. He heard Tony say something encouraging, but he could not make out the words.

Joey shouted from the bottom of the stairs. "Chad, Patrick! Get down here. Hurry!"

Chad sprang to pick up a lantern and Patrick grabbed his flashlight. They followed Joey's urgent call.

"It's the pavilion floor," he reported. "It blew onto its side against the veranda. The boarding and windows are blown out, but the pavilion is sheltering the openings and front door now!"

Chad and Patrick stood gaping at the damage and the unlikely shelter. Shattered glass, splintered boards, heavy drapery rods and fabrics lay strewn across seating. Air could blow through, but not rain.

The Whitehaven Community Center had the highest elevation of any building in the small coastal town. It was built to serve as a hurricane shelter and was crowded with residents who trusted that it was the safest place to be.

But in the wake of Hurricane Hugo, a corner roof section over some classrooms had already blown away. A tree rested on the floor of what was once a locker room. Residents were sheltered in the gymnasium and auditorium, where the mayor kept the gathered neighbors informed while fear and speculation bred a mounting chaos.

Finally, Pastor Payne jumped up onto a table and stamped his foot several times, raising his hands high. The surprised crowd hushed, leaving the raging storm as his only competition. With his palms outstretched, he exclaimed, "Aren't we losing our perspective? Who's really in charge here, huh? God is! Instead of cowering, wringing our hands, and frightening one another, why aren't we trusting Him and calling on the only one who can control a storm?"

Many residents looked unconvinced, but some nodded in agreement.

"I've got a family in my church whose children are stranded at Painter Place on White Island. It's clear that collectively, you need something positive to do. Get your focus off yourselves and start prayin' for Caroline Painter, who's in labor over there right now.

See how much worse your night could be? Join us to pray for her husband Chad Gregory, their baby twins, for Patrick and Natalie Painter, their son Noble and unborn baby, for Joey Grayson, Casey Austin, Maggie Jane, and Caroline's grandfather, Dr. Anthony Rush. A dozen lives, people that many of you know, are in more danger than you are. Make a difference by prayin' for them!"

The pastor jumped down and gestured for people to follow him to a corner of the cavernous room, where the Painters and Danny's family huddled miserably. The Payne family, Derrick Wallace's parents, and Maggie Jane's family sat with them. A young lady with a dark pixie haircut grabbed his arm and looked at him in alarm. "Excuse me—did you say Caroline's stranded on that island in labor? Like in the movies, havin' her babies at home, without pain stuff or anything?"

"That's right. Will you pray for her?"

"Oh, I—no, I'm pretty sure God won't hear me," she stammered, looking furtively around, fidgeting with a clasp on her backpack.

"I see. You don't know Him," the pastor stated, his eyes softening. "Would you like to?"

Clearly startled, the girl managed to say, "Know God?" She shrugged. "Well, of course—wouldn't anyone? Then He might change things."

"What's your name?"

The girl hesitated before she answered. "Krystal."

The pastor took her hand. "Krystal, what the Lord changes is you. Then He works with you to change the world."

"Oh. Well, I certainly need changing, but it'll take some work. How will that help Caroline tonight?"

The pastor looked at the gathering crowd around the Painters. "I'll tell you. Then I hope you'll join us with new assurance that Christ hears your heart's cry for her."

Maggie Jane was steadfast in her efforts to calm Caroline and reminded her that her daddy and Uncle Wyeth were born in this same room. "All these generations of Painters born here in this ole mansion, and none of 'em guessed that one day, some Gregory babies would be born here, too! Here you go again, honey, doin' somethin' new again tonight, somethin' that's never been done at Painter Place. All dark clouds are lined with silver, remember that."

Her tone changed as she looked up at Casey and the doctor. "Someone needs to go get Chad."

Casey ran to the empty landing. At the top of the staircase, she peered into the darkness trying to locate the sound of distant voices. Looking up to determine where the ceiling ended and the well for the stained-glass dome began, she went as close as she dared and called down for Chad.

In moments, he appeared at the bottom of the stairs, holding a lantern. One jean-clad leg rested his Nike running shoe on the first step.

"It's time!" Casey shouted urgently.

"We're right behind you. Go on!" Patrick told Chad.

Chad rushed up the staircase as Casey disappeared. He felt like he was taking a dive from a cliff as he briskly entered Gran Vanna's room and took Tony's place holding his wife's hand. He tried not to show how upset he was at her condition. She hardly noticed him as she tried to focus on Maggie Jane's guidance and soothing encouragement.

"I'm here, Baby, I'm here," he repeated as she made soulful cries that wrenched his gut. He ran his hand up and down her arm in a soothing caress, putting her fist to his lips. He wanted her to hear his voice, feel his touch. He wanted his children to hear his voice as they came into the world.

Outside Gran Vanna's door, Patrick took the pain reliever and water Natalie handed him. His face was drawn, but not from his returning headache. "You didn't do this in labor. Something's wrong with my sister! What if she dies here?"

She put her arms around him. "I was in a hospital and chose to have something for pain. But I had enough of it to remember, and this is making me crazy."

"I can't stand it. My grandfather should do something!" he exclaimed. "If this is what he calls 'taking the edge off' her pain, I'd hate to see what that edge sounds like!"

He looked over at Joey for support, but his friend had sunk to the floor against the wall miserably, his face in his hands. Natalie said, "Tony has to be careful not to give her anything that hurts the twins. He knows she'd rather suffer."

Maggie Jane's voice carried over the storm into the hallway. "Now, Caroline! Push!"

Joey dropped his hands to clench them into fists. Patrick grimaced and braced himself against a wall, pressing his forehead into it. At his side, Natalie's arms circled him again with her chin on his shoulder, holding her breath as she kept her eyes on the door expectantly.

Chad gritted his teeth, wondering how long Caroline could make that drawn-out sound. But when her cry ended, a different one replaced it. Stunned, he watched Maggie Jane laugh as she put a wriggling, wrinkled mess into a towel and handed it to Casey.

"Okay, Mommy! Rest a minute and give me the other one. We're almost done, sweetheart," Maggie Jane directed. "Tony, are ya writin' down the time?"

"I've got it. Ten thirty-three. Watch out for the cord—it can tangle."

Chad choked on his emotions and tears poured from his eyes. He was gulping in breaths, torn between watching the baby Casey was cleaning up and Caroline in her agonizing effort to deliver the next one. His voice was ragged and hoarse as he cheered Caroline on, and Maggie Jane swathed another wriggling, protesting baby into a towel four minutes later. Tony was checking over the first twin and writing down notes. He looked up at Casey. "Check for birthmarks. There's a tiny one on the outside of the right ankle over here."

"Outside of the left ankle for this one," she reported.

Tony glanced up at Chad and winked. "Lucky you! We won't mix them up. If they ever try to trick you, remind them you can call me for verification."

Chad let go of Caroline's limp hand to wipe his face with the bottom of his tee shirt. Her eyes were shut, and she seemed to be drifting in and out of consciousness, unaware as Maggie Jane worked with her.

Alarmed, Chad moved closer on the bed and ran fingers across her pale forehead. But she did not acknowledge him, and he felt a stab of panic. Maggie Jane handed him a damp washcloth to wipe his wife's face and hands with, and Caroline came around enough to attempt a weak smile before she drifted out again.

Tony looked up from a twin to see the concern on Chad's face. "She should be fine soon. She's remarkably strong and healthy. Her body's reacting to the trauma and pain. She may start shaking. We'll watch her."

Chad nodded at him, unconvinced. He moved his face closer to her, hoping his voice would make her fight to stay conscious. "You just blew the lid off being amazing," he whispered close to her ear. "Hear that? It's the sound of our babies cryin' in a hurricane. There's nothin' I can ever give you to top what you've given me, or what you just went through for me. You win, once and for all!"

Kissing her forehead, he let his lips brush against her skin as he asked, "Rest a little. But when you're strong enough, will you help me introduce our family? Everybody's worried about you, and they're waitin' in the hall. Patrick needs to see that you're okay before he decks your grandfather."

"Can I have some water?" she rasped.

Maggie Jane handed Chad a glass of water and a dose from the prescription bottle Tony handed over to her. Caroline still faded out as Chad carefully propped her up enough to sip it, holding the glass to her trembling lips when her arm shook as violently as the storm outside. Maggie Jane sang hymn choruses in her rich voice as she brushed Caroline's sweat-dampened blonde hair. She deftly twisted a strand into a wrap for a luxurious ponytail that cascaded across one shoulder. "Only my sweet Caroline could look so beautiful after all this," Maggie Jane cooed to her.

Casey handed Chad a baby wrapped in a light blanket with a red button sewn on it, and Tony placed a baby with a green button on the blanket into Caroline's lap, propping the bundle where it would nestle safely in her trembling arm. He grinned triumphantly from ear to ear, every bit a proud great-grandfather, as if he were invited to be there.

At a sharp clap of thunder, the twin in Chad's arms jumped and wailed, and the other quickly followed. A memory stirred Caroline. Weakly, she made a comforting sound that quieted the babies almost instantly. "There's nothing to be afraid of at Painter Place," she told them, just as she once told her doll Sabrina years ago on the stairs in the rotunda. "It's where we're supposed to be. God's here."

Maggie Jane smiled knowingly and wiped away a tear before she called over the din of the storm for the others. Joey looked haggard as he carried Chad's camera for some photos. Patrick gripped one of Natalie's hands and she clamped the other over her mouth while tears streamed from her eyes. They waited expectantly in the soft light of lanterns around the room.

Chad wet his lips, trying to find his voice. "We wish our parents were here."

He sniffed and pressed his lips tight while Caroline wiped a tear on her cheek with a shaky hand. "I'd like you to meet my children. I'm holding the firstborn, Rhett Montgomery Gregory. His brother is Rayce Heyward Gregory. You can tell them apart if you look at their birthmarks on the outside of their ankles. I hope that's not prophetic because on the day I asked Caroline's dad to let me court her, she asked me what my Achilles heel was."

Maggie Jane threw back her head for a hearty laugh. "Heaven help the baby girls being born in the next few years," she said, "With names like Rhett and Rayce, no heart will be safe. Look out, world!"

Chad grinned. "Maggie Jane's keepin' up with these little guys by red and green buttons she found tonight, and she says they feel like about a half cup more than the five-pound bags of sugar in her pantry."

Everyone collectively laughed, cried, and asked to hold the newest members of the family. Outside, thunder clapped. The wind howled.

Joey stopped shooting photos and embraced Casey, thanking her for being there to help. Then he went to kneel next to the bed by Caroline, his brown eyes swimming as he took her hand and leaned close to kiss her forehead brusquely. "This is an awesome day at Painter Place," he said. "I've waited years to see it. I promise, like a brother, I'll do all I can to be a good influence on the boys."

Patrick rushed to his sister's bedside behind Joey, waiting his turn. He kissed her cheek as he hugged her carefully. He murmured close to her ear so only she could here. "No more babies this way, understand? I thought you were dyin'."

He swiped a hand over his face and squeezed her arm. Thunder rattled the windows against the boards nailed to their casings. She weakly reached up for his hand, and he claimed it firmly. He whispered, "Chad will never get over what you just did. But please give him Savanna Caroline. She already has a name, and he's prayin' for her. We can string him along for the fun of it."

Tony proudly signed birth certificates he had packed in a sealed plastic bag, announcing that Maggie Jane's weight estimate was close. The packaging scales he brought in earlier from the studios weighed Rhett at five pounds seven ounces, and Rayce was five pounds four ounces. Both were nineteen inches long, and both were perfect.

Patrick watched Joey try the emergency television and radio again, sliding through the static. "You think we'll have a signal to listen to the race by Sunday?"

"Waltrip's takin' Martinsville," Chad remarked, trying to relax his back against a pillow at the wall as he sat on his sleeping bag. He was still uneasy about Caroline's physical condition and wanted to stay by her side. But the ladies scurried around to get his wife and Gran Vanna's room cleaned up from the birth, and Maggie Jane shooed him out the door to search the cooler for anything he could find to entice Caroline to eat. When he returned, she was surrounding his newborn babies with barriers of rolled towels to keep them on the bed near their mother.

Chad realized for the first time that he would be separated from his wife and children on a night they should have all been together. And after this storm, he wondered when life would ever be normal again.

Tony settled next to him on the landing in ghostly lantern light that exaggerated every shape into stretched shadows. "I've got something!" Joey exclaimed, motioning for his friends to come closer. They listened to a static-filled weather update that said the eye of Hugo was passing just north of Charleston, where spotty reports were coming in of horrific flooding and damage. The prediction was that the back side of the storm was even worse and would wallop the coastline above the three hundred nineteen-year-old city. The surge at high tide could be as much as twenty feet. Heavy winds and rain were expected in Charleston until midday on Friday.

Patrick covered his mouth with his hand and began pacing as they lost the signal. The three friends looked at one another with dread. Chad's voice was ominous when he said, "So they were right. The island will be under water—part of the ocean. Even if we're far enough away to miss the worst and only get, say, half that surge, this house is the only thing high enough above ground to make it. The old cottages are nearly sea level, so count them gone. The newer ones are like our homes, with ten to twelve feet of raised foundations, but if trees haven't already taken them down, rushing water and debris will. There'll be nothing else left if God spares our lives here tonight."

They jumped as the television suddenly picked up a major network that blared out a reporter's voice. A picture came onto the small screen, showing some flash photography taken in Charleston during the calm eye of the storm.

"Charleston and the coast of the Carolinas are being sledgehammered by the monster storm Hugo, which is carving a path of devastation far inland toward Charlotte during the night. Around the country, prayer vigils are being held for those in the storm's path. Many citizens are praying specifically for an historic little island that the locals call Painter Place, where Gregory Global heir Chad Gregory and his wife are stranded in the storm with his brother-in-law, pregnant sister-in-law, nephew, his wife's grandfather, and three friends. Dr. Anthony Rush is a prominent heart surgeon from Charleston who traveled to be with his granddaughter Caroline in case she went into labor with her twins. His fears were realized when she was reported to have gone into labor late this afternoon after they were cut off from the mainland by a boat accident that damaged the bridge. The local rescue squad calls the captain's survival 'miraculous' after Andrew Painter used his maritime life-saving skills to revive the same man whose boat stranded his children and grandchildren, leaving them to the mercy of Hugo."

Joey ran to grab Casey and Natalie to see the television. Everyone on the landing watched in shock at the devastation portrayed in Charleston in a news report plagued by static and interference.

"Americans first heard of the plight of the stranded residents at a televised banquet—" The picture became snow and zigzag lines. There was a huff of frustration around the group as they anxiously waited for more.

Chad gasped as a familiar voice blared from the speaker. "I'm honored by this award tonight, but my heart—it's with my parents in a shelter, enduring Hurricane Hugo, and with some friends who mean the world to me. They're stranded on an island that will likely be obliterated."

The little group on the shadowy landing watched Derrick Wallace choke up. A quick pan of the crowd he was addressing showed the surprised, compassionate reactions of attendees.

"I hope you'll excuse me for hijackin' the banquet, but at the risk of soundin' ungrateful, I need to leave so I can get to my hometown as soon as possible. My achievements are meaningless in the scheme of things. Those of you who are Christians, will you pray tonight? You've heard of some of my friends. Chad Gregory was on the cover of a financial magazine a few months ago, and his wife, Caroline Painter, is the niece of the artist Wyeth Painter. The last I heard, she's in labor with their twins on the island. She must be suffering—and so scared—" Derrick lost his voice and gulped a couple of breaths. He nodded at the attendees. "Again, thank you for the award."

Patrick groaned, exchanging a knowing look with Chad. The news cameras followed Derrick, a head above the others around him, shoving a huge trophy into the hands of an aide as he abruptly left for an exit. Stunned reporters began to improvise coverage, incredulous that such a sensation had just fallen from the sky into their laps.

Chad had to admit Derrick knew how to harness attention for a purpose. He never cared about awards or what anyone thought when he publicly talked about his faith. This time, he turned his notoriety into a means of raising prayer support for his parents and Painter Place. But the way he forgot himself when he mentioned Caroline, raw and unguarded, could raise questions Chad must face in media interviews in the future.

He struggled to stomp out a flash of hot jealousy. The spark had plagued him ever since the waitress glowed over Derrick and Caroline together yesterday.

Static filled the small television screen as a thunderous rumble and crash reverberated from the front of the mansion, so deafening that it momentarily masked the barrage of other objects being shot into the walls. Chad felt the jar of it deep in his bones, as the house must have before it made a sighing sound that spooked everyone. All eyes roamed the shadowy structure for what might come out of the darkness with the storm-scented rushing air.

Tony grabbed his flashlight and went to the staircase, unconcerned about the dome looming over his head. Chad quickly strode in the direction where he had felt the collision into the house. Gripping the handrail over the ballroom, he shouted over it. "It came from over here, Tony. It's the library!"

The young men held their lanterns and flashlights over the ballroom while drafts of sodden air rushed against their faces. Tony's gray head was in view when he came out of the library and looked up at Chad. His features were stern, eerily up lit from his flashlight, looking like an actor in a scene from a horror movie.

"It's like the damage on the other side of the veranda. The windows are blown out, boards and drapes down. Something huge blew up to crash into the house, blockin' the rain from coming in. It looks like roof beams crossing—like the underside of a roof, Chad. If I were a bettin' man, I'd put money on this bein' part of the roof of the nearest cottage, across the street. The other smacks we're hearin' against the house are likely the furnishings."

"Come on up. The first floor is dangerous. Could you see the water outside?"

"It's close, Chad," the older man answered soberly. "And we're still two hours away from high tide."

Natalie called Chad from the door of Gran Vanna's room. Chad rubbed his face again to clear his head. He must be careful about what he said to the ladies. That sickening grip of creeping terror teasing the edges of his mind had to stay out here on the landing.

Maggie Jane rose to let him have a seat beside his wife, who remained weak but roused herself to see him. She had regained some color as she leaned back on propped pillows. It was strange now to see her without a mounded stomach. The twins slept soundly beside her, and he dragged his eyes from them to meet her searching expression. "Did you know people all over the country are prayin' for us?" he asked.

She nodded. Her voice was low and raspy when she replied, "God works in mysterious ways. Chad, I want to know what happened to the front of the house."

He massaged her smooth, graceful hand in his rougher one, working around her diamond engagement ring and wedding band. "Your job was to deliver the twins. My job's not done. You need to rest."

"This is goin' to be my house someday. Tell me what's tearin' the front of it off. We're a team, like Wyeth and Phillip. We do this together, remember? When your dad hid something from Wyeth, it didn't end well, and they are still enduring the strain of it."

Chad gnawed his lip and lowered his gaze to keep her from reading him. "The pavilion floor and probably the roof of Juliette's cottage are lodged into whatever's left of the veranda, standing on end, shielding the front rooms from water damage. You're feelin' all the damp air because the mansion is—ventilated."

She closed her eyes and leaned back onto the headboard. "I knew we'd lose the pavilion, and if it's gone, so is the pier." A tear glistened in the candlelight and slid down her face, flipping his heart over. "Now the veranda and no doubt our cottage. Hugo's takin' everything, Chad—all we've known, all our special places!"

"We'll start over! A fresh canvas, remember?" He held up her left hand. "Remember what you said about your engagement ring? You wanted one like Grace Kelly was given by her Prince, because the emerald cut diamond is the shape of a canvas, flashing with fire in the pavilion and seemingly going on into infinity when you gaze into it. You said that's what you wanted in your marriage, a blank canvas to paint a lifetime together, full of fire and flash."

Caroline sniffed and swept another tear away before she failed in her attempt to smile. Chad squeezed her hand. "I'm committed to makin' that dream come true, but it takes time. A lifetime." He looked across her at his sons again. "They'll never know the Painter Place we grew up in. But it couldn't stay the same forever, Caroline. Nothing ever does."

In Washington, DC, a man looked thoughtfully at his television screen, keeping up with the movements of Hurricane Hugo. He'd been ready to turn back to the paperwork scattered over the expanse of his mahogany desk when he heard the news broadcast from the awards banquet, where Derrick Wallace made a plea for prayers for his friends stranded at Painter Place. The man scowled and picked up one of the phones on his desk.

"I'd like to see you," he said into the mouthpiece before hanging it up.

Another man came in, straightening a red tie as if he'd just put it back on. "Yes, sir."

"You're sure she made it off the island today?" the man behind the desk knit his white brows. "Some of the family is stranded."

"Yes, sir, I just saw that, too. The man that was sent for the update left the area immediately after he made sure she was in a shelter. Do you want him back in when the storm is over?"

The man behind the desk folded his hands, fingertips touching, and leaned back in his plush leather desk chair. "No. No, if she's off the island, that's all I wanted to know this time."

"Sir, he could blend in with all the traffic going to help the community with the cleanup. He'd be even less likely to be noticed as a stranger in town than usual. You may want to know where she will go if the house is destroyed."

The white-haired man pursed his lips, looking at the younger man thoughtfully. "Since my contact there on the island passed, every time I've put someone out to ease my curiosity, I've risked exposure for me and disaster for her."

"The men we send never know who they're working for, sir, you made certain of that. There are impenetrable layers of protection in place. She'll never be connected to you unless you reveal it."

The older man smirked. "When you've been around as long as I have, you'll know there's always a risk. There can be no vulnerability."

He sighed and drummed his fingers on the desk, eyes back on the television screen. "The media keeps them in their crosshairs. Now they'll be hot on the pro ball player's heels for a human-interest story. Let them do the work for us."

Chapter Eight

When Chad was a little boy, he used to wonder at a term Caroline's grandmother Savanna Painter used. But sitting on the landing in the grotesque shadows of lantern light, he knew now that he would never think of "tempest in a teapot" the same way again. Any reference to a tempest, storm, or hurricane would forever be measured against his new Hugo yardstick.

Patrick and Joey were motionless, save for the rise and fall of steady breathing. Sometimes he closed his eyes as they did, trying in vain to relax in the never-ending resonance of the storm. If the sea came pouring into the ballroom below, he wanted to hear it.

"Why'd you ever start investigating me?" Tony Rush asked from where he sat nearby.

Chad roused himself from another prayer for Baker Holmes and his wife Beth, who were on Caroline's heart tonight. "Your granddaughter accused me of being like you, only days after I came home and a model in London exploited a photo of me to get some notoriety. Caroline never even asked me about it, she just turned her back and planned to kick me off the island. It was a rude awakening when I realized what your reputation had done to her. I wanted to find out what was more important in your life than your granddaughter's love and respect."

They listened to the storm for a while. Tony glanced at Patrick to make sure he was asleep, then kept his voice low. "I never understood Christians. You make a big deal out of somethin' that's just natural—a primordial instinct."

Chad snorted in disdain, shaking his head. "Yeah, it's primordial when it takes a world full of women to get enough."

Tony leaned his head back onto the railing and closed his eyes. Soon, he said, "I married Audrey to have a family with a good bloodline, just like a lot of old families do. Bein' from different towns, she only knew what I wanted her to know about me. Her dad was in bad health and didn't expect to live long, so he pressured her into an arranged marriage with me, his childhood friend's son. I quit runnin' around as soon as I met her because she was enough, beautiful inside and out, and I loved her. I've never stopped. We were happy until I went to war as part of a medical team, after Valerie was born. I didn't know if I'd make it through a night, or ever get home. I wanted to feel in charge, alive, wanted. Nothing did that for me like a woman, and there were plenty of 'em. I didn't think I'd see Audrey and Valerie again."

The doctor paused for an onslaught of wind and rain. Once the clamor eased off, he said, "When I came back, Audrey realized what was goin' on, and that I wasn't a Christian. She refused to live with me unless I apologized and gave up the other women. I wasn't sorry and didn't want to stop. I respected her too much to lie. Besides, one lie leads to coverin' up somethin' else, and soon you can't tell lies from reality."

He waved a hand dismissively. "Plenty of women turn a blind eye to their husbands' indiscretions, I just didn't marry one of 'em. Audrey was devastated that she wasn't handed a fairy tale to live in with some adoring guy totin' a Bible. I was angry at being kicked out of my house after all I'd done to survive and come home. I couldn't even raise my own daughter, and I wanted more children. But my wife wouldn't let me touch her again. So, I decided to show her that beautiful women appreciated what she rejected, hopin' she'd be jealous and want me back on my terms. The women became my revenge, but there weren't nearly as many as the papers made it look like. Many of 'em were trophies to escort to a social event, and bein' married was my excuse not to be available for commitment. I did everything I could to keep Audrey from divorcin' me over the years, makin' her better off than if she were free, and I never stopped hopin' she'd take me back."

"You decided to make your own rules, like you had a right to do whatever you wanted at the expense of everyone else. Immoral women meant more to you than the love of a faithful wife and daughter, and more than havin' other children. But your life wasn't your own once you brought Audrey and Valerie into it, and you didn't have the right to make them miserable while you satisfied your ego."

Tony snorted defensively. "A lot of good being a saint has done you! You're about to lose everything you've worked and sweated for here, the life you dreamed of, on this island tonight. Is this how your God treats people who love him and do so much for other people?"

Chad's jaw and neck muscles flexed in caged anger. Tony was using the old trick of stepping sideways, trying to get the focus off the point by demeaning God's authority as a fair judge. "Remember the account of the disciples in a sudden storm on the Sea of Galilee, when they thought they'd die?"

"My parents made sure I went to Sunday School," Tony answered dryly. "Spare me the children's stories. I know about Peter walking on water if he had faith and sinkin' if he didn't. I don't have any, so I'd drown."

"What if he'd stayed in the boat?"

Tony's gray eyes became wary. "Spare me the traps, too," he scoffed.

"No traps and no faith required. It's just a simple question. Jesus was in the storm, as the Master of it, walking toward the boat. He could control the weather, but He allowed it. He didn't ask Peter to walk on water. That was Peter's idea. The disciples were never out of Jesus' protection, and despite their fear, everyone except Peter stayed right where Jesus expected them to be when He came toward them. The way I see it, I'm right where Jesus wants me. I'm stayin' in the storm-ravaged boat. That takes faith, too."

Tony was silent, so Chad continued. "What about the boat you're in? You've retired to have this experimental cancer treatment. Who's goin' to look after you while you recover? Spurned old girlfriends? Be wary when they hand you the meds."

The doctor growled. "I should've known you'd find that out! It's none of your business, so call off the hound. I haven't dated in a long time, so he won't find out anything juicy."

Patrick caught himself from opening his eyes in his feigned sleep. His grandfather had cancer, and Chad knew? He felt a pilot light of anger ignite. How long had this been going on?

Chad spurted, "Anything that concerns Caroline and Patrick is my business! Consider yourself forewarned that I'm their firewall, and I have limitless resources. Tell them soon, in your own way, or they'll hear my version. Maybe our hounds should just have lunch and exchange notes. I know you've had both me and Patrick watched on and off since college. I'm suspicious of anyone who investigates me. Are you disappointed that Patrick didn't trash Andy's rules by bein' like you? Would that have been more sweet revenge? Were you goin' to make sure Andy found out, and try to cause a scandal for Painter Place?"

Patrick's mind reeled as he pretended to sleep. He fought the urge to clench his fists.

"I wanted to hurt Andy for his seventh commandment fixation. College was when Patrick could finally be out from under Painter Place, and I hoped he'd join the real world. With his looks, his personality, his money, he'd have really been somethin'. But when he got there, it occurred to me that if he turned on Andy and sullied Painter Place, he'd nearly destroy Valerie. It would've broken her to have a son like me. She'd have blamed herself and thought she'd dirtied the gene pool for the Painters. My original plan to be sure

Andy found out if Patrick fooled around turned into a mission to cover it up so Valerie wouldn't know."

Patrick heard his grandfather pause and sigh tiredly. "Doesn't matter. He was what his parents raised him to be."

"So, why'd you spend good money settin' the hounds on me? Did you think I'd be a bad influence on him?"

Tony expelled a low, derisive laugh. "I was fascinated by you—the absolutely perfect storm. I wanted to watch when you broke over Painter Place and Caroline, like Hugo is doin' out there now. I didn't want to see her hurt—she's a treasure. But she'd get over it and find someone else. People always do, except for Maggie Jane, after her fiancé was killed in Vietnam. I wanted to watch Andy and the Painter Place aura take a hit that would change everything, ruining what his daddy and Phillip's had prayed for."

Patrick struggled not to get up and thrash his grandfather. His anger boiled and he imagined the thunder on Chad's face as Tony snorted and said, "I have to admit, the guy had guts to keep you away from Caroline. I never dreamed Andy would risk losin' her trust to make sure she ended up with the right man to carry on here. How can a heritage—a place, traditions, beliefs—be worth so much? I wanted to see his face when you failed. He'd have Derrick Wallace as one of the lords of Painter Place. That other guy, the preacher's kid, he wasn't cut out to stay here."

Chad barely held his fury in check and shook his head at the mention of Derrick. A mistake on his part in college could have meant a whole new reality on the island.

Tony smirked at Chad's involuntary reaction. "But like Patrick, you proved I misjudged you. I always wondered—why didn't you just take the beauty queen who chased you? You didn't have to like her."

Chad blew out an incredulous huff. "That fixation you say Andy has with the seventh commandment, well, my dad has it, too. He taught me that it's short-sighted to assume it only applies after you're married. I planned to marry Caroline someday, and if I handled women like they were my wife from God's point of view before then, that is as much adultery against my future wife as it would be after a ceremony. Not only that, but I'd also be breaking several other commandments. Jesus said the greatest commandment is to love Him with all my heart, soul, and mind—not to follow my own heart and mind, which would deceive me. Christ would never lead me to do something He'd already defined as sin in scripture. The second commandment is to love my neighbor as myself, and using a woman selfishly is clearly not considering her best interest, her future husband's best interest, my future wife's best interest, or any children that might have come about."

He gathered thoughts that came tumbling out, organizing them into something coherent. "Caroline deserved the man of her dreams, and I resolved years ago to be her dream. If I wanted the very first, the ultimate best, of her, she should have the same from me. Using Gloria or anyone else who chased me would've disqualified me from the honor of being the man Caroline waited for. I might still have won her, but she'd have been settling for less than she wanted, and I'd have proven beyond doubt that my lust was more important than my love."

He turned narrowed eyes at Tony. "Just because what you did is common and strokes your ego doesn't mean it's normal. Misled people acting on base instincts shouldn't define normal for everyone else. If I'd taken what Gloria offered, I'd have given her something irreplaceable that belonged to Caroline. I'd have handed her power over me—power to tell anyone and everyone what happened. Now I see that I'd have given you power over me, too, because you were havin' me watched. Sin is never private, even when you think you're alone, like Noah getting drunk and throwin' his clothes off. It always takes you places you never wanted to go, and you pay for that ticket over and over the rest of your life."

When the doctor didn't respond, Chad closed in. "If you want to know your family, you don't need private detectives, Tony. Stop holdin' on to your pride and reconcile with them. What do you want the end of your life to look like? What eulogy do you want from Valerie and your grandchildren?"

The wind abated as he waited for Tony's answer. Without the din of the storm, they were suddenly aware of another sound. It was like being on the pier when waves curled around it.

Stunned, Chad jumped up. Too quickly alert to have been sleeping, Joey and Patrick did the same. Tony rose more slowly, wincing and grasping his ribs, and joined them as they peered into the darkness over the landing. But the ballroom below was dry.

"It's not goin' to reach the first floor," Chad breathed, looking at his watch face.

"Can it erode the ground under the house away?" Joey asked.

"Yes," Patrick answered. "I'm tryin' to push out of my mind what we look like from the sky right now."

"But that's heaven's view," came Maggie Jane's voice behind them. They jumped in the dark shadows, whirling around to face her. "You're the men of the family now," she said gently. "If Wyeth, Andy, and Phillip were here, you know we'd be prayin' together." She gestured to Tony. "You can join us if you want, but the only prayers the Lord hears from the lost are for salvation."

Tony hesitantly trailed behind as the young men in the besieged mansion walked briskly away into Gran Vanna's room. Standing in the doorway, he watched Chad make a spot beside Caroline and the twins on the bed, reaching out for her hand and fussing over how she was feeling. Patrick took her hand on her other side, sitting in a chair Natalie vacated before she took his free hand and one of Maggie Jane's.

Caroline met her grandfather's eyes with a solemn beckoning, and Casey turned to him, motioning for him to take her free hand. Maggie Jane extended hers, gesturing to Tony to stand between her and Casey as they made a circle around the bed.

He felt awkward when Chad began praying, but he admired how unaware of himself Chad was. The young man wasn't posturing like the TV preachers he rolled his eyes at and flipped past on a Sunday morning.

Patrick prayed when Chad paused, and Tony's heart swelled. It was unexpected to crave the sound of his handsome grandson in prayer. *They talk like God's right here, and they have nothing to hide,* he marveled.

Joey prayed next. Praying was as natural to these young men as if they were talking to one another. They weren't afraid of God.

Tony felt something thaw inside him, and though he couldn't guess what it was, the warmth of it flowed into his heart. It swished like the sounds of the ocean under the house, and then he caught his breath. He could feel a peace, a presence, in the room.

His granddaughter Caroline prayed when Natalie and Casey finished. In a voice that was weak and still tinged with hoarseness, she asked for protection for their family and friends in the storm, if it was the Lord's will and brought glory to Him.

Tony felt resistance rise in his throat. How could protecting them not be in God's will? What kind of God would let this wonderful family perish? What glory was in it for Him in letting them be obliterated by this horrible storm?

He thought of Chad's words about staying in the storm-ravaged boat while Jesus was Master of the storm. But then his granddaughter's conversation with the Lord took a turn that left him nearly breathless. "My mama is so frightened for me and Patrick and her grandchildren tonight, and for her dad, too. Calm her and give her peace to face whatever path You choose for us. She loves us as only a parent can, and now You've given me a taste of what she feels. Painter Place will never be the same after the Atlantic is through scouring this island. Help us—help me—to be joyful and content with whatever blessing is left when the grieving is over. Since I only have one grandfather now, I pray You'll help him find his way to You, and back to his family."

The swell in Tony's heart sent a dam tumbling down, crashing, but not causing pain in the destruction. Instead, it was awash with long repressed feelings of love, desire, longing, belonging, sharing, and giving. He squeezed his eyes tight and struggled not to interrupt their prayers.

Beside him, Maggie Jane started praying, but he was distracted, fighting to breath normally. He acknowledged what he'd always known instinctively but could no longer deny. God was real. He was here. There was no turning back, no walking away as if this confrontation never happened. He was forced to decide what to do next, but he hadn't been tricked or trapped. This was just between him and God. No one else in the room knew any different.

Maggie Jane's conversation with the Lord was ending, and Chad would close the prayer session afterwards. That is, unless the only person who hadn't prayed—the only one who couldn't pray—did.

"Lord, I know You're here," Tony blurted out in the first prayer of his entire life. "I know You're real, and that all You said was true is true. I remember hearin' in church about Your promise—if I see I need You, and if I believe that You died for all the awful things I did, then I'm Yours. Nothing will separate us again. That's what I want. You're what I want. I don't care what happens to me here tonight, so do what You will with a ramshackle old man, and I'll be glad of it. But if my prayer means anything so quickly after just comin' across the threshold of heaven, I ask that You let my daughter Valerie have her children and grandchildren safe in her arms when this storm passes. They're her joy, and I—I certainly never gave her any. Thank You for—thank You for givin' me—You—instead of what I deserve."

Chapter Nine

Jordan Waters watched Derrick Wallace pace, pray, and morbidly stare out the window into blackness. They were the only customers in the remote airstrip terminal, and she kept herself out of sight behind a corner.

He thought he was alone. When no one was watching, he was exactly what he claimed to be.

She glanced at the big clock in the stark, shabby, industrial decor. It was three in the morning, and she'd been watching him for over an hour, unwilling to interrupt his prayers at what she knew was high tide at Painter Place.

Her legs ached from standing on the concrete floor, though she'd long ago removed the high heels she wore to the banquet. Taking a deep breath for confidence, she rolled her suitcase out into the open, heading for the only sofa and wishing it wasn't near the brooding basketball star.

Derrick Wallace was braced on one powerful arm against the wall of windows and glanced around at her dismissively before turning away. Relieved to have escaped a challenge, she settled and put her aching legs up on the sofa, stroking her hands down her silky stockings to relieve tension in the muscles. She hoped she wouldn't get spider veins and closed her eyes in gratitude as the circulation returned.

"How'd you find me?"

Jordan's eyes flew open. He hadn't moved, still facing out the window into the night, but he was watching her reflection in the glass. Meeting his mirrored gaze felt less threatening than answering to his face.

"Your driver turned right as if going to the airport. I went left, knowin' no commercial flight was takin' you into that storm. You fooled the rest of them, but I happen to know you can't even land in

Charlotte at Douglas International. It's my home, and the city's bein' ripped to pieces by Hugo right now. A small plane will eventually get you closest to Whitehaven. Maybe all the way if they clear that little airstrip to get help in there."

Derrick drew a weary breath. "Great. A stalker. You can't be the mother of my children and I don't drink or party—"

"Oh, please! You flatter yourself," she cut him off indignantly, narrowing her dark eyes. "As if that would cross my mind."

The star turned confrontationally, eyes narrowed, mirroring hers. "What do you want from me?"

"I want to travel into Whitehaven and get a story about Painter Place. I'm a huge fan of Savanna Painter, the famous novelist, and want to be like her someday. Freelancing in journalism is just a way to pay some bills until I can publish more novels myself. I live with my parents to keep down expenses and stretch paydays so I can write. I have two young adult novels on the Christian market and one Bible Study about purity for teen girls. So, I'm not bowing at your altar, or doing whatever else your ego dreamed up for me."

She fished in a sparkling evening bag and caught a card, which she brusquely offered him.

Derrick skeptically studied the young woman in a shimmering black evening gown, taking the proffered business card from a shapely toned arm he admired all the way to the shoulder. He smirked as he remembered that the words "long cool woman in a black dress" had played in his head when she caught his attention in the banquet crowd earlier tonight. She was only about an inch less than six feet tall before slipping on those enticing high heels on the floor in front of her.

She misinterpreted his smirk. "Spare me the jokes about my name. At least my last name isn't 'Rivers.' But I use my initials, J.C.

Waters, as my journalism pen name so I'll be taken seriously. I'd show you a reporter's card, but I had to give the last one out at the banquet. I have my credential badge if you want to see it."

He read the name on the card. *Jordan Waters, Christian Author.* Underneath was contact information in Charlotte, NC.

Turning on his heel, he abruptly walked back to the window. Suddenly, things were clicking into place. He needed to think, without her reading his face. Jordan Waters was the topic of the most recent scandal among his teammates, the dark beauty that walked in on her fiancé cheating with someone else. Derrick's teammates were wondering how to find this jilted jewel, and she'd just handed him her card.

"How's Dwayne these days?" he drawled, hoping to rattle her and see what she was made of.

When she was silent, he couldn't resist turning back. He met the cool gaze of eyes the color of mahogany, fringed with long black lashes that made something in his middle flutter, like before a big game when a lot was at stake.

"Let's lay it all out on the table from the get-go, shall we?" she began matter-of-factly. "Just so we know where we stand. You have something on me, and I have something on you."

Surprise must have crossed his face, for she paused and almost smiled while studying him. "I dated Dwayne on and off in high school and college when we could manage schedules. He went pro and bought me a ring with his first paycheck, proposing to me in front of who knows how many people at a televised game. While I giddily planned a wedding, he slipped into the party culture of his team. I delayed settin' a date to see if he'd pull out of a free-fall tailspin. I gave him space to adjust and remember who he is."

She swallowed and looked out the window. "I took a late flight into town for a date he begged me for. But he forgot about it after drinks with teammates in a bar. When he didn't meet me or answer the phone, I got a cab and asked the driver to wait while I stopped by his apartment on the way to my hotel. I heard music and his voice. The door was open, and I tapped on it and walked in. When I quickly walked back out, his ring was on the floor. He tried to stop me but couldn't follow me out the door because there are laws against being seen with no clothes in public. I didn't go to my hotel room or home, where he could find me, but held myself together until my flight landed near a friend's house. After a week of grieving at her place, I took another assignment, but never his calls. There's nothing to say and no going back. I'm a different person now. It's over."

Jordan turned back to meet his eyes. "So, you see, Mr. Wallace, we have something in common. I've done my homework. You'll always have a soft spot for memories of your time with Caroline, and I'll miss the Dwayne I once loved—the one who's not my future after all and wasn't destined to be that first kiss that I struggled so hard to save. You and I, we'll move on to something better along the way, something that was right all along. But we can hardly help it when they show up in a dream or a memory now and then. We're powerless to erase the past."

She studied him, and a tug at one side of her sad smile told him that his mask had fallen away. "So, what's your plan in followin' me here?" Derrick asked gruffly. "You want to take the same flight I do, hang around me for the tour and introductions, link up with the *Whitehaven Register*?"

Jordan blinked. "If that's your idea of a first date, I'm undaunted. I accept."

He clamped his mouth in a line to keep from grinning. "You're overdressed for this mission trip. I suppose this was your weapon of choice to get my attention. Got anything else in that suitcase?"

"I'll go change. Don't stand me up."

Dangling her high heels by a slender strap in one hand, Jordan pulled her luggage on its wheels toward the ladies' room. Derrick watched, getting a long look at her in the gown and admiring the leg that peeked from the slit up the side.

When she disappeared, he rubbed his face with both hands, asking himself what on earth he thought he was doing. The soft Carolina accent and straightforward attitude of this bewitching beauty was entangling him at an emotionally vulnerable time.

Dwayne was an idiot to lose someone like her. He remembered his last game against the guy who had tried to rough him up to get attention for himself. Derrick didn't appreciate rookies who put him at risk of a career-ending injury just to have their name mentioned in the same breath as his. He'd been wondering how to put this guy in his place.

Jordan said he tried to keep her from leaving, and she ignores his calls. Dwayne loved her and desperately wanted her back, badly enough to continue to crawl and beg.

He welcomed the unexpected adrenaline surge. Competition. What would his next game against Dwayne look like?

Brilliant colors teased the corner of Chad's eye. The colors hid as quickly as they peeked in. *Clouds must be blowing out*, he thought. The illuminated stained glass was playing hide and seek.

He bolted to sit up. The dome made it! The priceless, irreplaceable centerpiece of the Painter mansion was intact. "Praise God!" he whispered out loud. Silent prayers of praise and thanks began gushing from his heart, and tears stung his eyes. He had survived, and he was a father!

Seeing the other men asleep around him, he tried to be stealthy as he rose from the beautiful marble tile under his sleeping bag. He was uncertain if those tiles were the cause of a few aches and stiffness that surprised him as he stood up, or if it was from the jolt he took during the wreck yesterday.

After quick stretches to ease the stiffness out, he reached for his Nikon and tiptoed in athletic socked feet to see his wife and boys. He couldn't resist a bit of a slide across the marble, a rowdy indulgence he and Patrick had enjoyed for years when their dads weren't around. He leaned against the doorframe and gazed at his wife, sleeping with those impossibly tiny babies next to her. One of his sons had his fingers around a long blonde strand of her hair that spilled down onto the sheets. That must be a troublemaker, and now he had proof in years to come. He zoomed in some shots of his new family.

Maggie Jane awakened from her place in the upholstered armchair beside the bed. She smiled and stretched, then got up to tiptoe toward him. Standing at his side, she looked back. Casey lay on the floor beside the bed in a sleeping bag, and Natalie and Noble came in during the night to sleep close by.

Maggie Jane tapped his arm and nodded her head out the door. In the hallway, she looked over the railing to the first floor below. He reached for his gym bag and followed as she led him to the kitchen.

"You peeked out yet to see what's left?" she asked.

"No, I can't face it alone. I'll wait for the guys to wake up. Did I dream what happened with Tony last night?"

Maggie Jane beamed. "Those in the vine bear fruit. Only time will tell. But I believe he's one of us now. I'll make some breakfast from what we've got left of the picnic, though I expect we'll find a way to cook soon."

"Maggie Jane, we made it!"

She raised her hand and her sparkling dark eyes to heaven with a giggle. "Praise the Lord! He's got more work for us to do here before He takes us home." She touched the fingertips of both her hands to his temples. "Chad, these first moments of joy at simply bein' alive, burn them into your memory. This is what matters, not what you'll find out those doors."

"I'll try. Thank you for bringin' my sons out to meet me. Now I need to figure out how to take care of 'em."

"Remember Proverbs three, verses one through six. Don't rely on your own understandin' to raise those little hurricanes."

Chad washed up downstairs in Wyeth and Chrissy's room in the master suite, using water stored in buckets. When he reached the top of the stairs and gave his damp hair a shake, Joey was searching for a radio station with news reports. He had the volume set so only he would hear. Patrick rolled over and looked at them sleepily, but Tony was still.

Soft voices came from Gran Vanna's room, and Chad tapped on the doorframe. "'M'in," Noble sang out. He was snuggled into Natalie's lap with his favorite stuffed collie toy, hair tousled from sleep. He giggled when Chad stuck his head in and out as if hiding. "Unka Chad," he said, pointing to the bed. "Look—babies!"

Casey perched on the edge of the chair Maggie Jane had slept in, disheveled and looking tired as she checked Caroline's pulse and blood pressure. Chad stepped over her empty sleeping bag on the floor, then lowered himself onto the bed on his stomach and elbows to look at Caroline and the twins.

"How's mama this mornin'?"

Caroline smiled sleepily, and Casey laid her arm back down on the bed. "She needs to rest today when the boys will let her. They're so small that they are goin' to be hungry around the clock. Chad, can you watch the twins and Noble while Natalie and I get Caroline to the bathroom?"

Noble wriggled from his mother's lap as she rose, stepping on little bare tiptoes over to the side of the bed to look at the babies with awe. Hesitantly, he put a hand on the sheet.

Caroline gasped in unexpected pain as she reached for Casey's arm and slowly rose from the bed. Natalie held her other arm, and Caroline gingerly took a step. Chad noticed his wife's cute jazzy pajamas made her middle look closer to normal again. She winced and said, "It's not so bad since I'm up."

"Care awright?" asked Noble.

"I'm all right, Noble. I love you," Caroline assured him, smiling brightly. "Your mama's a great helper."

Noble nodded. "My mama helps. Love you." He absently blew her a flighty kiss and turned his attention back to the babies.

Chad scowled as he watched Caroline's struggle to move normally. But then he remembered to hide his concern in front of Noble, so he talked about the babies. "Look at their hands, Noble. Yours are bigger. You can help look after them."

Noble beamed at the compliment, and gingerly touched a finger to one twin's hand. The sleeping baby grasped it.

Though Noble was surprised, he did not pull back. Chad was reminded again of the day when newborn Caroline did the same thing with his hand. He was also two years old, and now he was startled at the déjà vu. His son Rhett might someday be the Gregory of the next generation to look after the financial interests of Painter Place, and Noble seemed to be the Painter who would work side by side with him. For the first time ever, they had just joined hands, and Chad was the one blessed to witness the future.

He gulped back his emotions. "The babies look the same," he managed to say. "Maggie Jane sewed a red button on this blanket, so she knows his name is Rhett, and a green button on this one so she knows his name is Rayce."

Noble studied the babies, knitting his blonde brows in concentration. He pointed to the twin with the red button that grasped his finger. "Wet?"

Chad grinned. "He might be wet, too, but we're goin' to leave that for the girls. Say the sound that makes his name. 'Rhett'. Hear the urrr sound, like a race car engine? Put it first. Say it with me."

Noble began shaping his mouth, his eyes on Chad's mouth, and they made the engine sound several times. "Rrret," Noble said when he put it all together. He repeated it several more times, and Patrick walked in. Noble looked over his shoulder to acknowledge his dad, who got on his knees beside him. "You say it, Daddy. Rrret. Rrrace."

Patrick's brows shot up as he looked at Chad. "You got him to use r's?"

Chad shrugged. "He wants to talk to the babies, right, Noble?"

Noble nodded. "Say it, Daddy."

Patrick obediently said the right name as Noble pointed to each baby.

Noble looked at the race cars on his onesie and pondered for a moment. Then he pointed to the green button and beamed. "Green flag. Rrrace."

Chad braced himself with Maggie Jane's warning to remember the elation of simply being alive before facing what lay outside the old mansion. The group's initial reaction of joy at surviving the night passed over breakfast trays of the remains of the picnic. Now, they brooded on what came next.

The ladies had work to do upstairs for Caroline and the babies, and Tony moved stiffly to freshen up. Chad did not like the idea of the injured older man using the stairs unless it was necessary. He asked him to stay upstairs near Caroline for any emergency while the young men went outside to determine if the house was safe.

Chad and Joey followed Patrick to the kitchen's back door. When the stairs proved safe, they descended onto the soggy sand.

Patrick convulsed and turned away from the sight behind the house. Joey said, "I feel like I stepped into an old Star Trek episode and beamed down onto a desolate alien planet."

Stunned, Chad raked his hand through the back of his hair. Patrick took a ragged breath and stepped up beside him. "You know how Caroline asks if somethin' is real when she can't take it in? That's how I feel. This can't be real."

Still speechless, Chad tagged along when they tested the pilings for the back veranda off Gran Vanna's room to see if it was safe to use it. They removed the boards from windows to get needed ventilation but did not stray from the battered house.

The hum of heavy equipment started across the water in Whitehaven. Joey ran out to the veranda when they heard a helicopter and spotted it across the waterway over his house. Chad rushed to him with binoculars.

"Whoa! It's a Blackhawk!" Chad exclaimed. He handed the binoculars to Joey.

"They must be reporting to Ben," Joey replied as the Blackhawk hovered low on the skyline, singling out Joey's house. The helicopter lifted and moved toward Painter Place. "They're checkin' the bridge. Ben's goin' to send help!"

The helicopter hovered over the site of the explosion for a few minutes. Then it flew low over the island, the chopping air pounding the wreckage from the Gregory Estate and heading south along the waterway to the Painter Estate at Brush Point. Eventually, it traced along the shore going north to Dog's Head before coming back to the beach near the mansion.

Casey came to see what the noise was about and followed the young men as they ran outside. A man in the helicopter threw down a bag on a dangling line while another helped him position himself with his back out the door, his right hand on the small of his back. He began rappelling down from the helicopter to an open spot on the ground where the bag landed. Chad grinned and snapped photos.

When the man hit the sand, Joey ran over to help. The man quickly removed layers of gloves and his helmet, dropping everything to grab Joey as if he might disappear. The chopper moved up and slowly lumbered over to the shoreline so that they could talk over the thundering blades that sliced the sky overhead.

"I knew it was you jumpin' outta that thing. You just proved what I've been sayin' for years—you're crazy!" Joey croaked, tears streaming down his face.

"Says the guy who's insane enough to get stranded in the Atlantic in a category four hurricane. Whose story's gonna sound better when we're braggin'? You scared the life outta me, Joey! Sandy showed me where I've got gray spots in my hair now. Chad, get over here! Good to see you, Patrick!"

The man sounded so much like Joey that Casey knew she would notice no difference over the phone. He kept Joey tightly gripped around the neck with one arm while reaching out for Chad with the other. His hair was the color of Joey's, but short, and he was older and more powerfully built.

Chad roughly hugged the man's other side, tears stinging his eyes. He was choked up and tried to hide it by joking, "Ben, who you tryin' to impress, showin' up at Painter Place in a Blackhawk?"

"I had to do somethin' to one-up that Lamborghini. It's bothered me for years." The man grinned and winked as he finally let Chad go. "That hug was from your beautiful sister, who's distraught over you. I need hard evidence for her that you're okay, so we're takin' photos. Where's the mother of your children?"

Chad sprinted to the stairs to get his family, with Patrick close behind. Joey reached for Casey's hand and pulled her over. "Ben, this is Casey Austin, a nurse friend from church. Casey, this is my big brother, Benjamin."

Casey lightly slapped her forehead. "Of course! Your dad's name is Jake and your mom is Rachel. Bible story names." She stepped up to shake Ben's strong grip. "I'd have said you were Jack Ryan."

Ben looked startled before he threw his head back and laughed. "I like her, Joey. Casey, did you deliver my nephews?"

"No, Maggie Jane did. I helped. You might know Dr. Anthony Rush, Caroline's grandfather. He was on hand to make sure the cord didn't tangle and choke Rayce."

Tony was quietly hanging around the back of the group as everyone came out onto the sand. Ben's eyes met his, and he nodded formally.

Chad held Rhett like a trophy, and Maggie Jane showed off Rayce before she handed him to Caroline and hugged Ben. He lifted her off the ground with powerful arms and swung her around. "Magnificent Maggie Jane, what a woman! You never told me you could birth babies in a hurricane!"

"I got some hair-raisin' skills jus' like you do!" she laughed as he set her back down and planted a kiss on her cheek. She took Rayce back so he could hug Caroline, which he did gently.

"Show-off!" he said to his sister-in-law. "You couldn't do this like everybody else, could you? And you're still as gorgeous as ever!"

Her smile was tremulous. "Dramatic circumstances call for dramatic action, a lot like you dropping out of the sky today. Are Sandy and Joshua safe?"

Ben kissed her forehead before letting her go. "Yes, but she can't rest until she knows you're all okay. Here, let me get a picture so I can prove you made it. She was a force of nature herself last night, roundin' up prayer support for all of you."

"That's my sister!" said Chad. "I knew she was in good hands with you. Take a picture with the last shot left on my camera, too. Get the film to Dad."

Ben quickly shot photos and pocketed the film. With a tilt of his head toward the chopper, he said, "They're gonna pull me up in a few minutes. This is officially a medical rescue mission in case any of you were hurt. I radioed engineers to see about inspecting that bridge until D.O.T. can get to it. They'll patch an emergency lane. You've got to have a way for help to get over here. It's not safe to land the chopper in this mess."

He turned to Noble in Patrick's arms and pointed at the helicopter. "I'm going to go up in a minute," he told him. "Promise to wave at me when I get into the door?"

Noble nodded, wide-eyed. "Kiss, too," he said, reaching to Ben.

When Ben let go of Noble, he turned to find the bag he had dropped from the line to the Blackhawk, handing it to his brother. "Mom and Dad are on their way home. The surge swept the house off the foundation, and I counted fifteen trees down, five of them on the roof. If you ever find what's left of your Harley, it won't be pretty. I didn't see your car anywhere."

He gestured for the group to gather around where he stood with his hands on his hips, assuming a military air of authority. The space between his eyebrows creased and his voice grew stern. "I've seen war zones that look better than White Island does right now. I dread reporting to Phillip what I saw and givin' him these aerial photos for the insurance. There's a lot of damage to the roof of the Big House, with some serious repair needed on the third floor. I don't want you goin' up to check it out before help arrives. The pavilion and Juliette's roof smashed the veranda off the front of the house, but it looks like they served as a bizarre kind of shield, diverting water and debris. I can't imagine what the impact must have been like for you last night."

Patrick asked anxiously, "What about the other houses and cottages?"

Ben looked away, weighing how much to say. "Assuming the impact from the pavilion and roof didn't make the foundation unstable, the mansion is the only livable shelter on Painter Place."

He looked back and pointed his finger around the group. "Do not—I'm serious about this, guys—do not try to go home, 'cause there's nothin' there. Your home now is the Big House, got it? Stay put. Help will come soon. You have enough food and water to make it here in the meantime."

He watched the dismay on Chad and Patrick's faces as the two exchanged looks, talking wordlessly as lifelong friends do. He waited to see if they would protest. When they did not, he continued. "Patrick, I'll radio Whitehaven police and have Sterling report to your family you're all okay. Boats are in a heap at the marina, so I imagine Andy's scramblin' to find somethin' that still floats so he can get here. The Castaway is standin' with a lot of damage, but the docks are gone. No signs of looting yet."

While Patrick groaned and rubbed his forehead, Ben looked at Chad. "Your family's stranded near Georgetown 'cause the Mercedes and your grandfather's car were trashed in a pile of everything in the parking lot. I stopped by and I have a friend in the National Guard posted there, waitin' on my radio report. Your grandparents are understandably upset, but everyone's okay. Your parents are distraught and haven't slept. They looked like death warmed over."

Casey snickered before she caught the startled looks at her inappropriate response. "Sorry," she said. "It just occurred to me that only a *man* would say somethin' like that. A woman would know that sayin' Phillip Gregory looks like death warmed over is like sayin' James Bond had a busy night with the bad guys. And Camellia? I can only dream of lookin' like a Bond girl after she's lost a night's sleep and worried herself sick."

The chopper began moving closer as Chad burst into laughter to hear his parents described that way. Ben studied her before he looked back at Joey, who was biting his lip against a grin. Ben shouted over the chopper, "I like her—a lot."

Then he turned to Casey. "Casey, I'm very protective of my little brother, and I've got skills. You've been warned."

With her hand to the side of her mouth, she shouted back, "I'm gonna make a move on him just to see you rappel out of somethin' intimidating to stop me. I assume you've got a gun somewhere under that jumpsuit. I can shoot, too!"

Ben grinned with delight at her, then grabbed Joey into another hug and shouted over the chopper, "If this doesn't work out, let me know. I have a friend who's been lookin' for her all his life. Take care of yourself. Love 'ya, man. Use that special radio in that bag if you have an emergency. Someone will find me."

Joey shouted that he loved him, too, and Ben prepared to ascend back into the helicopter, running toward the line that hung down. Noble put his hands over his ears, but when he saw Ben wave from the open door of the helicopter, he waved frantically, shouting, "Bye, Mr. Ben!"

Chapter Ten

The survivors at Painter Place waved at the departing Blackhawk until it disappeared. Without Ben's take-charge personality, the island was hopeless and desolate again. The deflated, somber group turned back to the mansion, taking a first long look around them. Caroline leaned on Natalie's arm as they picked their way over the debris and rough terrain.

Ben's right, she thought. *It looks like a war zone, except wars leave something.* Here, there was nothing, unless it was under the sand. Pavilion Way and Castaway Drive were gone. Juliette's cottage vanished, along with the Painter Gallery and studios. Nothing was left for Caroline to orient herself except the bedraggled mansion and the razed beach.

Trees that remained were uprooted or shorn off into bare trunks above ground. She squinted at the shoreline and saw scattered pilings where the pier had once been. Sea creatures lay dead in the sand, deposited and abandoned by the ocean.

She choked on an involuntary sob, her knees buckling. Beside her, Chad quickly reached out with one arm to grasp hers and handed Rhett to the closest arms to him, which happened to be Tony. Caroline went to her knees with Natalie, who started sobbing hysterically. As if on cue, everyone plopped down to the wet sand, shocked by the new reality that surrounded them.

Chad cradled Caroline's head on his shoulder, his chest heaving in his own grief, mingling his tears with hers. Patrick broke down with Natalie, who kept sobbing and clutching him desperately. Maggie Jane wailed and held Noble, rocking back and forth. Tony wiped his tears on the sleeve of the arm Rhett was not resting in. Casey bawled as she cuddled Rayce, and Joey let the dam break as he put his arms around them.

The Painter Place they knew was gone. And there was nothing in the world they could do to ever bring it back.

The remainder of Friday passed without any help arriving on the island, but the young men got the generators going so Maggie Jane and Patrick could cook dinner. Between the two of them, limited resources transformed into a gourmet meal for the subdued friends and family. But it cheered no one up.

After settling Caroline to rest on a sofa, everyone but Noble and Natalie gathered around her to see news on the tiny screen of the emergency television. The coverage out of Charleston and Charlotte was stunning in the scope of devastation. There was a twisted comfort in seeing the good side of human nature in people that lost everything yet looked ahead through their tears. But it was maddening to see the looters at work.

At a view of the Cooper River bridges, Caroline and Joey shuddered. "I'm not gettin' on Old Gracie anymore," claimed Joey. "How's that rust bucket still standin' after Hugo?"

Noble said little, sensitive to the mood of the group since their breakdown of grief after Ben flew away. He wandered from Natalie as she cleaned up in the kitchen, heading silently to the living room to grasp his dad's leg. On the news, he saw a woman and her children crying about the loss of her home before Joey noticed him and turned it off.

Patrick picked his son up to whisk him away. Noble reached up to gingerly touch the bandage over Patrick's eye. "Daddy let's go home now. I want my room. Where's my Nana Val'ry and Pawpa Andy? And TJ and Lady?"

Blinking back stinging tears, Patrick sniffed and rubbed his son's back. At some point, he must explain to his two-year old that he'd never go back to that home. He had no room anymore, and his toys, drawings, and special things were gone.

He reached Natalie as she put the last dish away, and his voice was thick when he met her eyes and answered his son's questions. "Remember, Mr. Ben came out of the helicopter and told us we have to stay here. Nana and Pawpa are comin' to find us. Maybe we'll see them in the morning, after you sleep tonight."

Natalie wrapped her arms around them from behind Noble, swaying side to side as she hummed the tune "The Lion Sleeps Tonight." Noble loved to sing the silly words at bedtime and was now effectively distracted. "Mama..." he giggled, leaning back into her.

"I saw some new books in the library on your shelf," said Natalie conspiratorially. "Gran Vanna went shopping again. Nobody else knows. Should we go get one and be first to read it?"

Patrick grinned at Noble's struggle to get down. He set him on his feet and impulsively reached for Natalie's face. He pulled her in for an ardent kiss.

"Daddy, Mama's goin' now," Noble informed him matter-of-factly, tugging at her.

"This isn't over," Patrick whispered to his wife. "Noble's not the only needy male in your life."

"Later," she whispered back, lavishing him with the look that always left him weak-kneed. He turned to follow her like a puppy and found his grandfather leaning against the wall, bemused.

Patrick's mood was dashed. Noble skipped beside his mother as they went to the library.

Tony held something out to him. "I brought these. Noble and I could play with them if you'll let me. Somethin' different might help."

Instantly, Patrick recognized the tin box molded and painted to look like a car. It appeared in old photos, open on the floor, and he was always playing with the contents. Sometimes, the lower body of a man on the floor behind him was also in the photos. His grandfather.

He drew a quick breath and reached out for the box, running his hands over the tin car—the hands of a grown man, no longer a child. His Adam's apple bobbed a few times in his throat, swollen from tears shed in an emotional day.

Summoning his courage, he pushed up on the snug-fitting upper half of the car to raise the lid. He stood staring at the classic old sports cars he remembered. Moments flew past on wings, fluttering with memories of the excitement he felt when imagining settings for them to race in.

His grandfather always carried them with him when he visited. Patrick had played with them the day his grandfather stopped by briefly to see his newborn sister Marina.

Tony parked that day at the nearly hidden turnaround at the top of the yard, leaving a woman that Patrick's parents did not know about waiting in his car. Patrick's grandmother Audrey, separated from Tony since Patrick's mom was a little girl, came in to spend the week helping with the new baby.

Grandma Audrey pulled into her customary spot around the back at the veranda, noticing her husband's expensive sports car and the waiting girlfriend. As she came through the kitchen door with her usual smile, Patrick and Caroline ran into her arms to greet her while the front door chime rang. A furious woman's voice berated his grandmother, accusing her of following Tony around and threatening her to leave him alone. Patrick never forgot that confrontation, but he did not understand the conversation until years later.

Patrick was upset about his granddad being friends with the lady who hated his beloved grandma. He remembered an overwhelming sense of dread as he heard his dad's anger explode in the living room while his mother and Grandma Audrey whisked him and his sisters from the house.

As they went down the steps to the yard and ran out to the long pier, his mom sobbed. Patrick heard his dad yelling at his grandfather to get out and never come across the bridge again, threatening him with what he would do if the man ever dared show up on the island.

He had never seen that side of his father and was afraid of him for weeks afterwards. When he was older, his dad told him it had broken his heart that Patrick overheard his fury at a time when he was too young to understand it would never be directed at him.

It was the last time he recalled seeing the tin full of cars, though he saw his grandfather for brief visits at his Grandma Audrey's house around holidays in his younger years, and he attended a few of Patrick's all-star ball games and high school graduation.

Standing there in the kitchen of the Big House, Tony's voice interrupted his thoughts. "They're just toys, Patrick," he said quietly.

Patrick looked up to find his grandfather studying his face. Tony's eyes swam as he said, "Noble doesn't have bad memories. He doesn't know who I am. For him, they're a fresh start. Please—I could use a fresh start."

Patrick slid his fingers lightly over the toy cars, their colors and shapes still familiar and exciting after all these years. Then he slowly pushed the box shut and handed it back as reluctantly as he must have when he was a boy.

"Okay. You can play with him."

Chapter Eleven

It is easier to forgive an enemy than to forgive a friend.
-William Blake

As Hugo plowed a path inland on Friday morning, Andy Painter wasted no time in recruiting help to move boats at Island Marina. He was unconcerned about straightening out his business, so the vessels in the roads and suspended in the side of Phillip's tower for Gregory Global would have to wait. He got equipment to sort through boats piled like pick-up sticks to uncover something that would cross to the island.

When he and his older brother Wyeth found one, it was nightfall. With no power, the town and the island were dark, so they bit back their impatience and went to spend another night at the community center.

Phillip arrived early Saturday morning at the Whitehaven shelter in a rental car with Camellia, his brother Justin, and youngest son Cole. His daughter Sandy had shown up at the shelter near Georgetown to take both sets of her grandparents back to her house in Charleston.

The boat Andy recovered from his marina only had room for the men, their bags, and a golf cart to get around in to inspect damage on the island. Danny volunteered to captain the boat, drop off the men, and then make a return trip for the women, food, and water supplies.

On board, Andy searched the altered northwest shoreline for a place to tie up. The old boathouse was gone. Everyone was supposed to keep alert for debris in the water that would sink them, but they were gaping at the shocking condition of the island. Even the topography of this west side was changed, so the eastern dunes on the Atlantic side were not the beach they knew so well. Bare, ripped tree trunks left the illusion of ribs on a carcass that was rotting and bleaching in a desert sun.

Settling for a spot under the damaged bridge, all but Danny disembarked. They set out the golf cart for the ladies to use when they arrived, assuming it would manage the terrain. Danny fought tears as he turned the boat toward Whitehaven again.

As the men neared the mansion, the graceful old beauty loomed taller, still standing with her chin up like a fortress that had survived being shelled in a siege. She was once like a belle dressed for a ball, but now there were no crinolines, ruffles, bows, or lace left. Her dress was ripped as if she had fended off a rakish rogue with dishonorable intentions.

By the time the men reached the raised foundation, now standing too high from the scoured sand, they all struggled for composure. Wyeth was grim and pale. He kept looking over where the studios and gallery had been, as if he could catch them springing back into existence.

Noticing a few of the familiar studio boards slung against the foundation of the house, he went to touch them, almost reverently. They were once part of the historic old stables his father, grandfather, and great-grandfather used when there were horses on the island.

The others watched Wyeth turn from the loose stable boards to reach out to the exposed piling that protruded up from bedrock to support the house. He gulped and slid his hand lovingly up to the foundation, squeezing his eyes tight as if speaking to it and comforting it.

Nearly choking on his own emotions, Phillip strode up to him, putting a hand on his shoulder. "We'll rebuild it, Wyeth. Together. Remember—best friends always, blood brothers—"

Wyeth spun around aggressively. Tony and the young men in the house had stepped outside to greet them just as Wyeth shoved Phillip and shouted at him.

"How dare you! You lost your right to remind me of old pacts made when we were boys. We didn't know what life would bring, or what real life was like—full of secrets! You betrayed me eight years ago and lived a lie for four years in front of me as if I was a fool. Now, you assume I'll trust you to rebuild my family's heritage. Forget it!"

Flushed, Phillip rose from the sand where he had stumbled at the unexpected shove. He growled as he threw his full weight against Wyeth, slamming him into the piling and pinning him. "It's my family's heritage too, remember? My first ancestor to this island lived here in the mansion, sheltered by yours. They helped each other, worked together. I meant that pact when we were boys, and I mean it now! I endured this disconnect from you for the last four years. You keep it under control, but it simmers underneath. You still doubt me, no matter what I do to earn back your trust."

Wyeth's furious struggle weakened Phillip's grip. He reeled back in the momentum, then steadied himself. Suddenly Wyeth faced his brother, who stepped between them.

Andy spread his arms out while Phillip rubbed his left shoulder. "I'm the one you want, Wyeth. All Phillip did was handle his son in your best interest, for Painter Place, for us all. It wasn't his idea to hide it from you or Caroline. That was me. It was me, Wyeth. He had to go along with me for his own part of the plan to work. I'm sorry. Come on, this is just me and you, like when you had to straighten me out when we were kids."

"That's easy to say now, after you've faced hours wondering if your children would survive the night, and how you'd robbed Chad and Caroline of four years more they could've had together!"

Behind Andy, Phillip nearly roared. Wyeth had hit a nerve, and Phillip pushed Andy away to clear the path to him. But Andy defiantly shoved Phillip out of Wyeth's reach to separate them, and Justin grabbed Andy to get him out of Phillip's way. But Cole knew his uncle could never subdue a man as strong as Andy Painter, and he rushed to help him.

Patrick bristled at what looked like Phillip's family ganging up on his dad. He took a step their direction, watching for a signal from his captive dad to intervene. But Andy stopped struggling to watch the confrontation between Wyeth and Phillip.

Chad pulled Patrick back and muttered, "They're only keepin' your dad out of this. It's time Dad and Wyeth spat out the poison."

Phillip and Wyeth circled one another warily, but Phillip glanced in Andy's direction to acknowledge him. "This isn't about you or your part in this, Andy. Wyeth got over that. He watches for you to do something unexpected. He can handle that from you."

He brushed loose sand from his cheek with his left hand as he kept circling with Wyeth, eyes locked. "But not me." He shook his head and blew out a breath. "No, that did him in. He thought he knew me, and that's what he can't live with, could never get past. I finally figured out what I did cut so deep because he trusted me utterly. He counted on me. He needed me."

He suddenly charged at Wyeth to force him to action, driving him back close to the piling again, but Wyeth was too strong. They stood locked, and Phillip's voice was steel when he said through clenched teeth, "I'm never lettin' go, understand? Never! So, get used to it. You're never gettin' rid of me! From my point of view, I didn't betray you. But I see your side. I'd have felt betrayed if it had been the other way around."

Wyeth was the one who roared now, surging in strength to slam Phillip into the piling, gripping his shirt collar tight with his left hand and his fist drawn back with the other. Phillip recaptured the breath knocked out of him, ensnared in the stark pain he found in Wyeth's dark gaze.

He dropped his hands limply by his sides and said, "You can't hurt me any more than you do every time I catch you unaware with that victimized look, Wyeth. What I did shipwrecked your security and your faith in me, and I've lived with a shell of my best friend for four years. I can't take it anymore—this ends now, today. What you said to Andy about wondering during the storm if he'd robbed Caroline and Chad of extra years together if they died here—that was me. I endured that nightmare for hours."

Now Phillip's voice gained strength and he shouted. "You think you can dole out more payback than that? Then do it, Wyeth! Give me what you think I deserve. Get this over with! You've tried to swallow it, to resolve in your heart and your mind to forgive me, and it hasn't worked. So beat your revenge out of me, and we can move on. I'll even make it a fight. Take a shot, and I'll get back up again. Then you'll get my best shot for doin' this in front of my sons. But when my blood's smeared on you and yours on me, we're blood brothers again, and I'm still goin' to be here to help you rebuild Painter Place."

"Uncle Wyeth."

Wyeth blinked at his niece's soft voice. She spoke as if they were alone, and he relaxed his fist, dropping it by his side. But he kept Phillip held in check by his collar, locked face to face.

The other men turned in surprise to see Caroline standing on the soft sand that masked her approach. Transfixed, they watched as she slowly went to stand at her uncle's side near the studio boards.

"'Truth is, everyone's goin' to let you down sometimes, and you'll disappoint them, too. Surround yourself with the ones who are worth suffering with. That's what Gran Vanna once told me. Your lifelong best friend is worth suffering with, even if things will never be the same."

Andy Painter choked at his daughter's words, the first he'd heard from her since before the storm. He drank in the sight of her and took the hit in his heart that her statement carried for him. For four years, nothing had been the same. He still prayed that someday, she would look at him with the trusting adoration she once had.

Wyeth slowly uncurled his fingers from the fabric of Phillip's polo shirt. He took a step back, wiping his hands on his jeans. "I've had enough," he stated gruffly. "It's over. I'm sorry."

Then he turned to Caroline, pulling her quickly into his arms and holding her tightly as he muzzled a sob. Fiercely, he blinked hot tears into submission.

Phillip straightened his collar and followed Wyeth's gaze of despair to where the studio boards lay on the sand over Caroline's shoulder. He stepped to put himself in Wyeth's line of sight again, leaning to touch a hand to the boards. "We nailed these onto the framing—me, you, Justin, and Andy, remember? Let's find more of these and use them in your next studio."

Wyeth nodded mutely, still clutching Caroline. Then he looked around and found Patrick. He sniffed, letting Phillip embrace Caroline, and briskly strode to meet his nephew Patrick in a bear hug as if he were a little boy again.

The poison evaporated. The reunions began.

Jordan Waters gasped and spun away from the window of the small Whitehaven airport where she and Derrick Wallace had arrived only fifteen minutes before. Derrick turned from the counter where he was arranging transportation to find his parents. Wide-eyed, she jumped up and down on her toes like a little girl, exclaiming, "The plane that just landed—that's Juliette Painter, the actress!"

"Don't tell me you didn't know that was Savanna Painter's daughter," Derrick drawled indulgently. "What kinda journalist are you?"

"Sure, but she doesn't live here. I didn't expect to see her face to face!"

Derrick raised his brows. This was the first time since meeting Jordan that he saw her flustered, and he liked it. Bemused, he stepped to her side, turning her around to look back out the window. "She was a late-life surprise for her parents, much younger than her brothers Wyeth and Andrew, and in extreme danger of being a spoiled mess. She turned out anything but that."

"Caroline looks like her. I bet people think they're sisters."

"You'd win that wager. They even wear a lot of the same clothes. Juliette loves working with a designer to create her own, but she can't be seen in public wearing some of them more than once, so she passes those along to Caroline. That's her husband, Cameron Fisher, the filmmaker. He flies his own Cessna, and he's probably as frustrated as we were at not being allowed to land yesterday. He's got to be worried sick about his sister, who is pregnant with her second child. She married Caroline's brother and was stranded with them. I haven't figured it out—is her sister-in-law Natalie also her niece by marriage? Or is Juliette her sister-in-law as well as her aunt?"

Derrick shrugged when Jordan laughed at his point. "Regardless, the doll-baby in Juliette's arms is their daughter Mia, and the lady with the little girl next to them is Whitehaven's mayor's daughter, Carly. She's Caroline's lifelong best friend, and we all ran around together in high school. Carly's husband, Jesse, is Cameron's cameraman of choice. Caroline did some matchmaking between Carly and Jesse when he came to help with a movie filmed at Painter Place four years ago."

The group from the Cessna entered the small waiting room, and the mayor's daughter's family went to the attendant to get news about the current state of the little town. Carly smiled brightly at Derrick and waved enthusiastically. Juliette led Mia by the hand to greet him warmly, getting a hug before he introduced Jordan.

"It's a pleasure to meet you, Miss Waters. This is Mia, my daughter," Juliette said with a smile down at Mia.

The little girl stared at Jordan with searching, incredible blue eyes before she said, "Happy to meet you, Miss Waters," and she added an adorable little curtsy.

"And I'm delighted to meet you, Mia," Jordan returned, adding her own curtsy, which surprised the girl. She beamed up at her mother.

Cameron came over for a hearty handshake with Derrick, who introduced Jordan and explained that she was a Christian author and journalist who was a big fan of Savanna Painter. As Mia wrapped her arms around her dad's jeans leg and cuddled against his hand on her head, Jordan gave Juliette her card. Derrick explained that Jordan traveled with him to Whitehaven to cover the personal side of Hugo's path over Painter Place.

Juliette's husband knit his brows. "Miss Waters, four years ago, reporters upset Caroline Painter's husband so much that they're only allowed on the island by invitation. Juliette may eventually get approval for you to write about Painter Place, but—"

"Cameron, she's with me," Derrick blurted. "She's—Jordan's my girl. I'll take full responsibility with Chad." He took Jordan's hand into his, feeling the elation of cornering Jordan into an official relationship with him. He had not had this much fun since the days of creatively cornering Caroline at every opportunity. Jordan would be stuck with him for at least a couple of months if she wanted to cover Painter Place, and there was a practice game with her ex-fiancé's team before then. Derrick would move the earth to have her there sitting with his team's wives and girlfriends.

Surprise passed briefly over the tall, dark-haired young woman's face before she smiled weakly. "It's a—recent development," she managed to say before her voice trailed off.

"Well, that changes everything, Miss Waters," Juliette said. She tilted her head, studying the journalist with a look that missed nothing. "Derrick is like family, and he's always welcome on the island. If you can travel to Atlanta, I'll arrange for you to have lunch with my mother, and she may grant you an interview. She's stuck there with friends while we sort this situation out. We're in disarray about the island, uncertain how to get over there. We flew over, and the mansion is all that's left. It will have to be inspected to determine if it must be torn down. We only know our stranded family members are safe and the twins are born. Would you like to release the report from a family member to announce their safety, and the boys' names? We want to publicly thank people for their prayers."

"Let me get my notepad!" Jordan turned to her bag.

Derrick's eyes met Juliette's with gratitude before the journalist had pen in hand. He slid his arm around Jordan's waist while she asked breathlessly, "What are the twins' names?"

"The oldest is Rhett Montgomery Gregory, and his brother is Rayce Heyward Gregory. Rayce is spelled with a "y". Their middle names are a tribute to Chad's maternal grandfather, Montgomery Heyward of Charleston, SC. Chad and Caroline will release a family photo when things settle down."

Jordan looked up from scribbling notes. "Heyward—spelled like the South Carolina signer of the U. S. Constitution? Whew! I hope I'm around to see what these boys are like twenty years from now. Just hearin' their names will make a girl swoon!"

Derrick rolled his eyes. The attendant called to him to say his friend Sterling arrived in a patrol car to pick him up. He looked at Cameron and Juliette. "I need to make mom and dad's place livable until repairs are done. We'll have to fly back out on Monday. Is there any chance I can get Jordan over to Painter Place tomorrow?"

Cameron shook his head solemnly. "I don't even know if I can get there tomorrow, Derrick. Unless Andy Painter finds something that floats to pick us up, we may sleep in the shelter or in my plane tonight. Conditions over there are dangerous and primitive, and I wouldn't want either of you to get hurt."

Juliette handed Jordan her card. "Jordan, while you're here, try to meet the owner of the Whitehaven Register to set up a working relationship. You'll like him. He's a Christian and tries to print a paper that reports just the facts, no spin. You can investigate the condition of my big brother Andy's business, Island Marina, beside the Gregory Global tower. My oldest brother, Wyeth, has no studio or gallery on the island anymore, if that helps your report. Both art venues were located in the historic old stables behind the mansion, but Wyeth had the foresight to have the artwork inventory evacuated prior to the storm."

She shot a glance over at Derrick, then back to Jordan. "If there's time, you and your boyfriend can go see the Castaway, my nephew's restaurant. Derrick is one of the owners and will want to see the extensive damage. Get in touch with me to approve what you want to publish, and I'll be your liaison for my mother and Painter Place. If we work well together, I'll have photos you can use to show the island as it is now, raw after the storm. Cameron and I have arranged to get his pregnant sister Natalie and my niece Caroline off the island for at least six weeks, while the men make it livable. Newborn babies and a two-year old should not be there in those conditions. It will be that long before we can give you access, but I can feed you information, if I have your word that you won't sensationalize any aspect of this."

Derrick's mouth fell open as Jordan gushed with assurances and gratitude. "Wait—back up." He shook his head as if to clear it. "Did you say Caroline and Chad will be separated for six weeks?"

Cameron glanced at Juliette. There was an awkward silence.

Derrick chuckled. "Ahhh, I see. Man, what I'd give to watch Chad's face when this goes down! He can barely make it through a day at work without her. I'm sure the evening news will fill me in on the next adventure she lands in, and I expect to hear he's on a plane to straighten somebody out."

Chad gulped. He was suffocating. The Big House was full of exhausted, emotionally charged people, elated at finding them alive one minute and despairing over being homeless the next. Caroline fed the crying twins constantly, and he was beginning to understand that they ran her life. She barely had time to sleep or even speak to him, and they were never alone. He was jealous of his own sons and frustrated at the communal conditions.

Upstairs was like a daycare—or more accurately, a zoo. Danny had ferried Maggie Jane from the island to Whitehaven to help her family, but he brought back Juliette's family on the return trip. Taylor Juliette, Mia, and Noble were the only ones in the house having a blast.

Where everyone would sleep tonight was beyond Chad, because the third floor was unstable due to roof damage. For all they knew, it would crash down on them any second. The six bedrooms left in the house would be occupied by the older couples, so he expected a night on the floor somewhere with Patrick, Joey, Danny, Tony, and maybe even Cameron.

As if the day had not been brutal enough with the showdown between his dad and Wyeth, now the men decided it was time to air out secrets in the battered, glass-strewn living room. Part of Tony's fresh start was admitting his perverse delight in setting up accounts for Patrick, Caroline, and Marina with Global and forcing Phillip to keep them confidentially hidden from Andy for years.

Now it was Andy, not Wyeth, who was incensed with his dad, who defended himself by explaining that he could do more with the money for Andy's kids than the competitor Tony was going to turn to. He conceded that Tony was trying to spite Andy and enjoyed the fact that Painters and Gregorys hid things from one another. But Phillip was looking at the end goal.

Next, Andy exploded at his father-in-law's admission that he followed Valerie's family via investigators over the years, and Phillip joined him when he heard Tony had watched Chad. The final straw was when Tony confessed that he was being treated for cancer that might be cured or at least held at bay with an experimental direction he was taking. If not for the fact that Tony seemed sincerely to be a new Christian who wanted to reconcile with his family, Chad knew Caroline's dad would be in a total meltdown and thrown Tony back into the water he had crawled out of during the hurricane.

Joey and Casey were out walking on the beach, getting away to clear their heads about news Danny brought back concerning their jobs. The physician Casey worked for was trying to reach all his staff to let them know they were unemployed until he decided whether to rebuild in Whitehaven. Joey learned that the radio tower was significantly damaged and off the air. Big Mike was in declining health and decided to sell the station rather than endure dealing with insurance to update the business.

Chad muttered to his brother Cole that he needed fresh air. He snatched up his Walkman and dove to the only safe exit, imagining himself descending through an escape hatch. He should have a couple of hours of daylight left for a desperately needed run to vanquish this tension.

The rousing rock beat of *Frankenstein* pounded out of his headphones at the push of a button. *Perfect.*

He was feeling like a monster himself and teetered dangerously on the verge of acting like one. Confidentiality was something he cut his teeth on as a Gregory, but the secrets that were besieging the island families made his stomach twist. Not only was it sickening, he was keeping them himself from Caroline only a few days ago. She was right—hiding things changed a person inside and affected all their relationships.

He guessed where Castaway Drive had once been and decided to see how far toward home he could get. Making sure he left a trail of prints in the sand so someone could find him if he got hurt, he navigated by keeping the waterway to the west at his right shoulder.

Tension uncoiled with each long running stride. His mental calculations of the financial losses around him would otherwise send him into despair.

Chad slowed to a stop where his house should have been and stood panting. His stomach clenched. The guest cottage he and Caroline had made their first home in either no longer existed or was reduced to rubble in a mess that was once the home he grew up in. Using his hands to rake his blonde bangs from his eyes, he stared.

He heard Ben's stern warning in his mind. He was a husband, a father. He could take no risks by going down there alone.

Tearing his eyes from the sight, Chad started his jog again, dodging tree trunks, debris from the destroyed cottages, and rotting sea animal carcasses. He reached the location of Andy Painter's estate.

The wonderful house would have been Patrick's someday, if there'd been anything left. Chad had spent his whole life, except for college, divided between his home, the Big House, and this house. Slowing down to a walk, he panted and carefully picked the safest path to see it better.

He rubbed his eyes to be sure of what he was seeing. Most of the house was gone, swept off the foundation, which remained. But the heart of the house—the replica staircase rotunda and stained-glass dome overhead, inspired by the Big House—remained. Tattered and solitary, it rose about four stories up into the air, open like a gazebo tower in a wilderness. The extra framework built into the house to support the weight of the rotunda withstood what the house never could.

Chad's chest felt as if someone dipped an empty bucket into a well of joy and started hauling it up. Other than the Big House, this was the first sign of any structural survival. He surveyed the rest of his surroundings. The basketball court, scene of a lifetime of Friday night Tarzan games, was nowhere to be found. But three of the huge oaks that shaded it had some branches left, like trees in a scary cartoon.

The memory of one evening when was angry at Caroline before a game with the girls popped in his mind. He had decided she'd have to come up with something extraordinary to get out of the trouble she was in. He was rough on her on the court, and shocked when he caught her lingering gaze on his mouth while guarding him. It was the heat needed to thaw the ice barrier he was churlishly punishing her with. When he asked her about it later, she admitted to wondering what a real kiss was like. She expected it to be dangerous, and she wanted that kiss from him.

Her first kiss. His first kiss. The one he saved for her, and she saved for him. The one they shared when he was told he could kiss his bride.

The kiss happened at the end of a pier that was now gone. The cottage where they spent their wedding night before flying to Hawaii was destroyed.

Caroline was right. Settings for their special memories now existed only in their head, or in photographs. God allowed them all to be wiped away by Hugo, even while He gave them their firstborn children.

The shadows grew longer. It was time to return run to the Big House. He decided to explore a different path now that he had his bearings. By the time the cassette in the Walkman ended, he reached the edge of what remained of the Gregory estate.

He slowed down to stop and flip the cassette over. His head shot back up when he heard his mother's voice, and he jerked off the earphones. Cautiously, he stepped forward. A massive sprawling oak was crawling on its hands and knees in front of him, and the impossible tangle of limbs and leaves were blocking his path. He moved closer to blaze a trail to navigate around it.

Then he froze when he heard his dad's tone. He could see them now in an open gap within the limbs. His dad stood in what was once the farthest front edge of his yard from the security gate, both hands behind his head and his face to the sky. His eyes were screwed up tight. Chad read the same anguish in his posture that he had heard in his voice moments ago, and it wrung his heart.

Chad's mother moved as if she was in a dream when she stepped out of the golf cart. She started crying, saying this was too much to cope with, and she was going to Sandy's to stay with her mom and dad.

With an agonized groan, Chad wiped his hand across his face, bracing for his dad's reaction. He watched him swing around, walk briskly back to her, and grab her shoulders to make her look him in the eye. Surprised, she abruptly ended her outburst.

His dad yelled that he was the one who took care of her parents the past few days instead of helping Chad and the Painters during the storm, and now he would be the one taking care of her. He shouted that if she imagined her dad could do better than him under the circumstances, then she could call Montgomery to come get her. He was too busy to haul her back to her daddy in Charleston.

Chad gaped while his dad let go of her and stretched out both hands wide, taking a step back, and then another. He reminded Chad's mother that when he met her at a concert on the Battery, her very presence in the crowd turned heads. She was the popular girl in diamonds who had everyone eating out of her hand, wanting to be near her. She exuded confidence, strength, and intelligence.

Angrily, Phillip shouted, "What happened to *that* Camellia? She's the woman I married! She was the one I knew I'd need someday! I always knew life wasn't a rose garden, and I chose someone strong to survive it with. Where is that person? A mere hurricane could never have daunted her!"

Camellia clamped her hands over her mouth and squeezed her eyes tight, stifling sobs that made her shoulders shake. Chad struggled, wanting to go comfort her, but siding with his dad. His parents never argued like this in front of him, though he had seen heated discussions on the far end of the pier out of his earshot. They always ended well.

His dad apologized for grabbing her, then turned his back and his attention to the rubble that had always been their home together. Chad mother hurried after him, taking his arm to turn him around and wrapping hers tightly around his waist. He held her just as fiercely, crying and kissing her desperately.

In the stillness of the late afternoon, Chad could hear his dad's voice, rough with emotion. "Stay here with me. You're my calm. I can't face this without you."

His mom nodded her head against his chest. Chad decided it was not the best time for him to go down and see if his dad wanted to scout the ruined house together.

As he backtracked to his former path, he knew Hugo was not finished with Painter Place. The aftermath was bringing out the worst in all of them.

Chapter Twelve

Chad and Joey could find no place to shave in the crowded house the next morning. They decided that if a scruffy shadow worked for Indiana Jones, it was good enough for them. The comparison inspired banter back and forth with some quotes about several particularly rough conditions Jones endured. They washed their faces and hair outside with a bucket of rainwater, putting the bucket back in the open to collect whatever water gifts might fall from the sky. Both had just donned the last of their clean clothes.

They sat on the trunk of a prostrate oak tree, surly, subdued, and stiff from another night on the floor. Their hair played in the breeze from the ocean, drying in any style it pleased in the early morning sun.

Joey glanced over at Chad and said, "Ben's bringin' Mom and Dad up from Charleston this afternoon to get photos of the house for insurance. I'll try to meet with Big Mike about the station."

"Tell 'im the Young Guns want a chance to make an offer, but I need an estimate of the cost of the upgrades. Marina and Danny are leavin' to stay with his parents, so you can ride in the boat over with them. Bring me somethin' to wear if you find your clothes under your house. I don't know when stores will open, or if I'll find any of mine in the rubble at the cottage."

Joey snorted. "This is ludicrous! You're a multi-millionaire, Chad—multi-billionaire if you count Global—and you're reduced to diggin' through rubble for your designer underwear. I have no home or transportation, and until the tower is repaired, no job. Casey needs to move away to find work. We were just mindin' our own business, doin' no harm before Hugo. Now we're campin' out for who knows how long, or how much money we'll all lose."

He miserably rubbed his hands over his face. The wheels began slowly turning in Chad's mind again, grinding roughly at first, and then chugging him out of his dark tunnel. "Casey can stay to help Caroline full time for now if she wants to wait until things settle down, so she can pay her bills and keep her room at the boarding house. Another medical facility will come to town."

Wyeth, Andy, Justin, and Phillip came out and walked to the front of the house, deep in discussion about whether to replace the old chapel where three of them had been married. Cameron, Cole, Patrick, and Tony wandered out after them, heading leisurely over to Chad and Joey, who stood up to see what the plan for the day was. Delighted squeals from the toddlers came from an open window.

Cameron furrowed his brow and looked Chad in the eye. "I'm on my way down to the Florida Keys for some work on a movie."

"They just filmed part of *License to Kill* down there, didn't they?" inserted Patrick.

"Yes." Cameron nodded before launching into his point. "It's a good time of year to take Caroline and the twins down with us until she's well enough to fly. Casey's invited, if she's still working for you. Juliette and Mia will love it, and we have a nanny who's excited about helping with the twins. I'll have access to a doctor for getting Caroline and the boys checked out when we arrive. From there, we'll be heading to Arles, France. I can give you at least six weeks to get the Big House repaired."

Cameron saw the instant resistance in Chad's posture and expression, so he let this sink in while he launched a plea with Patrick. "My aunt is begging for Natalie and Noble to visit her for a while. Let me put Natalie on a plane in Atlanta."

Chad and Patrick communicated to one another via expressions and demeanor, ambling from the side of the mansion to the front yard. Cole and Joey shot one another meaningful looks. They all paused near the massive front stairway to the destroyed veranda.

"Look, you're right. I have huge problems to deal with, in primitive conditions," Chad admitted to Cameron. "I'm overwhelmed, frustrated, stressed out, and suffocating in family togetherness. I'm lost about what to do with a wife and two very needy babies in this mess. The twins dominate Caroline's life right now. I haven't had a private conversation with her in days!"

He gestured around him. "It's hard to know what to do first! We've got to figure out our next meal and how to do laundry. We need to handle cleanup, repairs, insurance claims and settlements for the island and Global. With no phone service, I've got to get negotiations going on an offer to buy Big Mike's part of the radio station so Joey can keep his job. I don't know if I have a car and I may end up sleepin' on the sofa in my office for a while."

"Same here," Patrick exclaimed, running his hand through his damp blonde hair. "I can't shave or have a shower, let alone look after Natalie and Noble. Instead of focusing on gettin' the Castaway back open, I'm wondering whether to build an outhouse and carve a crescent moon on the door. Dad needs my help goin' through what's left at the house, the Tahoe is gone, and I don't know if my Corvette made it through the storm. I'm torn in a million directions! I'm drowning."

"You don't have to worry about me and the boys, Chad. Check that 'huge problem' off your long list."

All the men spun around in the direction of Caroline's frosty tone. She and Juliette stood together at the open double doors.

Chad opened his mouth to say something, but absolutely nothing appropriate came to mind. Their eyes met, his full of pleading panic, and hers perfectly matching the temperature of the ice water she just dowsed him with.

"I came down to let you know I'm leavin' with Juliette and Cameron. Can you believe I thought it would be hard to convince you to let me go? Turns out, this was the easiest thing I've done today. I know the calculations that must be going on in your head over the losses around here, and how you're tryin' to fix things for everybody. So, focus on business. I'll use my own money for the trip." Her eyes left his face dismissively and went to Wyeth's.

Chad's heart was in his throat, and he could not process what was happening fast enough to keep up. The love of his life could never have looked at him so coldly. She was not seriously thinking about leaving with his twins. And she would never refuse to let him be financially responsible for her, not in front of all the other men.

"Uncle Wyeth, I'll represent Painter Place while I'm in Arles, calling on some connections we might want to establish and painting at sites frequented by Van Gogh and Picasso. The Van Gogh Centennial at Arles will be the theme of my next body of work. I'll need supplies. When Global has power back again, watch for my fax receipts for the studio business credit card purchases. Don't approve any new studio and gallery plans until I get back to see them."

Wyeth swallowed. "Of course."

"Great, we all understand one another. Oddly enough, we're checkin' off problems at lightning speed. Danny, we're all on the demanding schedule of the very needy twins that dominate my life. Be ready at the boat for Whitehaven in less than an hour. Casey will travel with me. I need to pack, so I'll leave you fellas to brag about how big your problems are."

She turned on her heel, blonde hair swinging, and swiftly disappeared into the house. Juliette shot Cameron a warning look before following.

Shell-shocked, Chad stopped mid-step in the sand when Cameron grabbed his arm. The other men began to huddle around him as if in a team discussion on what play came next. Cole let out a long, low whistle, stepping up to pat Chad's shoulder sympathetically. "We all felt that one, big brother."

"Rookie mistake," said Cameron. "You just met the mama lioness. She heard, roared, bared her teeth, and unsheathed her claws. You've been warned—stay away from her den of 'needy' cubs. In my three years with my first wife before she died, two years dating Juliette, and four years of marriage to her, I've never messed up this bad. I regret to say that I have no words of wisdom for you."

Caroline's dad said, "I've been the jerk she put in his place once. At least she wasn't screamin' at you. My advice is not to try to touch her or plead with her unless you want worse than you got."

Chad's father scowled and blew out a deep breath. "What in the world would you say, Chad? You were speakin' your heart and mind. She knows it."

"But I have to stop her!" Chad protested. "I wasn't sayin' I wanted her and the boys out of my way! They're just—they're just—"

"A problem," finished Cole, nodding with pursed lips. "Misery loves company, so it's nice to have you joinin' me in a bachelor's life for the foreseeable future."

Patrick whistled. "I'm glad Natalie didn't hear me."

"I did hear you—from the window when I checked on Noble." They spun around again to the busy open doorway, where Natalie was now the feature act. She stood there with eyes flashing and hands on her hips. "I took care of myself and my much older brother before you ever came along, Patrick. I can certainly handle myself and a toddler. All you and Chad had to do was talk to us about it, instead of sounding off like we're a burden in front of the guys. Cameron, you're right, this is no place for me or Noble. Patrick, take a deep breath of freedom from me and your son while you build a cute outhouse and fix the mansion and the Castaway. While you're at it, fix your attitude."

Natalie slammed the double doors behind her. The men looked sheepishly at the other doors and windows. Tony chuckled, and Cole asked, "Should we get the guys to vote on which was worse? Chad will want to know who won."

Casey and Juliette took Rhett and Rayce from Chad's reluctant arms as the solemn group boarded the boat to ferry to Whitehaven. Cameron had arranged for a passenger van that waited for them at what was left of his brother-in-law's Island Marina.

Chad led Caroline out of earshot from the other goodbyes, pulling her into his arms to whisper in her ear. "You have to know I didn't intend what I said to sound demeaning. I meant that although Cameron is right that I'm in over my head, you and the boys were stayin' with me anyway. I don't know how I can face this," he whispered fiercely.

Caroline nodded against his shoulder, stiff in his arms.

"Talk to me," he begged.

"The boys need better living conditions, Chad. Love isn't enough right now. I'm dealin' with my own problems, but you aren't there for me anymore. You're out fixin' everything for everyone. I'm exhausted. I knew feeding the twins would probably be too much for me, but I hoped to give them a month. Now I have no home and will be traveling. I never dreamed I'd have no relationship with my husband during the worst crisis of my life. Like you, I'm smothering under so many people, and I feel—I feel like screaming!" Caroline whispered vehemently.

Startled, Chad held her at arm's length and found desperation all over her face. He had assumed she was a happy new mother enjoying lots of pampering from her family. The group's emotional breakdown had emptied him of the shock about their home after Ben left, and he thought she felt the same.

Now she looked away from his eyes. "I'm grieving for Painter Place, I miss you and me, and worst of all—I'm a terrible Christian. I have the foundation to know how to survive havin' the rug pulled out from under me, but I'm crashing. And I have no choice but to crash alone."

Chad shook his head in confusion. He had no idea what to say. He groaned, knowing a million things he should have said would come to mind after she was gone.

"Watch out, Chad," she whispered sadly, realizing he had nothing for her. "We're being divided, and we aren't as strong apart."

"Time to go, Caroline," called Cameron from the boat.

She quickly brushed a kiss on his lips and turned, but he grasped her arm to pull her in for one that had to last for six weeks. Then she backed away, her blue eyes forlorn and already lonely.

His heart lurched. He touched his finger to it and then pointed at hers. "Save your heart for me," he rasped through his tight throat.

"Always," she whispered.

She turned away and he watched the boat carry her and his sons across the waterway, out of his life for the foreseeable future. Patrick sniffed as he and Joey came to stand bleakly beside him.

The remaining group at Painter Place walked back to the house to have lunch until Danny returned with the boat. Chad mumbled that he was not hungry, and he never broke his stride toward the beach.

Patrick, Joey, and Cole stood watching his back. "It's not safe to wander off alone in this mess," muttered Cole. "There could be sinkholes. Anybody here who deserves bein' around him 'til he blows off steam?"

"This isn't my stellar day, either," growled Patrick. "I'll babysit."

"I'll bring out somethin' to eat in a minute," Joey muttered. "I'm bad company. Wish I didn't have to go back over to town this afternoon."

When Joey scouted out his friends, he held a paper bag stuffed with sandwiches in one hand and the necks of three juice drinks in the fingers of the other. He found Patrick leaning on an upright bare palm on the side of a dune, staring at a spot of twisted debris near the beach further south, where he could see the back of Chad's head as he paced.

Joey took a sandwich out of the bag he tossed to Patrick, setting down two of the drink bottles and taking his with him to find another spot where he could be alone. Without looking into the bag, Patrick pulled out a sandwich and sat with knees bent up, his Carolina tee-shirted back against what was left of the tree.

They silently chewed their lunch, listening to Chad's angry voice rise over the sound of the pounding surf. Joey winced when he heard him shout at the sea, "How could I have been so stupid?"

A glance at Patrick's back told him Chad was getting to him, too. It bothered Joey to have Casey go away for so long, disrupting his plan, but it was excruciating to see Patrick and Chad separated from their families. Caroline's face and demeanor sent a stab of fear through his heart, and he wondered what it meant. She was different. Would anything ever be the same after this?

He chewed the next bite of his sandwich and prayed, *God, help us. We're so changed, so raw! When will Hugo end? If this is happening at Painter Place, what's happening in Whitehaven?*

Patrick let the hot tears flow down his face. In his mind, he was lifting Noble up in his arms and answering a million questions. He was watching Natalie's lithe movements and soft expressions. He imagined her dark, silky hair in his fingers and her Mona Lisa smile, and put his hand on her stomach to feel his unborn child moving.

Chad's next shout at the sea brought him back to reality. Chad was wild with—whatever this was. Physical stuff calmed him, like jogging, working out, or their ballgames and golf. But this was different. The only other time Patrick had seen him off the charts like this was the day their fathers told him that once he left for college, he could not contact Caroline, or tell her why he would be out of her life for four years—for the ultimate good of Painter Place.

Patrick had listened, cried, and sat that episode out nearby, too, resolving that he would spend the next four years getting Chad through the ordeal. Somehow, they would get one another through this one, too. At least God had blessed them with a bond that few people had.

From an upstairs window in a guest room, Phillip Gregory looked out to the beach where his son was a raging storm in his own right, shouting at the sea, kicking debris, and throwing small objects he picked up from the sand out into the ocean to be rolled in again with the tide. He would wear himself out to the desperate praying stage, where his resolve was waiting. Chad had to vent this physically. Like father, like son, though Phillip was glad his daughter and youngest son Cole had their mother's temperament.

This was why Phillip understood, on a gut level, Wyeth's uncharacteristic outburst yesterday. It was certainly not behavior either of them would want the preacher or anyone from town to witness.

Nevertheless, Phillip was glad his best friend had finally broken under the shock of all he had lost. Wyeth needed to break the chains of repressed pain, guilt over his inability to forgive and forget, flex his power to remind Phillip of who the real boss at Painter Place was, and to draw a line in the sand. The incident was Phillip's warning that he would never get by with anything remotely like betrayal again.

While Phillip understood the depths that drove Wyeth's violent outburst, he also knew beyond any doubt that what the heir to Painter Place wanted more than anything was the restoration of the lifelong bond they shared. He sought confirmation and reassurance that all their childhood promises would be honored; Phillip tried to affirm it by repeating how solidly the blood brother pact rested in bedrock, like the foundation pilings of the Big House. He meant it when he told Wyeth he would never get rid of him.

But the same storm that finally gave Phillip his best friend back had traumatized his son and daughter-in-law, separating them from one another at a critical time for them both. Watching his son's emotional explosion on the beach, he scowled in concern.

Caroline and Chad were the next generation being groomed to take the helm at Painter Place. This recovery should have been a time to forge the kind of bonds that only getting through bad experiences together could do. But as much as he wanted his newborn grandsons in his arms, he knew Caroline was right to take them off the island.

He jumped when his long-silent mobile phone rang. At first, he stared at it, wondering if he was dreaming. But at the second ring, he fairly leaped to the dresser to pick it up, hearing his dad's voice from his daughter Sandy's house in Charleston.

PART TWO

Separation

Chapter Thirteen

In three words I can sum up
everything I've learned about life:
it goes on.
-Robert Frost

"It's good to see you're awake," said a petite dark-haired nurse in a nearby chair. "I'll let your father know you've opened your eyes." She pushed a button on a bedside table and smiled kindly.

A young man looked blankly back at her before his eyes roamed around the room. He was slightly propped up in a hospital bed, but not in a hospital. The room was enormous and beautifully decorated in a warm Spanish flair. A gigantic painting of a stalking jaguar hung over a long buffet of closed cabinets, its golden eyes intelligent and calculating. On another wall, tall glass doors opened to a balcony or patio. Sounds of jungle wildlife floated through them into the lavish room.

As the nurse began attending to what he guessed was a bandage around his head, two men walked in. One beamed at him with open arms, and the nurse moved to let him attempt a hug in which he did not actually disturb the position of the young man on the bed. When he straightened, he looked intently into the green eyes that studied him in confusion.

"You are safe at home now, son."

The older man spoke with confidence that such a statement would bring comfort, and knowing one is safe and well cared for is in fact a measure of it. But the young man did not know his caregivers, or where he was, and as he closed his eyes and slipped back into nothingness, it didn't even matter.

Behind the wheel of the rented passenger van, Cameron Fisher squinted into the black night along the roadside as Juliette searched for a radio station without static. His weary eyes strained as the headlights finally beamed onto the sign he was looking for. He exhaled a sigh of relief. The villa near the studios in the Keys was minutes away. A mellow tune slid smoothly out the speakers into the van, assuring a lover that he or she was the meaning and inspiration in the singer's life, and would be loved until the end of time.

A glance in his rearview mirror confirmed that Caroline was weeping quietly to the words of the song, and Casey was dabbing her eyes. Juliette was sniffling beside him. At least all the kids were asleep. The love ballad could have been written about Caroline and Chad, and the words made even him feel mushy. He regrated having the dirty job of tearing those two apart, but somebody had to do it.

Attendants unloaded their bags at the villa. He made sure everyone was getting settled with the waiting nanny before he went outside in the balmy Florida evening, letting a Gulf breeze play in his hair as he made calls on his mobile phone. First on the list was Chad.

"Sandy finally got through and said you'd been tryin' to reach me," Chad said. "I can't tell you how much it meant to them to have you drop by so my grandparents could see the boys. How is Caroline? Sandy hedged when I asked about her."

"She was outwardly calm and gracious, hemmed into her Southern manners. But she was quiet. She swings from being okay with the boys to being in a place even Juliette can't reach. I'll either qualify to be a counselor after this, or I'll need one. If I ever do a survival film, I'm putting a man in a van with four sobbing females experiencing a personal crisis, one of them pregnant and one post-partum, two toddlers who can't sit still and talk incessantly, and two newborns who scream to eat and have a diaper change every two hours."

Chad burst out laughing in spite of himself and ran a hand over the growth of beard on his face to wake himself up. He leaned back in his office chair, pushing from his desk. "You've gone way past the call of duty, Cameron. I swing between bein' furious at you for takin' Care away to knowin' I owe you. Did you visit Savanna Painter in Atlanta?"

"Yes, she met us at the airport due to Natalie's flight schedule, so it wasn't a cozy meeting. She brought the supplies Caroline asked her to shop for from an art supply store in the city. I'm afraid Gran Vanna is upset at the girls leaving Painter Place, though she agreed there's nothing for it. She says separation makes a playground for the devil. Those words rang so true that I was spooked. Step carefully, Chad."

Chad squirmed in his chair, uneasy. "Yeah, Caroline said somethin' similar when she left. We've learned to sit up and take notice when they say things like that."

Cameron cleared his throat. "I'm afraid seeing the kids was the only upside for her grandmother. She adores them. Seeing her seemed to help Juliette get past some of her grief over Painter Place, but it made Caroline worse. Savanna was pretty torn up herself by the time we said goodbye."

Chad frowned. If anyone could have reached Caroline, it would have been her grandmother.

"We stopped at a mall to pick up a change of clothes for Caroline, Casey, and the twins before we stayed at another motel overnight in Florida. I hoped some rest would give the ladies a new perspective. But today was still emotionally brutal. Just a half an hour ago in the van, Caroline started crying to a song on the radio, and on a dime, Casey and Juliette joined her. I was ready to cry myself!"

"Oh, yeah? What was the song?" asked Chad thoughtfully.

"'You're the Inspiration.' Why couldn't they have played 'I'm a Man' or the one about not caring what time it is?"

Chad snorted and grinned, wearily closing his eyes. "I'm losin' my mind without her. Is she around?"

"Let me tuck my head inside and check."

Waiting, Chad walked to the wall of glass in his office, which was sandblasted by Hugo and in need of replacement. He saw a single light glimmering through the darkness from the Big House, the only light on the island. He went to his desk for his binoculars, holding them up to his eyes with his free hand. His mom told him she would say goodnight to him and Cole by putting a lantern in Gran Vanna's window for a little while. He sighed at the comfort as if it were a hug.

She had not yet gotten over the night she feared he had been lost to Hugo. She also understood how hard this separation from Caroline was, and how much Cole missed Shannon.

Cameron spoke again. "Chad, Juliette said that Caroline's already asleep. She just lay across the bed in her clothes and conked out. Can I have her call you in the morning? Where are you?"

Chad swallowed his disappointment and turned to look behind him. "I'm campin' in my office at Global. Everyone is scattering to find a temporary place to stay. For reasons I can't grasp, Caroline's Grandma Audrey is lettin' Tony Rush have the guest room at her house down in Georgetown while he's in treatments, because his place in Charleston is trashed by Hugo. My uncle Justin got temporary backup help for the Global London office, so he's heading back to Charleston to stay at Sandy's. He'll help both my grandparents get their home repairs underway so my dad can concentrate on Painter Place and Global. We're supposed to have water here by tomorrow, and we have some power with the generator."

"Where's Patrick?"

"He and Cole will stay in an office across the hall from mine. It's the one Dad built for Cole before he fired him. He's just goin' through motions of livin' right now, really upset about Natalie,

Painter Place, and the Castaway. Joey's here in my office, sleepin' on the second sofa. He's been pretty down in the dumps, too, so we're a bunch of growlin' bears."

"Chad, I know this is tough, but make some fun memories of how you guys got through this together. You're blessed to have one another. I wonder if you know how rare that is."

"Thanks, Cameron. I'll take that advice to heart. Get some rest, and thanks for all you're doin' for my family."

A sunbeam warmed Caroline's upturned face, and she took a moment to simply be thankful for it. Squinting, she found more sunbeams bursting through open shutter vents and creating a playground for prism colors in her room.

She wondered what day it was. Life was a blur as one day melted into the next. She seemed to exist only to be a gypsy mother to two hungry baby boys.

A light knock prompted her to invite someone in, but there was such a profusion of people in her life she needed two hands to count who this might be. Juliette peeked in, smiling, and holding out Cameron's mobile phone. "Can you talk to Chad?"

Caroline nodded while Juliette handed her the phone and quietly closed the door. "Good morning," she said lazily as she opened the folding shutters to view breathtakingly blue water and a sugary sand beach.

"Good morning, beautiful." She could hear the smile in his voice. She smiled back, as if he could see her.

"It's always a good morning when I wake up to hear your voice. Where are you?"

"I'm in my office, looking at Joey sprawled out asleep on one of my sofas. I slept on the other one. We hope to get our first shower in nearly a week this morning. Dad couldn't have known when he built this place with showers in the men's room how much I'd appreciate it someday. I can't wait to shave. I look like Jeremiah Johnson."

"Of the two Johnsons, I prefer your Don Johnson look."

"Baby, I'll be any guy you want if you'll just come back to me. Sounds like my girl's feelin' a little better."

Caroline pushed the glass door open. "Yeah. I'm sure things will get better as time passes."

Chad frowned, unsure what to say. The woman he liked to think he had figured out had become a mystery again.

"Did any of our cars made it through the storm?"

Chad hesitated. Now she was businesslike?

"Are you sure you want to talk about stuff like this right now?" His frown had bloomed into a full-fledged scowl, and he absently picked up a pen from his desk to flutter rapidly in his hand.

"Yeah, I want to get it over with so you can be free to handle the details without me. The boys will wake up any time, and I'm hoping you can talk to them before we get off the phone. You know, like you did before they were born, when I put the phone on my stomach. Now I'll put it near their ears. They'll know you."

A pang of longing to hold his sons stabbed at Chad's heart. Realizing the pen's movement was like hummingbird wings in his hand, he stopped himself and set it back down, making it a point not to develop bad habits that betrayed his inner stress. He took a deep breath and said, "Great idea for ending on an up note. Okay, well, we still have a car for special occasions—the one that reminds me of you, and in which you finally revealed a long-anticipated secret to me right after our wedding. The secret you couldn't tell me unless you owned me or killed me, whichever came first."

"All right!" she cheered. "At least we have that left. Noble will enjoy more drawings of the Lambo."

"I'm in the realm of *ecstatic* about it! The Cherokee is still missin' in action, with no tell-tale oil slick to flag it. My old Porsche was unfortunately under the garage roof that was caved in by an oak tree. It's totaled."

"Oh, no, Chad!" Caroline groaned, then sighed with resignation. "That was your first car, and you babied it. I'm so sorry. It must've hurt a lot to see it smashed. What about my Mustang?"

Chad looked out the window, his voice quiet. "The Mustang was under the same tree."

Silence. He wished he could see her expression, put his arms around her to comfort her. "I'll find you another one, Care, or we'll have one built."

"No. It could never be the same. Dad did most of the restoration himself. Besides, he surprised me with it specifically for my sixteenth birthday to celebrate the year I was born. It was a sentimental gift, and that time in my life is past. Anyway, now I won't have to associate it with the year you went away."

Chad scowled again and sat up to rest his elbows on his desk, rubbing his forehead with his free hand. "Are you sayin' that my leavin' that autumn for college marred the joy in your gift? You never told me that."

"I'm sayin' the rest of that year was full of confusion, rejection, and pain. I want a new start. I'm a lumpy, humdrum mom now, so I'll drive somethin' sensible with room for car seats."

Chad was unable to keep up in this conversation, snagged on a branch back at the part about how his departure had effectively ruined her joy in the amazing gift her dad had poured his time and heart into. He chose his next words as if he were navigating a minefield. "Yeah, uh, I'll look for something we can all fit into when the insurance settlements come in. By the way, one lane of the bridge is being patched today so that help can cross over for utilities and repairs to the Big House."

"That's great news. Have you heard anything from Baker and Beth?"

Baker? Another jolting swing in the conversation. He felt dizzy.

"Uh... yeah, Cole caught him yesterday. Beth had a scary time, and she won't be able to have any more children. She was in surgery a while and he thought he might lose her. They named their little girl Stormy, because he said he was so frightened that night, for Beth and for us during Hugo. He said Stormy's name would remind him that none of us were alone, and it inspired another song he's working on. Looks like God put them on your heart that night just when they needed your prayers most."

A knock on her door brought Caroline in from the balcony. The nanny carried a fussy Rhett into her room, gnawing at his tiny fist, followed by Casey, who was cuddling and cooing to Rayce.

"Hear that, Daddy? Your boys are awake. Want to tell them you love them?"

Chad grinned at one of the photos on his desk of his sons on the day after the storm. Caroline held the phone to each of them, and they quieted at hearing his voice. His heart soared and tears stung his eyes.

When he hung up, he punched in a call to his dad's secretary in the London offices at Global. She enjoyed doing personal work for them to surprise their wives, and she was incredibly good at it. He marked his calendar as he made plans with her, on the dates he wanted to surprise Caroline, and gave the secretary the addresses of the villa in the Keys and the house in Arles.

Out on a balcony that opened from the living room with an ocean view, Juliette and Cameron were still eating breakfast after Mia had gone to play. Juliette finished off a strawberry with cream cheese. "Cameron, remember you once said you'd think about making

Painter Place our home, but expanding the old cottage wasn't worthwhile?"

Her husband sighed, putting down his empty coffee cup. "How did I know this was going to come up?"

"My cottage is no longer an obstacle. Can I talk to Wyeth? There's land between Andy and Phillip for me to build, but I only get to have it if it's my primary residence. It's gated for Andy's house at Brush Point."

"Honey, your brother no longer has a house on Brush Point. Phillip has no house, either."

"But they will. That means when we aren't traveling, you'll be your sister's next-door neighbor. She and Patrick will always live at Andy's house, since Patrick inherits it. Let's raise Mia there with her cousins."

Cameron's mobile phone rang. After briefly agreeing with someone, he put it down on the table. "Okay, I'll consider it again, and you can talk to Wyeth once he's not so overwhelmed. He's grieving right now. I have a car arriving here soon to take you and the girls shopping for clothes, and whatever the twins need. I'm leaving for a meeting. Any suggestions about how I can get Caroline to use Chad's credit card? He insisted on me taking it."

"I'll work on that." Juliette held her slender hand out, buffed nails poised.

Cameron's brows shot up, and he wore a smirk as he fished it out of his wallet. "He may not have given it to me if he'd known you'd get your pretty little hands on it. I'm certain infinity is its limit."

Juliette smiled patiently, snapping the card from his fingers, looking it over. The name Phillip Chadwick Gregory III barely fit across the front. "He trusts me, or he wouldn't ask for my advice about Caroline all the time. Besides, he has expensive, impeccable taste and loves to lavish it on his wife. I think sometimes he picks fights with her just so he can make up and show her how sorry he is by buying her something. She knew she struck his heart when she told him she was leaving and using her money, as if he wanted to use all his to fix his huge problems. She'll use his card for the boys, though, and hers to shop for Casey, who didn't need much besides nursing uniforms before now. Casey wants a makeover for the role of working for Caroline. Neither of them has luggage for the plane flight."

"But you brought Caroline the suitcase of clothes you wore while recovering from having Mia," Cameron said.

"She needs more than that."

Cameron stood up, smiling indulgently before bending to kiss her goodbye. "They're in capable hands, and the prospect of shopping and making Casey over is lifting your mood. I know you're still sad about Painter Place, but it's good to see you feeling better. You and the girls should eat dinner out and get in late."

On Thursday, it was lunch time before Chad could call the villa in Florida. Juliette answered and told him Caroline was out walking on the beach with Casey, trying out the new camera he had sent her.

"She took photos of the twins with your card wishing them a happy week-old birthday. I took some of her and Casey, and even Nanny. We'll get them developed and drop a package to you soon. I know you miss them."

Chad made a groaning sound in his throat. "Like crazy! Being a new dad hasn't gone at all like I planned. It's hard to believe they're a week old, and harder to not have them with me to celebrate. I had so many plans for enjoying the milestones with them. I hope they won't forget their old man."

"Eating and sleeping are extreme sports for these guys right now, so it would be seriously boring for a high intensity guy like you. Be glad you missed their total transition from mama to a bottle tomorrow. And Chad—Caroline was really touched by the card you sent for her, too. I wasn't there during the storm that night, but I can imagine the high drama of that experience. Don't be surprised if you're contacted about making a movie or a book about it."

Chad walked to the window wall in his office, staring out at the ravaged island for the millionth time since Hugo. He hardly recognized it. "Maybe someday she and I can talk about it to people, but not now. She gave me a handmade leather journal a few days before the boys were born, telling me to write about their birth and what my first days as a dad were like. I've been writing in it since she left, but I'll save some space for photos. Buckled spots are scattered on pages where I lost it as I wrote what happened."

Juliette's eyes swam. "Eventually, the passage of time will create enough distance for all of us to talk about it. I can't express in words what it was like to get the call when you were all stranded. And to see what the storm did all around you—"

Her voice broke, and he squeezed his eyes shut. "It's okay now, Juliette. We made it. But this changed Caroline. Coach me. What's goin' on?"

Juliette blew her nose. When she answered, she still sounded stuffy. "I'm workin' on that. It isn't just all that happened there, Chad, it's deeper."

"On the day before the storm, she told me that she and her mom talked about her uneasiness with the way God gives and takes away. Then, on the day you and Cameron took her from Painter Place, she said she's a terrible Christian. As close as we are, she still thinks she's facing this all alone. I don't get it."

"She feels alone because what's broken is inside of her, Chad, not you. She sees you deal with loss differently, accepting this and moving on, leaving her behind while she struggles. Don't give up trying to get her to talk about it, but don't corner her. She will clam up. In time, planning a new Painter Place will help her let go of my dad's personal stamp all over the island."

Chad smiled into the phone receiver the following morning. "I shamelessly admit my ulterior motive. I chose your favorite music to force you to think of me. You're being manipulated—a little tip my mom taught me in Charleston right after we became a couple."

Caroline laughed softly at the special delivery package, open and spread out on the living room sofa. A Walkman, headphones, batteries, and some cassettes lay around it.

"It's not manipulation if I love it! What made you think of such a romantic gift?"

"Cameron told me he was ready to cry with the rest of you in the van the other night when the radio was on, so I made sure to include that song."

"You know I miss you, Chad, without the music. You're part of me. That hasn't changed."

Chad blew out a quick intake of breath. "Then what *has* changed, Caroline? Something has, but it's vague, abstract, flying past too quick for me to grasp it. There's a—I don't know—a cooling off, a distance. And it's shakin' me to the core. I want the flash and fire back. I need it back."

He heard the nanny through the phone as she walked in with Rayce, who was complaining despite her efforts to calm him. "Sorry for interrupting, ma'am, but I thought since the little men woke up, you'd want them to talk to their daddy."

"Yes, I do, thank you so much," Caroline said. "Chad, Rayce wants to talk to you. He's the leader today, so Rhett will be here in a minute."

Chad was torn between talking to his sons and getting an answer to his question. His jaw muscle flexed, and he put up a hand in surrender as he forced himself to back off, remembering Juliette's advice about not cornering Caroline. "All right. But Care, think about what I said. Let's talk about it soon."

"Okay. I'm sure it's temporary. Here's Rayce."

It's temporary? Chad repeated in his mind. His heart skipped a beat and his jaw dropped. She had just admitted to feeling distance and a cooling off from him. *Cooling off!*

He wanted her to deny it, hoped he was just imagining it. He wanted assurances he was wrong, not confirmation of being right!

After taking a moment to redirect his focus, Chad composed one-sided conversations to his sons. He loved talking to them and hearing about their reactions to his voice. But he was distracted, and his arms felt even emptier.

When Caroline was back on the line, he opened his mouth to launch a seriously romantic goodbye intended to stoke some heat to her cooling off status. But his dad knocked briskly on his open door and came in, followed by Chad's good friend Sterling, an officer on the Whitehaven Police Force who graduated high school with him and Patrick.

Inwardly, Chad chafed against the seeming conspiracy that was preventing him from any privacy with his wife. This was worse than when they were dating and could never be out of sight. At least then they could get out of earshot.

He resigned himself to something simple to end the conversation. "I'll try to reach you tomorrow on the villa phone. Call me back here if you're out and miss it. I love you."

Reluctantly, Chad set the receiver in the cradle and looked up as Andy Painter led Cole and Patrick in. Phillip asked everyone to sit down.

"What's wrong?" Uneasy about the brooding demeanor on his dad's face, Chad cut to the chase from his seat behind his desk. His dad stood in the center of Chad's office, crossing his tanned arms over his chest.

It was not unusual for Sterling to be in uniform in his office. But seeing him in tow with his dad and father-in-law was starting to unnerve him. He stopped trying to read the expressions on the faces in the gathered group and stared at his dad.

"Back when I young, there were few families who could afford to pay a kidnapping ransom," Phillip began. "The heirs of those that could were on what was called a 'short list.' Wyeth and I were on it."

After a collective intake of breath from the young men in the room, he said, "Some others on the list were acquaintances and business partners. Over the years, Americans became wealthier. Kidnapping was less common. So I was stunned today when an anonymous warning showed up in Global's mail."

He turned to Chad. "I don't know if it's for me or you. There's no designation about the ending on our names. I got a similar letter when you were a baby, and shortly afterwards, there was an attempt to take you and Patrick. Andy never got one, so Patrick was probably an unexpected opportunity for a double target. Caroline wasn't born, so Andy's first child could be assumed to be his heir."

As Chad, Patrick, and Cole let this revelation sink in, Phillip cleared his throat and continued. "I quickly hired a bodyguard, but we were in a packed crowd at a classic car show in Myrtle Beach. Andy and I sponsored a car together and talked about it to bystanders. Your mom held Sandy while she talked to Valerie. The bodyguard couldn't move people quickly enough to stop two men who pulled you from your strollers, but he alerted security as he chased them. You both screamed and drew too much attention, so the would-be kidnappers shoved you into the nearest person's arms. They got away."

Chad was not the only one sitting slack jawed. Incredulous, Patrick turned to his dad. "You hid that from me all this time?"

"We decided if you knew it might frighten you from having a normal life," answered Andy. "Whitehaven police always kept an eye out for anything suspicious as you grew up. We built a new security station at the bridge and kept guards there around the clock. We gated the roads to our homes and scheduled random patrols from the water. I was ready to tell you about it anyway, then this letter came. I'm nervous about news reports that you and Chad are separated from your wives and kids while Painter Place is repaired. Someone might see this as an opportunity."

Cole huffed, shooting to his feet and pushing his hair back in frustration. He met his brother's eyes and walked to his desk. "Is it just me, or does anyone else think this should've been on the list while everybody was spillin' their guts at Painter Place the other night?" He tore his gaze from Chad's and spun around to his father and Andy. "Did you let Wyeth in on this one?"

This earned him a warning glare from his dad. Chad used his steel voice when he said, "I'm with you, Cole."

"No kiddin'!" Patrick exclaimed, coming to his feet. "Dad, what if Chad, Cole, and I hid things, like you two do? You demand openness from your sons, but you sure don't live it out in front of us."

Andy turned a resigned look to Phillip and responded, "Wyeth knew, and Poppy Noble and Gran Vanna, but not Juliette. Wyeth always alerts authorities when he travels. He and Chrissy never let Caroline out of sight at art events, since anyone interested in a ransom would discover it was her, not you, who would inherit the Big House. It wasn't just the possible damage to Caroline's reputation that made me furious when Wyeth let Caroline go out with Baker Holmes in Mevagissey. She ended up being a news sensation. I was upset that anyone with criminal intent now knew who and where she was. That mess was compounded by her connection to Chad, who ended up in the news at the same time."

Andy stopped to sigh and run his hands over his face. He looked at Phillip and said, "Then the stakes soared sky high when she married him. That may have been my dad's dream and his answered prayer, but it sharpened the razor's edge we live on. Now she's a Gregory as well—Chad's kryptonite—and they've mixed the bloodlines with the twins for two family ransoms."

The room was quiet for a few moments as this sank in. Chad said quietly, "I want to see the letter."

Phillip reached into his pocket and put an envelope into Chad's hand while Patrick and Cole came around to his chair. The envelope was typewritten, unremarkable, and addressed simply to Phillip Chadwick Gregory. He unfolded the blue-lined notebook paper that could have come from any school child's binder. Glued, cut out words from magazines looked like a first grader's school project, but no child would think up the message spelled out in that letter.

"How much are they worth? We'll discuss it when I call," Chad read out loud, then squeezed his eyes closed. The page trembled in his hand as icy fingers of fear crept up his spine.

Cole looked sharply up to his dad's face. "What did the letter you got years ago say?"

Phillip looked at him solemnly. "It said, 'How much is he worth? We'll discuss it when I call.' But no one ever called."

Shaking his head to clear it, Chad reasoned, "It's got to be the same person, or someone who knows him, and he's at least your age. How did you plan to pay the ransom?"

Phillip looked out the window into the distance for a few moments while the room was quiet. He finally looked back with resolve in his eyes. "We keep insurance policies for ransom demands."

Chad blinked. He recalled the conversation with his dad before Hugo about insurance, right here in his office, looking out over Painter Place. He passed a hand over his forehead, sweating now. "That's why you won't let me see the insurance coverage. It's one of the layers upon layers of insulation built into Painter Place and Global."

Cole reached out to put his hand on his brother's arm and hissed, "I told you! Your access to anything is limited because of all he's keeping from you—from us." He straightened and his voice was testy as he looked Phillip in the eye. "Now it's crystal clear. Under torture, we can't talk about what we don't know. Right, Dad?"

Chad watched the confirmation cross his dad's expression. Sterling looked down at the hardwood office floor.

Phillip kept his voice steady. "We have accounts from powerful clients that have to be protected. Some are undercover tryin' to snare the ones after them. Justin handles a few, but Dad and I are the only ones who have all the information their enemies might want. It's more efficient for someone to take us if they want access or ransom. Any leaks or spies from inside Global will know that, leavin' you two and your cousin in London out of danger."

Cole pushed dark locks of hair back, looking at the ceiling. "We finally get down to it. This is the reason why it was so serious when I snooped into Justin's computer with his password in London, and someone at the party took it."

Chad put the letter down on his desk and slowly rose from his chair, passing behind Patrick to walk over to the wall of windows. He stared over at Painter Place with both hands on his hips. "So today I learn what my legacy as a Gregory *really* is. I'm vetted to eventually be on an international hit list for kidnapping and torture for client information, probably by organized crime. My sons after me get the same honor, provided they haven't already been kidnapped and killed as children. And Caroline, well..." he huffed and clasped his hands at the back of his neck. "She had no idea what she was gettin' into, what it meant to be married to me, or that it was a risk to have a family. I danced her right in a circle of hungry wolves lickin' their chops. No wonder you and Andy wanted to know what I was made of when I went off to college. No wonder Andy wanted her to consider someone besides me for the future. Bein' a guardian of Painter Place has taken on a whole new meaning, and as for Global, I don't even know what to say."

Phillip went to stand beside him. "Can you begin to understand that I need all of your focus, Chad? You're divided. You can't do your best for Global or Painter Place while you run your own show. Sell me the Young Guns and make it a part of Global. I'll meet any of your terms, and Cole can come back as an heir with Global. Under you, he's proven himself."

He turned to Cole and Patrick. "Patrick, I know the Castaway is your biggest stake in the Young Guns, and Joey, Derrick, and the others have to be consulted. Cole, you delayed your last year of law school to be here to help your brother right now. But you never wanted to be an attorney anyway. You thrive on the Young Guns, on working with Chad. Shannon told your mom that she wants to be here at Painter Place to begin a family. Come back home."

Chad glanced at Patrick and Cole. "We need time to process this—all of this," he answered for the three of them. "Right now, we have to alert Cameron. He's had threats against Mia and has security, so Caroline and the twins are probably fine as long as they're in the villa. But this has just put everyone in more danger. I want Ben to find me the ultimate in a bodyguard to be in France to meet Caroline and the boys at the airport."

"This stays with the authorities and in the family for now," Phillip warned, glancing at Sterling's nod for confirmation. "Cole, Justin can make arrangements for security for Shannon in London."

"No more secrets between us anymore, and we start teachin' the kids to be cautious," Patrick said sternly to his dad. "This isn't directly about my family or Marina's, but most of the time we're all together. When everyone gets back home, anything could happen if the wrong people get on the island. I'm callin' Natalie. She needs to keep an eye open when she's out with Noble."

Painter blue eyes locked with Painter blue eyes, and Andy nodded. "No more secrets."

Chapter Fourteen

I think that everything which is really good and beautiful—of inner moral, spiritual, and sublime beauty in men and their works—comes from God, and that which is bad and wrong in men and in their works is not of God and God does not approve of it.
-Vincent Van Gogh, Letters, July 1880

Saturday was a new day, Caroline's first in Arles, France. It had been over two weeks since the storm at Painter Place. She was physically much better now after getting a lot of rest in the Keys before the flight to France, though she expected jet lag to affect her for a few days.

Still, her life felt directionless and upended. She reminded herself it was temporary, and she should just enjoy being a new mother, spending time with Juliette's family, and making the most of this unexpected trip for a professional direction. The boys slept so much that she could leave them with the nanny when she explored Arles.

It was rare for her to be alone, but that was when things she had no courage to face stood like leering giants towering over her. She was over her limit for how much she could handle all at once when she got the call from Chad last week about the kidnapping threat, so it was stashed on a shelf somewhere in her mind. Every time she let herself peek at what she'd lost, what she'd not known, and what her life had become, she became upset.

Somehow, France was where she was going to face down the giants. She was emotionally fragile, but she didn't plan to take them back home to Painter Place.

Today's surprise from Chad was a tour guide. He showed up at the door to announce that he was sent by Monsieur Chad Gregory to escort Madame Gregory and Mademoiselle Austin around town for sightseeing, to places of interest to artists. The bodyguard who answered the door cleared the tour guide after a call and some screening, and the guide cheerfully said that he had expected the guard to join them. Azariah's efficient handling of the situation was just what Caroline would expect from a man formerly associated with Mossad. She and Chad knew little about their bodyguard except that every close relative he had was killed in two different terrorist suicide bombings by Israel's enemies.

Caroline and Casey quickly packed small daytrip bags and cameras. Caroline handed Casey a nine-by-twelve sketchbook of acid-free handmade paper and a slender fancy tin of drawing pencils. "You're my guinea pig—my first overseas art student ever. Let me practice on you, and you'll get free lessons."

"Oh, Caroline, I've heard of those expensive trips that people take to study with artists. This is too much! Why waste this nice book on someone who doesn't draw?"

"People spend thousands to study with artists like my uncle, Casey—not with me. Lesson number one happens before we even get out the door. Always use the best materials you can afford. It profoundly affects your results and helps your mindset to treat your efforts seriously. You don't want to remember your first trip to France on sheets of discount store paper that will yellow and crack after a year."

Casey tagged after Caroline to the kitchen. "Paper makes that much difference?"

"Yes. Draw, journal, or write important letters only on acid-free paper. Something worth doing is worth doing right. I'll show you the difference later."

"But Caroline, I can't draw."

"Until you practice," Caroline added confidently. "Trust me, I've heard that a million times."

"Why do I have a whole tin of pencils? I only need one," said Casey as they put trail mix bars into their backpacks.

Caroline's laughter was a delighted sound that Casey hadn't heard from her in over two weeks. "There are numbers and letters on each of them that identify what sort of marks the graphite makes. I'll show you why that matters today. You'll begin by making a little chart."

On Saturday morning, Phillip knocked briskly on the doorframes of Chad and Cole's offices, singing out that it was time to rise and shine. Chad wandered for a moment in a dream in which he was still in high school, and his dad was waking him on a Saturday to work around the island. A nudge on his shoulder, accompanied by another encouraging reminder by his dad to wake up, sent the dream into the netherworld of things unfinished and unrecalled.

"Chad, come on, son, we've got an unexpected appointment. You need to dress for work for this one. Part of the order came in from the tailor in Charleston for you and your brother. This should do for a week while he works on the rest. Other things are in a box Andy's bringin' up."

Chad sat up groggily as his dad called to the other office again for Cole and Patrick to get moving. His dad narrowed his eyes, watching him and Joey shaking off sleep. "What's up, Chad? You're usually easy to wake. Joey, there are things for you in a box Ben and your parents sent up. Come to Painter Place with us and have some breakfast."

Without a word, Chad obediently headed to the open door in a tee shirt and gym shorts. His dad thrust some clothes into his arms and scowled at the beard on his son's face. "Chad, get your act together, okay? Hurry up and shower and shave. Next week, you need a haircut."

Nodding mutely, Chad started to the door again, almost bumping into Patrick as they stumbled bleary-eyed down the hall to the men's room showers. They shaved, trying to be quick so Cole and Joey could get in. Patrick finally spoke over the running water on the other side of the tiled partition. "No more junk food binges for me. Let's get Dad to take us out to fish for dinner and play some ball somewhere."

"I'm with you. I feel like a slug and was having the most convoluted dreams ever."

"Oh, yeah? I spent all night runnin' from Cameron's bodyguard. Half the time, I didn't even know what country I was in. Top that."

Chad leaned forward with his hands against the tile to let the hot water rain down over his neck and back, easing a vague headache. "Let me guess—he caught you with Natalie before you were married. At least you only had him to worry about. I was in my basketball uniform and Caroline had on that cheerleading uniform your dad almost didn't let her wear her sophomore year. Now I know why. We were playin' basketball in a mixed game on the court in your backyard. She was guardin' me with that smile, makin' me crazy. Suddenly we were slow dancin' at an Island Summer Dance. We left for a secluded spot I knew on the beach, and I swear I thought we were married. Too late, I figured out I was in college. I saw you, your dad, and Wyeth comin' toward us, and I warned all of you that you couldn't kill me because Caroline was pregnant with my twins."

Chad heard Patrick's delighted burst of laughter as he turned off the water on his side. "Okay, you win. At least we both made death worthwhile. Too bad it was only in our dreams."

They dressed and headed out the door to see Joey and Cole slumped against the wall, waiting their turn. "No more junk smorgasbords from a gas station, Cole," Patrick muttered. "Fish is on the menu tonight, and we're playin' basketball or somethin' to sweat this out of our system. Start hydrating this morning."

"Craziest dreams ever..." mumbled Joey.

Chad and Patrick exchanged glances and smirked at Joey's comment. "Hope it didn't involve Casey," Patrick quipped.

They walked into Chad's office, where their dads were talking. Phillip had his arms crossed over his chest and cleared his throat. "You guys get bored last night? The trash cans smell interesting."

"They're full of things that even law school can't teach your youngest son to pronounce on the labels," Patrick answered. "It was Cole's turn to plan dinner before some cards, games, and music, and he went for adventure. He doesn't get another turn. Trust me when I say that what's in that trash will still be around when archaeologists dig it up. Maggie Jane doesn't need to know about this, does she? I'm cookin' tonight. I hope Dad has a boat so we can fish for dinner and then play a Tarzan game. Our court's gone, but maybe the park has some goals and nets that survived."

"If I get what I want today, you guys will be back over at the Big House sometime next week for real food," said Phillip. "Chad, look this over so you have some idea what's goin' on. Andy and I will be outside about the insurance on the marina and Global. You four get this trash outta here and take your dirty clothes to the cleaners before you head over to the island. We'll meet you there."

Chad looked dumbly at the file his dad handed him. "Dad, do you know who this is?"

At the door, Phillip turned and looked at him levelly. "He's one of our biggest clients and he gave us the best deal. We'll change it after all this is over if you want to."

Chad drove his Lamborghini across the patched one-lane bridge to the island with Joey in the passenger seat, and Patrick brought Cole in his new Tahoe from a dealer in Myrtle Beach. They parked in a cleared area behind the Big House, and Chad parked as far as he could from an impressive Mercedes with a Georgia peach on the tag. Construction crews were crawling all over the mansion, and the rumble of bulldozers from down Castaway Drive made the sand tremble.

They ate a light breakfast in the kitchen and visited their moms, sharing phone conversation updates from their wives. Chad finished off a paper cup of pineapple juice and some water to start hydrating for the game later, then walked outside to wait for his dad.

He could no longer remember the last time he was in a good mood, and he definitely wouldn't find one until after this meeting. Of all the insurance companies in the country, his dad had gone with Lanny Smith Associates out of Atlanta. He saw Lanny a couple of times doing business with his dad. About three years ago, Gloria had worked for him and married him, and he had moved her parents there. He was at least a dozen years older than her, with salt-and pepper hair and the shape of a guy who spent too much time at a desk to bother with working out. Chad wondered what Gloria might have told her husband about him and dreaded the inevitable chit-chat about her today.

As he gazed around the barren island, he saw progress at the Big House. The boards salvaged from the Pavilion had been stacked as he requested, ready to be stored for the plans he had for them once the Gregory estate was built. He smiled, musing at how Caroline would love the private pavilion he had designed for date nights. Thinking of her sent his imagination to a place that unraveled his bad mood. He inhaled deeply of the salt breeze and let the calming lull of the surf massage the jagged edges of his emotions. Reaching up to clasp a bare oak tree branch with both hands, he stretched the tense muscles in his back and gazed at the sea, beckoning the wispy edges of the memory of his dream of Caroline last night. He wished he could see that look in her eyes, put his arms around her, kiss her...

Behind him, two arms encircled the waist of his white dress shirt. His reaction time was delayed as he awakened from his daydreaming.

"Lonely? You never had to be—still don't have to be."

Chad growled, letting go of the branch to brush away Gloria's arms, shouting, "I thought I was clear about this years ago. Don't touch me, or look at me like you're touching me!"

He spun around to face her. "Stop acting like there was ever anything between us, or ever will be!"

Her smoky eyes flared, and she yelled back. "Do you know who I am? No one talks to me that way! You'll be sorry!"

Chad was livid, setting his hands on his hips. "That's the best you've got?" he responded with a short laugh that sounded like a bark. "You've made me sorry for years, Gloria! Sorry that I was gentleman enough to meet you for an hour at the prom so you wouldn't be the first unattached Prom Queen ditched by a King who broke the tradition to be there together. There was no way I was goin' to start gossip by bein' in a car alone with you. You may've been popular, but it certainly wasn't because you were a lady!"

Gloria screeched and raised her arm to slap him, but he easily caught it on its way to his face. They glared at one another until suddenly her expression changed and she began leaning toward him. He dropped her arm and stepped back to keep distance.

Noticing a movement in his peripheral vision, he turned his head to see that her husband, the Painters, his dad, his brother, and Joey were all watching them. He instantly took another step back.

Seeing the look on his face, Gloria spun around. For a horrible frozen moment, all Chad could process was Lanny Smith's resolute expression.

"Gloria," said her husband mildly. "Please wait for me at the car. Jim," he gestured to a photographer that Chad hadn't seen. "Hand over the film."

Gloria slowly took a few steps forward while her husband handed a wad of bills to the photographer in exchange for a roll emptied from his camera. "Photos for the insurance claim are also on it," said Jim, resuming a position near crushed sea oats on the side of a dune. He fished out a fresh roll for the camera.

"I'll take care of it," Lanny Smith answered shortly as he slid the roll into his pocket. "I just paid for confidentiality, for both me and our clients. Understand?'

The photographer nodded. "Yes sir, Mr. Smith!"

Gloria hesitated. "Aren't you goin' to do anything about how he treated me? He insulted me and then grabbed my arm. I'll probably have bruises!"

Chad glanced at his dad and saw the anger level register in the danger zone. Like him, Andy and Wyeth Painter were flushed red in fury, and Wyeth bit his lip to keep from retorting. But Lanny Smith's face was a study in composure. "Mr. Gregory was only acting instinctively to defend himself. He was never a threat to you, and he has a throng of witnesses who saw and heard everything."

His eyes dismissed her and shifted to Chad's. "Mr. Gregory, my wife seems to have left her good Southern manners in Atlanta, so I apologize on her behalf and assure you this will never happen again."

Seething, Gloria stuck out a pretty chin, the highlights in her red hair catching the sun as she tossed her head and marched past her husband. When she was out of earshot, Lanny Smith met Chad's eyes. "I'm not a handsome man, Mr. Gregory, just a very rich one. I have no illusions about why Gloria married me. I'm not the least bit interesting, and I work long hours, so now and then, my wife lets me know she needs attention and romance. A vacation together to some secluded, exotic place is my usual remedy for times like these."

Chad reeled. He refused to look at his dad, who had awakened him early this morning and made him dress like a professional for this kind of humiliation. Well, he could hang his cool-under-pressure business protocol, and whatever advice he probably had about how Chad could have handled this better.

"Thank you, Mr. Smith. I'm sure you'll understand if I leave this meeting to the men who are actually in charge here," he managed in a civil tone.

He stormed away, avoiding walking in Gloria's footprints in the sand to the parking lot. The Lamborghini was in danger of losing the driver side door as he swung it open hard to get in, on his way to find a place to have another off-the-charts meltdown. Before Hugo, he went eight years without one, and now he was working on the second in as many weeks. He desperately needed Caroline. She was his calm, just as his mom was for his dad. He knew exactly what his dad meant now.

God, calm me down, he prayed silently. He felt desperate for self-control. After a deep breath, Proverbs 16:32 popped into his mind. *Better a patient person than a warrior, one with self-control than one who takes a city.*

Gloria sat in the Mercedes with the Georgia peach license tag. The passenger door was open so she could display her legs to the best advantage to another photographer she was talking to. The man's camera hung across his shirt, and he turned a sly look at Chad, who decisively slid on his Wayfarers and jammed his key into the ignition.

So, she had been walking the island, waiting for him to be alone, like a spider in a web. Savanna Painter said when Caroline left that separation was the devil's playground. Well, he'd certainly been played, and it infuriated him.

Joey caught up just before Chad backed the Lamborghini out, breathlessly jumping into the passenger seat without a word. Patrick and Cole raced to the Tahoe. Sand flew as Chad jerked his car out toward the bridge with the Tahoe after him.

In Arles, Caroline left a long message on Chad's office phone, thanking him for the tour guide that day. Casey joined her, enthusiastically thanking him for including her and praising Caroline for her sketching lessons. Casey said Azariah even looked interested, and she expected him to be doodling in his room later. That thought made her laugh before she told Chad that he was the best husband she'd ever heard of in the whole history of the universe. Then shyly, she asked if he would mind telling Joey she was learning to draw and that she said hi. Caroline chimed in again to tell him she loved him and was blowing a kiss over the line. That breathy sound and then two singsong voices saying goodbye ended the message.

The ladies hung up and plopped down on a sofa, waiting for Cameron and Juliette to arrive from a day on the set at the arena. Dinnertime in Arles began around 7:30, and they had reservations somewhere casual.

"I can't wait to show them my sketchbook! Who knew I could do this?" marveled Casey, thumbing through the first few pages. Caroline taught her to put her contact information on the inside cover in case the sketchbook got lost. Then at Caroline's direction, she made a chart on the last page to use as a reference for how her pencils should be used. She began a creative title page to designate that the first part of her book was done in Arles, then partitioned off four sections on the next two pages to do simple sketches of things that would not overwhelm her, like a door, a pot of flowers, a café window, and other small things she was supposed to observe closely as simple shapes. She followed Caroline's suggestion to initial or sign each sketch and note the date, then add notes about sounds, smells, and other impressions that made up the experience during that drawing.

"So, what did you learn today about art history?" Caroline quizzed. "You can look at your notes if you need to. It helps your memory when you recall things right away."

"Vincent Van Gogh was a nineteenth century Dutch Post-Impressionist painter—you'll explain what that means later—and this year, Arles had a Centennial Celebration for him that ended on April 30," Casey parroted. "He lived here from February 21, 1888, until May 3, 1889. The building where he lived, and the bedroom that inspired his painting *Bedroom at Arles*, was damaged in an air raid in World War II on June 25, 1944. It had to be torn down. Vincent used pure pigment and worked freely and instinctively. He used an impasto painting technique, and I think that means he put it on thickly. And that was lavish of him, because Vincent was penniless. He depended on his beloved brother Theo for support, yet two years ago in 1987, his painting *The Irises* sold for the world-record price of more than fifty-four million dollars."

She stopped and tilted her head. "Do you think Vincent was a Christian?"

Caroline sobered, looking at Casey thoughtfully. "No one has ever asked me that, but it's always the bottom line for any soul, isn't it? No matter what a person accomplishes on earth, it will end, and it turns out that the most important thing he or she did wasn't something they left behind. It was where they'd spend eternity."

"Vincent had some bizarre ideas about the Lord," observed Casey, scowling.

"People have had mixed up beliefs about Christ throughout history, and we can't all be right, so some of us are definitely wrong. Most books and articles published about Vincent at this point in 1989 suggest that his search for religious answers was a kind of pathology. They rarely mention that this cultured, well-read man wrote volumes of letters filled with Bible verses, prayers, religious stories, and discussions of Christian ideas. His father and an uncle were part of a group that believed that scripture was inspired, yet they denied that Christ was God, which is a stark contradiction to Christ's own claim to be God."

Caroline sat back into the sofa cushions, gathering her thoughts. "But when Vincent was twenty-two—sometime around 1875—he had what evangelicals call a 'born again' experience at a revival meeting held by Dwight L. Moody. He also read the sermons of Charles Spurgeon, and a medieval Catholic book called the *Imitation of Christ*, which inspired his idea of a suffering servant. But Vincent's personality was so intense and difficult that it made personal relationships hard for him. He was always lonely. He had a tendency toward willfulness and seemed unable to process balance in life. None of the doctors who treated him thought he was insane. I've never heard anyone say this, but when I look at his brush strokes, I wonder if they vibrate so much because he was outwardly expressing what it felt like inwardly to be him, like a constant motion, a driven feeling."

"That would have been awful. I like peaceful calm."

"Me, too. But Casey, what if that curse was his gift? What if he'd been a normal guy with typical relationships, moving along through life as just another face in the sea of folks wanting others to entertain them, and who only act and think within parameters? Would he ever have felt the passion to paint, to observe everything as if he were painting it, and would yellow have been his favorite color?"

"Wow, you've given me somethin' to think about."

"When Gauguin spent time with Vincent, he tried to get him to change his style of painting," Caroline said. "He made fun of him, remarking that 'his Dutch brain was afire with the Bible.' Wow, if only more of us could be worthy of such an insult!"

Casey tilted her head. "If he had a born-again experience, why did he struggle with all the confusion in Christian beliefs?"

Caroline bit her lip a moment. "The Bible isn't written to answer every question we have, and I personally believe the Lord left out details that would give His spiritual adversaries an advantage as history plays out. The basic truths are meant to be understood by simple people. It's important to pray for understanding as we read, and go with the most direct interpretation, putting it into the context we find in the passage or verse. Scripture says it is nonsense to unbelievers, so how could most people—those on the 'broad road' to destruction—correctly tell a believer what it means? Only the Holy Spirit can do that as we mature in our faith. We must compare scripture with more scripture when it's confusing, letting the Bible interpret itself. God won't contradict Himself."

She sighed and shook her head sadly. "No one has everything right, Casey, and incorrect beliefs about some things won't keep us from salvation. But we're meant to live victorious lives, and we don't want to influence other people to wrong beliefs. Most people follow traditions about doctrine without seeking truth firsthand. They never had an experience with Jesus as a person, or felt the fire He ignites in their spirits, like we read about in the book of Acts the day the church began at Pentecost, and in Matthew 3, when Jesus is baptized."

Caroline looked at the darkening view through the window. "God knows our hearts and minds. Jeremiah 19:13 says that if we seek God with all our hearts, we'll find Him. Vincent explained that his intention in using so much yellow was to represent the presence of Christ—of His light. The paintings he created of the sowers, reapers, and wheat fields are biblical pictures of how the fields of souls are white with harvest, but the laborers are few. In the last year of his life, he painted *Pieta*, *The Raising of Lazarus*, and *The Good*

Samaritan. Since yellow is a color associated with hope, it makes me hopeful, too—hopeful that Vincent will be in Heaven."

"Me, too. Our guide said it was winter when Vincent arrived in Arles, yet he thought in terms of color so much that he noticed yellow rocks, red soil, and lilac mountains. Spring arrived soon after that, and he loved the flowering fruit trees and vegetation. He loved and celebrated God's creation. It doesn't add up that he might have shot himself."

"I don't believe he did, Casey. There's so much that doesn't make sense about the account of his death that I don't believe it happened that way. But regardless of how the gunshot wound happened, it was just his time. Even an early death at thirty-seven couldn't snuff out what God had done and would continue to do with his life."

She sat up straight, folding her hands together, interweaving fingers and opening them several times with a far-away look. Casey closed the cover of the sketchbook and put it down. "What is it?"

"My Poppy Noble—Noble Painter, the artist—he died suddenly, twelve years ago. A heat stroke, the doctor said. He passed into heaven in the shade of a nearby oak when the men working alongside him pulled him under it. A South Carolina summer can be dangerous, and he shouldn't have been out there working at his age. He was sixty."

Uncertain about what to say, Casey watched the emotions crossing her friend's face.

"I blamed him for working on the island for other people instead of thinking of what would happen if he left me. I didn't understand why God didn't stop him from going out in the heat that day. He was a remarkable, godly man. We needed him—I needed him. Nothing was ever going to be the same. But now I see it was just his time. If it hadn't been, nothing could have happened to hurt him. If anyone was ever ready to leave here and enter heaven, it was my Poppy. In that knowledge, he blessed me."

She smiled tightly. "That was my 'yellow'—my hope. I'll see him again, but 'someday' is a long time for a broken-hearted girl. He died when the sunflowers at Painter Place were blooming. Chad was only fourteen, but he left a yellow sunflower at my easel in my grandfather's studio every day, knowing I'd go there, just as I did when Poppy was alive. I used to paint alongside him, but after his death, I went there to grieve. It was a while before Wyeth could get me to paint again."

Casey ventured, "Can you be thankful for the assurance of bein' with your Poppy again for eternity? Can you live your life the way you want to be remembered by your own grandchildren?"

The lock on the front door turned and Cameron opened it for Juliette and Mia. Mia joyously ran to her cousin Caroline, who welcomed her with a hug and kiss. As they gathered purses and sweaters to go out for their first meal in a French restaurant, Caroline whispered to Casey. "Thanks for listening to me talk things through. I think I can let go and live the way Poppy did."

Vincent the Painter in Arles, France
by Pamela Poole

Chapter Fifteen

If you can keep your wits about you while all others are losing theirs and blaming you, the world will be yours and everything in it. What's more, you'll be a man, my son.
-Rudyard Kipling

Phillip Gregory eased his new Mercedes into the parking lot of Whitehaven Point Park and pulled it up to Sterling's squad car. A young lady Sterling was interviewing leaned against the car, obscuring "White" from the town name printed on the side. Phillip rolled his eyes and smirked. "Haven" was an odd word for the side of a police car, and it certainly was not on the list of the descriptions he had for the town these days.

When the call came from Sterling to tell him his sons were in an "altercation" at the park, he and the Painters were just about to call the boys for some fishing. They had some serious things to discuss, and fishing was a relaxed setting in which to do it. Sterling would not expand on what the "altercation" was, but he asked to speak to Andy to let him know Patrick was involved, and that there were some minor injuries to all the young men consistent with a fist fight.

Sterling gestured with a tilt of his head in the direction of Patrick's Tahoe while he finished his interview. The Big Three, as the boys called them—Phillip, Andy, and Wyeth—got out of the Mercedes and started walking over. Two young men from the college class at church were hanging around the Tahoe, and one held the side of a cup of ice against his eye. The other held a cloth to his nose.

The stereo in the Tahoe poured out lyrics about there being no time for losers when you're the champions of the world. The Big Three tried not to smile at one another while Andy Painter opened his son's door and ducked his head in to look at him and Chad across the front seats.

Patrick turned the volume down on the music while his dad studied his ripped tee shirt sleeve near a bruise on his left arm and the bruised and swollen knuckles on Chad's right hand. Then his dad peered at Joey and Cole in the back and noted Joey was the worse for wear.

Andy pulled his head out of the Tahoe and turned to the college students from church. "You guys okay?"

"Yes sir, Mr. Painter," said the one on the other side of the open door, leaning on the hood. He warily pulled away the towel at his face and saw his nose had stopped bleeding. "We didn't do anything. They started it."

"That's right, ask anyone," piped up the other student on Chad's side of the car. "Sterling knows. He drove up and saw the guy with the broken bottle, and the gang ran off. Witnesses are tellin' him what happened."

Phillip stood at Chad's open door to take a closer look at his son's hand. "You delivered a strong punch. Any more injuries?"

"I took a hit in the stomach." Chad winced as he pulled up the edge of his tee shirt to investigate the bruising. Phillip clenched his jaw and narrowed his eyes.

"Joey, you look a little roughed up. We need to get you some help?" asked Wyeth, looking through the backseat window on the driver's side of the Tahoe. On the passenger side, Phillip was looking in at Cole to assess the damage on his younger son.

Joey shrugged. "Nothin' serious. My arms are bruised where they held me, they hit me once in the stomach, and I got a glancing hit in the jaw."

"They *held* you?" exclaimed Wyeth. "Come out here, let me see."

Joey hesitantly opened the door and stepped out. His tee shirt was ripped, and his arms had red welts on them. Wyeth scowled as he inspected Joey's jaw and ear.

Sterling made his way to the Tahoe and drawled, "Guys, I know you don't need your daddy, but you might need advice about pressin' charges, so I wanted them to be here. What I'm gettin' from you and the only witnesses who would speak up is that you were playin' basketball on the first court with a few other friends, only two of whom stayed long enough to be involved in the incident. A gang of other young men arrived, violating park rules by drinking alcohol on the premises, and they began harassin' you for the court space you were on. No other courts were bein' used, but you moved out of their way three times. In the last court, they began makin' obscene personal slurs and one broke a beer bottle against the goal post. He threatened to cut Joey while two others jumped him. The rest of you began trying to get Joey free and took some punches but gave as good as you got. I drove up on a routine route to witness the man threatening Joey with the broken end of a bottle. Someone shouted a warnin' about me and they took off. Is that right?"

The young men looked at one another and nodded. "Yeah," said Joey, who stood closest to Sterling.

Phillip looked at Cole. "Legally, what do you think?"

"We took steps to avoid trouble, didn't answer their taunts, didn't consent to fight, which wouldn't have mattered anyway once they made a weapon out of a beer bottle. They were seen by an officer, and we have witnesses in a public place. A few of us got in punches while tryin' to rescue Joey, but not to anyone's head or face. We have defensive wounds we need to photograph just in case, but I don't see how there could be any lawsuits against us for defending ourselves. We just need to decide if it's worth pressin' charges and keepin' this goin' a while, draggin' Global and Painter Place through an extended stay in the news, or walkin' away. We don't have to decide now. Joey's the one who was most directly threatened, so the station will be in the news anyway when the Whitehaven Register prints the weekly crime report."

Phillip told Sterling the boys would call him later with their decision, and the officer headed back to the squad car. The curious crowd began to break up.

Andy thanked the two college students for helping and asked if they needed a ride to the emergency room. They said they'd had worse in scuffles with siblings and cousins and would call him after they talked to their parents if they decided to press charges.

"Okay, but you call me later anyway to let me know if you're still feelin' all right," Andy said, handing them his card for Island Marina. "This is my mobile phone."

"Dad," Patrick said, leaning his head back on the headrest. "The guys who attacked us acted like we should be ashamed to be Painters and Gregorys. I never expected that, not in my hometown. And people in the park, they just watched and didn't support us at all."

"The gang didn't like it that all the girls were hangin' around watchin' us, instead of them," piped in Cole from the back seat. Phillip pressed his lips together to keep from smiling.

Andy bent down to listen to Patrick, eye to eye. "They said we don't have the right to hog up the park, puttin' on a show, and not to come back. Then they focused on Joey, warnin' him not to mention this on the radio. They said he was goin' to need his little—insert an obscene slur about Casey—nurse to sew him up. Dad, we need our own basketball court again."

"That's my new priority this week," interjected Wyeth, hands on hips. "On the parking lot I'm pavin' behind the Big House. It will do for now, and we'll build a real one later so we can invite your friends and the youth group from church."

Andy brushed his hand on Patrick's shoulder. "Let's all try to calm down. You four go change your clothes and come out to the island for some first aid and a fishin' trip for dinner."

Chapter Sixteen

For my part I know nothing with any certainty,
but the sight of the stars makes me dream.
-Vincent Van Gogh

Chad missed his window of time to call Caroline after his eventful Saturday, so he planned to try again on Sunday. It marked the second week to the day that she'd left. Being without her was no easier.

His answering machine was blinking when he and the guys stopped at Global to change clothes after church. He raced to it in hopes of hearing her voice.

But it was Cameron. "Chad, I got a fax today, a photo of Gloria cozily wrapped up around the back of you like a purring cat. It was sent to Caroline with a message that there were more where that came from. Call me."

Chad ran his hands over the nape of his neck, dismayed. "So, this is what Gloria meant about me being sorry!"

"I thought Lanny took that film!" hissed Patrick, slapping the top of Chad's desk. He quickly turned to Cole. "Check the fax machine, will ya?"

Joey tapped his forehead with his palm while Cole ran from the room. "Chad, that other guy with a camera, the one talkin' to Gloria at the car, he looked like he had somethin' on you. He was behind us somewhere yesterday. He could've zoomed a few shots for Gloria that Lanny's other photographer wouldn't have."

Cole came back in with a long whistle, holding up a fax of the photo Cameron must have gotten. Chad's mouth dropped when he saw what Lanny Smith and the others witnessed yesterday. Gloria's eyes were closed and she rested her cheek against his back as her arms encircled him. He dreaded explaining it to Caroline.

On the way to the island, he followed Patrick up Main Street toward the intersection of the patched bridge. He and Joey turned over the possibilities about who sent the fax. Chad tightened his grip on the steering wheel, a bandage over the knuckles of his right hand. "I might get to be the reason my wife finally snaps," he said gruffly. "On top of everything else dumped on her, now she has someone tryin' to make her doubt me. I'm terrified to even venture a guess at what else can go wrong before she can come home."

"At least she's with Juliette. You know she'll be on your side," Joey offered hopefully.

"She needs to be with me!" snarled Chad, slapping his hand against the steering wheel. "She warned me when she left that we were being separated and we aren't as strong apart, like she thought we were bein' tested."

The new topic of the photos set a stormy mood with the family at lunch. Wyeth paced, concerned about the impact on the gallery if his niece was portrayed in the news as a long-suffering new mother whose callous husband was playing around and got caught at Painter Place. Phillip was furious and called Lanny to demand he find who was behind this and stop it, before the press got it and damaged Global's reputation.

Chad went into the library for some privacy and dialed Cameron's mobile phone. He briefed him about what really happened the previous morning. Cameron sighed and then said wearily, "I guess I don't have to tell you Caroline didn't need this, Chad, and I'm pretty disturbed myself. My job is on the line if the media gets hold of this. I've got my hands full and can't handle their attention here right now. I'm trusting you and your dad to get on top of this. I'll go get Caroline for you."

Caroline soon answered, and her tone was subdued. "Hi."

"Care," he said breathlessly. "It is so good to hear your voice! I wanted to call yesterday, but I haven't gotten this time zone thing down yet."

"We were out last night anyway. We had our first authentic French dinner at a place with music. It was very folksy—accordions and guitar. They have some wandering orchestras here, too, and they play French bagpipes called 'bodegas.'"

"What's the food like?" Chad stroked his hand across his face, trying to diffuse the tension. He decided to tease her about her food habits. "Was there anything to bite into shapes or unroll?"

"I tried a seafood dish I can't pronounce, but it was good. I was able to cut away shapes to make it look like it had a fin." Her voice was taut, but she was making conversation instead of launching into him from the get-go.

"I'm glad you and Casey left us an answering machine duet. You should do that more often. Joey played it three times. Sounds like she's enjoyin' France."

"She is. Wait until you see her first travel sketchbook. And she's found clothes that really suit her. Joey's goin' to be pleasantly surprised at the changes in her under Juliette's influence. While we shopped in Florida, Casey bought some genuine cowgirl boots and helped me select a pair in an authentic brand and style. I wanted to cheer her up and honor her Texas roots. She's so much help. At night, she wakes up with me to handle one of the boys."

"I can't wait to see you in those boots, and to work the twins' night shift with you. Listen, Casey will want to know that Joey took a hit in the jaw and ear when we got into a fight in the park yesterday. I don't want to spend our limited time talkin' about it, but he'll tell her firsthand, and she can tell you. I only have some bruised knuckles and ribs."

"Chad! At least tell me what this was about. You got in a punch if you have a knuckle injury. I hope you made it count."

"It counted, all right. Some guys showed up at the park drinkin' and decided the 'privileged elite' Painters and Gregorys had no right to be on the public basketball court. They ended up jumpin' Joey with a broken beer bottle and sayin' something obscene about Casey. People must be thinkin' of them as a pair. They claimed she'd have to sew him up after they were through, so we stopped them just as Sterling pulled in."

Caroline's voice betrayed the tears he knew were in her eyes. "My great grandfather *gave* the town the land for that park! Chad, what's happening? Why are people rejecting my family? I made a breakthrough last night talking about Poppy Noble with Casey. My goal when I got here was to work through all this personal stuff and come back home for a fresh start at Painter Place with you. Then I got the fax this morning. If this thing with Gloria ends up going public, I'll explode!"

"I'm jealous that you're gettin' through this with other people. You don't know how hard it is for me not to jump on a plane to reach you," Chad said, ruffling the front of his hair. "But Dad depends on me more than ever at Global. My grandparents need Uncle Justin in Charleston to handle repairs on their property, so he can't be Dad's backup now. Dad needs to help Wyeth get the mansion repaired, for all our sakes. I can't just do what I want to, I've got to be here."

Caroline blew her nose, then answered, "I know that's the right choice. Stayin' there is oddly better for us than you comin' here. That's why I told you I'd have to do this alone." Her voice choked. "But I'm lovesick and homesick. What were you thinkin', Chad, lettin' that viper get close enough to touch you like that? This is huge! It could be the dynamite in every interview we both have for the foreseeable future. If this photo gets out into the media, it will never go away, ever. Did you get the fax? Is this blackmail?"

Chad winced. "I feel so lame sayin' I'm sorry. I never heard her come up behind me, Caroline, and I didn't know she had her face against my shirt. No one asked for money yet, and she sure doesn't need any. I didn't react quickly enough yesterday to beat the shutter speed on a camera, 'cause honestly, I was daydreamin' about a real dream I'd had the night before, starring you. I reached up for the tree branch to stretch out some of this constant muscle tension and stiffness from sleepin' on a sofa. There was a lot of background noise from the bulldozers and work crews here at the Big House. I waited on Dad and Lanny Smith, from the company handling the insurance for the island, and he happens to be her husband. When she spoke, I just blew up and said things that could've been expressed more tactfully, according to Dad. She tried to slap me, and I stopped her. Lanny Smith heard everything and told her to go wait at the car, and he handed a wad of cash to a photographer with him for a roll of film and confidentiality. The guy with the camera must make a fortune in hush money."

"Are you tellin' me this happened in front of her husband, and he's okay with it? 'Cause I'm sure not!"

Chad clenched his teeth at the strangled sound in her voice. He covered his mouth with his hand and took a deep breath before he said as calmly as he could, "Apparently he's used to it. He's a good bit older than her, and said he's not handsome or interesting, just very rich, and works long hours. He said this is how she reminds him she needs attention and romance. A vacation to a secluded spot is his remedy, so she's punished by having to spend time alone with him. The pre-nup she signed has to be a work of art on his part."

"Chad, what did she say to you?"

"Care, come on, baby, I don't want you playin' this out in your mind."

"Like you wouldn't?" she asked thickly. "Gloria had so little respect for me that she came to my home—my home, Chad—to trap my husband! This is more of a strike at me than you. I'll get the details out of Patrick or Joey if you won't tell me. I mean it. I'm goin' to be loaded with my own shots if the press comes."

Chad stared out the gaping hole where there had once been a window in the library. He told her everything, but before they could discuss it, they were interrupted by a little squawk for attention. He was relieved at the chance to change the subject. "Sounds like someone knows his dad's around."

"Rayce is first awake again. Nanny's off on Sundays, so I'm spendin' all day with them."

Casey's voice traveled the phone line in the background. "Rhett's eyes are open. He heard his brother and doesn't want to miss anything. I'll take diaper duty."

"Anything new with them this week?" Chad asked into the receiver.

"They look even more like you, and still sleep most of the time. Both seem to be fine with a bottle, despite all my concerns about failing them. It's so fun to watch them have their own conversations and eye contact, but it's in a code that the rest of us can't translate yet. I suppose it's a twin thing. Here's Rayce. Say hello!"

The baby coos and squeaks Chad heard as his sons recognized his voice made his heart swell. Caroline told him they were reaching to touch the phone in curiosity at hearing him there. They started fussing to eat by the time Casey brought a bottle for each of them, handing one to Caroline for Rayce before she took Rhett away to feed him.

"What time should Joey call?" Chad asked.

"Have him wait about twenty minutes," Caroline said as Rayce hungrily worked on the bottle she held for him. "Chad, my stomach's in knots. I need somethin' happy to think about before we say goodbye. I want to hear about that dream you had."

"I wish I could do more than that," he said in a throaty voice. "I want to hold on to you and tell you everything's goin' to be all right.

It will be, Caroline, somehow." Then he related the disjointed dream and heard her laugh softly.

"What in the world did you have for dinner?"

"Cole's experimental wifeless menu from the local gas station snack aisle. Patrick ran around the world all night from Cameron's bodyguard over Natalie."

Now Caroline laughed outright.

"See what you're missin'?" Chad's grin at the phone felt like an old friend she took with her when she left.

"You mean, what's happenin' with you clowns at Painter Place, or what happened in the dream?"

He closed his eyes. "I really, truly, deeply miss you," he said huskily.

"I miss you, too. When can I come home?"

"We're still on target for four weeks, but the Big House is full for months. We'll escape to Charleston sometimes to see my grandparents. Don't worry, I won't cross Old Gracie with you and the twins in the car. Help us plan a new house with Dad and Mom that has separate wings for our family and Cole's. I don't know how many years it will take to recover or whether we can rebuild cottages around here, since insurance on those old structures won't reimburse much at all. The financial side of this is a nightmare you can watch Wyeth face when you come home. As we already accepted, Painter Place won't be like the island we grew up on."

She drew a ragged breath. "So, we'll live with your parents. Are we goin' to be like Southfork and the Ewings on 'Dallas'? Promise me I'm not married to J.R."

"No worries, we'll make Cole be J.R. But Casey's got you started with those boots, in Texas tradition. I'm lookin' at some land nearby on the beach that's comin' up for sale, and we can build an escape for ourselves someday when the boys are bigger."

"I'll ask Casey to train me in whatever else I should know about the Ewings and Texas. Listen, Cameron's phone battery is low. Tell Joey to call Casey on the land line. I'll write you a letter after she fills me in on the incident at the park. Let Ben know that Azariah's workin' well, and I think you'll like him. Did you know his name means 'helped by God' and it was taken from Daniel 3:16-18, about Daniel's friends and the fiery furnace? You should see how he looks at the boys. I can tell he had a family once."

"Remember, he's guardin' you for me, not just protecting the boys. Try to call when you can and leave me a message. Your voice gets me through a day. I love you."

Beach volleyball with Painter and Gregory families did wonders for everyone's tension. His mom, Caroline's mom, and Marina did great in the mixed teams, but it was not the same without a guys and dolls game. He missed the secret looks Caroline and he exchanged in their own personal language, and the way they brushed into one another and set one another up.

If he closed his eyes, he could almost hear her laughter in the sound of the surf. He imagined the 'I'm gettin' ready to make somethin' fun happen' smile of hers that Krystal liked.

He stretched out on a lounge chair in the fading late afternoon light while the others went into the house to gather a picnic dinner. The cassette in the portable stereo ended, so he picked through cassettes in Joey's tape case and grabbed one. He knew just the song he wanted.

Leaning back, he gazed at the oncoming twilight as he did so often with Caroline. As he listened, his heart squeezed. The lyrics were nonsense, but the year "Nineteen Hundred and Eighty-Five" was the magic summer at Painter Place that no one would ever forget.

Joey plopped a cooler down onto the sand, handing him an iced tea. They listened to the song without speaking, but when it ended, Chad asked how the conversation with Casey went.

Shrugging, Joey replied, "Good, I guess. What the guys said about her in the park brought up an opportunity for her to throw what she thought was ice water on my campfire."

Chad braced himself. *Uh-oh.* "Okay. Is it something you can live with?"

Joey took another swallow of his tea. "Yeah. It's supposed to be a great thing not to have in-laws. Her recently deceased grandparents raised her after her parents died, when her dad crashed his truck after a night of parties. They were both drunk. Her dad was a rodeo star who got her mom pregnant and never married her. His parents refused to believe the baby was his and insisted her mom was a groupie trying to trap him, so she never met them. Casey assumes that considering my brother married your sister, and I'm so close to all of you, she's not the pedigree kind of girl that fits into my life."

Chad pursed his lips, looking out over the water and the darkening sky. "Did you tell her about Chrissy? And she's met Tony, so she knows how dysfunctional it was when Andy married Valerie."

"I told her Wyeth married Chrissy despite her having a fearsome, mysterious dad lurking around, and how her mom died under mysterious circumstances—shot by a sniper—before telling her who her father was. She understands how difficult Valerie's background is but heard people say around town that she's from the best bloodlines in South Carolina's history. Casey said, despite the dysfunction, Chrissy and Valerie were still socially high class, unlike a girl born out of wedlock to a rough cowboy and a small-town country girl who was raised better than she acted."

They were quiet for a few moments, listening to music, and Joey shrugged. "It was awkward when I realized we were talkin' about whether there were barriers to a future together. I didn't mean to get there, but at least now we both know the door isn't closed. This doesn't mean anything, exactly."

"What did you say?"

"I told her that wouldn't stop someone who appreciated her for who she is." Joey paused a moment, turning his scowl to the ocean. A warm breeze blew his chestnut bangs from his tanned face and suddenly he chuckled.

"We talked about the lines we'd both drawn in the sand, and since she's from Texas, I said one I absolutely can't cross is a girl who listens to country music. She said we were on the same page, then. With a few exceptions, she says country music in general tends to be attached to drinking addictions and glorifying promiscuity. She blames it for encouraging her parents to behave as they did. Casey also has a pet peeve about how so many country singers mention God in a song, then sing and live like they've never heard of His perspective on their party lifestyle. Her grandparents warned her that a lot of country songs had bad theology and they didn't want her to follow the influences that snagged her mother."

Joey shrugged. "Anyway, she knows now that we're both lookin' for the same thing, and I'm interested enough to check on her while she's gone."

The others began arriving on the beach with a picnic. Joey and Chad rose to join in the blessing. Patrick's mobile phone rang, so he picked it up while his mom motioned that she'd make him a plate. But his joy in greeting Natalie soon turned into a serious conversation with Noble.

"He came and put his hand on my face, turning it to the television," Natalie explained. "He told me to keep watching the cooking man and not to look at him. Aunt Grace and I knew he was up to something, but we let it play out. He was stealthy when he pulled the step to reach the kitchen counter over to the container that she hides cookies in. He took out about half a dozen to put in his toy bag before we stopped him. We told him how disappointed we were, and how unhappy you'd be. Can you talk to him?"

Patrick wished one of his few conversations with his son didn't have to be about discipline. He met his own dad's eyes when he brought Patrick's plate over. "Yeah, put him on."

Curious, Valerie came over to join Andy and listen as they ate.

"Daddy, where you at?" asked Noble into the phone.

Patrick's heart melted at hearing Noble's voice, and he had to build up his resolve to be stern. "I'm at the Big House, Noble, helpin' Pawpa Andy clean up all the broken things the bad storm did. I miss you, and I wish we could talk about somethin' fun. But you tried to trick Mama and Auntie Grace, so we have to have to talk about that instead. Would you have taken cookies if I was there?"

"You're not," Noble reasoned.

Patrick groaned and looked up at the darkening night sky, where clouds were beginning to obscure the stars. "Noble, God sees everything. He's everywhere, watchin' you. He helps Mama find out about the bad things you do because He wants you to learn how He would act."

"God's at heaven. The sky is far."

Patrick blew out a breath, covering the phone. "Dad, how did you explain God's omnipresence to me, and was I only two years old?"

Andy Painter joined the others as they laughed, then held out his hand for Patrick's mobile phone. "Noble, this is Pawpa. I'm sad to hear that you were sneaky today, 'cause that's the same as tellin' a lie. If takin' cookies without askin' a grown up is wrong here at home, it's wrong at Auntie Grace's home, too. It's wrong everywhere you are. Remember when we went to see the giant fish tank once, the one that was as big as your room, and it was full of pretty fish? We stood beside the glass and looked in."

Apparently Noble did remember. Andy listened before he continued. "Right, there were glowing striped ones and some seahorses. We saw all those fish in their home. To them, we seemed far away, and they ignored us. But we studied them for a long time, didn't we? We talked about what was special about each of them, and about what they were doin'. Jesus is watchin' us, too, Noble, except He can be in Heaven and here with us at the same time. He even knows what you're thinkin' about."

Andy listened patiently to his grandson while Patrick took another bite of dinner. "Yes, I'll tell Nana you're sorry, too. You tell Jesus you're sorry, and your Auntie Grace, and Mama and Dad, okay? Maybe you can draw something special for Auntie Grace. I'm goin' to give the phone back to your Dad now. Call me tomorrow and we can talk about happy things, okay? I love you."

Patrick took the phone with a grateful look to Andy, wrapping up his conversation with Noble with a warning and a bedtime prayer before spending time talking to Natalie.

Chapter Seventeen

You are not without allies, even though you know them not.
-Gandalf

Caroline engaged the tour guide for Monday, planning to see more of Arles and learn how to get to the Rhone for a few plein air painting night outings on their own. She wanted to attempt starry sky views from the locations Vincent Van Gogh had painted a century ago, and explore the places associated with Pablo Picasso. Picasso enjoyed bullfights at the ancient Coliseum, and she hoped to use the architecture to teach Casey some important things about perspective. That lesson would overwhelm her at this point, so Caroline kept the subject matter simple but charming. Some beautiful farm vistas helped Casey grasp foreground, middle ground, and background distances.

She watched with amusement as the tour guide often expressed interest in Casey. On the doorstep at the end of their outing, he asked them to consider dinner at a local restaurant that evening. He wanted to reserve a table for two, close to an outdoor patio for dancing, if Casey could separate from the group to join him.

Casey told the guide it sounded lovely, and she would talk to her host, but she warned him that she didn't drink alcohol and having it on the table would make her uncomfortable. The guide shrugged off what must have been an unusual condition in France for a romantic dinner, promising to call to confirm their date.

When Cameron and Juliette arrived later, Cameron's face was grim. He handed Caroline another anonymous fax with a photo of Chad holding off Gloria's upraised arm. The shoreline and the sparkling Atlantic were behind him. Her home. Her husband.

Caroline still felt a stab to see beautiful Gloria victorious in her plan to touch Chad, to make him touch her, and to insert herself into his life. *Please, God, don't let these photos get out,* she prayed for what must have been the hundredth time.

By the time they were enjoying dinner and the quaint, romantic ambiance at the restaurant where Casey met her date, Caroline's subdued mood had improved. They ordered different dishes of French cuisine and shared. Azariah sat across from her at their table for four with his back to the wall, watching the room, pleasant but not contributing much to their easy conversation. Cameron's guard and nanny were on duty at the house with Mia and the twins.

Occasional glances at Casey's table told Caroline the charming guide seemed to enjoy getting her to attempt French words with her Texas flair. When lovely strains of romantic music began, the Frenchman took Casey's hand and led her to join other couples on the torch-lit patio.

Cameron and Juliette rose to dance, and her uncle promised to come back for Caroline soon. But she did not want Cameron to split his time with Juliette, and a glance around the room told her there were other men noticing that she and the man at her table were not a couple.

Other women were watching Azariah with interest, so they both might soon be put in an awkward situation. She looked across the table at her bodyguard, whose narrowed expression said he was not thrilled with the attention she was getting.

She extended her arm toward him. "Azariah, will you dance with me?"

A flicker in his eyes said she had handed the bodyguard a situation he was unprepared for. Nevertheless, he rose, pulled back her chair, and suavely took her arm. For the benefit of onlookers, he tried to have a normal conversation with her while his eyes scanned and analyzed their surroundings.

Every man Caroline had ever danced with had some slight markers in their movements to tell her instinctively that something was changing, but dancing with Azariah was like dancing with a liquid substance. He moved her along until she picked up how to flow with him, keeping plenty of space between them.

Caroline caught a view of a man with an eyebrow raised quizzically as he watched. The man leaned over to say something to another man near him, who looked at them before smiling and making a reply that prompted a chuckle from the first man.

“People will joke that you act as if you’re being paid to dance with me," she murmured to Azariah.

Something akin to amusement crossed the bodyguard's face and tugged his mouth. "And they would be right," he said before his arm raised hers overhead in a fluid turn.

"I'm literally in your capable hands, and my husband would approve of my not meeting strangers here. Can we relax and act like good friends so no one will know I'm just a job?"

Azariah scanned the patio, street, and shadowy corners in one smooth sweep. "I'm not paid to be your friend."

When she was quiet, he glanced down into her face, where he became ensnared in the infinity of the blue in her eyes. She responded coolly, "Then do it for free. You need one."

Caroline knew pain when she saw it, and it ravaged the bodyguard's face like a lightning bolt just as the band announced the last song of the evening. Cameron touched her shoulder, asking if he and Azariah could change partners. The bodyguard tore his eyes from hers and hesitated, still unsettled.

"Just stay beside us," Cameron said, misunderstanding Azariah’s hesitation for lack of confidence in his ability to look after Caroline. Azariah nodded mutely and took Juliette into his arms.

“Should I be insulted that he didn’t want to dance with my wife?” Cameron’s voice was testy.

Now that Caroline could watch her bodyguard dance, she was reminded of a big cat melting into the next step. She half-smiled as the story of the Indian boy Sambo came to mind, in which the tigers ran around in circles until they became butter for his mother to put on pancakes.

"Not at all," she replied. "It's not personal. He just told me that dancing with me is only a job, and he's not paid to be my friend. I think he's terrified of getting close to anyone."

She felt Cameron tense and saw him frown. "He's not exactly socially graceful, is he? That was an inexcusably rude way to talk to a lady. Chad would fire him on the spot if he knew."

"He's not paid to be respectful, either," murmured Caroline. "At least he's forthright. We'll get used to one another."

Cameron's eyes swept their surroundings, catching the men watching Caroline and Juliette. "So, Chad hired a bodyguard who can dance to keep you out of reach," he mused. "You two doing a Mission Impossible episode together? I almost want something to happen so I can watch him in action."

"I've had too much action in my life lately. That's only supposed to happen in movies and books. I just want peace and quiet to raise my new little family."

A member of the band sang heartfelt words in French. Caroline could only understand a few of them, like *amour, je t'adore*, and *Cherie*. She sighed sadly, letting the empty feeling of missing Chad visit her heart momentarily. But the music ended in a soft trailing tempo, whispering, as if inviting her to follow its beckoning fingertip into a secluded setting. She gave in and allowed the ache for him to envelop her.

Tuesday morning promised another clear day in Arles, and the light was wonderful. Caroline lingered on the balcony over breakfast after getting the twins back to sleep. Azariah soundlessly passed through the French doors to scan the red tiled roof views below the iron balcony railing. She fleetingly remembered the Bible's description of King David, with his ruddy complexion. Azariah's hair was light auburn with red flashes if the sunlight hit it as it did now.

The guard hesitated when he circled back to the open double doors. "I was rude last night. It will not happen again," he said simply.

Caroline wondered if Cameron had spoken to the bodyguard or if this was on his conscience. "You were straightforward, and I respect that. I'm not easily offended. But I'm your friend, so do whatever you like about it."

The bodyguard remained a moment as if he wanted to say more, but Casey came out for breakfast with a bright greeting for them both. He politely wished her a good morning and disappeared into the house.

The ladies struck out on a sketching excursion with Azariah as their compass. Today's subject was a daylight view of the setting for one of Vincent van Gogh's famous paintings of the Café Terrace at night. Without the gas-lit glow on the awning and the drama of the dark sky, the street scene was unremarkable. It would be a good example of one-point perspective to demonstrate to Casey, who worked to sketch objects in the scene as they became progressively smaller until they receded down the street, as if they were flowing into a funnel.

Back home by late afternoon, Caroline found a huge bouquet of sunflowers waiting for her from Chad, with a message to call him. The vase was painted with a French countryside view. She phoned his office, filling him in about where she'd been the evening before and her outing that day.

"Casey had a—a *date*? They danced to love songs?" Chad sputtered.

"She said he recently had his heart broken. He's not handsome, but he's charming. It's an interesting twist on her trip to have a romantic Frenchman hangin' around. He wants to see her again and offered to join us for an outing to do a night painting I've planned at the river."

"Does she care if Joey knows?"

"Of course not! Casey's not sneakin' around. She and Joey have no commitments. By the way, the romantic music at the cafe made me wish you were here."

"I wish I was there, too, babe. Seems like every song I hear reminds me of you. Did you get my flowers?"

Caroline walked over to gingerly touch the fringe of one of the cheery sunflowers that brought a smile to her face. "Yes, and of course I love them—and you for sending them! I'm so excited about that vase. It will be beautiful if we ever get a place to decorate. Let me guess, your secretary found it at Christie's or Sotheby's and faxed you a picture?"

Chad laughed. "Yes, and like her, I knew instantly that it was the one. She's got you and my mom nailed."

"She's amazing. We should set her up with Dante Kent. They're probably about the same age."

"I never thought about her and Dante, but now that you mention it, it's not a bad idea for me to work on that angle—with Wyeth and some finesse, of course."

"I told Casey the other night how you left me a single sunflower in the studio every day the summer Poppy died."

"That was a special time between us. I had to cut the cash crop of Painter Place and then sneak the sunflower into the studio before you arrived. Back then, I was frustrated that it was inappropriate for me to be alone around you at the worst time of your life. Now, I'm your husband, and I'm still frustrated that I can't be with you in one of the worst times in your life."

"Things are a little better, Chad. Perhaps it's from being able to paint, and from all the prayers."

Caroline could hear Cole in the background telling Chad he had a call waiting long distance. Chad said, "I'm sure God's listening and mending the shattered places inside you, because He has a plan for Painter Place and you're the key. I've got to go, babe. Listen to music that makes you miss me. Love you."

Cheerful fires played in the old stone fireplaces to ward off a chill, creating a cozy dinner setting at home in Arles that evening. The friendly French housekeeper had prepared a meal and put on soft classical music before she left. Little Mia was delighted at having her family and aunt all to herself and set her favorite dolls and books in front of the fire in the living room for stories.

During dinner, Juliette said she would attend the dance training sessions for the film Cameron was directing and invited Caroline and Casey to come. "The leaders don't mind us joining in if we hang around the back. It'll be like a workshop for me and a workout for you."

The next morning's weather was dreary as Caroline and Casey arrived at the ancient Roman Arena to meet Juliette. The tour guide had previously taken them by the remarkable landmark, telling them it was over two thousand years old and was called *Les Arenes* by the French. Inside, they saw the space where twenty thousand spectators could watch concerts and bullfights. Caroline wondered where Picasso's favorite seat was.

In the makeshift dance studio, Juliette introduced them to the trainers, the other wives of the cast, and several dancers. The stretching and torso moves were difficult for Caroline so soon after having the twins. She, Casey, and Juliette were glad they already knew the basics of cha-cha, tango, and other steps that seemed to be the foundation of the dances.

A diva in the room named Baila oozed boredom, as if the sessions were beneath her. She tossed her head of glossy black hair proudly and commented that she should have private warm-ups and training. Juliette whispered to Casey and Caroline that the Spanish meaning of the diva's name was "dance."

The rest of that week was filled with sore muscles and some art excursions. Caroline visited several art galleries to introduce herself and to mention her intention of doing a body of work from her visit, promising to contact them later with examples. She continued praying that the press wouldn't get the photos of Chad and Gloria. Hints of scandal would end Caroline's interactions with the art world for a while and affect her income at a time when the Painter Gallery was in trouble.

On Saturday, the ladies spent the whole day shopping. Among their delightful finds was a quaint bookstore with volumes in English. Chad's favorite books in the cottage had been destroyed by the hurricane, so Caroline decided to help him get started rebuilding his library by selecting classics in leather covers and asking the clerk to ship them to Gregory Global in Whitehaven, South Carolina. She composed a personal message for the clerk to print up as bookplates inside the covers.

The moon was full on Saturday, October 14, three weeks after Caroline, Natalie, and Casey had left the island with Noble and the twins. A newly paved parking lot behind the Big House sported a basketball goal, but the men worked so long with cleanup at the Castaway that they were too exhausted to break it in. With water, power, and windows replaced, the mansion would now be home for

Chad, Cole, and Patrick. Joey would stay with his parents in a mobile home set up on their property while they rebuilt their house.

After dinner, Chad picked up his Walkman and headphones, then wandered out to the beach. Perhaps it was the full moon, but he felt particularly lonely tonight. He wandered to a palm tree log to sit, drawn to the shimmer of the moonbeams over the Atlantic. Then he looked up to the constellations, imagining the pictures against the dark navy backdrop. The breeze pushed his hair and the music in his headphones filled his ears with words about how the singer's wife's touch made his troubles all fade, and she was his lady.

Caroline. Chad closed his eyes, though the view was magnificent. He recalled romantic moonlight walks on the beach with his wife, and their time together afterwards.

It was after midnight now in France, so she was sleeping. Maybe she was dreaming of him.

Chapter Eighteen

There are few people whom I really love, and still fewer of whom I think well. The more I see of the world, the more am I dissatisfied with it; and every day confirms my belief of the inconsistency of all human characters, and of the little dependence that can be placed on the appearance of merit or sense.
-Jane Austen, Pride and Prejudice

Caroline quickly recovered her physical stamina and attended extra dance sessions. The dancers in the cast were practicing choreography for the film. She loved the Spanish flare in the moves.

After class on Monday afternoon, she gave in to satisfying her curiosity about the strain written all over Cameron's features and posture every evening. She wandered to the amphitheater on the sidelines to see her uncle in action, gazing at the entirety of the movie set and noticing her aunt standing apart from the cast.

Juliette wore headphones in her ears, attached to a Walkman in a pouch slung by her side. Caroline went to stand by her. Her aunt smiled, following Caroline's eyes to a dashing bullfighter in a flamboyant blue costume embroidered in gold. The short jacket was worn with a white shirt, narrow black tie, and a black sash knotted at the waist. His form-fitting pants ended in pink knee-high stockings and black ballet-style slippers. The actor held a black two-cornered hat that she presumed would soon cover his dark hair.

Captivated, she was snatched into a moment of aching to be a portrait artist. She analyzed the composition, colors, and his movements, desperately wanting to paint a picture with him in it, preferably including a bull with an attitude, kicking up sand flicked onto the canvas by pulling back the bristles of an old brush. The sight was simply too amazing to break it up into cubism as Picasso would. In fact, to reduce this actor in that costume to cubism would be a crime.

Juliette grinned knowingly at her dumbstruck reaction. She took off one of her earpieces and said, "His name is Alejandro Rafael. He demanded to work only with Cameron, but Cameron knew his reputation and named a ridiculous price to be out of reach. He was shocked to get it. Alejandro is too valuable to lose, so Cameron must entertain his every whim, as long as the movie itself isn't significantly changed."

Caroline watched the star become exasperated over one of his lines, shouting that it made him sound tame, and in Spain, tameness was not a positive attribute for either a matador or a bull. His voice was precise, with no discernable origin that she could pick up for the accent. It was a fascinating spectacle. With her eyes on the matador, she turned her face slightly toward Juliette when she commented, "My, my. He's runnin' without restrictor plates. Is he street legal?"

Juliette grinned at the racing jargon. "Not a chance. But there's no one to stop him." She wiped her earpiece and handed it to Caroline, who was now attached to Juliette via the cord to her Walkman. "This sums it up."

Caroline put in the earpiece, from which the words "everybody wants you" came crashing out. Now she was the one who grinned. "Thanks for the warning *not* to meet him! I have enough drama in my life with newborn twins, kidnapping threats, women chasing my husband, and a hurricane wiping out nearly every trace of my childhood home."

Juliette hissed. "Too late! He caught you lookin' at him. From his expression, he's misunderstood your—admiration."

Too late, Caroline realized she shouldn't have looked back toward the matador. He stopped his rant to look directly at her, his dark eyes intense and mesmerizing.

The Walkman cassette player crooned lyrics about paying dearly for your glory, but she barely heard. Her heart was in her throat, first with unexpected excitement, then with dread, wondering if he would pitch a tantrum about the distraction. She stood utterly frozen while the song in her single headphone claimed you can never get away because everybody wants you.

Juliette discreetly pulled the tiny speaker from her ear. It seemed to take an eternity for the bullfighter to reach her with a measured stride, chest out and chin up, ignoring Cameron's protests. The filmmaker signaled for the cameras to keep rolling, muttering that he wanted evidence if this jerk tried to get him fired.

The matador finally stood directly in front of Caroline, bowing elegantly without his eyes ever leaving hers. She felt hypnotized and breathless. He said something that sounded like "coo" and "foul."

Unsure how to respond, or if she could find her voice to speak, she remained locked in his expectant gaze. He stared unabashedly, waiting, a man who gets anything he wants.

Juliette cleared her throat, glancing at Cameron and back at Caroline. "He spoke in French, 'un coup de foudre,' which means either a strike of thunder or love at first sight."

Caroline's mind reeled. Cameron impatiently reminded Alejandro that time was money. Alejandro kept his eyes on Caroline but put his arm out to point back at Cameron, turning slightly in his direction to speak in English. "You do not tell me what to do." He swung his arm and pointed to Caroline. "This beautiful young lady does. She has only to speak to me, and I will return to do whatever you ask."

Then the matador lowered his arm and spoke in perfect English. "I must know your name."

Caroline swallowed hard to gain her voice before she managed to answer. "My name is Caroline. Cameron Fisher is my uncle."

Alejandro raised an eyebrow, slightly turning his chin in Cameron's direction again without taking his eyes from Caroline's. It was an astoundingly elegant, handsome pose that dripped with arrogance.

"Caroline..." Alejandro seemed to roll her name on his tongue and taste it. "I am charmed. May I kiss your left hand?"

As if in a dream, she slowly put out her hand. The matador grasped it firmly, breaking the staring contest by studying her engagement and wedding rings. He closed his eyes and pressed his lips to her hand, keeping it in his right as he looked at her again.

"A wealthy man's ring stakes his claim. You are married—the best kind of woman. Single women are too complicated. They badger men for commitment."

The spell was broken, its magical shards tinkling like glass around Caroline. She blurted, "Surely a man who wouldn't run from a charging bull wouldn't run from commitment. If so, he lacks the strength of character that marks him as having the kind of courage that ultimately means anything."

Alejandro flushed and drew a deep breath that nearly whistled through his white teeth. Gracefully letting go of her hand, he took a poised step back and bowed to her again. "It is as you say." He spun on his heel to make his way back to the set.

"The young lady wishes me to carry on for her uncle," he announced. "I'm ready to begin again."

The matador stopped on the set where his lines would begin and glanced over to find Caroline. But she was gone.

Cameron's group had dinner out again, and Casey's French tour guide friend asked to meet them and sit with the group. Caroline sympathized with Cameron's strained effort to relax and smile over good food. After what she saw in the arena earlier, she understood what a challenge he faced.

The confident, dashing matador was hard to put out of her mind, too. His arresting stare unexpectedly popped into her head, leaving her slightly breathless all over again. Then she felt guilty. Chad would not like how often she was composing paintings of the actor in a bullfight in her imagination, drawn to the scene by the danger, the colors, the movements...

Musicians played a mix of American big-band classics and French tunes. Caroline noticed that Azariah was on edge, and he ate quickly before he got up to blend into the background. She tried to look nonchalant as she surveyed her surroundings, wondering what it was like to see as Azariah did.

Caroline and Casey ordered Ratatouille because they giggled over trying to say the word. From the first bite, they both pronounced the stewed tomatoes, eggplant, zucchini, and onion as delicious, and Casey found no dirty rat anywhere in her plate.

Upon hearing Juliette describe the bullfighter to Casey, and Caroline commenting on what a fantastic painting the right artist could create from his role, the guide began telling them more about the costume and about bullfighting traditions in Arles. "The Toreros are the bullfighters, and the master is the 'Matador de toros,' or 'killer of bulls,' though the bulls are not killed here in Arles. He wears a costly 'suit of light,' elaborate and handmade, embroidered in gold. His assistants wear suits trimmed in silver. The most popular colors are red, black, green, blue, and white. Yellow is never worn, even by spectators, as it is considered to be unlucky. Toreros are highly superstitious. The black hat they wear is called an astrakhan. The costume has a cape, but it's only worn in the parade before a fight, and then is hung on the fence in front of a friend or a distinguished spectator."

"But the gold trim on the suit of lights is basically yellow," observed Caroline. "Maybe the Matador is flirting with a little bad luck, or maybe making a statement?"

"What about the way the spectators interact?" Casey chimed in. "Is it really like in the movies?"

The guide chuckled. "Perhaps part of the arrogance of the matador is that he can overcome bad luck, even if he's flirting with it on his suit. And yes, Casey, the crowd yells the word 'Ole!' when the bullfighter waves a cape at the bull in a series of passes, and they judge him on skill, grace, and daring."

Juliette put down her water glass. "What about the pink socks? Our actor was complaining about wanting his lines to be more masculine, but he doesn't mind wearing pink socks and ballet slippers."

Everyone laughed, even Cameron, and he reached over to stroke his wife's arm as they listened to the guide's explanation. "The Spanish word for 'bullfight' is 'corrida', or 'run', and the fighter has to engage in brilliant footwork. The almost fluorescent pink socks make it easier for the spectators to follow his deft movements. After all, they're judging him. Also remember that these traditions run back for about four hundred years, when it was a sign of wealth and masculinity to be confident that one's bright, expensive clothes wouldn't be spoiled in the ring."

He sat back in his chair, looking over at Caroline. "You remember when I told you that Pablo Picasso lived here and liked to sketch the twelfth-century church St. Trophine, the one with the sculpted Romanesque portico that represents the Apocalypse? He also loved to attend the bullfights and did many paintings of them."

"Yes, I remember. I've always struggled to understand the distortions in his work, but the bullfight paintings definitely have an aura of excitement."

Azariah came to Cameron and whispered before looking directly at Caroline. Cameron looked at him as if he wanted to know more, but then just nodded. "If everyone is finished, we need to call it a night."

The following afternoon, Caroline decided to rest after putting the boys down and having lunch. She skipped dance that morning and planned to take Casey out later to paint a night scene by the Rhone River, as Van Gogh had. Lying back in a lounge chair on the balcony, she put a cassette tape in the Walkman that Chad had sent her and turned the volume low. She was serenaded about the lady that the singer loved who was far away, but on his mind. Caroline let her own mind wander, wondering what her husband was doing. The song transitioned into declarations that the singer wished he could change his life to be with his love, but he had a job to do, and he did it well.

Loneliness rolled in over her then like a stealthy mist, but pride also swelled inside her. Chad was stellar at what he did. He once promised her he would always look after her home, just as his dad did for Uncle Wyeth. She suddenly understood that in a world where disasters affect good and bad people, rich and poor, God put Phillip and Chad in her life. They had an inner fire and a drive for managing Painter Place, because it was their home and heritage, too.

God did not let her down when He allowed Hugo to level the island. He provided a way to survive and carry on in a fallen world that knocks everyone off their feet indiscriminately. *Thank You, Lord, for opening my eyes and heart to this.*

Caroline later realized she was slowly awakening from a nap. Her headphones were silent, her sunglasses covered her eyes, and she felt the slight stir of a breeze on her face. She felt too lazy to rise, so she began praying again, asking God to help her stop resisting His plan by wanting her old life back. She asked for wisdom, strength, and courage to face her new reality. And as she prayed, she peeled back the bandage on her heart to see the cause of the ever-lurking pain. It was healing, but there would be a scar as a badge of courage.

Her mind strayed to Azariah. His family and too many friends had been killed by terrorists. She still had her children, her husband, her family, and friends, but most of Azariah's were gone. He had somehow come through the unthinkable and was now blessing her life by trying to protect her.

Her thoughts skipped to the way God had bragged on Job in front of Satan. He knew Job would emerge triumphant, however shell-shocked he would be. God proved to Satan that Job's faithfulness was not bought with worldly blessings or prosperity. At the time of his extreme trial, Job could not have conceived of God letting him live through it and using him for a blessing in the Bible for centuries to come. The story was not about Job at all. It was about God.

Caroline gripped the arms of the lounge chair when she realized that her children, grandchildren, and future generations, until the Lord returned, would have a family record of how the first female heir to Painter Place handled this monumental trial. She recalled the essence of one of her favorite scripture passages, from Job. She knew Chapter 40:1-9 loosely by heart.

The Lord answered Job:
Will the one who contends with the Almighty correct Him?
Let him who argues with God give an answer.
Then Job answered the Lord:
I am so insignificant. How can I answer You?
I place my hand over my mouth...
Then the Lord answered Job from the whirlwind
Get ready to answer Me like a man...
Would you really challenge My justice?
Would you declare Me guilty to justify yourself?

Do you have an arm like God's?
Can you thunder with a voice like Him?

When beaten down, Caroline had mistakenly lapsed into the world's way of looking at things, expecting justice in life to be like a reward for being good. But that was not what the whole of scripture taught. She was too limited to fathom justice from God's perspective, nor to fathom His ways of allowing the cursed world to play out in her life.

Tears tried to break behind her eyelids, so she opened them to blink furiously while she sat up. She set her headphones on a small table by her chair and saw Azariah at the edge of the balcony on one of his rounds. The bodyguard looked over the railing to the red tile roofs and streets a couple of stories below, his body tense and watchful.

"Do you see them again?" she asked softly. She wondered how many times he had paced the balcony while she slept, guarding her.

"Yes. They turned down a street to the market. But it was the same two men."

"Is it safe for me to go out tonight to paint?"

Azariah kept watching. "Yes. They're inquisitive but don't appear to be threatening. They have no weapons. I want the freedom to pursue the possibility that they are linked to the French tour guide. They made eye contact a few times at the restaurant."

Caroline considered. "Does that mean you're going to hurt him?"

Azariah relaxed and turned to walk the perimeter of the balcony railing. "Only if necessary."

"Azariah?"

The bodyguard turned to face her.

"Do you like the book of Job, in the Bible?"

Surprise flicked across his features at this abrupt change of subject, as it had when she asked him to dance with her. "Yes. The

Hebrew word for satan means an adversary, an accuser, or an opponent, so an evil being tried to make a fool of God. But God proved that was impossible. Job had bad counselors, like many of us do. I'm glad God set that straight in the end. It is God Himself from whom we should measure what is true, not the babblings of well-meaning people."

"I was just thinking—He shows us off, doesn't He? God, I mean. If we're His, He doesn't let Satan go any further than we can endure. He always gives us victory, but it comes with a price. Otherwise, how would struggles ever mean anything?"

Azariah looked thoughtful. "Yes. The bad times, the hard stories, those are the only ones that leave an impression on people. Job would be unknown to the world without his pain. Would he have chosen God's path to be significant for God's glory, or an easy life to be happy on his own terms, giving up his testimony and influence?"

Caroline, Casey, and Azariah planned to leave in late afternoon, hoping to walk to their destination and set up to paint in what remained of the fading daylight. This meant packing a light picnic dinner to eat at the quay on the east bank of the Rhone as they watched the sun set. The French housekeeper bustled gaily about the kitchen, concocting a grander picnic than they had time for, stashing gourmet chocolate into the basket.

As they organized essential painting gear for the outing, the phone rang. Caroline rushed over to pick it up, hoping to hear Chad's voice. But she was not disappointed when it was her little sister Marina, asking if Caroline would like her to open a letter that had just come for her from her friend, Sherrie Shepherd Hart.

"Sure, it's been months since I heard from her. I've got a few minutes before we go out," responded Caroline.

"Okay, I'm opening the envelope... I'll need to read ahead and give you my version until you get home to see it. Here goes. It's stamped from Florida... I didn't know she was in Florida now, did you? She starts with a greeting, asking how you are, and says that she heard about your ordeal during Hugo and hopes God is blessing you with healing and recovery... she's congratulating you on the twins... oh, no..."

Caroline scowled. "Marina?"

"I need a minute to get all of this. Hold on."

Caroline paced uneasily. She hoped the first thing that popped in her mind was not in the letter. *Please God, no.*

"Caroline, I wish I hadn't opened this," Marina said quietly.

Caroline braced herself. "It's Chris, isn't it?"

"He was pulled from his post to go help with Hugo relief work in Montserrat. But since his arrival on September nineteenth, he's been missing, and is now presumed...deceased."

Caroline put the phone receiver against her shoulder and gulped a few times to catch her breath. She heard Marina calling for her and put the phone back to her ear. "Caroline, are you there?"

"Yeah, I'm—I'm still here, Marina."

"Sherrie's in Florida, waitin' on her husband to return from searchin' for Chris. His bag was with the other workers' belongings, and they were all found in the rubble of a collapsed building. They heard a rumor that an American was badly hurt with a head wound in the collapse, and ruffians pulled him out before other men shot at them. They say a helicopter was in the area and could have taken him away, though there was no evidence of that, or motive. The robbers probably just hauled his body somewhere. There were no survivors in the rubble, and no trace of Chris."

The room spun, and Caroline grasped at a chair close to the phone. Marina could barely hear her sister when she asked, "Does she say where her parents are?"

"Only that they've joined her in Florida. We never heard where they went after Pastor Shepherd left Whitehaven to join the mission group. Oh, Caroline, I feel terrible. I wish I hadn't called."

Caroline shook her head, as if Marina could see her. "No, Marina, you meant to cheer me up. That's your heart. I'd rather hear this from you than anyone. You've always understood about Chris. We knew from the beginning that somethin' like this could happen. Poor Sherrie! I hope she is not givin' up yet. Do you mind tryin' to find out if anyone in town knows how to reach her on the phone?"

"Sure, but Caroline, are you okay? Can I let Chad see this today? This family needs our prayers."

"Yes, they do. Let everyone know but tell them not to call me. I'm not ready—I can't talk about it. And anyway, I'll be out painting tonight. I know that might sound cold, but—I need to paint. I'll be able to talk some other time." She quickly said goodbye to her sister and wiped away a stream of tears. Casey brought a tissue box, and Azariah watched nearby. The housekeeper stood wringing her hands on a kitchen towel and knitting her brow.

"Do you feel like tellin' us who Chris is?" asked Casey gently. "I'll call Juliette if you need her."

Caroline blew her nose. She put both hands over her face, seeing Chris' face before her. His golden-green eyes under brown brows had darker green rays like palm fronds spraying out from the pupils. He was the approachable all-American boy next door, not someone you'd notice in a crowd on the street, but handsome in a preppy way. She dropped her hands from her face and took a small glass of water the housekeeper brought.

"Chris Shepherd is—was—he's my former pastor's son, who came to Whitehaven after I graduated from high school. Chris and I were special friends. When he left, he said we were great at bein' friends."

And that I was the only girl he'd ever loved. Caroline swallowed some of the water from the glass in her hands.

"Just before we both graduated colleges, he asked Dad if he could court me. Dad hesitantly agreed, and I started to wonder if Chris might be the direction God was leading me in. Chad had been gone without a word for four years and I'd given up on him before Chris ever showed up."

Wide-eyed, Casey plopped down on a sofa. Azariah sighed and put one fist under his chin, crossing the other over his chest. The housekeeper shook her head sympathetically and continued to wring her hands.

"Caroline, are you sayin' this guy was your boyfriend? I thought that was Derrick," Casey said.

"Everyone thought of me and Derrick as a couple because we were often together for two years before we graduated. But I never let it become official—he didn't know where he'd end up if he went pro, and I had to stay at Painter Place. He understood he had to wait for a plan before we could talk about a future. He focused on his career and got consumed in his demanding college basketball schedule, and during my two years at a local junior college, Chris was the one who came home from his university a lot. I was distracted, tryin' to fill the aching spot Chad had left."

She tried to swallow another sip of water past the lump in her throat. She took a deep breath when the water trembled in the glass she held. "But Chris—he broke off our—whatever we were—after he accepted a call to be a missionary in places so dangerous that he had to be single and couldn't tell anyone where he was. I didn't know Chad was back on the island that night, but he saw Chris break the news to me at the old chapel. He parked in front of my house and watched me cry over Chris by the water around midnight, then asked me to dance with him at the Island Summer Dance the next day. By Sunday, he'd talked to Dad, and we began dating before

Uncle Wyeth spirited me away to England to help me get my perspective right again. A few weeks later, I learned why he'd had to stay away from me for four years, and what his plans for us were. He was always what I wanted."

Caroline looked up from the spot on the rug she had been staring at. She blushed at seeing she had a spellbound audience and handed her glass back to the kind housekeeper.

They all looked at her expectantly. She rubbed her forehead. "I lead a bizarre life. You'd think I'd get used to jolting surprises and difficult choices. God gives me a rest, and then it's time to get the wind knocked out of me again," she said shakily. "I'll be okay to go out tonight. I always knew something could happen to Chris."

The tour guide met the subdued group after finishing his last excursion, bringing a yellow rose for Casey. Azariah casually asked the young man if he knew the two men who'd been watching Caroline at dinner the previous evening.

"Sure. They work for an actor here with the film that Monsieur Fisher is doing. His name is Alejandro Rafael, and they screen anyone he's involved with."

Azariah looked at him steadily. "Involved with?"

The tour guide hesitated, glancing at Caroline's raised eyebrows and back to her bodyguard. "Look, I don't care what's going on. When I arrived at the restaurant, they asked me if I was with Cameron Fisher's party."

"Why did one of them give you a tip?"

The guide flushed, agitated now. "I did not ask for money, they just handed it to me! I'm an honest tour guide. They asked what Monsieur Fisher's niece's last name was, and I told them she was here as Caroline Painter, working as an artist, but her husband was Chad

Gregory with Gregory Global, who employed my agency to act as a guide to her and her friend."

Azariah peered closely at the young man's face in the gathering darkness. "Madame Gregory is not involved with Alejandro Rafael. There is no relationship for you to turn a blind eye to. If you wish to continue to visit Mademoiselle Austin, you will not cooperate with anyone else. You could unwittingly put Madame Gregory in grave danger."

The guide looked startled. "Danger? I see." He apologized profusely to the ladies and to Azariah, assuring him it would not happen again. Contrite, he sat back to watch them paint, and interacted with tourists as Casey and Caroline discussed the big shapes of the scene and how to simplify.

"It's not common to paint plein air at night, for obvious reasons," Caroline told Casey at her easel. "We're working under a streetlight, as Vincent did for *Starry Night Over the Rhone*, but it will interfere with our color senses. He once said, 'it amuses me enormously to paint the night right on the spot.' After we block in color for the big shapes to tame the white of our canvas, we're going to try to keep up the Impressionist approach. They painted quickly to achieve the sensation of immediacy. That includes dabs and strokes with expressive power, not concerning ourselves with details and accuracy. This painting will not be a masterpiece, so just relax."

On her own canvas, Caroline lightly brushed in the bones of the composition. "When Vincent described his work to his brother Theo, he said he painted the sky aquamarine, the water royal blue, the ground mauve, the town purple and darker blue, and the gas lights and their reflections yellow and russet gold. He changed the reflections to green bronze as they faded into the distance, descending. Notice that he didn't use any black, even though it was dark. In the sky, he tried to contrast the cool natural starlight with the warm gold of the gaslights. He painted the constellation Ursa Minor, the Great Bear, with cool green and pink."

Casey smiled. "I like the way he put the two colorful lovers on the shore. The figures remind me to experience the vastness of the scene."

"He hooked you because he provided you with scale, a reference point for proportion. Where did he place the lovers in his painting to get your attention?" Caroline asked.

"The foreground," Casey replied after studying the little brochure picture they'd brought of the original painting. "But he's confusin' me with his way of situating the middle and back grounds. You taught me to think of them in receding stages, as if a glass were separating the planes. I would've designated the water and some of the closer land as the middle ground, and the distant shore and sky as the background. But he's put the stars too large and close for background."

Caroline beamed at her student, pleased. "Yes. He broke some rules, so maybe he's makin' a statement about what the stars meant to him. Or that it's important to him that they are right over his head as foreground. Don't you wish we could ask him what he was thinking?"

Casey drew her outlines on the canvas as Caroline had, and the tour guide ventured up to ask where she was putting herself and him in as the two lovers. She rewarded him with a grin and purple stroke on his nose, and he began telling passers-by that he was in Casey's painting.

The ladies worked quickly. Now that she was working solo, Caroline's mind wandered to the heaviness in her heart. When she used the green-bronze colors in the distance in reflections running down, Chris' eyes flashed before her.

Caroline, I can't take you where I'm going, and you can't wait for me to return, she heard his voice say gently. She stood still and closed her eyes, fighting the unexpected knife of pain. She drew a deep breath.

I wanted to have a life that included you... now I see that I was running from what I was meant to be, and wanted you to run with me, away from what you are meant to be...

Caroline gasped and dropped her paintbrush, putting her hands to her mouth. Tears sprang from her eyes despite squeezing them tight.

Azariah grasped her arm and she heard Casey say her name. Her chest heaved with several gulping breaths before she could answer. Azariah pulled her over to sit while Casey quickly picked up her brush and put it into water.

"She just needs a minute," Casey told the tour guide and some people passing by. "She got some bad news about a friend right before we came out." She went to the picnic basket for a bottle of Perrier water and one of the chocolates the housekeeper had packed.

"Take a break. Nurse's orders," Casey whispered.

Caroline nodded, accepting what Casey handed her. "Go ahead," she said weakly, waving to the easel. "I got hung up by a color. It just surprised me. I'll be fine."

Casey nodded uncertainly. At her easel, she looked back at Caroline to engage her in a question about her composition. Soon both Caroline and the tour guide were at her side discussing the painting. Caroline moved to her own easel and immersed herself quietly in her work.

Chapter Nineteen

Chad jogged along the beach alone after escaping from the office early. Caroline's sister Marina stopped by to show him Sherrie's letter. Now, his focus was on nothing else. Running would help him think. He knew why his wife didn't want to talk to him, or anyone, about what happened. In her own way, she was running, too.

Wind gusts whipped his hair wildly as he headed down the isolated beach toward Brush Point. Fading sunrays melted over his bare shoulders and arms as they glistened with sweat. He ran, letting the air dry the salt in his tears on his face.

His life—Caroline's life—nothing would be the same, not even their love for one another. He reached his limit of just taking it, rolling over. He was ready to do something. Since Hugo, he'd been begging God to give him direction, to show him how to be what Caroline needed right now. He itched for action.

A memory flashed into his mind, of Chris Shepherd's handwriting on a message for Caroline four years ago. *Be who you are, and God will open the doors. Baker is only the beginning. As Jim Elliot once said, 'Forgive me for being so ordinary while claiming to know so extraordinary a God.*

"I'm ordinary, too," Chad gasped out loud to God as he ran. "But not You! You were extraordinary when you saved us here at the Big House. Maggie Jane told me to remember that joy. What happened, it's a—it's a landmark to remember Your greatness, like the hymn about raising an Ebenezer. Like Painter Place."

The melody and worshipful lyrics of the old hymn "Come Thou Fount" had been flitting around the edges of his mind all day, and his Bible passage to ponder on his desk planner was the first two verses of Psalm 90. As often happened, it was the message he needed today, even before Marina showed up at his office with the dreadful news of Chris Shepherd's death. He memorized the verses. *Lord, You've been our dwelling place through our generations.Before the mountains were born, or You created the whole world, from everlasting to everlasting, You are God.*

He slowed to a walk and then stopped to catch his breath, resting his hands on the hips of his gym shorts. Gulping deep breaths, he looked out to the Atlantic.

Moses had written that Psalm about the Israelites when they feared the giants in the Promised Land. Giants were not merely unusually tall people. They were the supernatural hybrid offspring of heavenly beings who rebelled against God by mating with human women, creating evil entities. These Nephilim traced back to the sixth chapter of Genesis and once deceased, their disembodied spirits became the demons who roamed earth because they had no place in heaven.

The Hebrews lived through incredible miracles to escape Egypt, having every proof that God existed. Yet they didn't trust Him to handle the giants, so He cursed them to wander homeless for forty years while that disobedient generation died out.

One thing about disobeying God that Chad took very seriously was that it was never a solo event. Everyone around you suffered.

For as far back as the Gregory and Painter families could trace, Christ was the dwelling place of their generations. Not estates in England, and not Painter Place, but God Himself. They could focus on the island or focus on the One who created it and allowed them to be stewards of it for a breath of time. If He wanted them to have the island, it could be like facing giants. Did Chad trust Jesus enough to walk a path of spiritual warfare?

He wiped his face with both hands. He preferred to just enjoy life with Caroline and his sons. But if he wanted to walk in obedience to Christ, that option was not on the table.

He looked back along the beach, where his solitary trail of Nike imprints came up like a tether to his feet. A tether, he mused. Yes.

It was a picture of his relationship with the island. He could never escape it.

Then a poem he memorized popped into his mind. It was another picture of his relationship with Caroline and her island. She wrote it in high school sometime after he went off to college, when she thought he'd left her behind. Assuming her dreams were dashed, she wondered who the Lord would send to fit in at Painter Place. Chad found the poem in her things when they married and moved to the guest cottage.

The stars were twinkling bright above
They seemed to wink at me
The man in the moon danced shimmering beams
On the swishing, foaming sea.
Alone in that enchanted world,
I walked along the beach,
And I left footprints in the sand
Just out of the water's reach.
Then you came, and together,
We built a castle in the sand.
You said someday we'd live in it
And then you held my hand.
Together, we walked down the beach
And I glanced back to see
Two sets of footprints right beside
The old ones left by me.

His footprints walked alongside hers. Whatever shelter they had together, it was their castle. Whatever giants threatened her when she had no sling and stone, her extraordinary God would use him and others to conquer. Chad was uncertain what came next, but it was time to cross the line, and he was itching to handle it.

Andy Painter wandered out to the beach, searching for his wife, and found her sitting on the sand near the water's edge. Panting, he plopped down beside her in the sweaty Castaway tee shirt he'd been jogging in.

"She needs me—needs us," Valerie told the waves in front of her. "This is too much to bear all at once. She's only twenty-four."

Andy nodded at the waves she had spoken to. "If I could take something off her shoulders, I would. I can only trust that God will prop her up for what she has to cope with and let the rest seep in as she matures."

Valerie held up a photo she held in her hand between her knees. Peering longingly in the fading light at her twin grandsons, she said, "She's afraid for them, afraid for Chad. Instead of loving them the way she wants to, she might keep distance around her heart, so it won't hurt so much if she loses them. Chris' death hit too close to home, and he was insignificant in the world's eyes, not under a kidnapping threat like her family."

Andy winced and sighed. "I know. She needs to talk about it. I called Juliette."

I know what I'm supposed to do, and I'll never be the same if I don't do it. Caroline slept fitfully with echoing memories of Chris' voice. *Don't wait for me... you belong here, at Painter Place... You know you're the only girl I've ever loved... I don't know how to stop thinking of you being my girl, or how to be without you...*

Rolling over again, she wiped tears from the side of her face with the back of her hand. She tried to divert her thoughts to something calm, like the rhythmic pounding surf at home.

Chris is in My hands. Nothing is wasted. Caroline sat up straight at recalling these words from the night when she sat by the water crying. Whether Chris was in heaven or hurt and wandering, not knowing who he was, he was in God's hands. And somehow, their time together had a purpose. It was not wasted.

She padded barefoot downstairs, turning on a night light in the kitchen and filling a pot for some tea. As it heated, she went to the French doors in the living room and looked out to enjoy the sight of moonbeams playing on the balcony tiles.

The moonlight and stars stirred the memory of a summer night when she and Chris camped with the church high school youth group at Dog's Head, on the north end of Painter Place. First, the kids wanted a scary story and asked her to tell the legend of King's Ransom. It led to a fruitful discussion Chris used to teach the truth about ghosts from a Christian worldview.

Caroline blinked in surprise now, as she stood looking out the glass. This was a way in which her time with Chris was not wasted, after all. They worked together in a ministry of sorts among the youth at church when he was home on breaks and for the summer. She was sure the teens would remember what he talked about.

Hungry to turn over more ways his outreach made their time together count for something, she eagerly reached back to that summer evening again. Chris had picked up his guitar to tune it, and the youth begged him to play some signature something with Clapton and Page. Shaking his head "no" while he adjusted his guitar, he unexpectedly let go with a riff from Page that made them gasp and cheer for more.

But he shook his head, saying he was not there to show off. Someone slyly suggested that he should show off for Caroline, which aroused giggles all around and envious looks from the girls. He grinned and winked at them, then pointed out that he just had. While they laughed, someone else piped up to ask if she was his girlfriend yet.

Chris blushed, chuckled, and kept his eyes down. He delighted them with the opening guitar solo from "Sunshine of My Love" and met her eyes as he joined them in the words to the first verse, about being with her when the stars start falling.

Abruptly, he looked away and swallowed hard. The kids protested.

Sitting across the campfire from him, Caroline remembered her face had flushed. Beside her, Carly discreetly pushed an elbow into her side.

"Okay, so you caught me showing off again," he teased, then gestured to his chest and added, "But I'm just the plumber and Caroline's the Princess. Princesses need a prince, not a handyman. I'm hangin' around in case Bowser shows up."

The kids who played Mario laughed, but another one announced that handyman heroes were just as good as princes. Chris pointed at him and replied that was true, but they had different skill sets for different roles God gave them, as they all had different spiritual gifts so things would work as a whole. He got the kids back on track when he asked if anyone knew the source of all the ideas for heroes and princes to save the day. Someone shouted Jesus, and he shouted yes and began strumming a hymn.

Caroline now closed her eyes, breathing an imaginary breeze off the ocean at Painter Place and an earthy whiff of pluff mud from the marsh. The glow of campfire light flickered around Chris' features, and she heard his rich voice singing as his hands slid over the guitar strings.

I love to tell the story
Of unseen things above,
Of Jesus and His glory,
Of Jesus and His love.
I love to tell the story
Because I know it's true,
It satisfies my longing
As nothing else can do.

Some of the youth group brought friends that night, and a few gave brief testimonies about the challenges they faced at school and at home. Chris was so disarming and approachable that others felt comfortable asking him hard questions about how Christianity and the Bible were still relevant in the world. Chris always seemed to know exactly what they needed to hear. He lived up to the meaning of his name, 'Christ-bearer.'

The campfire became glowing embers that summer evening while several teens in the group committed their lives to knowing and following Jesus. Even now, years later, Caroline's heart welled up with the joy of seeing him lead others to salvation that night. How had she missed knowing then that he was meant for a mission field much more extraordinary than a life at Painter Place?

The clink of a spoon on porcelain jolted Caroline back to France. She turned to the kitchen and saw Cameron, Juliette, and Casey as they brought out steaming cups of tea to the living room. Cameron put a small log in the fireplace. Azariah appeared, seemingly from thin air, and poured himself tea before padding to the Oriental rug in sweatpants and a tee shirt.

"Please tell me this isn't about me," Caroline said after thanking Juliette for the pretty porcelain teacup she handed her.

"Okay. It's about me," said Cameron.

"And me," Juliette and Casey chimed in together.

"And me," added Azariah before he tested the temperature of his tea.

Caroline allowed herself a tight smile. "Azariah, you're off duty. I'm not payin' overtime for this."

The corner of his mouth twitched as he put down his cup. "This one's on the house. I need a friend."

"I can't sleep."

"Because you're replaying memories in your mind," said Cameron.

"You need to talk about this," said Juliette firmly. "This is how you run when you don't want to face something."

Caroline bought a few extra moments by sipping her tea, letting the warm liquid slide comfortingly down her throat. "He was an amazing guy, and I feel guilty—about remembering," she said in a pained voice. "I try to stop it, to stuff it back down. Those feelings shouldn't be hidden in there. That's not who I am anymore."

"They're just memories, Caroline," said Cameron, turning from the fire with the poker still in hand, looking directly into her eyes. "Those feelings are associated with the memory, and it's past. You're not cheating on Chad. They're part of how you became who you are, part of the journey. Juliette helped me understand that. You can't live as if some wonderful things never happened to you, just as you can't pretend some bad things never happened. How long do you think it will take you to celebrate the twins' birthday without the feelings of fear and dread over the memory of Painter Place on the night they were born?"

Caroline covered her face in her hands.

Azariah's voice was low. "Maybe you can start by telling us why you think these particular memories about your friend are important to you. Then, if you feel up to it, I'd like to hear the details you know about his disappearance. I have friends in many—unusual places. They may help."

In her dance class the next day, Caroline was surprised to be asked by the instructor to team with a man whose partner was nursing her ankle on a bench. The dancers were practicing for a scene in the film where they would perform on a floor laid in the arena, and each couple had different moves.

But she found solace in the challenge. There was no time for memories. She focused on working with her partner so he could be his best in the movie scene.

The instructor stopped the music abruptly and clucked her tongue before she raised her voice. "What do you think this is, a chorus line? You're lulling me to sleep, dancers. Show me spice! Give me some salsa, some cha-cha, some flamenco, some Paso doble, some Spanish Gypsy, some tango!"

She clapped her hands sharply for tempo. In the moments before the music started, an explosion of shouting could be heard down the hallway. The owner of the voice was unmistakable.

"The witch will not be my partner! I'm the matador, *I'm* the star—she's only the cape. Baila fights me for attention on the floor. Off the floor, she can't keep her hands to herself."

Caroline followed her dance partner to the music in his routine, trying to block out the tantrum. She heard Cameron protesting as their voices grew closer.

The man she danced with whispered to warn her before he dipped her so low that she imagined she was only a foot from the floor. She knew it was higher than that and fought the urge to use one arm to hold his and help him support her. In practice, he told her to trust him and let go. She raised both arms gracefully over her head, posing her chin, hands, and feet artistically while holding her body in a straight line.

"I want her," The tempestuous actor's voice announced.

Caroline was lifted in perfect timing to the dance routine, and she stood poised with her partner for their next move. But at the door, Alejandro pointed right at her.

She gasped and started. Her partner instantly let go of her and took a quick step away.

"She's not with the cast and you know it. You're pushing too far!" seethed Cameron. He enunciated each word. "*Choose someone else.*"

Unfazed, Alejandro's dark eyes never left Caroline's, and as before, she was caught, trapped, breathless with the mystery of his next move. "Make the calls you need for a contract," he snapped with authority. "I will train her myself. Caroline is fresh, not molded into the predictable movements and rehearsed confinement of these others. She will not compete with me."

The matador turned on his heel and walked out the door.

Cameron's breath hissed through his clenched teeth, furious at the disrespect shown him in front of the dance cast. He turned an apologetic nod to the instructor and said with measured resolve, "Caroline, would you please step outside with me?"

She felt the heat of a flush as she scooped up her gym bag and rushed toward the door while other dancers muttered protests at Alejandro's insult about their movements. The instructor re-started the music and went to practice with Caroline's twice-abandoned partner.

Caroline joined her uncle, who slowly led her toward the waiting bullfighter. "How do you feel about this, Caroline?"

"It's absurd!" she whispered fervently. "Maybe once this guy sees I'm not good enough he'll get over himself."

When they stood in front of the actor, his arrogance evaporated. But his confidence remained, and he showed no sign of changing his mind. "On Monday, you introduced yourself to me as Caroline. May I call you that?"

She nodded, swallowing rising panic. Alejandro's voice became soft. "Caroline, I know what you're thinking, but this is not a position for a star. Cameron will come to agree with me. I merely need a young woman to follow me in some simple moves on her part, when I reach for her. Dance with me."

This confident command was how Chad always asked her to dance. She glanced up at Cameron, who was smoldering beside her.

"My uncle is in charge here. I'll try this only if he thinks I'm the solution, and if my husband agrees."

The matador smiled fleetingly, nodding to Cameron. "While you make the arrangements, we will begin." He took Caroline's arm and gym bag, leading her through an open door. An unruffled trainer greeted them with coolly raised brows.

"This is Caroline," Alejandro announced, sweeping toward a bench with her bag. "Cameron Fisher's niece. She is the Matador's Cape."

The secretary at Gregory Global told Chad he had an emergency call waiting from Cameron Fisher in France. With his heart in his throat, he hung up on another line with the office in London to take it.

"Chad, I know you're working, but I have a problem that can't wait," Cameron blurted. "Check your fax machine before we talk."

Chad's stomach clenched. Lanny Smith had assured his dad the photos of Gloria had been destroyed. This must be about Caroline or the boys. He pushed a button to tell the secretary to take messages.

"What's goin' on, Cameron?" His voice was clipped when he picked up the phone again, holding a contract and photos of an actor in a matador costume. He forgot to breathe when he saw the second photo. The actor was holding Caroline's hand in an astonishingly elegant pose.

She seemed captivated. His heart flipped over.

"First of all, Caroline is okay and doing much better now after the news about Chris. We all stayed up with her to talk, and it did a lot of good. What I'm calling about is what you're holding in your hand, and it involves her and my stormy star, Alejandro Rafael. He's a newcomer to American film, but you may have seen him in entertainment news or celebrity gossip. I'm being paid my price to put up with him like a lackey. This movie I'm directing was written with him in mind, and I must give him anything he wants. Today, he wants Caroline. He ditched his high-strung partner for an important scene. The quick version is that he met Caroline in an unusual way on Monday, sent investigators to watch her that evening, and now he's chosen her to replace a dysfunctional diva."

"*What?*" Chad pinched his eyebrows with one hand. "Caroline's not a dancer, we just—dance."

"She and Juliette have joined some other wives in rehearsals with the cast dancers as a workout. He must have found out. Juliette left the class as usual to help me and said Caroline was asked to practice with a guy when his partner was injured. I got called in to handle Alejandro's wild tantrum when he left a dancer shrieking filthy things in Spanish before he slammed the door in her face. It was like having two Tasmanian devils competing in the same room. I'm not sure I'll ever recover, and I almost exploded myself. I followed him down the hall where he zeroed in on Caroline. He's not negotiating, Chad, she's it. The only way out is if she messes up or you don't want her to take the part."

Chad felt disoriented, rubbing the fingers of his free hand over the tension in his neck muscles. "Why would he investigate her? Where was Azariah?"

Cameron explained that Azariah was on top of it. "Alejandro's persona is a dashing playboy to rich married women, conveniently never single ones. But it's all for sensation, and it gets him everywhere he wants to be. He's been seeing a British girl ever since he went to college there, but they're mum on their relationship status and his staged dalliances. His family heritage is matadors and dancers, and he trained as a matador but always planned to be an actor. He investigates a woman before he associates his name with her for publicity, and artfully makes sure the woman in question will not actually have a chance to accept his seeming advances. Women can't seem to help falling all over themselves to be near him. Except for Caroline. She rebuffed him."

Chad ran his hand over his face. "Do you know how bizarre this sounds?"

"It's more bizarre than you think. He didn't know who Caroline was. He was pitching a scathing tantrum with me about his lines being too tame when he noticed her, interrupted himself to walk over to meet her, and was cooperative the rest of the day after she left. Today, he dropped the attitude the instant he was alone with her. He was like a different person, and I've never seen this side of him. To say I'm baffled is the understatement of my year."

"Is this supposed to make me feel better?" Chad said testily. "What were they sayin' in this photo?"

Cameron related what Juliette told him. He waited tensely in Chad's silence.

"Let me get this straight. My sweet Southern princess joked about a guy she can't take her eyes off of as running without restrictor plates and not being street-legal, and he used French love language to tell her he's either thunderstruck or in love at first sight? What kind of racin' terms do they use to talk about us behind our backs?"

"I was dying to ask Juliette the same thing, but I decided I didn't really want to know if she thinks of me as the pace car."

Chad made a sound in his throat that indicated resignation. "I see what you mean. Cameron, seriously, can Caroline do this? Her art career depends on a reputation of excellence. I know you're from off, but Juliette can explain that Painter Place is at stake here."

"Alejandro Rafael believes she can, so I believe it. He's very calculated in career moves, like the women he stages for sensation to get his name and face in the news. Every change he insisted on in this movie made it better. Caroline can do the basic moves as his backdrop unless he gets creative and adds to the routine. The other dancer ruined the performance when she couldn't dial back.

She competed for the viewers' attention. Alejandro doesn't want the predictability of a trained dancer and insulted a whole room of them by saying so."

Chad groaned. "Will that stir hard feelings toward you and Caroline on the set?"

Cameron sighed. "It's hard to say. Alejandro welcomes Caroline's tendency for improvisation on her own, and the longer I mull this over, the more I see this as a good role for her reputation as an artist. You see, the performance is extremely artistic, a creative interpretation of a matador's series of passes with a cape to control a bull, without carrying a cumbersome cape around while he does other complicated moves. It's choreographed to cause her skirt to sweep with the drama of red flashing underneath, representing the raging bull."

Chad studied the costume and went back to the photo of Alejandro Rafael. The actor was too handsome to be real—surely the photo had been enhanced after a makeup and hair stylist finished. The guy had a commanding, no-nonsense expression. Black slashes for brows suggested speed and strength. His dark eyes were intelligent and intimidating. His mouth was full, a pout, and sat under a perfect Grecian nose. Straight, long black strands of hair fell roguishly over his brow.

Chad rolled his eyes. He could imagine women sighing and swooning in theaters.

He couldn't resist a pout of his own, mulling over the photo of Caroline interacting with Alejandro. "Convince me that this has a benefit for Caroline. He's not the only one who knows how to have a temper tantrum of biblical proportions."

Cameron snorted. "Remember what Baker did for her in Mevagissey? Multiply that exponentially. But we'll need to control the sensation of a romance, due to his reputation. I have some entertainment news reporters coming in to begin promoting the movie, and this will be juicy gossip among the cast. She's still known in Great Britain for her association with the rock star, and Wyeth tells me it continues to drive some of her sales and bookings for shows. Dancing as a hand-picked replacement of Baila by Alejandro Rafael, for what will be one of his biggest film moments to date, is unheard-of publicity. His heart and heritage are in this dance, and he's stunningly good at it. He won't risk letting Caroline dampen his moment. People will talk about this part of the film as art, even if they hate bullfighting or the film in total."

The memory of the note Chris had written to Caroline flashed into Chad's mind again. *Be who you are and God will open the doors. Baker is only the beginning.*

Yesterday, he decided during that jog on the beach he was ready for action, ready to do something for Caroline and Painter Place. He'd begged God for a chance. Now, he squeezed his eyes shut. He really needed to be more careful about what he prayed for.

Cole walked in to put something on Chad's desk and whistled low, snatching the photo in his brother's hand. He grinned with delight at Caroline's interaction with Alejandro.

"How much will she be paid?" Chad asked Cameron tersely, trying to ignore Cole, who slapped his shoulder and whispered, "No whining. You could've married a normal person."

Chad shoved him away with one arm while Cameron went over the details of the movie contract.

Chapter Twenty

Painting is easy when you don't know how,
but very difficult when you do.
-Edgar Degas

Sketching the arena facade at night was indeed the dramatic exercise Caroline anticipated it would be. The up-lit lighting exaggerated the shadows of the arches, creating a striking effect for black and white sketches. Caroline worked with Casey on the study of perspective and light and dark values as the arches marched in a curved line into the distance around the arena.

Unexpectedly, the French tour guide strolled up behind Casey and put his hands on her shoulders. He whispered a greeting close to her ear, then stood looking at the view from Casey's perspective. The guide shared insider information about the arena until he froze in mid-sentence.

Curious, Caroline and Casey looked up and followed his gaze to a young woman who was glaring at him, arms crossed over her body. She tossed her head and walked over to deliver a torrent of French that had none of the warm and fuzzy words Caroline had picked up in the romantic songs in the cafe the week before.

Obviously upset, the guide pulled the young French woman away, gushing out his own French response. His gestures and tone implied confusion, frustration, and passion. The young lady in the heated exchange pointed back at Casey and continued a furious French tirade. The conversation finally calmed down, and the young lady crossed her arms expectantly. The young man walked over to Casey and explained with a flush that the young woman was the girlfriend who had recently broken up with him, thinking he would miss her and realize how much she meant to him. She had pressured him for a commitment.

Casey smiled, first at him and then the young lady lurking in the background. "We're just friends from different continents. She may be confused about how to handle this, but you're both clearly in love. Maybe now she won't rush you."

The tour guide bit his lip and bowed slightly. "Thank you for understanding and for making the last week bearable. It has been a pleasure to spend time with you, Casey Austin." He smiled and wished a good evening to Caroline and Azariah before turning to the young French woman, and the couple walked away from the arena, hand in hand.

"The subject of commitment has been popping up in my life a lot lately," mused Caroline as she mentally measured how much smaller a receding arch on her paper would be. "Azariah, did you ever have a problem with commitment?"

"No. Go after the right thing in the first place. Don't just fish for whatever bites."

Casey turned to him, open-mouthed, then looked at Caroline. "He's a deep well, and you seem to be the only one who can draw anything up out of him."

The trio arrived back at the house to hear Juliette on the phone with Chad, and Caroline set her things down to take the receiver. Casey got them both a pastry and some hot tea left on the counter by the housekeeper.

"Hello, handsome," Caroline said as everyone left the living room. She plopped onto the sofa, leaned into some pillows, and stretched out her legs.

"Hi, gorgeous," he answered. "You and Casey were painting tonight?"

"Sketching. We were practicing perspective at the arena. The shadows from the spotlights are so dramatic! We'll paint another night when I'm not so tired." She nibbled the pastry and moaned a little in appreciation. "I'm getting hopelessly spoiled here, so you'll have to straighten me out when I get home."

"I don't want to straighten you out. I want to spoil you myself. Listen, uh, Juliette filled me in on how you're handling the news about Chris. When you're ready to talk about it, I'm here. Don't shut me out because you think you can't be honest with me."

She sighed. "Okay. I guess she told you we didn't sleep much."

"She did, and I know your emotions don't mix well with exhaustion. I'll wait on you. He was special. I saw that firsthand." Chad rose from his desk to look out at Painter Place. He braced for the next tough subject. "Did you sign the movie contract?"

"No. I don't feel settled about it and want to practice another day."

Chad ran his hand through the back of his hair. "Caroline, I saw a photo of you and Alejandro on the day you met. You didn't tell me about that. Is there any reason for me to be uneasy about this? You're not yourself. You're under a lot of strain right now, and something's still not in sync between us."

"Chad! You don't honestly think—wow, that must have been some photo! Look, the actor is—arresting. He forced me into a spotlight that caught me totally off guard. I've never met anyone like him, and the artist in me kept composing action paintings with him doing what matadors do."

His expression screwed up into a grimace. He was imagining her painting the guy in those tight pants.

"Seriously—the photo bothered you, yet you didn't discourage me from doing this?" she asked.

"Care, I want you to be whole again. If it means tryin' something new, like this movie role, then be the best you can be. Just save your heart for me."

"The actor is not a distraction. As for the role, I want to figure out who I'm dancin' with before I sign a contract. Alejandro had the manners of a Southern gentleman with me during training, and then he walked out of the room to play an insufferable temperamental persona. Other women chase him, but he knows I'll walk away."

Chad paced. His jealous streak was pulsing.

"Chad?"

"Yeah, I'm here," he answered shortly.

"I was raised around Nascar and Tarzan basketball nights on the island. I could never take a man seriously who wears fluorescent pink knee-high hose and ballet slippers."

He turned this over for a moment before he burst out laughing. "Yeah, well, I won't expect any for Christmas, then. Don't bother with the funny hat for Father's Day, either."

"But you'd be unforgettable in those tight pants and that little jacket. I'd never get over it."

"Caroline," he said huskily, feigning an admonishing tone. "I hope you're not talkin' like this in front of the kids."

"I've never met anyone as handsome as you, and you've been the man of my dreams for as long as I can remember. You have the only eyes in the world like the depths of the marsh shadows in the summertime at Painter Place. You've always owned my heart, and I miss you like crazy. I want to come home."

Chad sighed. "I'm lookin' out at it, right now." He could look out at home anytime, but she was a continent away. She had to imagine it, forced to wander while waiting for him to live up to his promise. She and his boys needed a place to come back to. They needed him, and he surely needed them.

During a quick time out after he scored, Derrick Wallace searched again in the stands for where Jordan Waters sat. She wore a blue sweater to support him in the pre-season practice game. Jordan was beautiful, beaming at him, still clasping her hands together from cheering.

Back on the court, he zoned out anything but the game. A flash of dark green from Dwayne's uniform blurred past him as he broke away into a play that never amounted to anything. Derrick's teammates saw to that.

Derrick did nothing on the court to deserve the glaring looks he was ignoring from Dwayne. Dwayne was so rattled that the coach might as well take him out.

During warm-ups, someone pointed out that the woman Jordan had caught Dwayne with was in the stands wearing green. Apparently, Dwayne never heard about Derrick and Jordan and did not expect her to be at this game.

Derrick hated that Jordan endured looking across the court at the woman who easily got from Dwayne what she waited on for years. The other woman was pretty in a brash, careless way. She wore heavy eye makeup and dressed for attention, with a figure that was sure to get it. He'd seen her in photos of the party circuit that got passed around, usually with a drink in her hand, and always wrapped around someone different. Dwayne was light years down her little blacklist, and it was tragic that a supposed Christian with a devoted fiancé had fallen as her latest victim.

But the bottom line was, Derrick was glad Jordan had the resolve to remain pure. Until there was a ring on his finger, he would do the same.

Jordan had reluctantly agreed to fly in and attend this game. It was a turning point he forced her to make about them as a couple, a public acknowledgement she was in a relationship with him. He booked her a hotel room with flowers and a round-trip flight, planned dinner at the most expensive place he could get a reservation at, and asked her to wear that black evening gown she wore to the awards banquet the night they met.

He felt empty on days when they were both traveling. She never called him, but he got a warm reception when he reached her. She was elusive, but she was not avoiding him. Her heart was still healing from a vicious wound, but the day was coming when she would be his—just as he claimed when he got her the story on Painter Place.

He saw in this game he could stand on the court beside Dwayne and still be her choice. She was his challenge. And he played to win.

Caroline went in early to dress for her training the next morning, hoping for a few minutes alone to loosen up and gather her courage. The matador's sanity had undoubtedly returned after a night's rest and this contract she was carrying could be tossed in the trash can. She just hoped he would be polite about it.

She quickly put on the leggings, tank leotard, and turquoise tank tunic she was given to train in. A look in the mirror made her laugh at herself. Leg warmers and a tight curly hairstyle were all she needed to star in a workout video.

As she drew closer to the door of the training room and opened it, the music told her she would not be first after all. Alejandro did not hear her and continued to stretch long, muscular legs. She guiltily ducked her face away from admiring them. He wore gym shorts, a tee shirt, and tennis shoes like any normal guy.

Closing the door quietly, Caroline put her bag down, breathing deeply to cage the butterflies set loose in her middle. She stretched muscles to a popular song about not really knowing a girl, only knowing her name.

Alejandro whirled in a practice move and noticed her. Stopping short, she stared wide-eyed, taking in the front of his "Invisible Touch" concert tee shirt.

He flashed a white grin at her reaction. "The secret does not leave this room."

"I wouldn't dream of destroying your hard-earned evil persona. Can you at least confess whether you drink something from a lab beaker or if you suffer from a split personality?"

Alejandro burst out laughing so hard he doubled over and leaned weakly against a wall. The coach Caroline met the day before came into the room with a female trainer, and they rushed to close the door.

"Alejandro, put on your training gear before leaving this room!" his coach admonished. "You have a reputation!"

The matador wiped tears of laughter from his eyes. "Yes, that's the understatement of the year. But it's hot in here. I want to relax this morning, and I'm sick of hearing all that triumphant Spanish stuff."

The coach frowned his disapproval and flipped on a box fan before he stopped the music. He replaced it with the training song, snapped his fingers, and then barked instructions to the actor.

The female instructor worked with Caroline separately, focusing on rib cage isolation and turns to make an imaginary skirt flutter. She demonstrated poses Caroline must memorize for pauses as she waited on the sidelines for Alejandro. Then, Caroline practiced movements with snaps of her head to one side for drama, as she once learned for tango moves.

After a break, the trainers told Alejandro to change his shoes, and they tied a practice skirt around Caroline's waist. They paced the couple to work together with the music. Alejandro used a lot of catlike walking steps, pulling and sliding his matador-slippered foot. When he reached for her in a tango move, she hooked her thumb under his arm. In other moves, they lunged with the palms of one hand together in the air on one side.

Alejandro stopped in mid-move after her third miss of a cue for him to grasp the silky skirt. He set his hands on his hips, and instantly, the image of the arrogant, rude bullfighter Caroline saw on Monday flashed in her mind. She flinched and braced herself. That image was swiftly swept aside by the sound of Hugo slamming the island into Gran Vanna's bedroom while she struggled in labor, and she caught her breath.

She turned and walked away a few steps. With shaky hands, she pushed the blonde fringe of her bangs up from her forehead. "I'm sorry—I need a minute," she gasped.

The actor stood waiting, a puzzled expression on his face. Finally, he walked to her and reached out to turn her around. He pointed at his face. "Look me in the eye, Caroline."

His dark eyes were calm and soft. There was no storm, no harsh words, no flying debris.

"See? Think of me this way when we dance. I'm not going to go off on you. Trust me. I did with Baila because that's her language and she was 'dishing it out,' I think you say. She was also—getting personal."

He gestured for the trainers to move away and told them to stop the music. Standing in front of Caroline, he intertwined his hands together, squared his shoulders, and relaxed. He lowered his head to talk to her face to face. "You are taller than Baila, taller than most dancers. I am not reaching in the right place for the hem of the skirt, even if you were on cue. It may seem you are the trouble, but I am making a mistake, too. We'll both adjust. Understand?"

When Caroline nodded, he continued. "You are a self-assured woman. Yet your eyes a moment ago—your reaction—it unsettles me. What went through your mind?"

She looked away from him and cleared her throat. "First, I imagined you in your tirade on Monday. Then, almost as quickly, I had a sickening memory of Hurricane Hugo bashing my grandmother's bedroom with what it had torn apart on my island, while I felt torn apart in pain, having my twins."

The female trainer gasped and slapped her hand over her mouth. Alejandro reeled back before he flushed. He looked away to collect himself. Moments passed before he looked back at her.

"I will not behave like Hugo, and I will not hurt you. Let's change the images in your mind. Imagine that you are like the fascinating substance in a lava lamp, a sculpture in motion, with a flowing skirt. This dance routine is an artistic depiction of a matador's skill in controlling a dangerous bull. I will have to use your skirt as a cape in a limited way, though honestly, the flash of red is to attract the spectators' attention, for a bull is color blind and does not care. He would appreciate your beautiful legs, though, and would stand thunder-struck instead of charging me."

Caroline's brows shot up. A moment passed in which she considered the teasing sparkle in his eyes and a tug at the corner of his mouth.

"Are you sayin' that if I let you wave my skirt at the bull so he can see my legs, I'm actually savin' your life?"

The trainers snickered from the benches, and Alejandro struggled to keep a straight face. "Precisely. Now, will you help me conquer that bull, or make me face a gruesome death?"

She sighed and rolled her eyes. "Well, since it's a matter of life and death..."

With a satisfied smirk, he turned to put his Genesis audio cassette back into the player. "All this triumphant marching music—it puts me on edge. We will practice with something you're comfortable with. I will show you the flowing moves, and you can put them to the other music later."

At noon, Alejandro's instructors called the session over for lunch so he could be at his afternoon filming role in the arena. He told Caroline he had arranged for a special meal with her because they had more to talk about and asked if she would follow the female trainer.

Caroline changed back to her street clothes. She wore her new chamois colored leather cowboy boots with faded blue jeans and an ultramarine blue sweater, then draped the neckline with a fabulous flowing silk scarf from a boutique in Arles. The scarf design was inspired by Van Gogh's famous painting *Starry Night*.

The female trainer led her to a large dining room just as Alejandro swept into it in full matador dress, with the disdainful air everyone expected. Other actors and actresses were rushing in and out for lunch as they greeted one another. Caroline and Alejandro sat at a table out of earshot, and on cue, someone brought out lunch for two.

"Salade Nicoise," the actor said in a low voice, watching her. "It means 'nice-style salad' and consists of more than greens and tomatoes. There are haricots verts dressed in vinaigrette, boiled potatoes, boiled eggs, olives, and seared tuna steak for protein. I'm a believer that you're only as good as what you eat, and it is obvious that your diet is healthy. I hope you find something in this that you like."

"It's wonderful, and I like all of it!"

He smiled. "Then please join me in blessing the food."

Caroline was glad for an excuse to close her eyes instead of letting them bulge in shock. It would be rude to show she was taken aback at the idea of Alejandro Rafael praying with her in a room full of people.

"Lord, we thank You for the provision of this meal and for the health we gain from it. Please guide us as we dedicate our good health to Your service. Amen."

"Amen," Caroline whispered.

"Now," he said, unfolding a napkin. "Have you decided to sign your contract?"

She hesitated while he deftly sliced a small loaf of fresh bread and placed a piece on a plate beside of creamy butter. Then he passed the plate to her. "Yes, I will see Cameron or Juliette after lunch," she said, a little distracted by being served by him.

He nodded, pleased. "Good! You have the moves now. Let's begin putting it all together."

"You're a patient teacher," she offered, and focused on enjoying the delicious salad. Alejandro seemed preoccupied as he ate, and finally spoke.

"Thank you for giving me proper perspective about commitment on Monday. I am struggling with a personal matter, and it was just what I needed to hear that day. I apologize for my manners. It is the way I compartmentalize and manage my life. This business will gobble up your soul if you let it. People use you up and spit you out, and women only see what's on the outside."

He took another bite of his salad and seemed to ponder something as he chewed it. Then he said, "There will come a time when I allow more of my true personality in my work world, perhaps after this film. You will help me make it a success, Caroline. I would never have felt satisfaction in my performance in this role if you had not been here. There are no words to convey how grateful I am, and how much you bring to this movie. Perhaps your uncle can explain it."

Caroline was unsure what to say. She blushed and ventured, "I'm sure it's true that much of what goes on in each setting or scene contributes to the whole movie. One of Cameron's cameramen once taught me how much could be done with editing to add impact when we filmed an art video. And I'm honored I said something helpful for your personal struggle."

They ate in silence a few minutes before Caroline asked, "Why did you stop what you were doing that day and introduce yourself?"

His eyes were serious as he studied her and swallowed the last bite he had taken. "I suddenly knew I was supposed to meet you, and it could not wait. It truly was like a strike of thunder, so to use that French term with a double meaning fit well into my work persona, serving my usual—uh—purpose. It gave me room to discover what I was supposed to be doing with you."

"How cozy," dripped a honeyed voice with a heavy Spanish accent.

Baila! Caroline felt a wave of dread and watched Alejandro's eyes narrow as he bristled. Glancing down at the face of the Rolex Chad had given her, she mumbled a thank you to Alejandro for lunch and started to push back her chair. He sprang to his feet to help.

"The naive little artist is wearing yellow stars in her scarf," purred Baila, inching up to the actor's side while he held Caroline's chair back for her to rise. "Yellow is unlucky for a bullfighter, Alejandro."

Alejandro took Caroline's elbow and pushed roughly past the dancer, who laughed spitefully. "She will make a fool of you in the dance, torero!"

Fascinated reporters stood around the perimeter of the room with a tour guide from the movie crew, snapping photos and asking for names. Alejandro stormed out with a sheltering grasp on her arm.

Caroline's heart sank. Not only was Baila probably right, but Chad might see her on the news tonight. He would not be happy.

There was a playful knock on Chad's open office door that made him look up and smile. He gestured to the postman to bring in three boxes stacked on a wheeled cart.

"They cut the tape on these downstairs for security inspection, but you'll have to sign for this," the man announced, handing him a clipboard. "They're all the way from France. 'Reckon your lady sent 'em?"

"Yeah, we're trading gifts from a distance these days. I wish she were in one of those boxes."

The postman grinned and winked. "Maybe she is, like on TV at those bachelor parties!"

Chad laughed. "Just in case, lock the door on your way out, will ya?"

The man slapped his leg and hooted. "Hey, seriously, hope your fam'ly gets back soon. Hope this whole town gets back to normal soon, if ya know what I mean. For the record, you guys go play ball in the park anytime you want to. You're one of us! They shouldn't be listenin' to trash talk from outside Whitehaven. It ain't right to turn on your own."

The postman slapped Chad's back companionably, and Chad shook his hand. He uttered warm thanks as his friend left, then he turned to look at the label on the first box. It was from a bookstore in Arles.

His breath quickened in excitement as he pulled back the flaps to the wafting smell of newly dyed leather. Inside were expensively bound, collectible versions of some of his favorite classics. He turned to his desk and pressed the button to tell the secretary to hold his calls for half an hour unless there was one from France.

Turning the books over lovingly in his hands, Chad inhaled the scent they bore. The stiff new binding snapped as he opened the front cover of the first one.

He blinked in surprise to see a handsome bookplate printed with a message:

"There's no story like our own, but these shaped who we are.
Those who read mighty books will do mighty things.

Remember, I've always loved you and always will.
Caroline
October 1989."

Chad brushed his arm across his tear-threatened eyes. After the photos of her with the actor yesterday, this assurance of her devotion went a long way. His heart ached to be with her, to tell her in person how much her words and this gift meant to him. He peeked into the next book and found the same bookplate. Caroline must have had each book personalized so he would always remember which ones came from her when she visited France.

Joyfully scooping up the classic volumes by Robert Louis Stevenson and other favorite adventure story authors, he arranged them in a row on the first shelf of a bookcase in his office before opening the next box. He put those on a shelf and opened the last box.

As he was wondering when he would ever have a home again to take them to, he noticed the titles mixed into the box of books for him and grinned. Caroline was restoring a few of her own books, and he cracked open the front covers to see they had no bookplates.

He stacked *Pride and Prejudice*, *Persuasion*, *Anne of Green Gables*, *The Hobbit*, *The Lord of the Rings*, and *The Lion, the Witch, and the Wardrobe* on a side table, brainstorming a personal message he could write in each.

Derrick's spatula clattered on the kitchen counter at the mention of Caroline Painter's name. He bounded to the television as the sports news gave way to the other side of the entertainment world. Now, film clips and publicity photos of a matador filled the screen, and the reporter's voice-over for this prime specimen of manhood proclaimed his reputation as a lover to rich married women.

Groaning loudly in protest, Derrick was riveted to the next photo—a gorgeous publicity shot of Caroline. Then, his eyes popped when the news flashed another photo of her, entranced as the matador kissed her hand.

"Sources on the set tell us that American artist Caroline Painter was discovered by the actor on Monday in Arles, France, when she appeared with her aunt, actress Juliette Painter, on the sidelines of a movie her uncle Cameron Fisher is directing," continued the reporter. "The actor, a trained matador named Alejandro Rafael, was quite taken with the artist, speaking French to communicate love at first sight. Later, he kicked a well-known dancer out of her role with him in a key scene. In a tempest that is part of his character brand, he announced Caroline Painter as his partner. She is not a professional dancer, raising questions as to the nature of their relationship and whether it is the matador or director Cameron Fisher who is in control of the film."

A cozy, blissfully happy publicity photo of Chad and Caroline together flashed as a reporter confirmed Caroline Painter as the wife of Chad Gregory of Gregory Global. It quickly gave way to one of the dashing matador and Caroline, with his dark expression a contained explosion as he shielded her from a fiery-looking dark-haired woman.

The reporter's voice barely concealed his excitement. "Alejandro Rafael and Caroline Painter were confronted by the rejected dancer Baila, who warned the matador that the artist was going to make a fool of him."

Next, a different reporter in Arles stood by an image of a chaotic bullfight scene by Picasso with blood and grotesque body shapes. Smiling, his orotund voice quipped, "In the city where Pablo Picasso enjoyed bullfights as subject matter, this painting seems to describe the mood here on the set."

Derrick collapsed in laughter. When he could speak again, he checked on his dinner in the kitchen, then picked up the phone. He reached Jordan's answering machine. "Jordan, sorry I missed you. Watch the entertainment news tonight. Remember when I told you Caroline would end up entangled in something Chad might need a plane ticket to straighten out? Well, it happened. It might make a good interview. I'll call again later."

Next, he called Chad's mobile phone, which was answered curtly. "Chad, I just saw the news."

He recognized Chad's steel voice. "I'm a little busy right now."

Derrick laughed. "Stay cool. This will all shake out to her good. You should be used to it."

"Yeah, well, you, Joey, and Cole should start a club. You all enjoy remindin' me I deserve what I get for not marryin' an ordinary woman."

"Jordan will help set things straight. She's not like other journalists."

"Are you sayin' this thing with the reporter is for real? We were bettin' you tricked her."

"As far as I'm concerned, it's real, and yes, I tricked her, but she's warmin' up to it. She came to my practice game and pulled for me over the cheating ex-fiancé. It was great watchin' him fall apart and lose the game. She's my secret weapon now."

"You're a sick man, Derrick."

Derrick's delighted laughter filled the phone again. He was having a great evening. "And I own up to it. Hey, don't get on a plane yet, Chad, as if you doubt her. I admit, the look on her face when he kissed her hand was disturbing, but let it play out. This is good TV."

"There's more to it, Derrick. I got a kidnapping threat that didn't specify the target. With her in the spotlight now, everyone knows right where my wife and boys are now. For that matter, the threat could've been for my dad about me and Cole. I learned there was an attempt to take me and Patrick when we were babies, and I didn't know until recently that Global has clients with secrets that people would kidnap and torture for."

Derrick sobered. "Oh, man, Chad! I just got chills. You got a security detail on this?"

"A bodyguard is with Caroline and the boys—hand-picked by Ben, my brother-in-law. Cameron had threats before and already had one for Mia, so they're workin' together right now. I'm watched by the Whitehaven police and Global's security, and I'm never alone off the island. The bodyguard will live with us when my family gets back, and I'm gettin' a trained dog."

Derrick wiped his hand over his face. "You're serious if you'd get a dog. You're not a pet guy. Well, you're all in my prayers, you know you can count on that. Keep me updated and let me know if there's anything I can do."

"I appreciate it, Derrick. Prayers are the best anyone can do for us at this point. It's also important that you keep the kidnapping threat under your hat from your girlfriend for now. I'm not sure when we're going public with that, but as one of my business partners, it was time to tell you in case somethin' happens. I'm livin' on the edge right now."

Chapter Twenty-One

It took me time to understand my waterlilies.
-Claude Monet.

Caroline stepped through the door Azariah opened at the new secret location for her rehearsal. She was grabbed from behind and spun around into a bear hug.

"Jesse! What are you doin' here?" she squealed as her face lit up.

"You're kidding, right? Would Cameron let anyone besides me film you? He made me work around the clock the past two days to finish a job, and I finally got some sleep on the flight here. I had to come in early to control the news hounds when we start capturing this dance."

"Tell me Carly is here!"

Jesse held her at arm's length, shaking his head. "No, I wish she were. Carly needs to be in Whitehaven to help her family. Her dad is overwhelmed with the hurricane cleanup." Then he whistled. "Hey, aren't you a new mother of twins? Look at you!"

"Ha, this is why I made you marry my best friend! You're great with compliments."

They turned back to the room, where Alejandro stood watching with a small smile. "Have you two met?" asked Caroline.

"Only by reputation—for both of us," said Alejandro carefully.

The two men warily shook hands. Jesse said, "I helped break Caroline into film in Mevagissey four years ago, when she accidentally became famous by changing a rock star's life and made it the best trip ever! She taught me far more than I taught her. Then she introduced me to the amazing woman I married, so I owe her more than I can ever repay. I filmed Caroline and Chad's wedding on her own island pier as an action scene in *Sea Spy*. When Caroline goes off script, we just turn her loose to see what happens."

Alejandro raised one eyebrow and half-smiled at Caroline. Then he looked at Jesse. "Are you with us for practice today?"

The two trainers walked past Azariah at the door, and Jesse replied, "Just long enough to see where you're at in the scene and get an idea of the best views to plan for the arena."

Then he looked at Caroline and tilted his head at Alejandro. "Remember, sweetie, he has all the pressure. You are background, like on the pier during the chase scene in the last movie. You've got this. Imagine you're at an Island Summer Dance in the pavilion with Chad."

A dark cloud crossed Caroline's face. "The pier and the pavilion are gone, Jesse," she said with a dangerous catch in her voice. "Everything on island is, except for what's left of the mansion. They're just—memories."

Jesse tucked his forefinger under her chin to turn her stricken face to him. His voice was low, but stern. "Everything that mattered made it off that island."

She burst into tears. Jesse pressed his lips together grimly and pulled her to him, rocking her slightly back and forth like an infant. He gestured to the trainer to begin with Alejandro while he walked Caroline to the far side of the room.

"That's right, just cry it out," he murmured. "I was careless to race in here and catch you off guard like that, reminding you about old times so soon. Unload your pain, Caroline, so you can live without limits."

Alejandro silently came to put a piece of paper in Jesse's hand and returned to his trainer. Jesse glanced over Caroline's back to read it. It was a room number and a note from Alejandro to his masseuse that Caroline would be using his appointment that afternoon.

Reporters trilled into microphones about the activity at Cameron's rented house in France. Caroline Painter's friends were descending on Arles. British artist Dante Kent arrived first, interacting congenially with reporters as he made his way to the front door from a limousine. He told them he was visiting his special friend Caroline Painter while she was next door to Great Britain, and he hoped they would join him when he painted plein air with her.

Shortly afterwards, British rock singer Baker Holmes and his wife arrived with their newborn daughter, telling reporters they wanted to take advantage of a chance to visit Caroline and introduce Stormy Holmes to her new friends Rhett and Rayce Gregory, who shared her birthday.

The house was quiet, and the curtains were drawn all Friday evening. The media had to be content with previews of practice that Jesse fed them. Alejandro was brooding and confident, every inch a matador in solo practice. Jesse released a photo of Caroline working alone with her trainer, conveying the idea that she and Alejandro had little contact.

On Saturday, the house party emerged after dark. The formally dressed group filled limousines on the way to dinner, surrounded by security and ushered into a private room. The press was ecstatic when Alejandro and his security detail unexpectedly arrived to join them. Camera bulbs flashed to catch the handsome actor in a tuxedo, while women openly sighed and agreed to be quoted about how dreamy he was. The actor arrogantly ignored desperate questions about his relationship with Caroline Painter.

"Alejandro Rafael did not confirm or deny that there is romance in the air," one reporter said conspiratorially into a camera. "Only one thing is certain—the matador is not a threat that warrants the formidable background of a Mossad bodyguard, and this over-the-top statement about security raises speculation about why

Chad Gregory of Gregory Global is taking extreme measures to guard his wife."

When limousines escorted everyone home, the reporters dissipated, assuming the house was buttoned down for the evening. Soon, Caroline Painter, Dante Kent, Casey Austin, and the bodyguard swiftly got into another limousine, into which the driver loaded backpacks and easels. Dante had arranged a secret outing to paint plein air at Saint Paul-de-Mausole in Saint-Remy, near where Van Gogh would have had the view for his painting *Starry Night*.

"The other starry night painting you did on the Rhone was perhaps the last of Van Gogh's 'happy' paintings," Dante told the ladies after they set up their easels. "But this view, when he was recovering in 1889, shows that he still had hope, hence, the color yellow glows in the sky and the village windows."

"The scene is different now," Casey observed.

"The view in Vincent's painting was partly invented, which is one of the best things artists do," Dante replied. "They take something ordinary and make it extraordinary. The moon tonight is barely a crescent, but three days ago, it would have been like the crescent in his painting."

"The movement in his sky is exciting for some people, and it may lead the eye around in the painting, but it always makes me feel sad that his world never seemed to stand peacefully still," commented Caroline. "The scene in the village is calm, with the church steeple, but the sky above it seems turbulent. I wonder if it reflected his view of heaven, or God, or faith, or his inner restlessness. The scene is sweeping and evokes wonder at the scope of the stars, but it also confines them. Perhaps he was trying to grasp them, but I prefer feeling an airy, peaceful, infinite depth in the heavens."

Cameron Fisher's house party did not emerge on Sunday, to the disappointment of the new camp of reporters. They saw security guards checking outside from balconies with binoculars, looking for badges in the crowd and speaking on radios about something they apparently found suspicious. The journalists and photographers smelled a story and began scrutinizing those around them, finding that their numbers had thinned by several people none of them remembered meeting.

Baker Holmes' family left for the airport on Monday morning while Cameron took his group to the movie set, stirring confusion by splitting the interests of the reporters. Upon arrival in the arena, Cameron announced that the media were not allowed on the movie set for the rest of the week due to possible unauthorized leaks of the final filming work.

Dante Kent threw the media a bone by inviting the press to join him and Caroline Painter when they painted plein air one evening. The artists would stage their own experience in Van Gogh's footsteps at the café site for his famous painting.

Chad sat in his red Lamborghini Countach with the stereo on, admiring the view from the huge new pavilion parking area. Twilight colors scattered over the Atlantic and made his heart ache for Caroline.

On the other side of that expanse of waves, his wife and boys slept. He felt particularly neglected and lonely today after hearing from his British friend Baker Holmes about how wonderful it was to see his family. He couldn't see his own children, but Baker had. He couldn't comfort Caroline, but Baker had. Baker talked about how she was changing, grieving, struggling, coming to grips with some deep things about her life—and all Chad could do was spend a little rushed time on the phone with her.

With a moody sigh, he reached over to the passenger seat for a package from Baker. The note said it was a tape of a rehearsal for a new song he wrote about the night their children were born and Painter Place endured Hugo.

Chad studied the rock star's handwriting on the cassette label, then pushed it into the tape player. Public Parking band members spoke, introducing the song and adding personal anecdotes to the recording about why it was important to them. Baker strummed some chords on his guitar as he mused, "We know this one won't make the top of the pop charts. It's for people who know who we're talking about—those who walk a narrow road. Few will find it."

Then he launched into the song lyrics.

Words are never enough
Whenever the seas of life grow rough
But never in any tempest
Will You abandon me.
Pain was not in Your plan
The day that Your breath gave life to man
But you let him betray Your heart
And Your perfect world.
When the wild winds buffet
Lord, help me to wait.
When I see nothing else
Help me see you are great,
Breathe on me (breathe on me, breathe on me),
Breathe on me.

Chad's throat ached as he choked up during the rest of the song. Brilliant sky colors evaporated on the horizon of the ocean before him as memories flashed through his mind about the night Hugo ravaged his home, right where his car sat now.

All over again, he was struck with wonder at how his little group had survived that night. He had never questioned miracles and knew he was the beneficiary of one right here on Painter Place. In his heart and mind, time would never dim how astounding their escape had been.

He played the song again, this time thinking of how Caroline must have felt in France when she heard it. Then he swiped trails of tears from his face and glanced back to the mansion, where more lights were coming on inside.

Chad pulled out Baker's cassette and put in one to soothe his raw emotions before he joined everyone for dinner. He settled back and relaxed as Styx cooed "Babe" in the darkness.

There were a million things he wanted to tell Caroline. He wrote many down in the journal she left him, but the rest of them were in his head—things that were theirs, things he wanted no one to accidently read. He closed his eyes and smiled.

The mobile phone made him start when it interrupted his imagination. He saw the number and his heart rate jumped. "Cameron, it must really be late there. Everything okay?"

"More than okay, Chad. Things are terrific! I'm working overtime tonight with Jesse, watching the sequences we filmed today of Caroline as the Matador's Cape."

"It's working out?"

"Chad—she's wonderful! I had to get used to seeing blonde hair instead of Baila's black hair. But it's better. Her fairness adds a contrast to his darkness, and it helps her become background with the sand colors of the arena. It focuses the viewer on the cape movements of her costume. Alejandro was right on target with the changes and brilliant in his performance."

Relaxing and sitting back, Chad closed his eyes to imagine Caroline again. "That's my girl," he murmured.

"Jesse will tell you more while I try to wrap up here."

Jesse took the phone and asked if Chad could work out a flight the following week and bring Carly in with him to attend a cast party as the filming wrapped up. Alejandro and Caroline were performing the Matador's Cape to kick off the party, as an insider preview, and he could watch it without her knowing. Chad could surprise Caroline and escort her home.

Chad felt a rush of hope and excitement. "I'll see what I can do."

"Get over here. It's great on film, but you'll never forget seeing her do this live, if you can take your eyes off the matador's performance."

On Saturday evening, Dante alerted the media that he and Caroline would be painting their versions of Van Gogh's view in *Café Terrace at Night.* When the starry sky overhead was dark, the café awning glowed with light.

The two artists painted the big shapes of the scene on their canvases. Using small pictures of Van Gogh's 1888 version taped to their easels, they tried to capture his spirit of the setting. Chunks of time were designated to paint, then Dante took breaks for questions. Curious bystanders and tourists created a crowd.

Some onlookers simply gawked at Dante Kent's elegant wolfish appearance rather than his art, speculating among themselves about which movie with a castle they saw him in. Caroline clamped her lips tight to keep from laughing when Dante gave her a sidelong look and smirked. She had stared at him the first time she met him, then tried to cover her rudeness with the lame comment that he reminded her of someone. The British artist had smiled and asked if it was the Big Bad Wolf.

Artists were an interesting and challenging group to be around, she knew firsthand. But Dante was one of the most approachable, easy-going, unpretentious people she had ever met. For him to show up at her Uncle Wyeth's request was a testimony to his close decades-long bond with her uncle. His presence as a business partnership with Caroline and the Painter Galleries was proof to the media that she had no time or opportunity for dalliances with a dashing matador.

Dante had never married and had an heir to his ancestral estate, which did have a small castle on it. But she was playing matchmaker for him to meet Chad and Phillip's secretary in London when he returned home.

During the first painting break for questions, Caroline was asked what appealed to her about Van Gogh's painting of the café scene. She replied that it was full of the light and peace that the artist sought all his life. The warm glow under the awning suggested a haven and imagining the warmth of a cup of chocolate there was comforting.

The next question was for Dante. A reporter asked, "Are you glad this was a coffee shop? It's well known that you and the Painters don't drink wine."

Dante's black brows shot up, but he had a reputation against drinking alcohol and was ready with responses in public. "It wouldn't have mattered what the patrons were drinking. I simply liked the view enough to paint it. I have artistic license to leave out anything I wish in my compositions. Have you ever seen Van Gogh's painting *Night Café*?"

Most looked bewildered and jotted down the name, but a few nodded. "It's the opposite of this wonderful scene in the coffee shop. It records the ugly truth about alcohol, in garish light. In *Night Café*, there are drunks lying face down on tables. It's a shame that people deaden their God-given senses instead of embracing them as gifts in the scope of life's joy and pain. Their minds, muscles, and tongues will be loose. They will lose their manners along with the control of their motor functions, making non-drinking people around them uncomfortable and in harm's way. But they care nothing for the welfare of those around them and will insist on their personal right to infringe on the rights of others. They will do things they'll regret the rest of their lives. Some will be ruined, and many will become controlled by the next drink."

Another reporter blurted, "But you're a Christian. Isn't it true that Jesus turned water into wine? That crowd was 'well-drunk' after a wedding."

Dante studied the man. Caroline held her breath, wondering if the artist's wolfish elegance would come off as arrogant and cold about his faith and convictions.

But Dante's gaze softened, and he replied mildly, "This is an outing to promote the art and history of Arles. But please call my agent tomorrow. I'll be glad to sit down with you to discuss my convictions about alcohol throughout scripture. To address your public assertion about Jesus, however, it's appropriate for me to respond publicly. So, I ask, are you stating that He would create a way to sin? For the Bible continually teaches against the sin of drunkenness, and the scenario you propose would show God contradicting Himself. Scripture says that's impossible. Therefore, if Jesus created the kind of drink you assume that He created—our modern idea of strong wine—wouldn't that be as if He were in a bar and bought drinks for people who'd already had too much? Wouldn't that be unscriptural?"

Dante paused, putting his paint brush in the water jar next to him while the reporters murmured among themselves. He looked up and said, "The word for wine in scripture does not always mean alcohol, but also refers to juice, and to using wine in water to purify it. The Biblical passage not to even 'look at the wine while it is red' would be a warning against wine as alcohol, undiluted, retaining its red color. Looking long at it is the first step to consuming it. That's the way most of our sin begins, isn't it? Azariah, tell reporters what is cleaned out of Jewish homes during Passover, inspiring our term 'spring cleaning.'"

The bodyguard answered, "Leavening. Biblically, it's associated with sin, so we clean it away. The unleavened bread of Passover represents Christ's sinless body, so it would be a contradiction to drink leavened—fermented—grape juice turned to alcohol to represent His blood."

The reporters and the crowd either stood open-mouthed or buzzed to one another. Dante calmly announced that the break was over, and he turned to resume painting.

A reporter asked Azariah if he had the same convictions about alcohol. The bodyguard looked at him levelly. "Yes. I believe Jesus turns water into wine all over the world in vineyards, where the showers from the heavens get soaked into grape vines and they produce health-giving fruit. Every part of our body serves a purpose and function, including our ability to think and react, and impeding those functions with alcohol intentionally works against God's purpose for our well-being. I would add that apart from any religion, merely on a professional or life lesson level, if you never take a drink, you never lose your head. Other people's lives depend on me being the best I can be."

Chapter Twenty-Two

I've lived through some terrible things in my life,
some of which actually happened.
-Mark Twain

It was the first day of November. Chad had a hard time writing down the date all day, marveling that the holidays were almost here. Tonight, he would jot it at the top of the last entry in the journal he kept for Caroline.

When he thumbed back to the beginning, he was sure he had never been so transparent in his entire life. It was one thing to speak these things to her but proclaiming them on paper made him vulnerable. And that was exactly why he expected her to cherish it.

Chad inhaled the new scent of the Jeep Cherokee as he pulled onto the repaired causeway bridge. The insurance settlement on the destroyed Cherokee, Porsche, and Mustang sent him car shopping this week. He tried out the volume on the new speakers, and lyrics about taking care of business and working overtime made him smile.

His own overtime rolled into his day job recently when he sold his side business to his dad. The Young Guns, as it was affectionately referred to, was officially part of Gregory Global now.

Dad's right to demand my entire focus, Chad thought as he crested the bridge. Phillip paid Chad off the charts more than anyone in his position with competitors—not because he was his son, but because he had the attention of the financial world and it reflected on the company.

He pulled into an empty parking space and heard laughter ring out from open windows. Anticipation surged in his heart at scooping Noble into his arms and seeing Natalie again. Savanna Painter traveled home with them, and when he could talk about it, she would want his first-hand account about what happened in her bedroom suite on the night her great-grandsons were born during Hurricane Hugo.

Caroline's grandmother must have been stunned at the condition of her home and the island. But there were silver linings and blessings tucked away all over the place, such as the doll she gave Caroline as a little girl. On the spiraling marble staircase in the heart of the mansion, Gran Vanna had overheard young Caroline assuring this doll that they had no fear of storms at Painter Place, because God was here. Beloved Sabrina had survived Hugo. Valerie found the doll in the rubble of Andy's house and repaired her as best she could, making a new dress for her out of similar fabric. Now, Sabrina sat on the bookcase in Gran Vanna's room.

Savanna would remain on the island to manage the work while everyone else headed to Charleston to catch the secure private flight his dad chartered to France. Since he was paying for a plane, he wanted to fill it with anyone who wanted to go.

On Friday afternoon, Chad was in emotional overload. Rhett and Rayce could hold their heads up and were very social, smiling and reaching for him when he talked to them. They stared at him unabashedly with the familiar Painter blue eyes. When others in the family held whichever baby was not in his arms, the baby would turn to Chad's voice as he spoke.

When they arrived at the arena for the party, Jesse whirled Carly off the ground for a long hug and a kiss full of missing her. He escorted them with their armloads of roses to seats with a good view of Caroline.

They had barely decided on seats among them when the bullfighter stepped into the arena and walked over to a stereo. Chad stifled a groan, and Cole, Patrick, Joey, and his dad all turned to him with raised eyebrows. Even his mom joined the other females in their group who exchanged wide-eyed glances at one another. Patrick lightly slapped Natalie's leg to divert her stare and scowled comically at her.

The actor practiced some strong, fascinating poses in the first two verses of the song "Amanda." Chad gulped. That was Caroline's middle name! Did it mean something to the actor?

Then a movement caught Chad's eye. *Caroline!*

She seemed to float to the actor, who took her smoothly into his arms for some practice turns. Her endless skirt whirled from her hips, flashing one long leg through a slit when the actor guided her into the deepest dip Chad had ever seen. Her arms were overhead, her chin held high to reveal the column of her neck to best advantage, and her hands were posed.

It was a move of complete trust in the matador to hold her, designed to heighten suspense. It worked. Everyone in the family gasped, and the lead singer in the music sang about not wanting to lose Amanda.

Upright again, Alejandro circled Caroline, dragging a lingering hand around her waist—her slender waist, not the post-baby waist Chad remembered from six weeks ago. Then she followed him into a swift lunge, and they pressed their hands together.

The matador's face was cheek to cheek with hers. Cole snorted and Joey leaned forward, wide-eyed as he looked down the aisle at Chad and Patrick. They never learned moves like this in cotillions or dance lessons in the ballroom at the Big House while growing up. The actor was like a magician, pulling Caroline's fluid skirt to make it flutter like a matador's cape. She responded instantly to his confident touch.

Juliette came up to sit behind Chad and Camellia just as Cameron beckoned the dancing couple. Men brought out a magnificent white horse in beautiful gear to the edge of the arena.

"They'll be takin' Caroline and Alejandro for their entrance," Juliette explained. "The remaining cast and crew will be allowed to come in to see the performance before everyone mingles for the party. Baila left as soon as her part was over this week, so there shouldn't be any awkward moments to mar your reunion."

Caroline was being escorted off the floor on Alejandro's arm, and Chad listened to Juliette over his shoulder while studying his wife's costume. It would have been strapless except for jeweled ribbons the color of her skin that encircled her upper arms, decorated with what appeared at this distance to be single red rosettes in the center. A glittering black ribbon and rosette circled her neck, and a rosette decorated a comb that pulled back one side of her long blonde hair. The gown was shimmery black, form-fitting until it reached just below her waist, barely creating an hourglass curve before falling into folds that seemed too sleek to extend as far as they did in Alejandro's hands. Her shoes were the color of her skin, as if she were barefoot.

Cameron spoke to the cast as the crowd grew. The lights in the arena faded to let the inky darkness overtake all but the spotlight.

Chad's stomach fluttered like Caroline's skirt in Alejandro's hands. The matador sat on the back of the decorated horse, with Caroline walking beside him in measured steps. She now wore a feathery-light shawl with long fringe to match the horse's mane. Her arm was outstretched to hold one side of the brim of his hat, while he held the other side.

Music filled the arena, like the well-known "Bullfighter's Song". It had a marching beat, triumphant and exciting, stirring anticipation. The matador slid off the horse without taking his hand from the connection to Caroline, pulling her slowly closer until their torsos touched the hat between them, facing one another and pausing. Both extended only the toe of one shoe to their side, tracing a half circle on the ground toward their backs. With a snap, he took the hat from her, and she whirled away, sending the fringe of the shawl fluttering around her before she smoothly floated it to the ground.

The horse was unobtrusively led away. Caroline became the background, sometimes remaining still and sometimes moving fluidly.

Alejandro began a solo dance of moves used to maneuver a raging bull. The effect was so mesmerizing that Chad forgot to look for his wife. The matador followed a change in the music that seemed to become more like a combination of "Classical Gas" with bridges of "The Lonely Bull."

Then he grasped Caroline, and they flowed into some of the turns Chad saw them practice earlier. At one point, Caroline froze gracefully like a statue, her head dramatically profiled like the snap in a tango.

The matador, looking at the crowd instead of at her, ran his hand around her waist once before snapping his hand to her skirt without a glance. He went to his knees beside her as if waiting for a bull to brush his suit of lights as it charged past him. The skirt flashed red, and everyone gasped with applause as they imagined a bull charging through it.

Chad's chest felt like it would explode with pride as Caroline posed calmly while Alejandro made a few more breathtaking moves with her skirt as a cape in an all-out bullfight. As the dance concluded, the matador let go of the 'cape' to hold Caroline's face in his hands for a moment, then sent her into the plunging, dramatic tango dip.

On the edge of his seat, Chad watched Caroline hold the pose, her body in a beautiful line with her arms and hands posed over her head. The music ended, and everyone erupted in applause and whistles. Alejandro continued to hold Caroline in the dip, an interpretive sign of conquering strength in the arena, and the crowd reacted as if it was an encore.

The Painter and Gregory group were on their feet in applause and cheers. Chad marveled at the strength it took for Alejandro to hold a woman Caroline's height for so long. Finally, as if in slow motion, the bullfighter raised Caroline back up, and they held hands and bowed as one entity to the crowd.

The cast applauded and whistled enthusiastically. In the distraction, Juliette quickly moved her family group down to the sideline in the shadows to wait.

Alejandro gestured for Cameron to come stand beside Caroline, then pointed at them while he applauded. The cast and crew took his cue, and when they quieted, he raised his hand to speak.

"My respect for Cameron Fisher made him the only director I would work with in this movie. He is a man of faith and honor, and it is my fault that he wears more gray in his hair than when we began. It was a distinct privilege to work with him. And his niece, Caroline—what can I say?" He turned to face her. "You have been God's answer to prayer at just the time I needed you."

She blushed demurely and he turned to the cast again. "Thank you, everyone, for your creative efforts and hard work. A film is only as good as the contribution of everyone involved in it." The actor pointed to the cast and began applauding appreciatively, whistling at them, and they joined him.

As they quieted again, he cleared his throat. "There is someone here tonight who did me the honor of traveling a long way to attend. Amanda, will you join me so I can introduce you?"

A young and pretty blonde woman with a short fashion-model hairstyle and a gown the color of his suit covered her mouth with both hands. She recovered enough to walk up to join him.

The matador got down on one knee with a ring that flashed in the pale-yellow spotlight bathing the couple. "Amanda, I can face a raging bull fearlessly, but this takes all the courage I have. I am at your mercy in front of everyone here. I want to go through my life with you at my side. Te quiero siempre. Please marry me."

The young woman was unable to speak through a choking sob. She merely nodded, and he put his ring on her finger before standing to hold her against the suit of light. The cast cheered and buzzed with excitement at this unexpected event, and Juliette walked out to the spotlight to take Cameron's hand.

Cameron got the attention of the cast and congratulated Amanda and Alejandro. "This is a great time for an engagement party, and we have more to celebrate tonight. Caroline, Juliette, and I haven't seen our American family in six weeks. Please join our reunion!"

The spotlight shifted to the sidelines. But Chad barely heard the cheers. His eyes met his wife's, and she froze in disbelief. He knew she was asking herself if this was real, and he watched her go through the phases of accepting that he was not a dream.

Wait for it, he kept telling himself as he tried not to run to her. And there it was. The look.

He was unsure how, but he reached her. "Did you save your heart for me?"

"Always, just like I promised," she blurted back.

Cameron introduced Chad as Caroline's husband while Jesse and one of the film crew quickly came out with bundles of red roses and baby's breath. The cast waited, spellbound, when his arms were full of flowers.

Chad heard his own deep Southern drawl echoing in the acoustics of the ancient arena. "This isn't the only place you've been dancin', Caroline. There's a rose here for every day we've been apart—forty days and nights—and they represent you as the star of my dreams. The baby's breath is for the twins you gave me, who also filled my dreams. I've always loved you, and I can't wait to get you home. We'll start over at Painter Place, buildin' a new life together."

Caroline's eyes swam as she reached up to put her hand on his face, mouthing that she loved him. The cast was sighing, oohing, whistling, and clapping.

The party began with a spotlight dance for Alejandro and Amanda to honor their engagement. Caroline pulled Chad along to reunite with her family and introduce him to Azariah. When their dance was over, Alejandro and Amanda came over to meet the American families.

While Chad and Alejandro respectfully sized one another up, Amanda warmly smiled at Caroline. "It was no coincidence that you were here while Ali was making this movie," she said in a British accent. "Ali and I had broken up again. I couldn't give any more years of my life to his career without a wedding. You brought us together."

Caroline reached out to hug her. "God brought you together. All I did was watch Him prove to me that He's still working. Congratulations on your engagement."

Chad and Alejandro shook hands and exchanged comments about Caroline's participation in the dance. The actor said he learned to expect serendipity, and that life with her must be fascinating.

"You have no idea," Chad said with a smirk that Alejandro appreciated in an exchanged look. Then he reached for his wife's hand and said, "Dance with me."

The romantic tune of "Ladyfingers" filled the arena, and Chad finally felt the rightness of holding Caroline again. He closed his eyes and rubbed his cheek in her hair as the music box sound of the song flowed into a sweet, mewing sound. When he opened his eyes again, he met Alejandro's gaze as he watched them.

"You're actually here," Caroline whispered into his ear. "You came for me."

"Don't ever leave again," he whispered back. "I'm nothing without you. Ask anyone who has endured being around me lately. You're the best half of us."

She pulled back to look him in the face. "Talking like that will get you brownie points until the end of the decade, Mr. Gregory III."

"That's only a few weeks from now, my dear," he said in his best Rhett Butler imitation. "I have some things stored up to say that should earn brownie points far into the next decade. How long before we can leave?"

She laughed, and it was the sound that teased his mind the last six weeks. The extraordinary sparkle in her eyes was back. "We'll have to walk if we don't wait for everyone else. Azariah might ask for a raise if you're goin' rogue like this often."

"It's not far," his voice trailed off. He glanced to the side of the arena. "Let's at least get away from the crowd." Taking her hand in his firm grasp, he led her off the floor and found an open door to a hallway in shadows.

"So, you're recklessly goin' to test Azariah's nerves—" Caroline's teasing warning was cut short with missed kisses as Chad started to catch them up.

They were both breathless when they were quickly interrupted by a couple from the movie cast with the same intentions. The couple found a place not far away in the shadows.

Chad's life had been bursting at the seams with too many people ever since Hugo ravaged his life. He groaned a little in frustration, running his hand down his wife's arm. His hand reached for hers and he put it to his lips.

Caroline pushed away from the wall and kept his hand, leading him further away from the other couple and around a corner. She nudged him back against the wall, leaning into his side and tiptoeing to kiss his neck, inhaling his cologne.

"Drakkar Noir," she breathed.

His skin tingled and a quiver swept over him. "Mmmhmm—just so you'd mention it. You make it sound like you're sayin' somethin' you shouldn't."

"'Black dragon ship'... the name stirs my imagination. It sounds and smells like an adventure."

"I'm a big fan of your stirrings, imagination, and adventures, so run with that," his deep voice drawled. "Speakin' of black dragons, do you get to keep this dress?"

She ran a finger over his tuxedo jacket lapel. "I'm glad you like it," she whispered. "But I'll have to ask Cameron about that. It's goin' to be too large anyway if I can ever manage to get to my former size."

"Then you could wear it again after you have Savanna Caroline," he whispered. "We'll both feel like dancin'."

She sighed playfully and pushed his blonde hair from his brow. "I haven't agreed yet."

"That reminds me," he said, reaching into his jacket pocket. "Hold out your hand."

She obeyed, and he placed something in it. He met her eyes a moment before uncovering her hand.

Caroline blinked and scowled. "It's a lot smaller than it looked in the magazine. Did it come with the miniature guy modeling with it?"

Chad looked up at the ceiling, biting his lip. "I know it's small, but you gave me something small, too. Rhett and Rayce were like bags of sugar in Maggie's Jane's pantry."

She turned the yellow Hot Wheels Ferrari over in her hand doubtfully. He said, "If you're still lookin' for the guy, he's not in there. I decided to make sure you won't miss him." Then he pivoted in one easy move to be in front of her again, pinning her between where his hands pressed against the wall. He went for an ardent kiss.

A few minutes later, he led her back around to the party and pulled her toward the door through which he remembered arriving. His eyes scanned the dance floor for Cole, Patrick, or Joey. He signaled Patrick, who laughed, mouthing "bodyguard."

Chad rolled his eyes but glanced around to find Azariah watching alertly. It was obvious the guy had known where they were every second, and this was going to take some getting used to. He tilted his head toward the door, and the bodyguard moved that direction.

They were barely through when he saw another shadowed recess in the wall. He impulsively pulled her there for another kiss, whispering, "When we get to the house, I'm goin' to forget to tell you some of the things I've been savin' up, so I'll get started on the way." He launched into the best one.

Azariah followed discreetly as the couple made their way along the few blocks to the house. He scanned for anything unusual in the passers-by. Caroline pulled Chad over into another shadowy space and whispered something that earned her a spirited kiss. The bodyguard sighed and glanced around. The street was too open for him to cover everything.

His earpiece blurted, making him jump. "Azariah! I've got activity here. Are you still in the arena?"

The bodyguard tensed and answered, keeping his voice low. "I'm following Chad and Caroline back to the house. We're a block away. This had better be legitimate activity. We need a bucket brigade for this fire."

The other bodyguard chuckled. "Yeah, well, I warned you some Southern Belles like their sweet tea hot. Hurry up and get here. I had the nanny lock herself in the nursery with a gun, and I'm investigating. Someone was around the windows in the back, and now they've knocked out the streetlight. At least two men, one medium height and one big guy."

"Want me to call it in while I'm on my way?" Azariah asked, jogging toward Chad and Caroline as they walked along the street in view of the house. Chad had whisked off his dinner jacket and draped it around her shoulders before he pulled her tightly to him.

The blaring security alarm sounded like stereo from inside Azariah's earphone and in the outside air. Chad and Caroline turned startled looks at Cameron's house and quickly back at Azariah for confirmation.

"Get over here, *now*!" shouted Mia's bodyguard into his ear. "I've unlocked the front door for you and alerted police!"

Chad was already running, shouting for Caroline to listen to Azariah. She looked desperately from her husband's back to the bodyguard, slipping her costume dance shoes off. Azariah grabbed her arm, and they ran to the open front door.

"Call Cameron!" Azariah commanded just as the alarm went silent. Caroline grabbed the phone, and the lights went out. "The line's dead!" she shouted.

The bodyguard had efficiently cleared the room and gone to the next one. The sight of him pointing a gun set her teeth on edge. He returned to go upstairs, gesturing to a small half bathroom under the stairway. "Lock the door. Don't stand in front of it."

She nodded just as Chad's voice shouted upstairs, threatening to kill someone. She heard the conviction in his voice. Now she understood what people meant when they said their blood ran cold. Gunshots exploded upstairs and sirens blared on the street before she could fully close and lock the powder room door.

Caroline slid to the floor in the complete darkness of the small bathroom, both hands clamped tightly over her mouth to stifle her screams. She shook violently with adrenaline and desperate prayers, torn between her instinct to run to the twins or to obey Chad and Azariah.

Hugo had taken Painter Place. Someone in the dark upstairs could take her husband and children.

Phillip tore through the crowd outside Cameron's rented house in Arles. Lights flashed on police vehicles and reporters gathered in an energetic throng. He made it almost to the front door before a French policeman attempted to stop him.

"My son's in there—I'm Phillip Gregory. You can't hold me back." The blunt authority in his voice proclaimed he was used to getting his way, and he boldly pushed against the officer's arm. He broke through while the officer quickly spoke French into a radio.

Patrick Painter, his dad, and Cameron ran up to the officer next, shouting that their children were inside. The officer relented, but Wyeth, Cole, and Joey had less success. They waited outside for the ladies to arrive in a car from the arena.

Phillip rushed into the living room to find Chad. His stomach clenched when he saw smears of blood marring his white dress shirt. Caroline's face was composed as she sat beside him on the sofa, but the way she nervously laced her fingers in and out of his hand betrayed her. Two officers stood in front of him, asking for details.

Phillip quickly crossed the room to sit on the other side of Chad, investigating the blood coming down his son's collar from the back of his head and the swollen bruise on his hand. "I'm okay, Dad," Chad assured him. "But he got away. He said he'd come back."

Phillip scowled and watched Chad's face. He was shaken up, but clear-headed. One of the officers asked in a heavy French accent, "Mr. Gregory, you've told us how you came to be here at Mr. Fisher's house. Now tell us your version of shooting the intruder. Begin with what happened up the stairs."

"I saw the security guard fightin' with a big man dressed in black before the lights went out. The bodyguard shouted my name as he kicked the guy's hand. A gun slid across the floor."

"The gun you gave us when we arrived?" asked the officer who was taking notes. "It is not your personal firearm?"

"No, I didn't travel with mine," Chad said. "I shot the second man with the one belonging to the big guy."

"So, you own a gun and are trained to handle it?" asked the other officer.

"Yes, I have a collection, but they're at home in the States."

The officers nodded. One recorded information and the other asked Chad to continue. "I grabbed the gun from the floor while my eyes adjusted to the darkness. There was enough light through the windows to help me see the archway of the hall where the bedrooms are, and I shouted to the nanny that I was there. But another guy heard and came in after me off the balcony, pushing me back into the bookcase. That's when I hit my head. I was a little stunned, but I held on to the gun. I don't think he knew I had it. He laughed, sayin' he'd been sent for mere silver and found gold. He said—"

Chad's voice broke and he wiped his hand over his face, collecting himself. "He said—" he opened his mouth, forming words as if trying them out. "He said, if I'd leave with him, he wouldn't come back for my wife and kids."

Phillip inhaled a sharp breath. Andy Painter gasped from nearby, then covered his face with his hands. Chad swallowed. "I shouted for him to stay away from my family, or I'd kill him, then everything seemed to happen at once, so I might mix the sequence up. He cursed and tried to grab me. I turned out of his reach, and a shot flashed in the darkness from where the bodyguard was still fighting the big guy. The other one took a shot at me, too, but someone pushed me out of the way. I stumbled, heading back toward the arch where the nursery is. The guard was down, and I realized Azariah was goin' to help him. The man who shot him ran out to the balcony when he saw Azariah. I turned to the other man and saw he had his gun locked on me, so I—I pulled the trigger to hit his right arm. Dad always taught me to hit the shooting arm first, and I got him. He cried out and cursed again, then disappeared into the darkness, shooting wildly at Azariah with his other hand. I felt dizzy so I leaned against the wall in the hallway and slid down to the floor, hopin' Azariah could catch him. The kids were all cryin', so I called to the nanny that everything was okay. Azariah was suddenly there to check on me and he told the nanny it was all clear to open the door. Then I heard the police shouting in the house."

One officer stopped jotting down notes and furrowed his brow. "Sir, are you saying there was someone upstairs besides you, the security guards, and the two intruders? Who pushed you out of the way of the bullet?"

Chad looked bewildered for only an instant before he answered. "I don't know. But I've played contact sports all my life, and I know when I'm pushed."

The officers glanced at one another furtively. Phillip watched their doubtful expressions and asked, "Is there a bullet hole where he said the intruder shot at him?"

One officer nodded. "Yes, sir, but everyone is accounted for who was in the house. There was no one here to push Mr. Gregory out of the way."

The other officer said in a gentler tone, "Look, Mr. Gregory took a hard hit on the head. It needs to be seen to. The medical team has Mr. Fisher's bodyguard stabilized, and they can look at Mr. Gregory now. He reports feeling dizzy, and I'm sure that accounts for the sensation of being pushed, but we will make a note."

"Have the intruders been located yet?" asked Andy Painter from behind them.

"No sir, but all medical facilities have been alerted because they sustained injuries. Would you like me to make a statement to the press?"

Andy and Phillip looked meaningfully at one another for a moment. Andy nodded and Phillip said to the officer, "Before you do, I have to tell you something. It's important to your investigation. The press will begin rumors and speculation, so it's time for you to just put the facts out. This isn't the first time Chad has been a target, and we recently had a threatening letter sent to our office in the States."

Casey had a nursing assignment. She would watch Chad all night for signs of trouble with his head injury. She set her clock to get up and check on him and keep paperwork for the physician. The upside was that Chad could feed the boys on night duty, if someone else brought them down the stairs and he sat in a chair when holding them. Cameron's bodyguard was recovering from surgery in the hospital, and two French officers were stationed outside so Azariah could sleep.

Caroline dozed off on a sofa but awakened sleepily to see Chad with one of the twins. He sat in a yellow upholstered chair near the dining room, and Patrick held the other twin as he slowly paced, rocking his upper body side to side with a bottle held in the baby's mouth. Her brother was talking in hushed tones, as if telling the baby secrets, and the twin stared at him with nearly identical Painter blue eyes.

Chad's eyelids were closed as his baby's face rested against his shoulder. He gently rubbed his bruised hand in circles across the twin's back. "I'm never goin' to let anyone take you," he promised huskily. A tear slipped down his face, and Caroline's throat tightened. The baby gurgled and held his head up at his dad's voice.

With a sniff, Chad looked down at him, shifting his son to rest in his arms. The twin reached for Chad's mouth, instigating a smile. The baby copied him.

Chad glanced over at Caroline, expecting her to be asleep, and his eyes lingered when he found her watching him. He wiped the drying tear from his cheek and smiled again. "Everything's goin' to be okay," he drawled. "We have angels lookin' over us."

PART THREE

Seimpre
(Always)

Chapter Twenty-Three

"There are far better things ahead than any we leave behind."
- C.S. Lewis

"Hugo changed Whitehaven forever," said the mayor. "Some sold out instead of rebuilding, and two developers are plannin' to give us a war over gettin' vacation condominiums built by the waterway. That may lead to a fight for bars and entertainment. City council is scrambling to talk to other coastal towns that keep a family atmosphere. I'm goin' to cut right to the chase. A seat on the city council is vacant due to an illness, and we need at least one of you to accept an appointment to fill it."

He looked over the room, where he had gathered Phillip, Wyeth, Andy, and Savanna. Sterling stood at the door, volunteering duty as a security guard.

"Savanna, it would be a gentler influence if you'd consider," pleaded the mayor. "You helped Noble back in the day, and both the boys when they served. You know how this works. And it might keep the talk down."

Wyeth snorted, his brother Andy huffed, and Phillip smirked, all reminded of the gossip against them in town. The mayor sighed and lifted a hand from the table.

"I know. The discontents have no clue about what it means to own anything, how business works, or how to see past tomorrow. But the gossip that really sticks in my craw is the one about Andy. They speculate he resuscitated the man who blew up the bridge and stranded his family all for media attention to raise money for Painter Place. Then he and his father-in-law Tony put the guy through rehab just so Andy could hire him at the marina to get a big humanitarian story against the evils of alcohol and drive traffic to his business."

"What would they have done—let the guy die?" spurted Andy. "I can't handle all the business I already have—that's why I hired the captain! Painters can't do anything for anybody now without raisin' suspicion about our motives. What's gotten into everybody? We aren't any different than we've always been!"

"I haven't gotten over the incident in the park with the boys," interjected Sterling as he leaned on the doorframe. "From that handful of bullies, there's an 'us' and 'them' mentality that never used to exist here. When you add all the comments from the outsiders who are only here to make money on cleanup, and those who are bitter and need someone to bash over their storm losses, I'm seein' outlandish snobbery against the Painters and Gregorys. Yet, they point at you as bein' the snobs. As for Chad—" Sterling shook his head and chuckled. "Well, they don't know what to make of him. The ladies wanna kiss 'im, the guys wanna kill 'im, and those who want 'im to make a big mistake still sit salivating. But they've all got one thing in common—they wanna *be* him."

The room was quiet as everyone reflected on this observation. Phillip said solemnly, "They'd better stay out of his way right now. Everything he touches is turnin' gold, tangible and intangible."

"Narrow escapes from death twice in six weeks has changed him," agreed Savanna, her Georgia drawl resonating as its softness seemed to round off all the hard edges of the room. "The police in France may dismiss his account of bein' pushed out of the way of a bullet a few days ago, but I agree with him that it was divine intervention. Caroline's changed, too. She's off the leash that bound her up after my Noble died. Facing the worst that night in France broke her free. She's only twenty-four, yet she's ready for a new vision at Painter Place, and that's not all. She's goin' to hit the art world as a bold up-and-coming leader now. The boost in Arles from Dante

Kent and the movie role helped, but now she's writing an article and an illustrated book of her observations about Vincent Van Gogh. It will be unique in the market because of her Christian perspective. What does it matter to her if she faces criticism for her views? Bring it on! She survived havin' twins in a hurricane that should have killed them all, and the kidnappers were foiled as they tried to kill her husband and take her children."

Andy nodded. "When she left, she was defeated, broken. She came back with her head up and conviction in her heart. She's the driving force the new Painter Place needs."

Phillip laughed. "The look on her face when Chad took the cover off the Ferrari was priceless. She thought the Matchbox version was all she got unless she had another baby."

From the doorway, Sterling grinned. "I can't wait to pull her over as if she'd been speedin'. She'll probably dare me to cuff her and take her to the station. I'll write her a creative ticket to let Chad win ten ping-pong games at the community center in front of everybody."

The mayor laughed with them and reached out to touch Savanna's hand. "Can she and the other ladies smooth the rough edges on your family's reputation around town right now? The editor at the paper says Juliette's workin' with a journalist from Charlotte for some interviews about Painter Place and the recovery. Will you consider playin' up the emotional side of the losses endured by the Painter women and Camellia?"

"I'll propose this to them and let you know. Juliette will be brilliant at orchestrating the interviews, Chrissy's forte is the role of elegant ambassador, and Camellia's the one in the group who owns every crowd she appears in. Valerie's the approachable warmth that makes people feel she understands them."

The mayor leaned forward, clasping his hands on the table. He looked directly into Savanna's eyes. "The interviews about you by that journalist—Miss Jordan, I think her name is—have been perfect timing. Promise me you'll pray about the appointment to the city council."

A card table was transformed into an elegant romantic dinner setting beside the wall of glass in Chad's office. The inviting glow of lights from the mansion in Painter Place beckoned everyone home from work, but Caroline and Chad planned several evenings here during her first week back home.

The glow of a single lamp created a romantic ambiance in the spotless office, but otherwise, it oozed masculinity. A pair of huge nautical paintings by Caroline's grandfather hung above twin oversized blue leather sofas, complementing the deep contrasts of natural beach and ocean colors in the room. One of Wyeth's largest works was of his catamaran, the *Artistic License*, and it hung over a beautiful chest that deceptively housed a filing system in perfect order.

Saved from the cottage before the hurricane, *Tall Ships and Sunflowers* was now part of a grouping of Caroline's homeless paintings on the wall behind Chad's massive desk. The strong lines of the natural wood he worked at were softened by the images behind it. His valuable tall ship collection graced a large bookcase, where the new books from France were arranged by leather binding colors in descending heights.

Caroline saw hers stacked separately on a table. While he went to change into jeans and a polo shirt, she picked up the one on top. On the inside cover was a hand-written note in his strong, bold style.

"Fiction or reality, it's all the same.
You've always been my fantasy.
Your knight in shining armor,
Chad
November 1989"

Biting her lip, she ran her fingers over the ink. She opened the next one and saw the same message. He had written in each one.

Slowly setting the book back down on top of the neat stack, she fought the urge to arrange it off-kilter for an artistic effect that would drive him nuts. Instead, she went to his stereo system. On top was a cassette labeled *Songs for Caroline 1989*. With a smile, she put it in. A haunting melody would soon be followed by the chorus, "I've been waiting for a girl like you to come into my life."

Closing her eyes and sighing, Caroline let the music touch that deep place inside her that appreciated beauty. She felt swept along as if carried by water, and imagined colors blending to the song's powerfully intimate mood.

Chad reached around her from behind, holding a bouquet of sunflowers out in front of her. He pushed her hair from her neck with his nose to plant a kiss in a little spot he knew. He swayed as if they were slow dancing, taking her arm to turn her for a kiss before he murmured, "Want to put those in a vase? I'd like access to both your arms."

"You read my mind," she said and kissed a little spot she knew below his ear. He caught his breath, and she turned with a smile to carry the bouquet to one of the vases he sent to her in France.

She turned around to find him lighting candles in two unusual antique candlesticks she assumed were purchased by his secretary in London. He carefully carried them to the little card table and strode back to his desk to pick up his leather journal.

"My thoughts and notes while you were gone," he announced, presenting it to her. "Maybe you can read one entry a day until Christmas."

"You've filled the whole thing already?" Caroline hugged the journal. A waft of his cologne mixed with the scent of the leather cover, either from him or his handling of the book. "Drakkar Noir..."

Chad groaned. "Vixen. You leave me weak-kneed with your Southern Belle French accent."

Caroline laughed outright, putting down the journal and resting her hands on his shoulders. "Then you'll love my Southern Belle Spanish. I asked Alejandro to teach me how to tell you something. 'Te quiero seimpre.'"

Chad's brows shot up. "Wow, that sounded authentic. You rolled the r's. I remember from high school that 'seimpre' means 'always' because it made me think of you." He leaned closer. "Help me with the rest but do it while nuzzling my ear."

She tiptoed up as he lowered his head, whispering. "Te quiero seimpre. I'll love you always."

Chad took a deep breath, pulling her closer. Music by the band Journey seemed to come from everywhere in the huge office. "Then dance with me," he whispered back.

She whispered, "It's the first time you've ever danced with me in cowboy boots."

He chuckled softly and kissed her forehead. "Does something unexpected happen?"

She leaned back to smile up at him. "If I tell, it won't be unexpected. And by the way, I'm givin' you a pair for your birthday in a few days. If we must live like the Ewings, you have to dress the part."

"As long as you understand that I'm not J.R.," he reminded her as they swayed to the music.

"And you understand I'm not married to him."

"Let's try that tango dip, the one you did with Alejandro," Chad suggested softly as the stereo cooed lyrics about being forever faithful.

Caroline opened her eyes and traced a finger along his lower lip. "But I like our way, Chad. Besides, you'd have to support me on your knee. I'm not holdin' on like I used to."

"It's not just my arm in a dip that you're not holdin' on to anymore. You've learned to let go of the things you mentioned the day before the storm."

She looked startled, then thoughtful. "I did, didn't I?"

A duet came through the speakers, declaring one another to be their first love, their last, their future, and their past. Caroline held out her empty hand, closed it, and slowly opened her fingers so her palm was face up.

"Remember when I wouldn't open my hand for you to take out the rings you gave me, and you pried up one finger after another until the ring was lying there in my open palm? Those rings didn't do me any good while I clutched them in a fist. But when I opened my hand, they became blessings that didn't control me. That's what you tried to show me. I have to live with my hands open, no matter what comes in and out of them."

Chad smiled indulgently as they swayed to words about how men follow rainbows, silver, and gold. "Teach me how to do the dip, Care. I can't allow you to only have that memory with a dashing matador."

Her eyes were mischievous when they sparkled up at him. "You're jealous!"

"And admit it, no one has better reason to be, so do somethin' about it," he retorted. "I warned you on the pier the day of our first date that you're my Achilles heel, and jealousy of you is my second weakness."

Joey had managed to see Casey daily since dominating her time in France. Her new wardrobe played up her coloring and best features as if she either discovered her own style or found the courage to be herself. Her confidence, maturity and mannerisms became more refined over the six weeks they were apart, but there was little refinement in the havoc it created in Joey's life.

Casey's first step to getting back to her life was returning to her room at the patched boarding house. She would work for Caroline and Chad until she found another job in the health care field. A new physician was coming to Whitehaven. She turned in her resume with him, but she was really hoping for a position with a chiropractic wellness center that was opening in a refurbished historic building downtown. The Gregorys leased the building, and it was a short walk from the boarding house.

For now, she helped Caroline and Chad handle a wave of correspondence about the hurricane's effect on Painter Place and the kidnapping attempt in Arles. She continued art lessons with Caroline, and Joey was impressed with her work. He had taken drawing classes from Wyeth with Chad and Patrick when he was younger, and his praise was sincere.

Chapter Twenty-Four

Love sought is good
But giv'n unsought is better.
-William Shakespeare

There was a new address in the Painter Gallery's future. It was an historic brick building on Main Street in Whitehaven, parallel from The Castaway at the bridge. The Painters owned the building and usually leased it, but Hugo left only a wrecked shell to work with and little to preserve of what was once the old Coastal Corner Pharmacy and Soda Shop.

The former intimate, historic personality of the island gallery location was impossible to recreate without the old Painter stables. Heightened security limited traffic for the foreseeable future, so Wyeth and Caroline sadly acknowledged that circumstances forced them to be the first generations of Painters to set up the family gallery off the island.

It was Caroline who nudged her uncle to design a sleek, modern facility. The long-time gallery manager, Shelly, and the studio and classroom manager, her husband Zachary, were enthusiastic about Caroline's vision. Massive glass windows in the design would fill the space with light, create a sense of a connection with the coastal sky, and share tempting views of artwork that would lure the townsfolk inside. Purchasing the ruins of the adjacent building provided space for an art library to read in and a permanent exhibit on the history of the Painter art legacy. The new Painter Gallery would be unique to the Atlantic coast.

There was more than Painter Place and the contemporary Painter Gallery on Wyeth Painter's list of all he had to oversee. He and Caroline had nowhere to paint, and all workshops, retreats, and events scheduled at Painter Place had to be cancelled. He was also forced to cancel other professional appearances and travel so he could rebuild the island and business.

The daunting cost of the new facility far exceeded insurance settlements for the former gallery and the ruined corner building, at a time of greatly diminished income. And worst of all, the personality of Painter Place changed when there were no beach cottages left standing for creative people seeking a retreat.

Caroline watched her uncle with concern. No one could recall hearing Wyeth's jovial laugh since before Hurricane Hugo.

She worked with Shelly to brainstorm how to bring income to the business and keep it from obscurity while the gallery was under construction. Her collaboration with Shelly and Gran Vanna on projects from her trip to France had progressed, but it would take time before there was a meaningful profit.

Phillip Gregory's suave demeanor fell away when he was with Wyeth. They drew strength from one another, facing sorrow and challenges they had never imagined. Wyeth wore the weight of the leadership of Painter Place with a solemn, beaten-down expression that only eased whenever Phillip enthusiastically enticed him with new studio designs on a raised foundation to weather storm surges, featuring skylights and views of the ocean and the marsh. There were enough of the old stable boards being salvaged to design some furnishings. Phillip kept reminding Wyeth they would build it together, just as they built the last studio as boys, decades before.

Caroline hummed a lullaby as she put the twins down to sleep in the bedroom that she shared with Chad on the second floor of the Big House. Fresh air came through the open door to the veranda balcony, and she picked up Chad's leather journal and wandered out to a rocking chair. It was her first Saturday back home, and she hoped to enjoy a beautiful autumn day with temperatures in the low seventies. But the ever-present hum, roar, chomp, buzz, and grind of heavy equipment and machinery on the ravaged island destroyed any trace of solace she might find in the rhythmic sound of the surf massaging the shore.

With a few minutes to wait before Casey's art lesson, she opened the journal. So far, she had read Chad's account of the storm and the two days afterwards, crying through his passage on the birth of his sons. His witness to her grandfather afterwards in the hallway amazed her, and she had no doubt it softened his heart for the group prayer when he became a born-again believer. Now she was at the entry for Sunday, and she braced herself to re-live it.

Sunday, September 24, 1989

Caroline left today. I can't believe I even had the guts to write that. It looks so permanent. The detached expression in her eyes cut me to the quick. She's resolved to face what's ahead on her own, and for me, that's rock bottom. I thought there was nothing we wouldn't face together.

I hurt her when I badly handled Cameron's invitation to take Caroline and the twins away for six weeks. I know she didn't want to go—probably wanted me to forbid it—but she overheard me foolishly worrying about how to take care of her and the boys. She snapped, taking charge and removing herself from my reach. Caroline knows she can confidently manage her life quite well without me. And I can't stand that.

Hugo has wreaked havoc in all our emotions around here, even between my parents. I felt so smothered in the tension that I escaped by going out to run. Now I see that Caroline needed an escape, too. I've been so wrapped up in the camping-out conditions and complex relational crossfires that I only focused on how to deal with it myself. But I can't pretend I didn't see the desperation and grief in her eyes, and her loneliness for me. I didn't fight to be who she needed at one of her darkest hours. I was intimidated and distracted by the dynamics of having both families crowded into one place and allowed myself to be kept at bay in her life. Lesson learned, the hard way. Now I must get that look in her eyes back—the look that restores my place.

It's been years since I had a meltdown like I had on the beach after she left. I'd promised her I'd always be what she needed, then I failed her at the first real sign of trouble. I promised to take care of her home, and when it was destroyed, I acted helpless and complained about how to take care of her.

So much for bravado. I was pitiful, and I'm embarrassed. In front of her family, she had to face the futility of my good intentions and take life into her own hands when I let her down. I never touched the ground since seeing her for the first time when I came home from college, but God let me fall flat on my face today."

Casey came out onto the veranda to find Caroline, but she paused at her reflective mood and the book in her lap. Caroline smiled distractedly at her, closed the book, and rose to look out over the marsh.

"I haven't been here long enough to understand how different the marsh is since the storm," Casey observed. "Can you describe it?"

"Well, the tide is low right now, so there's less water. That means the main arteries are more defined. There are fewer of them, and they've been carved larger. They run toward Dog's Head more than before, and many of the wonderful ancient trees are down."

"Is Dog's Head the name of the north point of the island?"

"Yes. It looks like a retriever's head from the air, like Hilton Head and Isle of Palms have larger shapes on the north end. The waterway side is where the campground used to be, where we let church groups and scouts hold retreats. They always tell the campfire legends about the island. Oddly enough, the north side is where a shipwreck involving a retriever named King is supposed to have happened. There are other legends about the island, like the one about how the magical wind songs came to fill the trees of the marsh. I used to listen, sitting here with my Gran Vanna. Since Hugo, I can't hear them anymore. I suppose it's because of the trees being gone or broken too far down to have branches for the wind to whistle, moan, and rustle through, and I'm sad that the configuration of the new growth may not be right for the same wind songs."

They were quiet for a few moments, straining to hear, but the sounds of cleaning up the island overpowered anything else. "Caroline, you need new songs," Casey finally said. "Songs uniquely for your time here, 'for such a time as this,' like the Bible says. You know that the trees have changed growth and location since the legend. The songs have always changed and returned."

Caroline sighed, her gaze at the marsh full of sadness. "You're right. I'm sliding back into wishing I could hold on to things whose time is past."

"Look, we don't have to paint today. Will you tell me the legends about Dog's Head and King, and how the wind songs came to Painter Place?"

Caroline looked out solemnly over the marsh for a few minutes more. "Okay, but not here, with all this construction noise. Bring your sketchbook and let's take a ride."

Caroline put on her running shoes and picked up the camera Chad had given her, along with her sketchbook. Downstairs, she told her mom and mother-in-law where they were going and asked if they would watch the twins.

Valerie and Camellia glanced at one another before Valerie reminded her daughter that she was supposed to take Azariah wherever she went. But the bodyguard was with Chad, who had meetings in Whitehaven about the radio station and with contractors at the Castaway.

On a clear Saturday afternoon, the park would be busy with locals, and Camellia and Valerie hesitantly agreed it was generally a safe public place. So, Caroline and Casey drove across the waterway in the new Ferrari with the windows down and the ocean breeze in their hair.

Casey found the Myrtle Beach station on the radio and brightened to hear the upbeat song "We Can Work It Out."

"I love this! Can we play it loud?" she asked. "I wish our station was repaired, and Joey was on the air today."

Caroline nodded, grinning smugly at Casey's wish about Joey. Then she sang along with her at the top of her voice. "We can work it out," they sang, harmonizing on the subject of life being too short for fussing and fighting.

Chad and Patrick's cars were among several others in the parking lot of the Castaway as she pulled up to the stoplight at the end of the bridge. When that meeting was over, they would go to the storm-damaged radio station. The light changed to green, and she turned left, heading toward White Point Park while she and Casey sang backup for John, Paul, George, and Ringo.

They left their sketchbooks in the car to walk the trail first. With the intention of shooting photos of the ravaged view of the island from the park, Caroline hung her camera around her neck. She told Casey some of the legends of Painter Place and stood pointing over to where her home had been.

"On the day I found out Dad and Phillip had made Chad stay away from me and Painter Place when we were in college, I was so furious I considered leavin' the island. I ran away for the day, upset at how Painter Place controlled my life. That night, Chad brought me here in the Lamborghini—his trophy from his dad for making it through the ordeal—and he parked it where we could see the lights of home. He told me we weren't like the people who come here and look across, wishing they were us. They think we just do anything we want. But the truth is they could never live like us. Other people up and leave a job, a situation, or their family on a whim to chase something else they see and want, but we marry forever and are always bound to the island. They blow a paycheck on a weekend of partying, expecting family or friends to bail them out, but Painters must plan for generations ahead, with layers of protection and firewalls so the staggering cost of keeping the island is paid. They think we live on a playground, but for us it's a lot of work in a harsh environment, like how I told you my Poppy Noble died."

They turned at the sound of a heated argument. A big young man in a Tech jersey was bullying two teens, who eventually huffed and turned to leave the basketball court. A group of guys with the bully surrounded Caroline's Ferrari, and one bragged about how the artist chick would love his artwork carved into the side. The others laughed as he reached into his pocket.

Caroline took several steps toward her car and shouted, "This will make a great photo for the Whitehaven Police!"

Her camera clicked while the startled man held the key in his hand. The others whirled around. She clicked again to capture their faces.

The young man who bullied the teens away came up to grab her camera, which she jerked out of the way as she stepped back. He hesitated when some passers-by stopped and waited to see what would happen. Two other bystanders warily headed to their cars, and Caroline saw one pick up his mobile phone.

"Well, well, well, looky what we have here," sneered the biggest of the young men in the gang. He sauntered toward Caroline and Casey. "The hot-shot's candy, newly fallen from heaven to earth on her trashed island. Maybe Gregory wouldn't like her so much if I ran this key across her face." He swiped the air in front of Caroline with the key, but she didn't flinch.

"Is that what happened to yours?" she replied calmly.

He clenched his jaw and narrowed his eyes as he took a menacing step toward her. Casey moved protectively closer to Caroline and taunted, "If you think that's intimidating, you clearly don't know she grew up with a big brother. And if she came here in her old Mustang, you wouldn't have looked twice. You're just jealous of her car. If you touch her, Chad's gonna kill you, and her big brother's gonna drag your sorry dead carcass behind his Corvette all over town as an example to others. Then her dad's gonna drag it behind the *Artistic License* for the sharks, and her uncle's gonna hang what's left from the bridge for the vultures."

A few of the guys shifted uneasily, and one said, "Hey, she's got a point. Painters and Gregorys fight together, like a clan or somethin'. Joey Grayson's one of 'em, and they got the mayor and police in their pockets, too—and Derrick Wallace. I don't want no trouble with any of them, 'specially Wallace."

The bully mocked them with a sneer before he turned to Casey. "So, Grayson's feisty little nurse is back in town. I'm feelin' like she's the answer for my ragin' fever."

He made a crude gesture that Casey ignored as she stared down a young man she recognized. The leader didn't like being dismissed. "We heard you're the unfortunate backfire from some fun a bull rider had with his groupie, a pretty little Texas cowgirl. Maybe I need a lasso to get your attention, huh? Wild times run freely in your hot blood, girl, and they'd be wasted on a self-righteous stiff like Grayson. You're not his type."

Caroline glanced over at Casey. Her clenched fists were the only sign that the insults hit their mark. Her eyes drilled holes into the guy she recognized, and she retorted, "Back in Texas, where I come from, men defend women and win them with compliments, not insults and intimidation. Maybe that's why Billy ran off, so he could gang up with his kind in Whitehaven's scourge. Or did you hear that this was where I found work, and you came here to make a better life, too?"

The young man blanched. The leader snorted, impatient now. He grabbed Caroline's arm, trying to reach for her other arm to get the camera. She held it away on the wrist strap for Casey. The bully jerked her roughly into his chest just as Casey slipped the camera off her fingers.

Caroline's arms were instantly pinned behind her with one big hand. The man pulled her head back to his shoulder by her hair with his other hand, and Casey's expression relayed her restraint from trying to intervene, weighing whether Caroline would rather she protected the camera. It was a prized gift from Chad after she left the island, and the roll of film inside had photos of the twins on it. She anxiously waited for Caroline to give her a signal.

The bully nuzzled his face into Caroline's hair, sniffing, and she shuddered. Her reaction brought a snicker. "What's the matter, you so used to your highbrow hotshot you're scared of a real man?"

"A real man wouldn't hurt me or steal from me," she hissed through clenched teeth. "You're an animal!"

Unable to move her head, Caroline's eyes looked wildly into the gathering crowd for help. Her arms burned in the young man's cruel grip, but if she tried kicking back into his legs, he would twist harder. She wanted to cry out in pain, but pride made her bite her lip instead. If no one respected her enough to help, she would not give them the pleasure of seeing any weakness. Her only hope would be from above, and she silently prayed for a rescuer.

In her peripheral vision, she saw movement from the trail and heard a familiar voice shout to the crowd, "What's wrong with you people! Are you crazy? Help her!"

Krystal. She knew that voice from a phone conversation before the storm. In a moment, Krystal was wildly trying to wrest her away. The man increased the pressure to keep Caroline and it hurt more to be in this tug-of-war. Caroline was unable to contain the cry that escaped her lips, and she repeated her silent prayers for help.

One of the men in the gang rushed to push Krystal back while she flailed against him. She resorted to screaming hysterically for someone to call the police.

"Grab the camera from the cowgirl so we can get outta here," growled the bully. A couple of the guys made a move toward Casey, but Billy protested and stopped them. "Wait, we're drawin' a crowd. It doesn't matter if she has a photo. We didn't do anything to the car. Let's go!"

"Yeah, well the crowd doesn't act like they care about their homegrown rich and famous anymore, do they?" snarled the gang leader. "I can get good money in a pawn shop for that camera, and we'll split the profits."

He eyed the disconcerted, murmuring, but non-interfering crowd in scornful delight as tires screeched in the parking lot behind him. "They'll enjoy this—give 'em somethin' to gossip about," he said with relish. "They want the artist to get marked up so she's not the fairest in fairy tale land anymore. Maybe all her money can buy her a new face. Hurry over here with that key!"

The young man who threatened to key the Ferrari came forward with a malicious grin. Krystal shrieked dreadfully in protest, pounding on the guy holding her back. He clamped his hand over her mouth. This earned him a ferocious bite that made him yelp and curse.

Casey stood defiant, staring back at the leader, camera in hand. She raised it quickly to snap a photo of him assaulting Caroline.

"Press the side of that key against her cheekbone," he commanded, leering at Casey. "Now, cowgirl, give me that camera and I might not fillet your friend's face."

Caroline braced for pain. Instead, her assailant grunted and staggered as she heard a thud from behind. Her arms were suddenly free, leaving her off balance as she fell to the grass on her palms.

She winced and cried out at the shock in her wrists. Turning, she saw Azariah take the man down with a move she wanted to learn. Then she heard Chad bellowing in rage while the guy threatening her with the key landed on the ground nearby. She tried to scramble out of the way when the guy got up to fight back. Chad caught a glancing blow to his cheekbone but was too busy subduing his attacker to notice.

Caroline choked on a sob, frightened for Chad. Billy backed away while Patrick, Cole, and Joey took on the others in a furious flurry of arms, fists, grunts, and roars. Casey and Krystal pulled Caroline away just before the guy who had held Krystal landed in that spot. Cole was on top of him with a primal shout of victory.

She saw her brother get hit in the face and she screamed his name. He did not acknowledge her, but she heard the breaking bone when he made sure the aggressor's arm would not hit him again. The guys always avoided hits to the face and head if they were forced into a fight, but the gang followed no rules. Blood dripped from Joey's nose onto the guy he pinned to the ground.

Sterling's squad car was trailed by two more that raced into the parking lot with sirens blaring.

Billy ran.

Phones were buzzing in Whitehaven as word spread of the attack on Caroline and Casey. The mayor made a lot of calls and scheduled an emergency town meeting for Monday evening. Then he gathered city council members to ride with him to the island, hoping this assault on the future heir of Painter Place would not stop Savanna from announcing that they could make her appointment official.

Andy Painter paced like a caged wildcat in the parking lot of the Big House as Chad drove in. He swiftly opened his daughter's door and helped her out, flushing in anger when he noticed the red marks on her arm. She flinched from his touch.

"They stood and watched," she said, on the verge of tears now after her initial indignant anger at the incident. "Only one person tried to stop those guys, except for the man who went to his car and called the radio station and police. I know some of those people, and I'm sure the others knew who I was. But they wouldn't help me!"

"I know, baby, it's not like it used to be around here. Come on inside. Your granddad is on his way to help Casey with first aid for the guys. You're sure you're okay?"

"Yeah, but my arms, wrists, and neck hurt," she answered, looking at the grass stains and scrapes on her palms. "Patrick got hit in the face. Dad, I'm worried about him. And Chad has a bruise on his cheekbone near his eye."

She turned back to Chad, who joined a gathering group of men outside as they parked at the mansion. He met her eyes and nodded at her to follow her dad while Azariah pulled in with her Ferrari.

Wyeth was on his way out as they came in, holding his mobile phone at his ear. He pulled Caroline to his side in a sheltering hug with his free arm, ending his conversation. "Get here as soon as you can. We're in the parking lot behind the house."

He set the phone down and scowled at the marks Andy showed him on Caroline's arms. She saw them exchange a look charged with meaning. Her sister Marina ran up, teary-eyed and fussing, and Casey came through the door to join the expanding group of ladies in the kitchen.

Maggie Jane wrapped her arms around Casey, who sobbed uncontrollably into her shoulder. "Shhhh, nobody's gonna hurt anybody now, child," Maggie Jane said soothingly in a singsong way, running her hands over Casey's hair. "It's gonna be okay now, nobody's gonna hurt anybody now. You'll see."

From her Aunt Chrissy's embrace, Caroline blurted, "Casey, those things that guy said—that doesn't define you, and anyway, what would he know about Joey's type?"

"What's goin' on?" asked Maggie Jane. "Ya tell us so we can help. Hidden things, they just get rotten in the dark."

Through her sobs, Casey blurted, "Joey already knows, but he brushed it off. Now he'll hear why it matters, what other guys think of me, and his parents will hear. I'll have to move away and start all over!"

The older women were bewildered. "Casey, can I tell them?" asked Caroline.

Casey sniffled and nodded into Maggie Jane's tear-dampened shoulder. Maggie Jane rocked her gently side to side. Caroline explained that the younger part of the group at Painter Place thought they were the only ones who knew about Casey's background. She told them that one of the guys in the gang at the park was from Casey's hometown and apparently told them about it, and now, everyone in the crowd in the park knew and would spread it all over town, adding any flourish and embellishment they wanted to make it juicy.

"What's so bad about her background?" asked Camellia, walking over to hand Casey a tissue and pat her hair soothingly.

Caroline explained, and told them the demeaning things the bully said in front of everyone.

"Oh, Casey," said Chrissy sympathetically. "I've never even known who my dad is. Worse, he knows who I am and won't acknowledge me. I wish everyone could have a childhood like those raised on this island, but most people in that crowd didn't. You pray long and hard before you run away from a life here just because of this."

Maggie Jane would not leave for home and was at her best, a mother hen herding her chicks under protective wings. She worked to put together an impromptu meal for an unknown number of dinner guests, directing Natalie and Shannon in the kitchen. Audrey Rush arrived and joined them while Tony sat in a lawn chair in the parking lot, weak from a cancer treatment.

As dusk gathered, floodlights automatically came on. Savanna Painter came inside after a brief meeting with the mayor and city council members, refusing to give them an answer until her sons were satisfied with how this assault and the aftermath were handled.

Peeking out the window, Savanna knit her brows. Three of Whitehaven's ministers, including their own pastor, plus the mayor, Sterling and the police chief, city council members, Joey's dad, and the Painter and Gregory Global attorneys were gathered. Chad, Phillip, Cole, Andy, Wyeth, Patrick, Danny, and Joey were stolid, arms crossed, feet spread, and wearing stony expressions. Azariah stood watching in the background behind Tony Rush's chair.

Little Noble eventually stopped playing with his cousin TJ and wandered into the main group, confused at the prevailing tension and the unusual situation in the house. He went to the window, trying to wave at his dad and asking to go outside with him.

"Daddy's hurt," said Noble. He pointed at his own face.

"Papa Tony said he's going to be all right. He's takin' care of Daddy," Natalie assured her son. But Caroline understood that Noble was disturbed by his intuition. Maybe his dad was all right, but his Aunt Caroline was hurt, too, and Casey had been crying.

She tried to divert her nephew's attention by asking if he would draw with her and Casey. Immediately, he took Casey's hand to lead her to the library table and spoke over his shoulder to Caroline, telling her to follow them. Caroline smiled at how he took charge of Casey in an innocent sign of acceptance that Casey desperately needed tonight.

Caroline's grandfather found her in the library and gestured for her to follow him out of the toddler's earshot. Checking over her arms and shoulders, he observed, "Nothing's broken. You'll be mighty sore, but this is small stuff for a girl who had twins in a hurricane. Ask Maggie Jane for her remedy for bruising. It wouldn't hurt to get your neck and wrists checked out next week."

"Is Patrick okay? It scared me to see him hit in the face like that. What about Chad and the others?"

"He's showin' no signs that he's not okay, so I'll go with that. He's in no mood to be babied right now. Chad, Joey, Cole, and Azariah are banged up, but nothing's broken."

Glancing at Noble, he kept his voice low. "Don't go to town anymore without a gun, a bodyguard, or that mutt your husband's gettin' for you, okay? I think things will get better, but I'm buyin' a place I found on the waterway and movin' me and your grandma to town to keep an eye open. She needs to be closer to Valerie when somethin' happens to me, anyway."

"What does that mean—when somethin' happens?"

He smiled wryly, reaching into a satchel he brought. "We all have to go sometime." He showed her a book he was returning to the Big House library. "Your mama told me to read this, and it opened my eyes to a whole new way of thinkin'. I'm borrowin' some more if you don't mind me lookin' around."

Caroline saw the title. "Yes, it's profound and prophetic. I believe we'll see it played out as my boys grow up. If you liked that, borrow the books by Henry Morris, over there."

He looked again at *The Genesis Solution* in his hand. "If I understand the Bible, things will get worse before the Lord comes back, so all this has to happen. I'm just thankful that I'm not blind anymore. Your grandma Audrey told me God starts where we're at and takes it from there if we let Him teach us. A lot of people are laughin' at her for takin' me back, but she holds her head high and smiles like the gracious belle she was raised to be. And Patrick—he was so tough in the parking lot meeting tonight, defendin' you. I must've been glowin' like one o' those floodlights in pride. But he—you know—he keeps me at arm's length, and I understand. I'm just grateful he lets me be a great-grandpa to Noble."

"He needs to know you're for real before he allows himself to feel emotions. Everyone protected us from the newspaper society pages when we were younger, sneakin' them out when we looked at local stuff and Patrick and Chad's ball scores. But we saw the looks passing between the adults, and Patrick would go out to buy or borrow another paper to see the news about you. Chad tried to discourage him, but finally he just helped him get it over with so they could go play ball or somethin' to blow off Patrick's anger. I saw the news sometimes at Carly's house."

Her grandfather sighed and looked away. "He's like his mother. Valerie held my feet to the fire all her life, never lettin' me forget what I was doin' wasn't okay, and that she'd never accept it. I know those wasted years are gone, years when none of you related to me with love and respect, like your Poppy Noble gave and got from you. All I have left is to start over now."

Savanna entered the library, smiling at Tony and beckoning Caroline to her side. She lit up with a special smile for the drawing Noble waved in front of her. Taking his hand, she told him she wanted to show them all some lights across the bridge.

The toddler's eyes sparkled at the prospect of adventure, and he skipped toward the door with her hand. She led them up the stairs to the long veranda balcony across the back of the mansion.

Tony picked up Noble so he could see the shoreline of Whitehaven across the patched bridge. "There?" the toddler pointed.

"Yes. See all the lights? People are in The Castaway parking lot, Daddy's restaurant. They're holding those lights up to be sure Aunt Care and Casey see them. A friend named Krystal started callin' people and drivin' around town to invite everyone to tell Aunt Care and Casey how much they are sorry that somethin' bad happened in the park today."

Chad came up to the balcony, slowly walking to Caroline's side and putting his arm around her. She linked hers around his waist. "They want to see you," he said quietly. "You and Casey."

Caroline drew a ragged breath and Casey blinked back tears. Noble reached out a little hand from Tony's arms and ever-so-carefully touched Chad's face. He was fascinated with a swollen bruise on his cheekbone. His big blue eyes studied Chad's to see if he was crying. "Be more careful," he stated matter-of-factly. "You'll be all right."

Chad grinned at his nephew, hearing Patrick's words and manner. Joey came to stand with them, looking out to the lights and then at Casey. When their eyes met, hers darted away. He sighed and reached out to take her hand.

"Let's turn on all the lights in the house, even the third floor, so they can see," Caroline said, looking up at Chad. "Then let's drive over."

Chad hesitated, then nodded, and she leaned forward to look at Casey. "Remember what I told you this afternoon, when we looked across from the park to Painter Place? That applies to you, too, if you're not afraid to be our friend. Are you ready for this?"

Music boomed from a stereo in the Castaway parking lot and floated in the clear night air over the waterway. Raised voices sang with gusto as if pushing the words to songs about friendship across the bridge to Painter Place.

Applause erupted as the Painters and Gregorys crested the bridge in a caravan of vehicles two lanes wide. Azariah led the convoy down the middle line, driving Caroline's yellow Ferrari. Once parked, he and the armed island security guard opened the doors and alertly scanned the crowd, the street, vehicles, and the buildings. He gestured behind him, and Chad and Joey got out of Chad's Cherokee. They went around to the passenger sides to open doors for Caroline and Casey while the crowd waved their flashlights and lanterns.

Everyone on the bridge followed Azariah and the security guard to the bottom, where cars were parked with headlights shining across it. Joey held Casey close to his side for the crowd to see.

Friends gasped as lights revealed the bruises on the young men's faces, proving that Krystal's version of the incident was not exaggerated. Valerie gently handed Rayce to Caroline, who winced as she shifted the baby with her sore arms. Camellia handed Rhett to Chad. Patrick carried Noble, who turned from investigating his dad's face and was wide eyed at the lights, music, and singing. He waved with excitement at his Sunday School teacher and other friends he recognized from church.

Danny stood on one side of Patrick as he held Taylor Juliette close to Noble, and she clapped her little hands together to mimic the crowd. The Whitehaven Register photographers and reporters got some photos of the family illuminated by car headlights at the foot of the bridge.

Krystal shouted, "We love you, Caroline and Casey!" Others began shouting, adding the rest of the family's names. Caroline and Casey waved. Caroline mouthed "Thank you" to Krystal and gestured for her to come past the car barricade.

Krystal sprinted over and breathlessly tried to hug her while not smothering Rayce. "I'm so, so appalled at how no one helped you today. Before Hugo, I was always hearing how much this town thought of your family. I don't understand all this, but I knew there had to be plenty of people left who weren't jealous of you. They were just so busy with their own troubles from the storm that they haven't spoken up. They're still here, Caroline. Not all could come tonight, and some had to leave already, but I found them."

"Will you invite them to come over to the island on the first Saturday in December for a bonfire, hot chocolate, coffee, donuts, and caroling on the beach? If any have something small that's ruined from their old life before Hugo, and they want to throw it into the fire as a token of being ready to start fresh like we are, tell them to bring it. They can also bring guitars or whatever instrument they play for the carols. Will you let them know it's a personal invitation from us?"

With a restrained version of jumping up and down, Krystal exclaimed, "You bet I will. I'll spread the word here and have them tell the others. Thank you so much for inviting us!"

"Soon the Castaway will be open, and we'll have that lunch date I promised."

Krystal flashed a smile and nodded, then attempted another semi-hug around Rayce. She backed away, waving goodbye, and then turned to enlist friends to help her spread the invitation for the bonfire.

Once everyone was back in the mansion and gathered in the living room, Joey said, "By now, you know why the guys in the park were insulting Casey. They brought me into it, so I'm speakin' up in front of her. I knew weeks ago about her parents. My family knows, and they're ready to deal with the flack like the rest of us. It might be rough at first. They got a call right after the incident in the park from someone askin' if they knew I was hangin' around with a—uh—"

Standing there awkwardly, Joey wondered how he managed to get himself into that predicament. He would never say the word or think of Casey that way, but having people blast it into your life made it pop into his mind.

Cole shrugged. "Your dad set them straight on the phone, just like we will. It could've been much worse. Darth Vader could've come wheezin' up and revealed that he was her father. Neither Skywalker nor Casey will ever turn to the Dark Side."

The guffaws and laughter died down enough for Joey to be heard again. "So, Casey," he said, pausing until she looked him in the eye. "People can make fun of me, my family, or anyone else here, but it won't change who you are to us. Don't avoid us or talk about movin' away."

Chapter Twenty-Five

If it weren't for painting I could not live.
I couldn't bear the strain of things.
–Winston Churchill

In Washington, DC, a red phone vibrated in its cradle as it rang on a massive mahogany desk. The white-haired man behind the desk answered. "Yes. Hmm... interesting. Any ideas?"

He relaxed back into his plush leather chair and looked out a window at a clear blue sky. He occasionally contributed to the conversation before he sat up straight. "What?"

The exchange lasted a few minutes more and he hung up. Then he sat silent a moment, fingertips pressed to one another in front of him and a far-away look on his face. Eventually, he picked up another phone receiver on his desk and told his assistant he wanted to see him.

The door opened to admit his aide, who was straightening his tie. "Yes, sir?"

"I need some extra research about a place no one else knows about. Something unexpected, and extremely complicated, has come up."

The aide smiled conspiratorially. "Does it involve travel, sir? I can have someone there tonight."

The older man looked at him indulgently and smiled as he took a notepad and jotted down some things. "No, not yet. I need some history from four years ago, and some records of a missionary organization."

The air ripped above the page as he tore it briskly from the pad and handed it to his assistant. "Burn this when you're finished and use the code. We need to keep an eye open. A situation has arisen that is connected to our—place. It will be a while before there is any action, and it is currently out of our jurisdiction. But the situation could spill over to the States and it's not too early to make all the preparations and have a plan."

The assistant's eyes were popping as he looked up from the notes. "The Jaguar, sir?" he squeaked.

The older man's eyes looked at him solemnly. "If life is anything, it is an adventure."

The tropical jungle created an endless sea of every conceivable hue of green to surround the walled grounds in view of a flagstone terrace. A small table was set with breakfast for two, where an older gentleman and a younger one sat together. The elder was jovial and positive, but the younger was quiet and ever watchful as he ate, often lapsing into a bewildered look that haunted his eyes.

A dark-haired man came out onto the terrace. He walked up to the old gentleman's side, handed him a note, and warmly smiled at the younger man. The elder man read it, looked up at him, and nodded in a gesture only they understood. He turned to the younger man and smiled before he put his napkin by his plate.

"I'd rather sit here with you, son, but an urgent matter means my day must begin. I dare say yours is harder than mine by far, but they tell me you're building up strength and doing well in your training. It will be a matter of months, perhaps a year, but eventually you'll be out again. Many people need you. Set your eyes on the goal, not the daily drudgery of getting there."

The younger man blinked. "I wish I could just remember everything. It would save so much time. How can I wake up one day in what feels like someone else's life?"

Chad stifled a groan from the bruises he sported from Saturday's fight in the park, rolling over to hit the button to turn off the soft music on the alarm clock after the first few notes. The sound was barely discernable so the twins would not wake up, but a tiny sigh from Rhett's bassinet made both Chad and Caroline freeze.

In a few moments, Caroline ventured a look at Chad, who looked over at her, waiting. She felt like she was going to giggle, and she put her hand over her mouth. It was totally irrational to giggle about something that would not be a bit funny if it happened. If Rhett cried, Rayce would copy him, and her whole day would be doomed to their upset schedule.

Chad winced as he rolled over, and then traced his forefinger over her face. She knew he was thinking about what could have happened to it in the park barely two days ago.

Many rounds of ice and Maggie Jane's special tea poultice had taken the swelling on his cheekbone away. Hopefully, the bruise would be gone by Thanksgiving next week. Chad pulled her arm out from under the sheet, inspecting the bruises near her elbow. He gritted his teeth. "I can't stand seeing a man's finger marks on you like that," he whispered fiercely.

"Does your face hurt?" she whispered back.

"It aches a little, but mostly just when I forget and touch it. My hand and ribs hurt." He sighed as he shifted his weight. "But Noble promises if I'm more careful, I'll be all right."

They snickered as silently as they could manage. After a swift peck at her temple, he stiffly, but stealthily managed to get out of bed.

She lay quiet, gathering her prayers to begin the day. It would be Thanksgiving next week, and instead of counting her blessings, she was wishing for some peace, quiet, solitude, and calm. Lonely people longed for family and friends over the holidays, but she could appreciate a deserted island right about now.

Chad soon emerged from his shower to find her standing and staring out to the view of the distant waterway and Whitehaven. He put his arms around her waist and kissed the back of her head. "Let's do dinner at the office again this week. It's your turn to choose the music. I'll wear my cowboy boots," he whispered.

"Let's try shaggin' in our boots. I'm goin' with beach music and oldies," she whispered back, turning around to face him. "You were a heartthrob in them with your rock music on your birthday."

He grinned and pushed her hair behind her ear. "Maybe Casey will have us in ten-gallon hats next," he whispered near it. "I'll have to look into which brand JR wears. Listen, be prayin' about the outcome of the town meeting tonight. It's goin' to be in the news, since Derrick's girlfriend will team up with Juliette and Mia in Charlotte to fly in this afternoon. She's stayin' with his parents. He'll be here this week for a day before gettin' back for another game."

Caroline sighed. Unless they found a place in town to stay, Juliette and Mia would add to the crowd in the house, and Mia's bodyguard would be with them. Cameron would be here next week for Thanksgiving. More people. More noise.

"The crew with the monument will be here at ten," he continued to whisper. "Wyeth's handling the new veranda construction, but you know the design details if he's called away. Let me know if somethin' comes up."

"Chad," Caroline blurted in a whisper. "I need a place to be quiet and paint. Sometimes I feel like I can't breathe."

His calm green eyes searched the desperation in hers, seeing a hint of the look she had the day she got on the boat to leave. Panic flitted through his chest, and he instantly grasped a plan. He quickly whispered, "Global has an empty office with a big window. Make time to paint and bring what you need. Don't leave the island without Azariah, though. Our dog's gettin' socialized and will be here soon, so think of a name you like."

"Everyone expects us to call him 'King,' after the legend, so let's be unpredictable. Let's call him 'Lancelot.' It means 'servant' and he's a working dog who's goin' to serve us by guarding us."

"That's very—French/British."

"No more than 'King.'"

"Great point."

Caroline spent some quiet moments reading more of Chad's journal. She had to cover her mouth to keep from laughing aloud and waking the twins. Chad and Cole's offices were unlikely motel rooms, and Chad's version of their coping skills was hilarious.

Some of their bonding brought tears to her eyes, and she planned to tell Natalie and Shannon about it. The guys held nothing back with one another about how deeply they loved and missed their wives, and they had not known Chad was going to write about it. They even shared their grown-up fears and insecurities.

Despite their daily exhaustion from the storm recovery efforts, the men took turns planning short Bible studies or devotions. A strong running theme was debunking the accusations people level against God because He allows suffering and destruction. Cole and Patrick came up with a great illustration during one of their board game nights. If God controlled everything, He was only playing solitaire. Yet scripture is clear that God's purpose in creating man is to interact in a loving relationship with Him. Being made in God's image, man necessarily had to be given the characteristics of that image, such as feeling, thinking, and interacting. God wants a heavenly family, and a true relationship is impossible with a programed robot. He allowed His spiritual enemies to tempt men against Him so they could decide who to follow. God created a sinless, ideal world, but man's gift of independence brought down a curse on creation that will remain until the Lord sets it right again—on His terms.

Caroline thoughtfully closed the journal. She had to go meet the crew hauling a monument to the site of the old chapel. It was reduced now to the foundation footings, yet generations of weddings, difficult decisions, and heartaches had been wrestled with in prayers on that spot. Her parents, Chad's parents, and Wyeth and Chrissy had a triple wedding in the chapel, so she knew it was heartrending for them not to rebuild it.

She drew a sad sigh. The old Painter Chapel was where Chris Shepherd once struggled in prayer for strength to say goodbye to her. The building was erased by the same storm that erased him from this life.

But Chad had been in the chapel praying about her, too, just before Chris arrived. He was praying for strength in plans that included her. God knew what Chad and Chris needed and wanted before they asked, and he had been working through their prayers. He was not confined to a building. Anyone could seek God anywhere, and every Christian was His sanctuary.

Caroline and Azariah left the monument crew to work and went returned to the Big House. They met a stir of excitement in the parking lot, and she groaned. Azariah turned from the driver's seat with a knowing look and a faint smile.

"Azariah, you don't say much. Have you decided to be my friend yet, for free? I'd love to confide something, as a friend."

He laughed. "I thought we settled that in France, the night you talked about your friend Chris. I'm your friend—for free—and I know what you want to say. You wish your life wasn't so interesting."

"Interesting. Is that what you call it?"

"As your friend, for free, may I say something?"

"Only if it doesn't involve more people sharing every breath I take."

"Don't feel guilty about your need to be alone. Embrace it as part of your gift and look for balance again instead of starving it. Being sociable drains your energy and spends your creativity. Painting is vital to your joy and sense of purpose. When you're deprived of that, you resent it. In Arles, you glowed. Even your heartache lost any power to weigh you down when you were teaching Casey about art, or painting, or dancing."

Caught off guard at her quiet friend's insight, Caroline opened her mouth to tell him they would soon go to Global to paint. But Wyeth appeared and swiftly opened her door. "Caroline, will you get your camera to document something for me?"

She and Azariah exchanged a look and a grin. Then they followed her uncle to the front of the mansion, where a construction company worked to rebuild the double verandas. Wyeth signaled the supervisor, who used a lift to elevate Caroline and Wyeth up to the huge front doors.

Beside the doorframe was an opening in the siding where new lighting was being wired. Wyeth and the supervisor directed Caroline to snap photographs as they proceeded to pry open the area. "Ya see this?" the supervisor drawled, pointing with a dirty gloved finger. "Now we're down to the original facade of the house. I don't have to tell ya how old that is."

Wyeth pointed to a flat wooden board. "And this is what you're sayin' isn't supposed to be there? Caroline, can you get a few shots of this?"

Curiosity brought the rest of the construction crew over to the lift. Wyeth knocked on the door of the house so Chrissy would answer, and he asked her to bring Savanna, Valerie, and Camellia. When they gathered, he asked Camellia to get Phillip or Chad on the phone, and said he wanted them all to watch what he would uncover in case it was important.

The supervisor carefully worked to pull back boards. His rusty laugh was triumphant when he stepped back, gesturing to Wyeth, who grasped the top of what appeared to be two squares of wood with something in between. With some effort, he loosened it and pulled it out.

They all saw the humble object in Wyeth's hands. Caroline photographed it while Camellia described what they found to Phillip over the phone. "It has very old metal thingies around the sides to bind it, like a book," she told Phillip.

She met Wyeth's excited eyes. "He says to try to open it."

Wyeth struggled with a clasp, an effort that finally paid off. The top slab of wood moved, so he carefully lifted it.

They gasped. It was a folder, with documents inside. They appeared to be of leather or skin, with elegant, spidery handwriting.

Camellia described it to Phillip and then blurted, "Wyeth, he says this is big—it may be what the Gregorys and Painters have searched for ever since the house was built. He's callin' the attorney and drivin' over here right now. Chad's comin' out and bringin' Patrick from the Castaway."

Saws buzzed and hammers pounded while construction continued at the mansion at Painter Place. Wyeth had approved Caroline's request that the original façade design of the house be reconstructed now that there were hardier materials on the market, and the supervisor was trained in historic preservation. He hovered over the process of pulling back old surfaces.

Maggie Jane circled the massive dining room table, unobtrusively serving small chicken salad sandwiches that were disappearing without anyone really thinking about eating. They stood leaning on the table to see what Wyeth, Phillip, and the gray-haired attorney were studying with such relish.

The attorney eventually peered over his reading glasses at Wyeth. "The document trail should be solid, and if you're on track that this is your friend's place, you've already been there. Now that we have proof of the name change to protect the property, and the name of the stewards left over it, we can claim it. I've never seen such shrewdness in liquidating assets into hidden places. Chadwick Gregory and Beauregard Painter were geniuses!"

He pointed at the documents with the magnifying glass held in his hand. "With this personal letter bundled with the deeds, there's no doubt about anyone's intentions."

"The list instructing us to pull back the covers on certain paintings for more documents—what if the stewards had to sell them for upkeep on the property, or they were confiscated during wars?" asked Phillip.

"Then we look at a database to try to find them. There should be records. This might take years, and some may have been destroyed, but they are separate holdings, not dependent on one another. New owners may feel entitled to what we find."

Caroline walked back over to the letter they found when they opened the wooden covers pressing the pages together. The container miraculously served its intended purpose of protecting its contents from humidity. She felt sad that the original Patrick Painter never found this communication from his brother. It was cleverly hidden from pursuers, but it was intended to get the attention of someone who often went in and out of the front doors. It had seemingly slipped further down into loosened siding than it was meant to, perhaps with the slamming of those doors.

She re-read the beautiful, flowing script of a remarkable, well-educated man, wishing she could meet him right now. It was a comfort that as a Christian, she would see him someday in heaven.

My dearest brother Patrick,

You'll never know how I'm struggling at this moment not to knock on your door. It is a torture indescribable! The house is blessedly dark, so it is not seen from the sea. Keep it that way at night. I know Mother and Grandmother are asleep, and I hope old Gregory is also here. Oh, if I could hear all your voices again one last time, it would be worth facing what I suspect lies ahead of me! I dare not draw any attention to this fine house, for you would all be murdered by my selfish folly.

When I got word by a messenger from Father about what happened and where you are, I did everything to get here. You must think me dead. Pirates captured the ship I had passage on, and I was among men forced into their crew—a better fate than those left on board. But as God would have it, He blessed me even then by surrounding me with uneducated fools who saw no value in my written words, disguised in preserved wooden boards. They allowed us to keep our meager personal belongings. A mate on watch took a bribe to let me sneak off in a small boat to land here tonight, while the captain sleeps off a drunken stupor. I told him honestly that I wanted to hide a personal item that would surely get me arrested if the ship was ever boarded by the English. No doubt he thinks it is evidence of some crime.

The truth is, little brother, my worldly treasure lies in this book, my crime simply being that I am the eldest son of a man condemned for his faith by a government that merely wants to steal his wealth. On the run and living little better than an animal, I gained passage as crew on a foreign ship to the Americas, in hopes of meeting you here. We have an estate, the details of which are contained herein, under a legal name I set up to hide it. I have a steward who knew old Gregory. He will live there and watch over it until it is safe to return. It is yours, brother, for I do not dare hope I will survive. It is not the first time I have secretly come ashore before to quickly hide on this beautiful island my share of some pirate raids. I did not participate but acting as ship physician allotted to me a portion. My crude map is drawn by moonlight and the glow from a candle stub behind a dune, and I am not certain on the topography. God willed that I get it here, so I trust it to be discovered in His good time.

Give my enduring love to our mother and grandmother. Carry on the Painter name and faith in honor, Patrick. Take a good wife of inner beauty who possesses all the qualities our parents taught us to look for, fill this house with children raised to carry on our legacy with determination and God's grace, and make Gregory stop working long enough to do the same so that his brilliance, foresight, and vision are passed along and shared with the world. Alas, brother, I regret to say I heard our father's life on this earth is over, but in this we are certain: we will all reunite in heaven. For what are we in time, but dust in the wind? When eternal bliss stretches before us and we have nothing to fear and no one to run from, that is when we truly live.

Your eldest brother, forever faithful and true,
Beauregard Painter

Caroline's eyes stung and her heart overflowed with gratitude and love for this man she never met. Her musing was interrupted by something the attorney suggested to Wyeth. "I think you should call your friend while I am here and tell him what we've found. He may have questions for me, and I need access to his attorney."

She moved closer to her uncle, watching the emotions on his face. He nodded and picked up the phone to make a long-distance call to England. He drew a deep breath and closed his eyes before he spoke into the phone. "Dante, this is Wyeth. Do you remember when we first met, and you told me you felt a sense of destiny about our friendship?"

Chapter Twenty-Six

Even the wise cannot see all ends.
-Gandalf

"If this undercurrent of change gone wrong is Whitehaven's new personality, find someone else to run for mayor next election. I refuse to travel this muddy road with you." The mayor sternly scanned the crowd he addressed at the emergency meeting in town hall on Monday evening. "The Painters and Gregorys don't need you—you need them. They've always been gracious enough to go out of their way to include you in what they're about. There's not a person here who can give me an example of a time any of them have snubbed you or treated you unfairly. They support your businesses. They even split up to try to cover each of your car dealerships! Did it ever occur to any of you that they could drive to Myrtle Beach or Charleston and get what they really wanted?"

Many in attendance turned their eyes down or looked at one another.

"They were willin' to forget the Saturday when the boys were attacked, but last Saturday changed everything. Caroline's the next Wyeth, and they absolutely will not tolerate this attitude toward her. The face those thugs threatened to cut up is the future face of Painter Place! Now the Painters are lookin' outside Whitehaven for their business, where there's no prejudice against her. Maybe you noticed the construction crews weren't working on Wyeth's building at the bridge today."

He paused and looked around the room for effect, nodding. "Yeah, you're right to look concerned. That gallery plan is state of the art, the only place of its kind on the whole coast! It would have lured a lot of culturally minded tourists here. He stopped construction on the Painter Gallery location on Main Street. He's lookin' at property in Charleston and Georgetown now. Don't you get it? Caroline Painter doesn't have to put up with insults and snubs in her own hometown. You need her, but she doesn't need you—or your distain. In case you've been so caught up in yourselves that you haven't taken your blinders off, she and Chad are puttin' this place on the map. Derrick is, too. Patrick Painter and the Castaway are gettin' attention in culinary circles. We have some wealthy families tryin' to build or vacation here now because of them. Do you want their taxes and business?"

His audience stirred with sheepish expressions, but no one spoke up. The mayor nodded and said, "Maybe you forgot that Gregory Global was settin' up to expand here in Whitehaven. New internet capabilities are makin' it possible for them to shrink or phase out London's offices. But I got a call from Charleston today tellin' me that Phillip's father was scoutin' commercial property in Charleston this afternoon for that expansion. And Andy Painter was overheard makin' calls to Myrtle Beach about property, downsizing the reconstruction plan for his marina here and sendin' his business up there. Is that really what you people want?"

Alarmed conversations buzzed across the room among the gathered residents and leaders. One man spoke over them to the mayor. "But they have money from insurance and their own wealth to pay for their losses, while most of us have next to nothin' left this year for the holidays after the storm. Back where I come from, that's called a hard candy Christmas. I thought those days were over for my family."

The mayor shook his head in disbelief. "Back where the Painters and Gregorys come from, people tried to kill 'em and take everything they worked and sacrificed for. When they escaped and came here, they hoped those days were over, too. But look at 'em now! They can't even walk in the park they gave us!"

The crowd's responses to one another grew in volume as they argued among themselves. A City Council member raised his hand and stood up to speak. "The Painters are Whitehaven's George Bailey, not their Mr. Potter. This is ridiculous!"

"That's right, they ain't been nothin' but good to anyone in this town," said one business owner. "I went to the Castaway parkin' lot on Saturday night to join their friends, and they came out to show us they appreciated what we were doin'. They coulda stayed in their house with those lights ablazin' to thank us, and no one woulda blamed 'em. Instead, they came out personally and invited us all to come to sing Christmas carols at a bonfire on the beach soon. We can burn somethin' from our life before Hugo to show we're not defeated and we're ready to start over. If you'd been over there to see that place, you know they lost way more than anyone here did, and insurance won't cover it. That island will never be the same. When you have a lot, you lose a lot."

Another man spoke up. "I used to be on the city finance committee, and I just want to say that if it weren't for the folks on that island, this town would be nothin' more than a trail in the sand for influential people to get past on their way to Painter Place. I never understood prejudice against people who have money to work with. They provide us with jobs, roads, and amenities. God blesses some with the means to be His hand to bless others. He decides who the best stewards are. If you have a problem with Him givin' more to the Painters and Gregorys than He gave you, take it up with Him and leave them alone. God didn't appoint us to say He made a mistake or try to correct Him."

There was applause from some in the room, while others looked sheepish. A lady in the crowd spoke next. "My nephew is on the construction team out there rebuildin' that huge veranda on the front of the house, and he told me they found somethin' historic today when they pulled off some old siding. He heard Wyeth mention some deeds and property in England, and someone heard through the window that there was a treasure map. I say we'd better appreciate the Painters, 'cause they could isolate themselves from Whitehaven to other places who embrace 'em. This will put 'em in the news again, and we need a new hotel just to handle all the folks they're bringin' in here already. My nephew could use the construction job on a hotel and my niece would love to work there."

The meeting went on for an hour and a half before the mayor had organized team leaders to begin re-building the relationship with the Painter and Gregory families. The first idea was to create a symbolic bridge between them, repairing the damaged connection to Whitehaven. They would place luminaries to run the length of the causeway bridge on the night of the caroling bonfire, with the name of a Whitehaven friend written on each one.

Derrick got into Whitehaven for a quick day to visit his parents and Jordan. He tapped lightly on the frame of Chad's open office door, but he stopped short when he saw the bruise on Chad's face.

As he stood there gaping, Chad smiled tightly from the other side of a telephone receiver. He ended the call and stood up to shake his friend's hand. Derrick held out Chad's arm to look at his knuckles. "So, this is what came of Caroline's walk in the park that Mom and Dad told me about," he said, whistling and looking back up at the bruise on Chad's face. Cole came in from across the hallway, getting Derrick's most common greeting—a hug.

"Cole, you too?" he asked, examining Cole's nose.

"Ouch!" Cole exclaimed. "Still ain't as bad as yours, bro," he said. "And a girl didn't do it."

Derrick glanced at Chad. "Yeah, well... I'd like to see the guys on the other side of this. Good for you, takin' care of our—I mean, takin' care of Caroline," he corrected.

Chad pursed his lips, hearing "our girl" in his mind. He went around to his desk for a contract in a neat stack of work. "Everything's ready. I know you're in a hurry to see Jordan. Savanna's really impressed with her, so I hope she's feelin' good about this assignment."

Derrick took the pen Chad handed him and signed. "Yeah, she is. She was gushin' about it all over the phone last night."

"Hey, will you sign something else for us? Come to my office before you leave. I've got two fresh basketballs for our new court Painter Place, for our Tarzan games."

Derrick grinned. "What, you hopin' some of this rubs off on ya? My signature ain't magic."

"Hey, I'm hedgin' every advantage," laughed Cole. "You want to come out to the Castaway tonight for dinner? We re-open this weekend, but Patrick pushed to have it ready for the family, you and Jordan while you're here. Bring your parents."

"Give me a time and we'll be there. Is Jordan at the Big House now?"

Chad nodded. "I can call and have her come get you."

Derrick shifted his weight, hands on his hips. "No, dad left his car for me at the airstrip. I'll just—I'm goin' to ride out there. I haven't seen it since the storm."

Chad studied him, and Cole snorted. "Expect the worst. Then go backwards exponentially. The Big House is the only thing that's remotely the same, and we're doin' an exterior makeover to take it back to the original design. We got delayed with a significant development."

"Jordan mentioned it," Derrick chuckled. "There's always excitement around Painter Place, so we'll have to double it now with a British castle. Seamure, I think it's called? When are you takin' your sand buckets out to the beach to dig for that buried treasure?"

Chad grinned. "We're tryin' to figure out where to look. The map of south side back then is different from the island now. It looks like it should be close to where Andy's house was. Maybe it will pop up in construction. Juliette and Cameron are buildin' right next to him, so who knows? We need places to live more than we need a treasure hunting hobby."

Cole said, "It still hasn't sunk in for me that Dante Kent is the last of the stewards who were looking over the estate that Beauregard Painter set up, and just happened to become a close friend of Wyeth's. He has no children to pass the estate on to, and claims he knew the owner would come forward in his lifetime. He was always intrigued with Wyeth's story of the Patrick Painter who settled the island."

Derrick's eyes popped when he got to the crest of the bridge to the island, and he was unable to stop shaking his head in denial as he whispered "no" over and over. He blinked back tears and recovered enough to chat briefly with the security guard about his game performance the night before.

He did a double take at the sparkling yellow Ferrari in the parking area behind the Big House, and he cringed to think it was almost keyed by the gang at the park. Caroline's car. He laughed out loud. She's the only person on earth that could get a Ferrari out of Chad Gregory.

Derrick whistled to himself in appreciation as he shielded his eyes with his hand and bent to look inside. Suddenly, his own red Ferrari seemed out of date.

He sobered when he straightened and looked around. The gallery and studios he used to visit to see Caroline had disappeared.

The pavilion, where he danced with her at Island Summer Dances, no longer existed. Closing his eyes for a moment, he conjured the image of magical nights under the moon.

He walked to the edge of the parking lot to look at the beach in the distance, then he gasped. The magnificent pier was gone. In fact, the island looked nothing like the place in his romantic memories.

He shook his head in disbelief and ran his hand through his hair. So, this was what happened while he was praying at the airport for Caroline and Painter Place. The night Jordan followed him.

He wiped his hand over his forehead, imagining what this island had looked like during high tide with Hugo. "Thank You, God, for saving them," he whispered. "I won't forget it, ever."

Strolling around back again, he made his way to the kitchen door and tapped lightly. A huge grin split his face when he saw Maggie Jane at work through the glass in the storm door. She returned the grin and put down a stirring spoon, wiped her hands on her apron and came to let him in. He swept her into a bear hug.

"Here to pick up your girl?"

"Yeah—" he began, then looked bewildered. Coming into this house again made him forget he was not there for Caroline.

Maggie Jane watched him orient himself. "Yeah—sure, of course," he tried again, forcing another grin. "I hear you're winnin' her over."

"She's winnin' us over, too, just like she did you. Let's go find 'er."

Derrick followed into the rotunda, where he stopped. Hesitantly, he walked to the bottom of the magnificent marble staircase, letting his eyes roam up until he gazed at the stained-glass dome. "It made it," he said reverently.

"The front windows were all blown out. It was a dreadful crash. That's where God put the pavilion and Juliette's roof, against the front of the mansion, to guard us. He knew the foundation would bear the force. If He tells me in heaven that He had an army of angels holdin' on to this old mansion in that storm, then I'll understand how we made it."

Entranced, Derrick walked to the replaced front living room windows. He squeezed his eyes shut at imagining what it must have been like for Chad, Patrick, and Joey when this happened. And Caroline, who must have been in so much pain with the twins before she heard the crash that could be the beginning of the end of their lives.

"Derrick, she's in the library, where the other windows were blown out."

An image of a younger Caroline popped into his mind before he corrected it. Maggie Jane was referring to Jordan.

He heard children's laughter upstairs as he went slowly through the ballroom. He spun around as he tried to look everywhere at once, his mind filled with music from the incredible New Year's Eve parties. But Caroline was not in his arms, and his steps were not leading her in a dance. They were taking him through the huge double library doors, toward Savanna Painter's musical accent.

The room was enormous, lined on three sides with bookcases up to the tall ceiling. Massive ornate easels displayed the more notable paintings by past generations of Painters, and the deep window seating in front of huge windows was not yet stained to match the woodwork after being recently rebuilt.

Savanna sat in that wing chair she liked so much, with the white animal fur throw, holding a baby in her arms. Jordan sat on a sofa with a notebook in her hand. He returned the smile that told him she was glad to see him.

Caroline turned from the new window, her face lighting up. He instinctively lingered in that look a moment but blinked as her grandmother got his attention.

"Derrick, how wonderful to have you come by!" greeted Savanna. "I believe an introduction is in order, for two new members of my family. Come over and say hi to Rayce Gregory."

Derrick obeyed, as everyone who heard Savanna felt compelled to do, and he diminished his height down to his knees to be beside her arms. "He's—incredible," he whispered.

The little boy stared at him with blue eyes just like Caroline's. His tiny arm jerked a little when he reached out to Derrick as if to greet him, and he made a friendly croaking sound like he wanted to say hi.

Enchanted, Derrick became lost in his sparkling gaze, and before he thought about it, he reached out to the baby. Rayce grasped at his hand. Derrick felt his heart swell and his eyes sting. He smiled to cover his emotions. Rayce smiled back.

The next thing he knew, Caroline was standing beside him. "Derrick, meet Rhett Gregory. Rhett, meet our local star, Derrick Wallace. Maybe he can teach you some great basketball tips someday."

Rhett looked like the same baby that held his hand, but he did not reach for him. Instead, he stared with curiosity, sizing Derrick up. Like his dad.

Derrick looked from the baby to Caroline, gazing into the same sea blue that sometimes left him breathless as he seemed to sail into infinity...

"They look so much like baby photos of Chad," Savanna's musical voice observed. "When their eyes are closed, Phillip acts like he's holding his baby boy again. As they grow, they'll change into whatever the Lord intends. He didn't mix the Painter and Gregory bloodlines after all this time unless it was for somethin' amazing."

She laughed softly and Derrick blinked, tearing his eyes away from Caroline's. He slowly stood up, collecting himself.

"I was just goin' to take Jordan out to see the Thanksgiving monument, where the chapel used to be," Caroline said warmly. "Join us. We'd love for you to do us the honor of reading it out loud."

"Yes, do," encouraged Savanna. "Jordan was finishin' up with us so she could spend the rest of the day with you."

Jordan came to stand beside him, and he smiled at her. But her eyes were thoughtful as they met his. He reached for her hand and said, "We've been invited to meet everyone for dinner at the Castaway tonight for a private re-opening celebration. I wanted to show you off, so I hope that's okay."

"I'd love to!" she answered. "I hope Patrick himself is chef today. I've heard he's become quite the local food celebrity—after Maggie Jane, of course."

Caroline and Savanna led them into the rotunda, where Camellia had come down to the foot of the stairs. "I thought it might be time for the little ones to be ready for a nap," she said, reaching out to take Rhett. She extended one hand to Derrick and said brightly, "How delightful to see you, Derrick!"

Juliette descended the stairs. "Hi, Derrick! Want to take a ride with us?"

As he stood before a giant column that led his eyes to heaven, Derrick listened to Juliette explain the purpose of the monument. "After a loss such as the island has never known, we want to celebrate a special Thanksgiving Day here this year. God saved our family in a remarkable way. Chad has always loved this prayer by Sir Frances Drake, and we thought it was appropriate."

Derrick went closer to touch the engraved letters gingerly, considering them. He stepped back to view the whole thing at once.

"Go ahead, read it out loud," encouraged Caroline.

He hesitated, feeling unworthy to utter the prayer. Then he cleared his throat and spoke solemnly.

The Prayer of Sir Frances Drake, 1577:
Disturb us, Lord,
When we are too well pleased with ourselves,
When our dreams have come true
Because we have dreamed too little;
When we arrived safely
Because we sailed too close to the shore.
Disturb us, Lord,
When with the abundance of things we possess,
We have lost our thirst for the waters of life;
Having fallen in love with life,
We have ceased to dream of eternity
And in our efforts to build a new earth,
We have allowed our vision of the new Heaven to dim.
Disturb us, Lord
To dare more boldly,
To venture on wider seas
Where storms will show your mastery;
Where losing sight of land, we shall find the stars.
We ask You to push back the horizons of our hopes;
And to push into the future
In strength, courage, hope, and love.
Amen.

Derrick's voice choked with emotion before he was halfway through, but he struggled through and finished. Jordan cried and fished for tissues in her purse, forgetting to write down the prayer. He put his arm around her and pulled her tightly to his side.

"I was just off balance when I saw the island and the mansion today, that's all," Derrick explained as he and Jordan took a walk by the waterfront at his parents' house in Whitehaven.

"No, that's not all," said Jordan quietly, looking into the distance at the island. She turned a penetrating look his way. "I have access to the island and the stories now. Whatever chivalry possessed you to tell them I'm your girlfriend isn't necessary any longer, and frankly, I respect them too much to deceive them. Let's just say we've decided we're better as friends."

Derrick stopped their stroll abruptly to take her shoulders. "I'd be lyin' to them, and they'd know it. I told Chad my intentions. He knows I'm just waitin' on you to feel the way I do. I crossed that bridge today to say a final goodbye to all the memories so I can launch in a new direction. I'm ready to move on, Jordan, just like everyone at Painter Place is."

Jordan's mahogany eyes studied him dubiously. But he saw a flicker of hope in them. She wanted to believe him.

"Look, it hasn't been long since—Dwayne—and I've been rushin' you. But can I call your dad today and ask for his blessing to see you as my girl, with an end goal in mind if things work out, and tell him I would never hurt you like Dwayne did? Are you ready for that?"

He watched her swallow and look out at the tatters of his parent's pier. He squeezed her hand. "I have a lot of games around Thanksgiving, but I get a few days off at Christmas and New Year's Eve. I could meet your family and try to start takin' Dwayne's place. I can handle it when they accidentally call me his name for a while."

Her expression softened and a smile played at the corners of her mouth. Then she rubbed her temple and said, "I understand your struggle now. I've never met anyone like Caroline, and she never did anything to betray you, to make you turn your back and let go. I saw it in your eyes today, Derrick. I'm not your first choice."

"And I'm not yours, Jordan!" he retorted in frustration. He huffed and looked away, dropping her hand. "Like you said the night we met, no matter how we feel about it, our first choices weren't the right ones. We have to move on."

She reached out to grasp his hand again. "Today, I was jealous. I guess that means it's time for you to talk to my dad."

He turned a startled stare back at her. "Jealous?"

She nodded solemnly. He gulped at the smoldering look in those lovely eyes. "I don't like it much that you acted so cool and suave about it," he said hoarsely. "Are you goin' to let me see what jealous looks like when you're officially mine?"

She leaned into him and rested her head on his shoulder. "Don't give me a reason to."

Derrick's parents mingled companionably with the Painter Place families in the dining room while he took Jordan on a tour of the Castaway, saying hello to the cooks in the kitchen and inhaling Patrick's recipes for dinner. She asked how he got involved in the Young Guns, and he laughed.

He told her the story of a Sunday more than four years before, when he met Chad for the first time since he returned from college. Derrick came to town to persuade Caroline to let him talk to her dad after he got his contract to go pro, but Chad was back and had a different plan for Caroline. She was driving Chad's Lamborghini and he had just put a Rolex on her arm. He drove up in her car and warned Derrick to stay away. But rather than risk a friendship over the confrontation, he handed him his card for the Young Guns and invited him to join them.

"He didn't try to fence off Caroline from being your friend anymore?" she asked, puzzled. "Wasn't he jealous?"

"He was ready to explode!" Derrick chuckled. "I think he's still a bit jealous, but my parents probably remedied that tonight with their announcement about us."

Derrick glanced at the open door from Patrick's office out to the dining room. He kept his voice low. "Caroline and I—we have a connection, an affinity. I hope you understand that it's not a threat. Chad never tried to keep us apart. That would be admitting that he wasn't man enough on his own to keep her. He had to show me I was neutralized as a threat." He shook his head in admiration and grinned. "We understand one another. He thrives on winning, and to win, you need competition. He's brilliant. Not only did he win her, but he won me over as well, recruiting me to his professional team while keepin' her out of reach personally. He didn't know how close Caroline and I were while he was gone or he'd have been back here to stop me, and if she'd known he was forced to stay away, she'd never have spent so much time with me. He was her destiny, and I tried to make her forget him."

He looked from the door back to Jordan. "No one on the planet can take Chad's place to look after Painter Place for her, and nothin's goin' to happen to stop the plan. Just in case anyone missed that when he survived Hugo, God reiterated that point in France. He was divinely protected."

"Derrick, what you said about how alike you and Chad are—you were doin' what he did when you showed Dwayne you were enough on your own to neutralize him, right? I see it now—that's why it was so important to you to have me at the game!"

He laughed and pulled her to him to kiss the top of her forehead.

Chapter Twenty-Seven

Far away there in the sunshine are my highest aspirations.
I may not reach them, but I can look up and see their beauty,
believe in them, and try to follow where they lead.
-Louisa May Alcott

On the Saturday morning of the caroling bonfire event on the beach, Azariah, Caroline, Chad, Patrick, Natalie, Marina, Danny, Çole, and Shannon went out to jog the beachfront. Caroline stashed her camera in a bag belted around her waist, hoping to get some shots of their young German shepherd, Lancelot, in his first beach romp. Marina's collie, Lady, followed on a leash.

They waved at some teens from their church gathering limbs for the bonfire near the old chapel foundation. Tonight, there would be a lighted trail of luminaries out to the monument for guests to ride out to see it. Spotlights kept the granite column illuminated after dark, a landmark to be noticed by sea. Next spring, special landscaped gardens would be organized to enhance the setting for guests. As the new grounds and gardens supervisor, Danny had a daunting job ahead on the nearly barren island.

Lancelot looked mildly curious of the teenagers, then barked and strained at the leash, interested in something farther ahead. The men slowed down, wondering whether it was worth stopping for. Lady panted as she walked up beside Lancelot, nuzzling his head, and he acknowledged her with some licks to her ears. Then they both barked at whatever it was, and a rustle of brush moved.

The group decided to stop to catch their breath. "It's an animal," speculated Cole. "Looks like it's hiding in that mound over there.

Must have been deposited by the storm, since the tide hasn't been this high since."

"Likely a snake," agreed Patrick.

"I say we investigate anyway," drawled Danny. "Let's see what's botherin' this expensive guard dog."

They plowed through loose sand off the smooth shoreline, following the pull of the dogs. When they came within six feet of an object, they carefully looked around it. It was covered in dried seaweed and one side was up to the top in the loose sand. It had the shape of a box.

Caroline circled the object, photographing it from all angles. Lancelot watched her curiously, his ears flicking up every time her camera clicked.

"It looks like it was metal, before all those barnacles grew on it," observed Cole.

"It's open. Broken open," reported Azariah from where he squatted down close to it. "And it was chained to something." He touched a barnacled chain in the sand, and then looked up to Chad.

The young men looked around at one another. "Someone's got to investigate," Patrick said. "Might as well be us."

"I'm not touchin' it. We don't know where it's been," said Cole. "If there's trouble, I'll get blamed for it."

Danny nudged Chad's arm. "Chad, you're the one who always imagined we'd find treasure here someday. Wanna go first?"

Patrick and Chad scouted for any snakes before they squatted near Azariah. Chad resorted to quotes from Treasure Island to ease his nerves. "It's not likely from the *Hispaniola*. But if it were a treasure, I'd swoon like a lady of quality, I would."

Patrick grinned and drew a spot on the sand. "You have 'til ten tonight," he said in a rough pirate voice.

By now, the others were bent over laughing, and Lady yapped. Chad got on his knees in the sand in front of the box, where a padlock had broken off.

"Open it, Chad," Cole urged. Even the dogs stared at Chad, waiting with their ears up. He exhaled a quick breath and looked at Caroline. She smiled and nodded so he put his hand on the lid and pushed.

He stared, speechless, at a tumble of gold and silver bars. The others crowded close. "It—it really is—treasure..." Shannon's voice trailed off.

"We didn't have to dig? It's not supposed to happen this way," stammered Marina.

Caroline put her hands on the top of her head. "Is this—real?"

They all wondered the same thing, and they were unsure what they were supposed to do next. Azariah picked up a bar in the box, weighing it in his hand. His voice broke the spell. "This is real. I'm radioing back to the house to get help. Look in the sand around the box for bars that might have spilled out when it was bashed open in the storm. If this was from a shipwreck, there could be more artifacts scattered around. Caroline, keep a record with your camera."

Marina exclaimed, "King's ransom—it could be from the legend of Dog's Head! Maybe it's the lost dowry, the price that was supposed to buy the groom's plantation in the Colonies. He called off the marriage because his investment would fail without the dowry."

Wyeth, Andy, and Phillip soon rushed to the site when they got Azariah's call. Once again, phone calls were made to attorneys. Wyeth phoned someone he knew with the state historical society. By noon, they loaded the box and other objects they found to store in the house, safe from foot traffic to the monument for the event that evening. Caroline drew a rough map to note where each object was found, and they roped off the area.

On Monday, teams from the historical society would arrive to evaluate whether an underwater search for a shipwreck was warranted. Hugo may have dragged one closer to shore.

"It's breathtaking," Caroline said, looking across the bridge from the second story veranda. Guests from town spaced out luminaries across one side of the bridge while making their way to the bonfire. "We still have friends, Mama."

Valerie sighed and nodded. "But we also still have security at the bridge, extra security in the house, and Azariah and Lancelot, honey. Never let your guard down. The intruders in France escaped with no leads, and our enemies are most effective if they blend in with our friends. The danger has increased dramatically with the discovery of that sea chest today and the possibility of something hidden by your ancestor somewhere on the south side of the island. Until the historical team is done, we'll need patrols on the shorelines, where people will try to sneak in by boat. It might cost us that fortune in gold to pay for protection unless Sterling and Wyeth can raise a force of volunteers."

"It was one thing to think like this in France, but it's an adjustment to think of my hometown this way. I've always been troubled that we guard the *Artistic License* constantly when she's docked here. I wonder if it's worthwhile to have anything, Mama. People just want to take it away from you, vandalize it, or hate you for havin' more than they do."

Valerie stroked her daughter's hair back from her shoulder and smiled sadly. "If you didn't have anything, baby, you couldn't be in charge of this island someday. And if you aren't in charge of this island, it will never be shared as the Painters do. People can't see they'd rather have you here than the alternative. They have no vision—they live for the moment."

Caroline leaned into her mother's shoulder, and her mother put her arm around her waist. They watched more guests set up luminaries on their way across the bridge to Painter Place. Valerie said softly, "There's a price to pay for being a watchman, Caroline. You'll be misunderstood and maligned, but you've been raised to come through. I know you will while God keeps it for you. The island is a gift, and you're a steward, much like Dante Kent is. Sometimes a gift can feel a whole lot like a curse. That's why you must always look outside yourself at the big picture. When you shy away from the spotlight, remember it's not about you anyway."

Savanna came out to join them and overheard. "Every Painter in your shoes has faced down their own giants, Caroline, for they rise up in every generation. Look back in the journals and records sometimes for the encouragement they left you. To live is to face conflict. It shapes who you are. But we're blessed, because every Painter has had a Gregory. They were never completely alone, and someone always understood."

"What about your giants, Gran Vanna?" Valerie ventured, stretching her arm, taking her mother-in-law's hand to invite her to Caroline's other side. "I heard the mayor called with a list of people who won't be here tonight. They oppose your appointment to the council."

Savanna smiled. She squeezed Valerie's hand before stretching her arm around Caroline. "I'll do what all Painters do—pray while I pull out my sling, stone, and sword. We don't back down from spiritual warfare, girls. Those who want their own ideas for Whitehaven have the same right to speak as others, but not all their ideas are equal. Some ideas are clearly about selfish ways they want to live, or power they seek, or about making money for themselves, not about the welfare or quality of life of Whitehaven's residents. Someone must be the bad ol' judge, and I can take it if they want to insult and rough up an old lady."

Chad and Caroline took the twins down to join all the children for the bonfire, pulling out a double stroller so their hands were free to shake and their arms free to hug. Azariah and Lancelot remained with them constantly in the crowd, and Patrick, Cole, and Joey stayed close by.

Joey's eyes popped when he saw Billy from the gang who assaulted Casey and Caroline in the park. The young Texan was in an earnest conversation with Casey as they walked onto the beach. When Joey stood in front of them, and Casey introduced the two young men.

Billy nodded politely and put out his hand. With a narrowed gaze, Joey reached out stiffly to shake it. "Sterling let me onto the island to apologize," Billy began in a drawl as authentically Texan as the boots he wore on the sand. "I turned myself in, and he's been helpin' me get straightened out. I just—I wanted to tell you face to face that back home, the guys put Casey on the shelf to date once they were ready to get married. She's not a girl you take out for a good time. What the guys in the park said—I had no business bringin' up how I knew her, but I never insinuated the things they came up with."

Joey turned his gaze to the doe eyes that always sent something somersaulting inside him. He sighed and reached out to touch Casey's face, lightly brushing his thumb across her cheek. "I know. I'm not wondering about it, but thanks for doing this for her sake."

He gestured for Billy to join them as the caroling began. The firelight cast a cheerful glow on the guests' faces, many of which were sometimes moved to tears, singing words about the incomparable gift of Christ to the world. Hearts were as full as the cups of hot cocoa and light as the marshmallows, and a new bond, stronger than ever before, formed between the attending Whitehaven residents and the island's inhabitants.

The Painter and Gregory families tried to spend personal time with guests, silently thanking God for friends. But everyone was making mental notes of who was not there. It might matter a great deal someday.

Krystal made a yummy sound and closed her eyes as she savored a bite of Patrick's chocolate éclair at the Castaway. Caroline watched her with a knowing smile. "I told you it would be worth it to save room for dessert," she said. "Patrick came in early to do this himself in the huge commercial pans before opening today. He tries to do something different that is exclusively his own about three days a week, instead of the staff making everything from his recipes. People in town are intrigued by the mystery of it all. They don't know what to expect. They only know they want it."

"Oh, Caroline, this dessert has to be sinful! It'll turn up in one of Pastor Payne's sermons."

Caroline laughed. "Only if you resort to idolizing it, or to gluttony." She took a bite from her own plate, enjoying their lunch together. Krystal spoke of her salvation experience on the night of Hugo and the change it had made in her life.

"If every meal in here is inspired by Painter Place, how in the world do you stay slender?" she asked between bites.

Caroline swallowed water with a slice of lime. "Most of the credit goes to Maggie Jane, who limits the fattening stuff and makes vegetables interesting. We consider her as much a Painter as the rest of us, and she sees us as her family and her responsibility. She says health is in food and shows us off to everyone in town as evidence that she takes care of us. In case you haven't noticed, the guys at Painter Place are fiercely competitive, so we do a lot of walking, jogging, volleyball, basketball, and working out together. Chad deals with stress by working out, and I'm a little like him, addicted to a rush I get from it."

Krystal polished off the last bite in her plate. "I guess my workout is walking a million miles in and out of the Sand Dollar, carrying trays of food. Chad's job and the stress—he doesn't do a day's work and forget it when he comes home at night, the way Patrick and Joey do. That's why he's so—" She hesitated.

"Wealthy? And in danger?"

Krystal smiled sheepishly. "I know in the South it's impolite to mention money. I'm just trying to sort things out, like the attitudes and prejudices, and what people here are missing about him."

Caroline looked at her thoughtfully and then out the window. "The most dangerous threat to Chad isn't the local prejudice and jealousy. That's what hurts his heart. The lethal one is organized crime."

Krystal's mouth dropped open and her brows shot up. She recovered to say, "Caroline, would you have still married him if you'd have known what your lives would become, what danger your children would live in?"

Brooding as she traced the tip of her forefinger around the top of her water glass, Caroline finally looked up to meet Krystal's eyes. "God didn't give me that choice. He decided. So here I am, with the right man, come what may. Krystal, I haven't told anyone outside the family this, but I'll include you because you saw the incident in the park."

She glanced at her bodyguard, who was out of earshot. "I've known how to shoot for years, but lately, I've begun doing some self-defense training without guns and asking Azariah to help me understand the best way to handle being held captive. It's not all about physical and emotional reactions, but mental, as well. I have a feeling it's important. It can't hurt to be prepared, and it will keep me from being fearful."

"I think you are the smartest and bravest woman I ever met, Caroline. Being ready will give you peace of mind and confidence." She tilted her head at Azariah. "I wouldn't want to be the one holding you captive if that guy was coming after you."

Caroline's laughter inspired Krystal to do the same, and the serious mood was broken. "Okay, back to what we were talking about," Caroline said. "Oh, yeah, attitudes and prejudices among the locals. Chad has a gift, a vision, and he uses it to make money for people. He can't just turn it off when he leaves the office, and it pays more than an ordinary person's salary. He likes to build things, imagine things, begin things, and restore things. He loves to do stuff for people, especially when they are unaware. One of his spiritual gifts is giving. Most of Whitehaven has no clue what they enjoy because of his family. They get all tangled up in Chad's movie star looks, his clothes and cars, and his life on a private island. They decided it's not fair, and though they don't even know how many zeros are in the numbers for millions or billions, let alone how to be responsible for that kind of money, they resent people who do. They treat Chad as if he should be ashamed of his job."

"Like all the people I see in the news who are worse than broke after they win a lottery and blow it," Krystal interjected. "And the pro athletes who end up with nothing, after making millions."

"Exactly! So, as long as there are misunderstandings about wealth, there will be prejudice against it. Wealth is not a sin in the Bible until money is a controlling idol. When it takes big money for a big job, God provides it, as he did for Noah to finance the ark, and Job, Abraham, David, Solomon, the man who provided a temporary tomb for Jesus, and all the other examples in scripture. There will always be good people as well as corrupt people, no matter their income."

"I'm afraid I don't know how to manage money more than getting by," Krystal said. "But I don't blow it on alcohol and entertainment, and I figured out how to tithe without starving."

"Would you like to see if Chad can help you organize your budget so you can save a little?"

"You'd—you'd trust me around him?"

"Krystal, every woman breathin' will notice Chad Gregory, but it doesn't mean she'll act on a lustful impulse. If women admire him, I only ask that they stay on their side of the fence." An image of Gloria with her arms around Chad on the island flashed into her mind. Rumor was that Gloria was pregnant, so that little vacation to punish her paid off for her husband.

Caroline sipped her water, then said, "You may have heard about the matador I danced with in a movie scene in France. When the movie comes out, you'll see he is absolutely a dream, and trust me, as an artist, I noticed. I imagined paintings with him in them, but never about bein' alone with him. We were friends in a working environment, both of us in love with someone else in committed relationships. But I saw firsthand how complicated it is for my aunt to perform with other actors. She's never done kissing or intimate scenes and it limits her parts to being suggestive of a kiss happening. Christians don't have to hide in isolation to live our convictions. I know I can trust you around my husband, but I'm sure you understand that he can't afford to ever be alone with a woman who isn't family. If you have friends at Tech who might be interested in budget advice, Chad could talk to everyone at once. We could meet here, or at church."

"I know some who would love the help!" Krystal gushed.

Part of the fun of the annual New Year's Eve party at Painter Place was getting dressed up. It was a formal affair, with plenty of photos of family and guests taken on the rotunda stairway and in front of a towering Christmas tree. Even the twins would make an appearance this year in tiny tuxedos to match their dad's. A few hand-picked reporters were invited, leaving Jordan free to relax and enjoy the evening with Derrick, and Azariah supervised a well-oiled machine of tuxedoed bodyguards and security.

A dapper DJ was training with Joey. The Tech student would graduate from studies in communications, and he did apprentice work at the radio station in hopes of settling there. Joey went over last-minute details in the music corner of the ballroom.

"The main thing to keep in mind for Painter Place is that the selections are based on more than just the family-friendly guidelines of music from the station," he explained. "At Painter Place, no one can appreciate dancin' to a song like 'Evil Woman,' even if it's free of offensive language. We do a lot of events here, and I keep lists of acceptable songs to change things around."

He waved a list of selections for the evening on a clipboard that he laid on the table. They heard a commotion through the doors into the rotunda, and he winked at the young DJ.

"Prepare to be dazzled. The ladies are on the stairs, and tonight, it's no exaggeration to say Painter Place is the center stage for some of the South's most beautiful women."

The DJ grinned. "Oh, believe me, I've heard! Hey, did I tell you I'm interested in girl from school? I just need to get up the guts to ask her out. Her name's Krystal, and I think she knows some of you. Maybe you've seen her—she's a waitress at the Sand Dollar. Cute little dark-haired thing, really friendly and sweet. Do you know who I'm talkin' about?"

Joey blinked and smiled. "Yeah. Yeah, I think I do. She goes to my church. Why don't you visit Shoreline next Sunday? Maybe you could sit with her."

He was still chuckling to himself when he joined a crowd of men gathered at the bottom of the enormous marble staircase. All the Painter and Gregory ladies, plus Casey and Jordan, had come down at once, making a fairy tale appearance, like queens and princesses amid tiny lights that glittered all the way up. The array of stunning formal dresses made the scene breathtaking, and Joey's eyes quickly found Casey's strapless magenta gown.

He inhaled sharply and stared. His brother Ben came up behind him and whispered, "Your heart's on your sleeve. You may want to rethink flashing it like a neon sign."

Joey turned to speak over his shoulder. "Says the guy who embarrassed me by being tongue-tied whenever Sandy Gregory was around. I'd say her name, and you'd be worthless for half an hour."

"How do you think I learned not to act like you are? I gave her total power over me, and I never got it back. I should've been cool under fire, like I was trained to do for work. Mom and Dad will be here soon. Is tonight the night?"

"Don't rush me," Joey growled.

Ben laughed and clapped his little brother on the back as the cameras flashed and the ladies posed. They came down the stairs to meet the men, gathering as couples and families for photos before the party began in earnest.

Natalie was radiant but felt as if she might go into labor at any time. Patrick was ever attentive, asking that they be first for photos in case he had to leave with her for the hospital. They might not win a prize for the local New Year's baby, but they would begin the first few days of the new decade with one. At Thanksgiving, they decided to announce the baby's gender and name, since the letter discovered on the veranda was such a significant event. Their son would be Beau Painter, to honor Beauregard, the original Patrick Painter's elder brother. Following the tradition of interesting names in the Painter lineage, the baby's name would mean "beautiful painter," as Beauregard's name had meant "beautiful view painter."

At Joey's signal, the DJ played soft instrumental background music as guests arrived. The families were granting interviews, so conversation and greetings filled the mansion with a subdued roar.

Wyeth, Chrissy, Juliette, Cameron, Chad, and Caroline were the busiest with interviews, though Patrick fielded a few about the growing reputation of the Castaway. Wyeth was asked about plans for his gallery and career, which had been waylaid while he filled his role as heir to rebuild Painter Place. He brought over his gallery managers, Shelly and Zachary, to talk about how they settled on a location in Whitehaven for the facility after all. Wyeth moved on to other questions about what was next for the family as they took their estate in England under wing, and how his friend Dante Kent would remain in charge there. He was asked about Dante's sudden appearances in London with a secretary at Gregory Global, and he smiled when he told them Dante would answer that question for himself.

Cameron dealt with questions about the upcoming movie premier and whether he had considered making a movie about his family's survival at Painter Place during Hugo. Reporters were forewarned that Caroline would not accept questions about Alejandro Rafael if they implied a romance between them. An arts and entertainment reporter engaged her in an interview about plans for a Van Gogh Centennial theme in her paintings when she had a studio again. Chad had been asked so many questions about his survival of the hurricane and threats to his family that he had brief responses waiting like an arsenal.

The children were made much of before being taken upstairs by ten o'clock, with two college students from church helping Mia's nanny put them all to bed. Mia's regular bodyguard had recovered his gunshot wound and returned to duty, standing at the top of the staircase. Delighted to have him back again, Mia joyfully took his face in her dainty hands to soundly give him a good-night kiss on his nose and wish him sweet dreams. He smiled and answered that they had to be sweet because she was in them.

Wyeth led Chrissy to the center of the ballroom floor to kick off the party. "Most of you heard accounts of what happened in this house during the hours when Hurricane Hugo hit on September 21. That night, in this ballroom, our courageous young survivors gathered together. The thunder and lightning crashed, the wind howled, tornadoes whirled, and an endless depth of ocean pounded relentlessly all around them. So, what did they do in the face of such danger?"

Wyeth's pause had the intended dramatic impact as guests stood spellbound. Then he said, "They danced."

The crowd applauded, then he raised his hand for their attention. "I don't know what the rest of you who endured Hugo did that night, but I can tell you that dancing never occurred to me. They danced to celebrate the loves of their lives, their friendships, and their memories of the island that would change forever. They danced to help Caroline deal with her painful labor with the twins. They knew it could be their last dance. And as the night wore on within these walls, the same storm that was destroying their home was being used by the Lord to build reconciliation in a longstanding broken relationship. We want to thank all of you who were praying."

Guests reacted with applause once again, and he waited to speak. "Tonight, we'll start the party with the songs they danced to, closing the decade the way they closed a chapter in the history of Painter Place. But after midnight, we'll turn to the new decade on the island with hope—and more dancing!"

He gestured for those who had been in the storm to come stand with him, including Tony Rush and Maggie Jane. They waved to everyone, and Joey signaled his apprentice. Maggie Jane's song choice during Hugo began, and guests laughed in surprise while joining partners to rock to "Roll Over, Beethoven."

Joey kept Casey close to him, appreciating how she looked in the deep pink of her gown and saying so. She told him he looked like a handsome prince in his tuxedo. Before "Danger Zone" was over, Casey said, "I'll never hear this song without rememberin' this place, on that night, with you."

"It's a long way from Texas to Painter Place," he responded. "What's the chance anyone travels that far to be in a situation like that, with a guy like me?"

Joey grinned at a Beatles song about holding hands as he brought her through a turn and held their clasped hands out for her attention. "We look good together," he announced as he swung her closer. "Even our hands fit together just right." Then he sang lyrics near her ear about feeling happy inside and unable to hide his love.

Casey blushed at his focused attention. He let the last notes of the song end and asked her to step out to catch their breath. He led her to the table for punch, mainly because he needed the security of holding on to something. Then he led her out to the rambling new veranda, where fairy-tale twinkling lights enhanced the impression of the mansion as a magical castle.

She sighed, immersing herself in the vista of sea and stars. "I never get over how beautiful the view is from here, night or day." She rested her free hand on the railing, studying the design. "And I like Caroline's decision to restore the veranda to the original house plan. It must've been so difficult. She painted the view from the old one in *Enchanted Summer Evening* because of years of memories she and Chad shared on it."

"She doesn't know Chad restored boards salvaged from the old veranda and the old pavilion. He's goin' to build her a private gazebo, big enough for a dozen couples, with the boards as the floor. He'll start when they build the new Gregory estate. It's our secret, okay?"

Casey's eyes sparkled. "I like being in on the secret."

"The new pavilion will be massive, for the public dances. We outgrew the old one long ago," Joey mused, looking into the distance where footings were being poured to begin construction. "I see everyone here struggle with memories they cherish but tryin' to move on with new plans."

They stood listening to the surf and the music floating from within. Casey ventured, "But, you've been here all these years too, Joey, like a second home. You loved it, and you miss everything. Everyone thinks of you as a Painter Place guy."

Joey emptied his cup and set it on the railing, then turned Casey to face him. "Yes, I do miss it. After months, I still get caught off guard by a stab of pain when I look for somethin' that's not there. I often have dreams where the setting is the old Painter Place, no matter what the dream is about. But I have to let go."

He took both her hands in his and held her eyes. "I wanna begin the new memories of Painter Place with you, Casey. There's nobody left in your family for me to ask if that's okay, so this is up to you. Can we be a couple, gettin' to know one another better?"

Casey looked down at their clasped hands. "How is that different than what we've been doin' as friends?"

"As your friend, I can't stop you from goin' out with French tour guides and dancin' all evenin' to romantic French music. As friends, I don't have the nerve to ask what you meant when you told the girls none of the Painter and Gregory men are as 'hot' as me. I'm goin' crazy wanting to play that up to my advantage. And as your friend, I couldn't do this."

He crushed her to him and wrapped his tuxedoed arms around her, kissing her temple. "I'm way past friendship, Casey. I'm ready to see if this is goin' to work out for the rest of my life."

She whispered up to his ear, raising one finger to push long chestnut hair away. "I'm past friendship, too."

He ran his hand over her shoulder blades and kissed her forehead this time. He whispered with lips against her skin, "So, I let you in on a secret, now you owe me. Tell me what you meant when you told the girls I'm 'hot.'"

She burst into giggles and pulled back, looking into his eyes. "That was a private conversation, eavesdropper! Shame on you for listening in on a ladies' Bible Study, of all things."

"Give it up. I've waited for months."

Several other couples suddenly poured from the front doors, greeting them, and praising the new style of the veranda. Joey dropped his arms from around the back of Casey's formal dress and squeezed her hand as he led her back inside. "You're not off the hook. I expect an answer by the time we're on the front porch of the boarding house when I take you home."

"On the first day of 1990?" she asked as they entered the ballroom.

He grinned. "My decade will begin with a bang to rival the fireworks."

She laughed and gave him a coy glance. "I don't know. Keepin' a secret is turnin' out to be a lot of fun."

He wound his way through the couples on the dance floor to his brother and Sandy, who were dancing near his parents. As he and Casey danced, he gave Ben a smug look.

"You finally asked?"

"There wasn't anybody to stop her," Joey joked, looking triumphantly at Casey. "She doesn't know any better yet."

Caroline danced in Chad's arms. With her hair up and sweeping over one ear, she wore a single earring in the other. It was a gift he gave her in Charleston on the anniversary of their second week as a couple. Three diamond sprays dripped and dangled, swinging with her movements to the music.

She asked him if he remembered the night on a yacht in the harbor of Mevagissey when she committed to be exclusive to him. He laughed. "You know I'll never forget it. I had to corner you to say it so I could win."

"Do you remember when I said that painting *Tall Ships and Sunflowers* helped me work through how to think about us?"

He led her in the beat a few moments, pondering. "I think it was along the lines of how nothing at Painter Place would be simple anymore, as it was when we were growing up."

"Right! While I painted, I suddenly realized that sunflowers and tall ships in bottles could be appreciated in a different way. It didn't have to be exactly like when we were kids, as long as we're together."

He pulled her close a moment before a turn to end a song. "That's my girl. Hold onto that truth as we face a new decade. Painter Place can be appreciated in a new way as times change."

Another song began, and he noticed Joey and Casey. He leaned into Caroline to say something before he spun her around in a turn to see, and she laughed. He got Patrick's attention and nodded in Joey's direction, and they both caught Joey's eye. He grinned and they mouthed 'congratulations' to him.

Chad bumped into Cole on purpose as his brother danced with Shannon, telling him about Joey. Cole grinned and maneuvered his wife to dance in Joey's direction to harass him.

Spiral Staircase sang thanks to the Lord for love that was growing stronger and promised to be true. Derrick noticed Chad, Patrick, and Cole making their way to surround Joey. Leaning close to Jordan, he chuckled and said, "Joey and Casey are finally a couple."

Jordan laughed. "Things need to slow down around here. I have novels to write." Derrick's dad came up and asked to switch partners so he could dance with Jordan, and Derrick winked at her and took his mom.

Midnight would soon end the decade of the 1980's. With seconds to go, the DJ began the countdown to twelve o'clock, then he played the music to Auld Lang Syne. Kisses, good wishes, and hugs were exchanged all around the ballroom among the guests. Shouts of Happy New Year and various blessings for the new decade rang out, and confetti showered from the balcony. Toasts of sparkling juice and punch were made to the prosperity of Painter Place. Cameras flashed and laughter filled the same mansion that had been buffeted and threatened by a fierce hurricane just over three months before. The DJ got everyone dancing again to the song "Beginnings," and guests sang along.

Then the DJ announced that he was ending the evening by playing some special requests before everyone was invited to go out to the veranda or the beach for a firework show. The first song request was from Chad Gregory, to celebrate Caroline's role in a movie to be released in the New Year.

"What did you do?" Caroline asked Chad under her breath. Chad smiled smugly at her before he drew the attention of the guests to Cameron, Juliette, and Jesse for their part in the movie. The crowd applauded and quieted in anticipation as he pulled Caroline to the center of the room.

"My gorgeous wife didn't know about this. The truth is she doesn't like the spotlight. But she always comes through like a natural, and she's a good sport about it."

He smiled down at her and squeezed her to his side, making the metallic gold on her gown shimmer in the light. She smiled weakly at the guests as he continued. "I owe it to a matador that I learned a new way to show her off. My family surprised her by attending her movie performance in France before bringing her home. I was about to burst with love and pride, and I want to share some of that joy in an exclusive peek at what you'll see her do on a movie screen this year. She'll dance to a different song, and the matador will mostly be a solo act, since the dance is about him. But in *my* dance, here at Painter Place, Caroline is the star, shining brightest in the end when she trusts me completely."

The ballroom resonated with the sweet sounds of "Ladyfingers" and Caroline felt transported back to the arena in Arles, when it was her first slow dance with Chad after Hugo. But this time, he led her with the added moves they had been practicing on date nights in his office, moves that she and Alejandro performed when they danced together. At the end of the romantic music, the crowd encircling them was unprepared for the daring dip.

When Caroline expected Chad to bring her up as they rehearsed, he kissed her instead. And at that moment, it was just what she was in the mood for—a dangerous kiss.

Epilogue

Summer, 1990

The Rock the Island Dance was in full swing at Painter Place. The expansive new pavilion throbbed with happy couples and cascades of laughter to accompany the music.

"Joey arranged a break for me to use the microphone," Chad said as he danced with Caroline.

She smiled indulgently at him. "Why don't you just put up a billboard at the bridge, or arrange a press conference?"

"It crossed my mind," he quipped. "But then I realized our real friends in Whitehaven should get the privilege of hearing first."

As the DJ played a song about having fun with the one who was still the one, Casey's diamond flashed from her hand in Joey's. A dazzling ring on Jordan's hand around Derrick's waist exploded in the beam from a nearby Japanese lantern. "There's a lot of new bling in this pavilion tonight," commented Chad as the song ended and Joey signaled to him. He pulled Caroline by the hand while the young new DJ asked everyone to listen for an announcement that pertained to Painter Place.

Chad took the microphone. "How do you like the new pavilion?" he asked to the delight and boisterous response of the attendees. "This is the first Rock the Island event to kick off the decade of the 1990's, and we appreciate your help breakin' in the dance floor and celebrating a turn of the page for a new era at Painter Place."

Everyone clapped, shouted, and whistled. "It's exciting, even magical, around here on the island from spring through the fall," Chad continued with his deep Southern accent. "But for those of us who live and work here, it's really busy, and you'll understand if we get nervous from now on during hurricane season."

The crowd roared in laughter, nodding appreciatively while Chad cleared his throat. "So, winter is the best time on the island to have babies, and God willing, next February, Caroline's goin' to give me a little girl she's carrying."

Caught off guard, the audience erupted in shouts of congratulations, laughter, and applause, and Chad beamed as he raised Caroline's arm in the air, hand in hand with his.

Did you like this book? Then you can do something wonderful for other readers by taking a minute to write a short review or rating online at your favorite bookseller. It helps the reading community and authors really appreciate it!

Want more from the Painter Place Saga? Check out Southern Sky Publishing[1] *to continue the story! Sign up for my author newsletter for monthly fun, freebies, and insights.*

Be sure to see the book club discussion question. Also, feel free to visit the artist's website for updates, coloring pages, music, and newsletters!

Connect with Pamela Poole:

YouTube Channel: Pamela Poole, Artist and Author[2]

Artist Website: Pamela Poole Fine Art[3]

Publisher Website: Southern Sky Publishing[4]

---

1. *http://www.southernskypublishing.com*
2. *https://www.youtube.com/user/PamelaPooleFineArt*
3. *http://www.pamelapoole.com*
4. *http://www.southernskypublishing.com*

Beneath the Surface

Discussion Topics for Book Clubs

* White Island is the fictional setting for Painter Place. It represents faith and family. While it's portrayed as an island, it's not self-sufficient or isolated. In *Hugo*, the bridge crossing the waterway from the island to the coastal town of Whitehaven plays the role of being a passage to both safety and danger.

* What does your Painter Place (your family) look like? Do you have ideals, hopes, and goals for how your family lives in a world where the concepts of morality are considered taboo? Are your ideals worth the extra personal cost as you struggle to live them? Are you hesitant about training your children in your morality because you fear they will face persecution for being different?

* If you are committed to living on a higher plane than most of the world, what areas of your life are most affected?

* Hurricane Hugo was a real event. In this novel, it obliterates Painter Place, sparing only the mansion, which was set into bedrock. Hugo represents the real storms of life that hit your family. Is your faith grounded deep into the bedrock of Christ, as is mentioned in Matthew 7:24-25?

* The prayers of generations of Painter ancestors for future generations are mentioned during the storm preparations to encourage the family. Do you pray for future generations? How would they describe your spiritual legacy?

* Biblically, the concept of adultery is much more than just having an affair after marriage. Discuss what you think about how purity before marriage relates to the seventh commandment. Look

up scripture passages in which we are called adulterous in our relationship with the Lord.

* A lot of confusion exists over Christian doctrines. This novel brings up how artist Vincent Van Gogh often wrote about his search for truth. Do you just accept whatever traditions you were brought up in, pick and choose what you find comfortable, or put your beliefs under the magnifying glass of the Bible?

* Christians will have unexpected opportunities to be used by Christ, for His glory. Can you think of a time when He brought something or someone into your life to help you?

* If only unbelievers ran all the companies of the world, or held a political office, or taught school, would that be a good thing for Christians?

* Discuss the reasons people tend to resent those who seem to have been given a better life in terms of material wealth.

Other books in the Painter Place Saga

Novels

Painter Place, Painter Place Saga Book 1
Hugo, Painter Place Saga Book 2
Jaguar, Painter Place Saga Book 3
Landmark, Painter Place Saga Book 4

Legends (Short Stories)

Wind Songs of the Marsh, Painter Place Saga Legend 1
King's Ransom, Painter Place Saga Legend 2
Coming Soon! The Mermaid's Treasure Hoard, Painter Place Saga Legend 3

Devotional

Inspired Artistry – Embracing the Creative Calling

The Strange Sands Suspense Novella Series

The *Strange Sands Suspense* series by Pamela Poole follows architectural historian Mercedes Annalee Ellison as she investigates historic properties along the South Carolina coast—only to discover that the past often carries spiritual consequences into the present. Routine preservation projects quickly become encounters with hidden passages, ancient vendettas, and unsettling artifacts tied to the unseen realm.

Rooted in a clear Christian worldview, each faith-filled novella blends mystery, suspense, and spiritual warfare with themes of obedience, calling, and trust in God. Clean, gripping, and thought-provoking, *Strange Sands Suspense* is perfect for readers who enjoy inspirational suspense where light confronts darkness and faith makes the difference.

The Old Cedar Chest

Strange Sands Suspense 1, Hilton Head, SC

The Hidden Hallway

Strange Sands Suspense 2, Savannah, GA

The Freedom Staircase

Strange Sands Suspense 3, Charleston, SC

The Dark Passage

Strange Sands Suspense 4, Bluffton, SC

The Devil's Drawer

Strange Sands Suspense 5, Beaufort, SC

Book 6 is coming in 2026! St. Augustine, FL

About the Author

Inspiring Southern Fiction

Pamela Poole writes inspirational romance, mystery and suspense that explore the intersection of faith, history, and the unseen spiritual realm. Her stories are grounded in a clear Christian worldview and shaped by a deep respect for both historical preservation and biblical truth.

Pamela writes inspirational stories that bring together Christian faith, historic places, and hidden truths. Her novels reveal how the past can press into the present, where faith becomes essential to discernment and courage. Her characters are ordinary people facing extraordinary challenges, learning to trust Jesus when darkness threatens and answers are not easily found.

Pamela is the author of the Strange Sands Suspense series and the Painter Place Saga, blending richly detailed settings with themes of calling, obedience, redemption, and spiritual warfare. Her fiction offers clean, thought-provoking suspense designed both to engage the imagination and to encourage the heart.

When she isn't writing, Pamela enjoys research, painting in her art studio and on location along the Southern coast and making memories with her family and friends.

Accolades for the *Painter Place Saga*

Painter Place, Painter Place Saga 1

"If you are looking for a well written, CLEAN, sweet romance with a good story-line included this is for you! Would I recommend this book? ABSOLUTELY!"

-Liz, Top 100 Reviewer

Hugo, Painter Place Saga 2

"Another tremendous read by this author Pamela Poole. Book 2 in the Painter Place Saga doesn't disappoint as we remember the category 4 hurricane that came in with a vengeance in South Carolina. Continuing with family drama we are captured with the lives of Painter and Gregory families. I highly recommend reading this saga. You'll never want it to end."

-Gingy, Reader Review

Jaguar, Painter Place Saga 3

"This is the first book I've read from Pamela and the first I've read in the Painter Place Saga. Whew, there were things in this book that just left me speechless they were SO good!!!"

-ASC Book Reviews

Landmark, Painter Place Saga 4

"For young and old alike, this beautifully written story dares to hope that relationships can stand the test of time - without sacrificing personal modesty, integrity, and values."

-The Pen, Reader Review

www.ingramcontent.com/pod-product-compliance
Lightning Source LLC
LaVergne TN
LVHW050923080826
845145LV00001B/188

* 9 7 8 1 9 5 6 0 8 9 1 1 0 *